Bad in Bal........ .... by
K.A. MITCHELL

Bad Company

"…an entertaining, emotional, sometimes funny, of-tentimes sensual story with two likable MCs…"
—Love Bytes

"This is a great read that I'm adding to my favorites. Thank you, K.A. for bringing these men to light."
—Rainbow Book Reviews

Bad Boyfriend

"I really really loved this book. It was sexy, fun, quirky, heartwarming and everything amazing."
—Gay Book Reviews

"Fake boyfriends, a little age play, and a whole lot of chemistry between Quinn and Eli come together to make this an unputdownable read."
—The Novel Approach

Bad Attitude

"I really loved this book, it's an interesting look of opposites attracting and finding out that they're not that different after all."
—Diverse Reader

By K.A. MITCHELL

BAD IN BALTIMORE
Bad Company
Bad Boyfriend
Bad Attitude
Bad Influence
Bad Behavior

READY OR KNOT
Put a Ring on It
Risk Everything on It
Take a Chance on It

Published by DREAMSPINNER PRESS
www.dreamspinnerpress.com

BAD
BEHAVIOR

K.A.
MITCHELL

DREAMSPINNER
PRESS

Published by
DREAMSPINNER PRESS

5032 Capital Circle SW, Suite 2, PMB# 279,
Tallahassee, FL 32305-7886 USA
www.dreamspinnerpress.com

Bad Behavior
© 2018, 2020 K.A. Mitchell.

Cover Art
© 2018, 2020 Kanaxa
Cover content is for illustrative purposes only and any person depicted
on the cover is a model.

Digital ISBN: 978-1-64080-423-4
Mass Market Paperback ISBN: 978-1-64108-077-4
Trade Paperback ISBN: 978-1-64080-424-1
Library of Congress Control Number: 2018934234
Mass Market Paperback published January 2020
v. 1.0
First Edition published by Samhain Publishers Inc., December 2014.

Printed in the United States of America
∞
This paper meets the requirements of
ANSI/NISO Z39.48-1992 (Permanence of Paper).

Thank you to everyone who helped me tell this story:
B.F.S. for trusting me, Erin for making me go deeper,
and Beach and Tai for the lovely inspiration.

Author's Note

WARNING: THIS book is kinky. I mean kinky. With lots of sex. It describes a fully consensual, intense D/s relationship that changes a character's life. It includes impact play and bondage along the way to a very happily ever after.

Chapter One

THE PREMATURE ejaculation of a Second of July firecracker exploded out of the night. Without a backward glance, Beach stepped from the steam of a Baltimore summer into Grand Central and took a deep breath of sweat, spilled booze, and sweet, sweet testosterone. The opportunity for a nameless fuck on the nearest convenient surface was one of the reasons Beach loved having sex with men. Women were not without their charms, though the maybe/maybe-not dance could get tiresome. But men, especially the men who came to Grand Central, weren't there for that kind of dance.

After waving over the bartender, Beach paid for a local bottled beer he would be scrupulously obedient about not drinking and scanned the sparse weeknight offerings. He knew exactly what he wanted—or at least, he would when he saw it. He could never say for sure what would catch his eye. All he knew was he had to find it.

Tonight more than usual.

His gran always said Beach had ants in his pants when he fidgeted, unable to keep still or hide his boredom at being stuck anywhere for any length of time.

And stuck he was. In Baltimore. Until his lawyer managed to work a deal with the DA over something that had created far more inconvenience for Beach than it had for any of the birds on the sanctuary he'd allegedly trespassed on.

But the trapped feeling wasn't all that had pushed him out the door tonight. He was looking to forget the voicemail he'd gotten while in the shower.

Hope you'll take some time during celebrating the Fourth to think about your old man spending his twenty-fifth year in exile from his country.

As if Beach could avoid thinking about his father, when an effort to bring him home had taken him to the bird sanctuary and was the whole reason why Beach now possessed a cane and custom-fitted ankle jewelry courtesy of the Maryland Department of Public Safety and Correctional Services.

And this jittery sensation that he had to do something *right now* or come out of his skin.

The itch burned like an infection in his blood, a desperate fever heat. Without any chemicals to take the edge off, not even a sip of beer, it was impossible to ignore.

But there was always something better than beer or chemicals if you knew where to look. Something exactly like… that. A crinkle at the corner of an eye. Warm tan skin over a broad cheek.

Beach shifted off the barstool to make a better appraisal. The object of his fascination leaned over a pool table. Jeans showcased a firm ass, and a tank top showed off intricately patterned black ink from shoulder to elbow. Though it also served to draw attention to the massive muscles on the arms and the breadth of chest that turned the hot ache under Beach's skin to fire. Whether a guy was a top or bottom, Beach had never had any trouble getting exactly what he wanted. And he wanted that.

The man became aware of Beach's greedy stare and glanced over. If Beach hadn't already been determined, the smirk would have done it. The eyes, the not-quite-smiling lips, the black slash of his brows. All of it together promised he could bend Beach in half, make him beg the Lord for mercy, and smile all the way through it.

Beach tipped the bottle toward the man, then brought it to his lips, suggestion in the way his mouth covered the rim. Without losing any of his smirk, the man turned back to his pool game, lining up his shot. Beach didn't know much about pool, but he had a fair understanding of physics, and the shot was at a difficult angle.

When the man spread his arched fingers on the felt to make a bridge for his cue, the strength on display from fingertips to shoulder made Beach's mouth water. He barely refrained from fanning himself in an imitated swoon. A dip in the music let him hear the sharp click of the colliding resins, the softer thud of ball on bumper. The resurging volume of music couldn't drown out the groan from the man's opponent. Beach's target lined up another shot, and with a shake of hands, the game was over.

As the man rounded the table, Beach transferred his weight to his good leg and contemplated leaving the blasted cane against the bar. He already felt hard muscles under his palms, heard the slap of their flesh as their bodies pounded together. The itch that had driven him here rushed to his cock, pulsing hungry and insistent. Catching the stranger's eye, Beach tipped his head in the direction of the bathrooms.

The smirk grew more promising, more pronounced on his handsome face, leaving Beach more determined to see him follow through on it.

Then the man plucked the plastic triangle off the wall and began racking the balls for another game. He might as well have racked the ones hanging heavy under Beach's dick. The bastard had turned him down in favor of another game of pool. It was a damned sorry state of affairs when men came to Grand Central to fondle billiard balls instead of each other's.

Beach dragged his bad leg back up onto the barstool and had almost opened his mouth to order several double Maker's Marks when the ankle shackle on his other leg caught the footrest. Right. Even that consolation was denied him. And nothing but the threat of the absolute loss of freedom was enough of a deterrent to keep him sober.

With a disgusted sigh, he slammed down the bottle he'd been using as a prop and placed a different order. "Bourbon and soda. Hold the bourbon. And keep 'em coming."

Beach grew aware of a few other approaches as he drank his utterly impotent soda. But he wasn't interested. All he could see was that damned smirk. The mesh-and-block-patterned tattoo on the solid shoulder. He had developed a craving, and nothing else would satisfy, though his wounded pride kept him from glancing back toward the pool table.

When three glasses of soda made another need equally insistent, he clamped a straw between his teeth and slid off the stool, propping his cane under the bar. Affecting the rolling stride he'd developed to mask his limp, he headed for the men's room. He should probably get it checked out again, but a few weeks in a coma and then surgery to put a rod in his snapped tibia had exhausted his tolerance for doctors for the foreseeable future.

The day he needed support to stand long enough to drain the snake was the day he went off a bridge headfirst on purpose. He was shaking himself dry when he heard the door open, but before he could tuck and zip, a hard body clamped around him and a hand covered Beach's on his cock.

There couldn't be two men in the bar with a chest like the one Beach felt against his back. But he snuck a glance at the arm around him to be sure. There was the same intricate tattoo, ending at the elbow.

He felt the voice before he heard it, gravel-rough and smoky-smooth like the best bourbon. The voice alone could harden a man's cock at ten paces.

"Give you a hand?"

Beach's dick had never had much pride. It was all ready to forgive the earlier insult, jolting forward at the offer. "Near missed your chance. Thought you weren't interested."

"Like hell." Sweet Lord, the voice was sin. "But *I* make the first move."

"You can move it anyway you like if your cock can cash the check your mouth is writing." Beach pulled his own hand away.

The hot grip was all his cock needed to shift from leaping to lunging for attention, dragging his hips forward in search of friction.

An arm wrapped around Beach's hips and pinned him back, denial and promise in the press of a cock against his ass.

Beach's friend Gavin would probably be able to predict the exact inches and circumference from that brief grind. All Beach knew was it was solid, hot and thick, and felt damned good. He pushed back to indicate he was on board with the plan.

All he got for an answer was a grunt as he was dragged backward into the end stall. The wider one with the rails. The man wasn't rough—not by Beach's standards—simply forceful as he shoved Beach face-first against the tiled sidewall. There was a stone window ledge to lean on or to grip if things got as wild and fast as he hoped they would. That the other man wanted to take charge was no hardship. The more responsibility someone else took, the more Beach was free to focus on how good everything felt.

Except there wasn't any feeling good at first. Beach had been ready to go since he set his eyes on his prize, but a hard dick didn't automatically make his ass soft. He hadn't been fucked since before his coma. This was where chemicals were so damned useful, right here when he was trying to trade the discomfort of a thick callused finger jamming lube into him for the tingle he knew would happen if that finger curled the right way.

It didn't.

His jeans were snug enough to stay bunched under his ass after the man had shoved them out of the way, and they made it tough to spread his legs to accommodate the added stretch of another finger. Beach wiped his forehead on his forearms where they rested on the window ledge and tipped his ass up, looking for that good pressure, the way the muscles would give and the nerves would start singing praises louder than the Sanctuary Choir on a Sunday morning.

He didn't get it.

He shifted more of his weight onto his whole leg, wondering if he wanted to turn around and see the size of what the man behind him was sheathing in latex before it went up his ass. Then the man grabbed one of Beach's hands and put it on the smooth, covered flesh. Maybe the guy meant to prove to Beach the condom was on, maybe it was to give Beach some lube on his hand to help him work his own cock, but as Beach's hand closed around the dick a few inches from his hole, all he could think of was the heft and the width spearing into him. The strain that had been balanced between a throbbing hunger and a gut-churning tension snapped. Beach spiraled into a hot, dizzy space where pain and pleasure were all part of the same beautiful sensation to send him out of his head, better than any drug ever could.

He released the man's cock and held himself open, rocking back onto the blunt head, wanting to push them faster into the rhythm of the fuck, those few moments of perfection where nothing existed but pleasure.

Beach wanted to rush them, rush himself past the first moment of I-can't-take-this, but a bruising pinch on the swell of his ass made him lurch forward. Before he could spin around with an affronted remark about not being a cocktail waitress, the man wrapped an iron-muscled forearm around Beach's waist.

"I make the first move, remember."

It was a statement, not a question, but Beach nodded. Beach didn't know how he could forget anything said in that voice. He should have had it available to read him his textbooks in school. Should hire the man to record the latest board of directors' update.

He wished there'd been a need for more negotiation, the kind of dance he'd come here to avoid. Because then the voice would roll over them, fill the air like fog, the kind thick enough to grab on to. He waited, hoping he'd get rewarded with more of it.

When it came, it curled inside him, an added sensation to build the agony of waiting. "Good." The voice trailed over him, a hand stroking down his back, rubbing the pinched spot for a soothing instant.

Then the arm around Beach's waist pulled him back, forcing his hips out so torso and legs made a comfortable angle. Beach smiled, imagining the man lining himself up with the same care he used on his pool shot, and hoped his skill translated.

It did.

It really did.

The first push had the head in, smooth and easy at first, until the man held them there. Beach's nerve endings, his pulse, his muscles all screamed a reminder that they were doing this without any of the usual enhancements, that this was the only part about getting fucked he wished he could skip, the sting of too tight focused right there in too small a spot, straining tolerance to the limit. This was the part so easy to forget once everything was friction and heat and pressure.

A harsh breath stuttered, echoed into the tiled space, and the rasp in Beach's throat let him know it came from him. He'd half a mind to tell this smirking prick what he could do with his first moves and weird pauses. But they were almost there now, and hell if Beach would back down from a challenge.

The man moved, finally, but it seemed to take forever for him to work it in. The scrape and burn had faded, leaving an even emptier craving. The damned bastard better have stamina to make up for the torturously slow entry.

Beach gripped that window ledge with all the strength in his fingers as his ass swallowed up the thick length. By the time the man's balls swung into Beach's, his manicure was shredded.

Beach shifted a bit under the grip keeping him tight against the other man's hips, wanting more—more room in his ass, more movement between them, every bit of sensation. One of the man's hands was flat on Beach's chest, the other pinning them together at the hips. Beach was sure the man felt the leap of his heart as someone came in to the bathroom, letting in a blast of music before the door swung shut, muffling it again. A scrape of shoes, the sound of a zipper.

No patron of Grand Central would be shocked to stumble over men fucking in the bathroom, so Beach couldn't explain why tension had his muscles locked, his teeth clenched to hold back any sound. After all, fucking had been about the only item not on the list of things forbidden until his trial.

As the stream splashed into the urinal, the man behind Beach used his mouth to shift aside the hair from Beach's neck, kissing away the sweat, then drawing the already tight skin into teeth, sucking a burning mark to make Beach's ass throb harder around the rigid heat inside it.

The chuckle the man outside the door gave as he washed and shook dry his hands made Beach's cheeks flush, as if this was the most outrageous thing he'd ever done—instead of something mildly impulsive.

His exhale as the door closed behind the other man was full of relief.

"What's the matter? Didn't want to share?" The voice purred against Beach's back, across the bite on his neck and into his ear.

Something insaner than usual had gotten into Beach since he'd glimpsed the crinkle of eye above tanned cheek, leaving him damned near broken to saddle, but he found his footing.

"Starting to think there's nothing here to share. You all talk? Have to go that slow to keep from shooting soon as you get it in?"

Beach expected a rough, if not violent reaction, a quick withdraw and a slam forward, finally getting the pounding he'd been looking for, what he'd known he needed when he parked his car down here on Eager Street.

But despite an even tighter clamp of the man's arms, it was only a long, smooth, and—damn him—perfect stroke. He shifted Beach, lifting him up and back a bit more. No wonder the guy was so good at pool. He knew his angles, that was for hell sure. And Beach didn't care if the guy was playing Beach's body like he owned it; that was what Beach wanted. This, all of this, was the answer to the itch that had been driving him out of his skin. Steady, deep pressure, exquisite burn on the backstroke. The hand on his chest found a nipple under Beach's shirt and pinched until Beach gasped, dropping a hand to work his cock. He could manage to whisper all kinds of sweet things to a partner when he was the one driving his dick into them, but right then all he could handle was an endless repetition of harsh breaths and moans.

The build inside made his lips and tongue start to shape the word *please*, as if he couldn't manage his own climb. It was like he'd forgotten his dick was in his hand. He shivered and started working it, hand and fingers providing all the friction he needed to turn the pressure inside into one hell of an explosion.

The grip of fingers around his wrist was as tight as a handcuff but warm and alive. It didn't bruise as it tugged, dragging his hand back up to the ledge to join the other, leaving his cock bobbing and pushing on nothing but air.

"No."

Beach considered himself a pretty open-minded individual, but if there was one word he was down-right prejudiced against, it was that one. The barest hint of it had him either openly defiant or looking for a way to dance, charm, or twist his way around it.

He chalked up his reaction to the voice. Had to be the purr of it that made him suck in a gasp as his balls grew tighter, instead of the word creating the urge to tell the guy to fuck himself from now on.

He didn't even yank his hand free, although the pressure of the other man's hand atop it wasn't enough to keep it resting on the ledge. Since he hadn't been disappointed this far, he'd see what the guy had in mind.

"Better be worth it."

The answer was a faster thrust, a renewed sting of skin against teeth on his neck, and a drag of nails against his nipple as a hand found its way under Beach's shirt. All of it drove electric jolts to spike into his cock without the answering friction of his hand to ease him through it, to give it a place to build to.

Too much and not enough. But damn, it felt good. He rocked back to meet the thrusts, not caring anymore if the angle was perfect. He needed. Needed rougher and harder to hold back the hunger to come, spilling from his cock and balls, shaking into his hips and belly and arms and chest until he trembled with that much want. The sensations kept building without a crest to ride them out.

What was the plan here? Because Beach was pretty sure orgasms were the endgame, and he was more than ready to collect his and say thanks and good night.

He started to tug his hand free, and the man's fingers interlaced with his, cock still slamming into his ass deep and hard. It wasn't that Beach couldn't get himself off with his left hand; it just wouldn't be as much fun. And as much as he wanted to defy the bossy son of a bitch, his curiosity won out. Maybe the guy would come and then suck Beach off, which was an appealing scenario.

Beach tightened his ass against the thick pressure, earning himself a gasp that heated his ear.

"Yeah."

Okay. Beach worked his muscles and drove back harder, increasing the burn of friction for himself and earning the pleasure of constant strokes over his gland. So hot, melting with it, drowning in it. He gave up trying to free his hand, breath whistling out of him.

"Come." That voice.

He wanted to. Fuck how he wanted to. But he couldn't. Not without— "Now." There was a threat curling under there.

It sparked something inside him, cranked the urgency way past the red line, and still Beach couldn't. He'd fucked guys who could. He didn't happen to be one of them.

"I can't." The admission dragged at him, sinking him into a chill of disappointment and shame. His body remembered there was a big fat cock in his ass, that both his nipples hurt, that his balls were aching and full.

"Don't have a choice." Despite the harsh command, the man's hand soothed and petted across Beach's chest, soft lips and soft beard teasing at his neck under his ear.

The man released Beach's hand and laid a hot palm low on his belly, so damned close to where it would be of some help, and kept fucking him.

Beach looked at his freed hand with fascination, wondering why he didn't simply grab his dick and finish, then shut his eyes as the man's rhythm shifted, short quick hard.

"Now." The man growled it.

Tension and yielding in a giant tangle. Straining for it, knowing one thing would be enough to free him, but he didn't know what it was until the solid punch of it shocked him. It was everywhere. In his ass. His balls. His dick. Oh God, so sweet and hot and electric in his dick. A powerful jerk wrung the first shot out of him in a burst of light behind his eyelids, and then all the aftershocks, each one its own slice of heaven as he came back down. Beach found himself wishing their audience had stuck around, because that certainly deserved a round of applause. He'd clap himself as soon as he got his coordination back and got what now felt like a cannon out of his ass.

His bad leg was shaking with exhaustion. Hell, everything felt shaky. Still, he could manage a hand job, though, or even a suck if he sat on the toilet to do it.

The pleasure faded away. There was no high on earth like an orgasm, but the price was that you didn't get to stay there long, and there was no way to up the dose right away. That was the only downside to sex. The sorry, sagging aftermath. He leaned forward in an effort to get the man's dick out of his ass and found himself wrapped up in something between a hug and a restraint.

"No."

There was that word again. "I could—"

"No." He stretched Beach's hands back out to the ledge and fucked him.

It hurt. Not in a God-I'm-dying-get-it-out way, but it definitely wasn't comfortable. And there was no reason Beach couldn't stop it. The man obviously could have won in a battle of strength, but Beach knew he would let him go if Beach made it an issue.

No. It had never been a sexy-sounding word before. And even if there was no way Beach was going to be getting off from it, something about this felt good, despite the scrape of the cock in his ass. The man's hands trailed down his arms, his shoulders, the sides of his chest to land on his hips.

"Good," he murmured in Beach's ear, following the comment with a choked groan. "So good."

Beach's dick ached as it tried to get back in the game, but he had to content himself with the tingle from the man's pattern of caresses, the way his breath and beard tickled Beach's neck. The surprising warmth from listening to the man's control began to shatter. Beach put a hand back, urging the man closer. Faster.

"Yeah."

The raw feeling in the smoky voice made Beach tighten his muscles around the cock fucking into him, dragging out another stuttered *good* before he felt the man come, the lock and snap of muscles, the convulsive jerk of hips. Beach rode it out with him, and when the man finally pulled out, Beach swallowed back the burn of disappointment. He wiped his forehead on his forearm, still holding on to the ledge to relieve the pressure on his leg.

The condom hit the water in the bowl, and the roar of the flush echoed around the stall, but Beach thought he heard "That was sweet" before the man brushed a kiss against his cheek and left.

It took a few minutes before Beach was ready for the world. His leg throbbed, a spiking pain underneath like a fresh break. His next round of sex would be horizontal, definitely.

By the time Beach decided he didn't look or walk quite so rode-hard-and-put-up-wet, the man with the tattoos, goatee, and velvet-sin voice wasn't lingering around the pool table or anywhere in the barroom. Which may have saved Beach the humiliation of forcing his number on the man and begging him to schedule a repeat.

After retrieving his cane, Beach made his way out to his Spider and dropped the top as the engine purred and rumbled. He'd always imagined the sound like a tiger getting a belly scratch. Now it reminded him of the gravelly notes in the voice that had whispered in his ear in the bathroom. The one that had told him *no* and made Beach listen. He was shaking off his stupidity and putting the car in gear when his phone went off.

He let himself enjoy a few more moments of a fantasy where the man had recognized Beach somehow, found his number, and was calling to set up something blissfully horizontal and twice as hot. But it was only a computer-generated voice. Female, impersonal. But to Beach it always held a bit of a derisive sneer as it told him to report to the probation office for testing tomorrow. Thank God sex was the drug that didn't leave any traces.

TAI'S COMPUTER had barely finished moaning and grinding to life that morning when Sutton dumped a bunch of files on his desk.

"Here's your latest share from the Bob fallout."

Tai scanned the pile. "Eight?" And two of them were thicker than average. "Overtime authorization come with them?"

His boss shook his head. "Sometimes you gotta take one for the team."

"Or eight." Tai hauled the files closer. Everybody had more shit now while Bob was suspended and Leslie was out on medical leave. His mom was fond of saying the only reward for a job well done was another job, but Tai hadn't ever noticed her slacking off, house or hospital.

Top file was some sixteen-year-old busted for shoplifting. When Tai flipped through and got a look at the parents' occupations, he was surprised they hadn't been able to make it all go away. Then he got a look at the priors. Some people loved wasting second chances, and third, and fourth. But that wasn't something he had to get to right away.

The next one was a mess. Bob must have been shoving it to the back while he spent his time drinking and driving around underage girls. Tai was still sorting through the file when the switchboard called to tell him David Beauchamp was reporting in. The name meant nothing, which meant he was one of Bob's. Tai yanked out the file and ran through it.

David Beauchamp at thirty-four was where that sixteen-year-old was headed. Charges dismissed, violations and misdemeanors all reduced by the intervention of more money than everyone in this office would make in a lifetime. Beauchamp's sole occupation was to keep the family lawyer in business. Tai moved through to the present. Christ, Beauchamp had been the one to take the header off the bridge back in March, then get busted in May for criminal trespass out on Fort Carroll. The office got one or two of those cases every damned year. Most of them urban adventurers looking for online fame with videos of the dangerously crumbling fort. Tai wished the island would sink the fuck back into the bay. Failing that, become Anne Arundel County's problem. They had enough shit to deal with here.

Beauchamp had been seen as a flight risk and had substance-abuse issues, so they'd slapped a monitor on him to track his whereabouts and to read alcohol intake. Tai checked the monitoring system on the computer. No ethanol alarm, but Beauchamp had been flagged for location last night.

All the chances in the world, and all the advantages, and Beauchamp still had to act like an asshole. Maybe Tai would just throw him back at the judge for violating probation terms. Except given the way things worked for a guy like Beauchamp, he'd be back in Tai's office the next day with a shit-eating grin on his face.

As the man made his way in front of Tai's desk, Tai glanced around the computer screen enough to catch a glimpse of a cane. The grip on it, the light drag in his step, said it wasn't only decoration, but it could be a sympathy game.

A vocal gasp made Tai think the limp and cane were part of the same pity ploy.

"Sit down," Tai spat out before he flipped through the file again, looking for the medical reports. Coma, fracture of the tibia—the jump off the bridge? No, the trespass on Fort Carroll. So Beauchamp wasn't just a party boy, he was a klutzy one. Tai went back to the monitor.

"Want to tell me your whereabouts last night?"

"I would think you already know the answer to that, Officer Fonoti." Beauchamp's voice was amused. These cases made Tai sick. Give him a street punk any day over someone who'd had everything handed to him and threw it away. "Since our whereabouts happened to coincide so forcefully."

Tai snapped a look at the man in the chair. No. No fucking way. Admittedly he hadn't been paying much attention to the guy's looks after ascertaining the basics—fuckable and asking for it. It had been a good time, the guy playing along like he knew the ropes. He'd bet it wouldn't have taken much to get the guy to drop to his knees and kiss Tai's boots.

But last night there hadn't been a cane. Tai hadn't been interested in a lot of details beyond getting his dick up a nice—God, he'd been tight—ass. Tai tugged on his pant leg to free up space. He couldn't get his brain to connect the smug bastard in front of him with the eager, obedient screw he'd had last night. The way he'd groaned and shook and how hard he'd clenched down. Tai had to tug on his pant leg again.

Despite all the evidence, Tai took another look at the program on the monitor. Beauchamp, David A. had been at 130 West Eager Street from 8:52 until 10:38. Tai had gotten there at seven thirty.

"I was informed my probation officer would be closely monitoring my activities, but I didn't realize how closely," Beauchamp said with a slow blink, a smile curving over an unshaved chin.

Tai had been threatened by gang leaders, self-labeled drug lords, and your basic foaming-at-the-mouth douchebags with anger issues. He'd listened to sob stories about hungry children, cheating girl-friends, and backstabbing friends. If any of that could screw with his judgment, he wouldn't have been able to do his job. And he was good at his job. He knew the rules, knew about the boundaries with clients. Hell, it didn't take the Parole and Probation Officers' Manual to figure out the rule on fucking probies. Just one word. *Don't.*

"Mr. Beauchamp—"

"Call me Beach. Everyone does."

Tai looked away from where white teeth bit down on a pink tongue in a cheeky smile. "Mr. Beauchamp—"

"Beechem. That's how you say it. Beech. Em."

The heat in his gut drove Tai to his feet. He glanced down at his hands on the desk, knowing he had slapped them there, but only from the sting in his palms, the echo of the sound. He stared a little longer, taking a deep breath for control, battling the instinctive desire to put his hand on Beauchamp's neck and remind him where the power really rested and do it in a way that had nothing to do with supervising a client. Of course, if Tai allowed himself such an extreme reaction over the slightest challenge, Beauchamp was the one in charge. He peered down. The amiable expression on Beach's—Beauchamp's—face didn't change at all. But his gaze made a leisurely journey from Tai's thighs to his face before he raised his brows.

"According to the conditions of your pretrial probation, you are to remain out of bars."

"But I didn't have a drink of anything… fun." Beauchamp's eyes focused on Tai's crotch. "Didn't my lovely ankle jewelry tell you that?"

Tai glanced over at the monitor, though he already knew the answer.

"Where's Bob? Not that it isn't charming to run into you again, albeit under these circumstances, but I thought I was working with Bob."

Bob? "Officer Meade is not working with this department right now."

"Now that is a shame. We were getting along so well."

Tai had been about to resume his seat, but the phrasing made him wonder if Beauchamp hadn't been getting more from Bob than supervision.

"Drug test. Let's go." Tai grabbed a sample kit from the cabinet and started for the door. Having to piss under supervision like a toddler was humiliating enough to take the starch out of most of the assholes Tai dealt with. But as Beauchamp pushed open the men's room door, Tai realized how epically this was going to backfire. He busied himself in tugging on his gloves, avoiding the memory of his last trip to the men's room with Beauchamp.

Beauchamp stepped up to a urinal and grinned at Tai. "Hold it for me?"

"Excuse me?" Tai stepped away from where he was blocking the door.

"My cane." Beauchamp held it out. His tongue caught in his teeth for an instant before he added, "Well, it's either my cane, the cup, or my cock, but I was trying to keep things professional."

Tai snatched the cane and handed over the sample cup. Beauchamp faced him as he unzipped. Tai tried to glance away, but the action made him appear more pathetic.

Beach shrugged. "Not like you haven't seen it."

"Get on with it."

It was only a small hitch in Beauchamp's breath, but in the tiled room it echoed. And the echo reverberated right to Tai's balls. Tucking the cane under an arm, he kept an eye on the mirror set up to make sure the probie couldn't sub out from a tube secreted somewhere and waited.

When a minute passed, Tai leaned back against the doorframe. "Shy bladder?"

"Not as a rule." The response was sharp. "Uh." There were a few variations on that sound before Beauchamp said, "Tell me what happened to Bob."

"It's none of your business." Tai pushed away from the wall and turned on one of the faucets. "Some inspiration."

"Yeah, thanks." Beauchamp's voice was polished, smooth as silk with a hint of the Carolinas in it, and an ever-stronger promise of a laugh waiting to happen.

"Relax and concentrate."

"Not helping."

Tai made a living reading truth, fear, or desperation in people's voices, their faces, their body language. Right now Beauchamp was projecting all three. And that came overlaid with the awareness Tai should never have of a client. To know he liked it hard and dirty with a commanding voice in his ear.

The sooner this was over with, the sooner Tai could be in Sutton's office, passing Beauchamp onto another PO. That was what he told himself, but it was only half the truth as he took a step to put himself close enough to growl into Beauchamp's ear, "Do it. Now."

There was the sexy hitch in his breath again, and then Beauchamp obediently filled the cup, lifting it away as he splashed the rest into the urinal. He held up the cup, cheeks pink, looking at Tai's shoes. "Uh."

With a heavy sigh, Tai handed him the cap and a paper towel. "Wipe it off."

"Right. Sorry."

When the cap was twisted on and the outside was as clean as it was going to get, Tai took it, slapped on a label, and they both signed the seal on it before he passed back the cane. "Your curfew is eleven, and you're due for a home visit. Better be there. And stay out of bars."

"That's it?" Beauchamp sounded disappointed.

"That's it."

With a raised-brow leer, Beauchamp used the cane to swagger out as Tai held the door. "I can't tell you how much I'm looking forward to that home visit, Officer."

Chapter Two

TAI WATCHED Beauchamp turn the corner for the elevator before he sprinted to Sutton's office. Tai had worked for Sutton for five years, never asked for shit, always took the crap cases. Hell, he'd take two to unload Beauchamp, as long as there were no questions asked about why.

The doors always stuck; too much fucking humidity. He shoved it open, the argument already spilling from his head. "I'll take—trade any other client, but I can't work the Beauchamp case."

"Just a second, sir." Sutton glared at Tai, then jabbed a button on the phone. "What the fuck is with you, Fonoti? You don't know how to knock? You think I got time for you to whine while I'm on the phone with the goddamned DA?"

Until that moment, Tai had Sutton's leadership style categorized as lots of bad jokes and backslapping encouragement, but right then he could have given the

scariest defensive line coach lessons in heckling. It
hit with the same shock as the day Tai had realized he
wasn't going to the NFL.

Sutton sagged in his chair. "Look, be a miracle if
Bob doesn't take the whole fucking department with
him. Just do your job, Fonoti. Is that too much to ask?"

There wasn't a good time to say *I fucked a client
and wouldn't mind doing it again*. But this, this was
a supremely bad one. "Got it." Not that Tai had been
about to spill the truth. No way in hell could he do his
job if every probie he hauled in for a drug test claimed
Tai was staring at his dick.

He dragged the door into the jamb as quietly as he
could and lowered his head against the wood before
heading off to do the parts of his job that didn't involve trying to forget how every hitch of David Beauchamp's breath showed how very much he wanted to
give up control.

BEACH SWORE the Spider had an insulted in-
quiry in its purr as it rounded the corner where the
GPS had led them. "Yeah, baby, I'm not too keen on
this street either."

A cargo container, the top of which was covered
with trash, occupied half the driving lane on the one-
way street. He must have misheard Gavin, but there
was his friend's Bentley, tucked into the alley behind
an Audi. Beach might have spent a good portion of the
spring in a coma, but he'd been awake long enough to
have heard if there was some urban renewal real-estate boom going on in West Baltimore. He pulled his
Spider in behind the Bentley and patted her steering
wheel. "It's okay, baby. Daddy won't make you sit
here long."

He rounded the front of the building to see Gavin nodding and talking with a woman who screamed *realtor* from the tip of her sleek bun to the heels on her four-inch pumps. Beach did a second go-over from the hem down. Nice legs. A lickable line of muscle cut in the sleek brown calves. He was considering pretending to take a look around the side of the building to get a read on the rest of her package when Gavin caught his eye and pursed his lips.

Gavin was decidedly less fun these days. He'd always been a bit of a melancholy-poet type, but Beach had been able to shake him out of that. Now that Gavin was fucking a cop regularly, he seemed to be infected with a fatal case of law-and-order morality.

"What do you think?" Gavin said, turning to Beach and cocking his head at the pile of white bricks they were apparently there to inspect. "Eden Hadley, my friend, David Beauchamp."

"Mr. Beauchamp." The realtor offered a cool, soft, and exquisitely manicured hand.

Beach allowed the firm business shake, feeling her size him up, appraising him as a potential ally or threat to her sale. As her grip relaxed, he gave her hand a gentle turn and bowed over it. "My absolute pleasure. Call me Beach."

Her lashes dipped. To make it clear he and Gavin were not that sort of friend, he let his gaze caress the purple lace edging of the camisole under her gray-striped suit jacket. Turning back to Gavin, he asked, "What do I think of what? This oversized prison guard tower?" To Eden he offered a wink and a grin.

Not mollified, she straightened, pointing at the odd glassed-in top. "The solarium was a former art studio. The chain fencing was required by code enforcement, but of course you would be free to re-place it with a more decorative safety measure."

Gavin cocked his head at Beach. "I meant the neighborhood."

"In the daytime I'm only slightly terrified to leave my baby unattended. I know you want to move out of the manor as soon as the latest Montgomery has debuted. But—"

"It's for a foundation."

"Ah." That explained everything. Some sort of guilt complex for having been lucky enough to be born with a platinum spoon in his mouth made Gavin the belle of the ball in the charity circuit, popping up on boards and committees. Beach wrote out donation checks and showed up when there was a ticket to something that sounded fun. Gavin's level of hands-on sounded like martyrdom. Worse, it sounded utterly boring. "I'm sure the foundation will love it." He delivered himself to Eden for redemption and received an open-mouthed smile in return.

"Do you ever read your emails?" Gavin asked.

"Every one of them," Beach lied without a blink. "So, Gavin, fond of you as I am, I actually was look-ing for your pet policeman."

"Lucky you. He said he'd meet me here if he could. Shall we?" Gavin said to Eden, who produced a key that admitted them to the building.

As Beach held the door for the lady, he passed her his card. Gavin moved on ahead of him, inspecting the wood-paneled hall.

"If you ever have trouble contacting Mr. Mont-gomery, I'm sure I can track him down for you." She accepted the card and his flimsy excuse with a coquettish nod. Last night had been amazing—even if the morning had held a rather rude reintroduction. This was an entirely different kind of game, and Beach liked his odds of winning, especially when she tucked the card inside her camisole.

Gavin finished his inspection of the stairs and came back toward them. The entryway was solid, at least—the stairs free of gaps or holes, with double-sized archways to either side—but through the archways, stacks of rotted boxes decayed against peeling walls.

"It's fortunate to find a gas-furnace conversion in a building of this age," the realtor pointed out. "A real savings in the long run."

"And what age would that be?" Beach asked.

"The original building dates back to 1894."

"Any problems with the original owners?" Beach poked his cane at the boarded-up window.

"Excuse me?"

Beach was getting that a lot today. Must be his charm was in need of rebooting.

"Beach is referring to ghosts. He's a little obsessed with them," Gavin explained.

"They are obsessed with my family home. Can't stand to share it."

Eden split her attention between them as if she were watching a tennis match, no doubt trying to determine if this was a scam to drive down the asking price. "There's been no report of—"

One of the boards Beach had poked snapped in two, making all three of them jump.

"This is really a charming place, Gavin. What does your foundation expect to do to get it at all useful?"

Gavin clapped Beach on the shoulder, forcing him to put more weight on his cane. "We're looking forward to a lot of volunteerism. I know you've got all that free time on your hands, given your inability to leave the county."

"Thank you so very much for mentioning it." Beach could read faces like Gavin read poetry, and Eden was about to leave his card on the floor with the rest of the ancient rubble. "I don't have a phobia or anything so dire," he offered in clarification, then stopped, realizing a phobia might sound eccentric, while being bound with a tracking anklet in lieu of sitting in jail came off as dangerous.

"Christ, Gavin, what the fuck are you thinking with this shithole?" The complaint could only be from Gavin's bantam rooster of a boyfriend, stomping his way in. Clouds of mortar dust sprouted under his shoes, glowing in the single beam of light from the window. For the first time in their brief acquaintance, Beach was happy to see the arrogant prick.

"Actually"—Beach turned to Eden with the first genuine smile he'd felt all day—"I'm thinking I'll be able to take my yacht out on the bay very soon. Or perhaps make a weekend trip to Saratoga when the races start."

There was a slight thaw from Eden as the belli-cose presence of Jamie made it clear she would need additional allies.

"It's a multiuse space. Some of it could be turned to investment opportunities." Eden indicated a side door that appeared to have at one time been a ga-rage-sized opening, now bricked to a standard size. Judging by the sheer amount of crap left behind, Beach was guessing a former life as a warehouse.

"We won't be renting any of the space." Gavin's voice was firm.

"You never said what your foundation intended to do with the building, Mr. Montgomery." Eden led them back toward the hall.

"The foundation is establishing a shelter—"

"For rats?" Beach murmured to Jamie. As sweet as the rear view of Eden Hadley was, Beach had come here to pursue a more pressing need, and as much as he loathed the necessity, he had to make an effort to endear himself to stompy and short.

Jamie snorted a laugh, and Gavin tossed a glare back at them as he continued, "—for homeless LGBTQ teens and young adults."

The realtor's reaction was somewhere between an *ah* and a *hm*. While Beach couldn't see the point in wallowing in so much guilt you felt you had to take on the world's problems, he also couldn't imagine anyone would object to sheltering homeless children.

"Is that a problem, Miss Hadley?" Gavin's voice dropped the room temperature several degrees. Considering that it was an un-air-conditioned space in Baltimore in July, the chill was almost pleasant.

The realtor rushed in to take the edge off. "Of course not, Mr. Montgomery. Though with that information ahead of time, I would have guided you to a space more suitable for that sort of living arrangement."

"I'd prefer a space we can adapt to our needs. You said there was a kitchen on this floor?" Gavin's strides moved him ahead of the realtor. He was playing it cool, but Beach had known him for over twenty years, and Gavin wanted this place.

The space to the left of the entryway was much less debris-filled, empty and dusty. "You've never seen him like this, when he gets involved in a project." Beach stopped and leaned on his cane, leaving Jamie with the choice of walking around him or kicking the cane out from under him. Based on the narrowing of Jamie's eyes, Beach had better make this fast if he didn't want to find out how the mortar dust tasted. "Our Gavin may not be very expressive, but he does feel things deeply. When he finds something worthwhile, he gives it his full commitment."

As the disgust curled Jamie's lip, Beach wondered if perhaps that was the wrong opening for a conversation with the boyfriend.

"You think you gotta tell me that? Hell, you're not even worthwhile, and he's still friends with you. Though you tried to kill him twice."

"I wasn't—" Beach began, but he knew Jamie wouldn't hear the facts, that Gavin had chosen to come after Beach both times, that there was honor at stake. Something he doubted was part of whatever passed for a policeman's training. "And I am heartily suffering for it," Beach assured Jamie with a palm raised in surrender and a cane thump for emphasis.

"Not nearly enough." Jamie heaved a sigh, sending some more dust swirling, his gaze already moving past Beach, on to his homeless-shelter-obsessed boyfriend.

"But I am." Beach tugged on his jean leg to reveal his anklet. "Worse, the probation officer they've assigned me has serious boundary issues. I do believe he's coming on to me."

"Christ, Beauchamp, you get any more melodramatic, you'll be fanning yourself and fainting. What the fuck you mean, coming on to you?"

At least Beach had secured Jamie's complete attention. "I mean, the way he came up behind me, pressing against my ass while he was *helping* me get a sample for my urine test. And the things he said." *Come. Now.* The memory of that voice sent heat pouring over him like Carolina sunshine.

Jamie studied Beach's face. "That's out of line. Illegal kind of out of line. You're technically in custody."

"I thought so. If I were to report this—"

"He'd be screwed. What office they send you to?"

"Dundalk."

Jamie reared back. "Aw hell. They're already so fucked over with the drunk-driving mess. They'll be all over that like flies on shit."

"On the other hand, maybe he'd be willing to loosen the ball and chain." Beach tapped lightly on his ankle cuff.

"God, you don't take responsibility for anything, do you? Half kill your friend, drag him into burglary—"

"We weren't stealing anything. I was merely making an effort to retrieve my family's property."

"What would you call it if people were wandering through your house?"

"A reason to reach for a rifle."

"Exactly. Because it's burglary. You're lucky the charges aren't worse, lucky as hell Gavin's not going down with you, and you still think you should walk free because you know how to shake your ass?"

"I never knew you'd noticed," Beach cooed.

"You disgust me." Jamie stomped away.

Beach smiled at his short-legged progress. He had his answer. Nothing Jamie had said meant things wouldn't go exactly as Beach planned.

Chapter Three

THE NEXT time Bob decided to go on a bender, he could fucking well get some paperwork out of the way first. After the adventure with Beauchamp that morning, Tai's day had been quiet. His spot-check on his teenagers found them both in summer school where they were supposed to be. With only him and DiBlasi, they couldn't do much out of the office, so Tai gritted his teeth and started clearing through Bob's files.

At six thirty that night, Tai slammed the drawer on his filing cabinet and punched the lock. Before he could get the hell out, Sutton popped up in his doorway.

The field director looked like shit, and Tai could almost feel sorry for the bastard, if it wasn't his own damned fault for enabling Bob's fuckups until everything hit the fan.

Sutton pinched the bridge of his nose, shoving his glasses sideways. "What was that case you were bitching about this morning?"

"David Beauchamp, some asshole with more money than brains. He—"

Sutton held up a hand. "I don't give a shit what's got your panties in a twist. You wanna switch it with one of DiBlasi's, tell him I said to do it."

Tai nodded.

"You're welcome, Fonoti. They don't do manners where you come from?"

"Washington Hill?" Tai squared his shoulders.

"Really? Thought you were Hawaiian or something."

Or something fit. Tai had been checking the "Other" box under ethnicity all his life.

Black, yes. White, yes. Pacific Islander, yes. "Samoan."

"Yeah? How they say 'thank you' in Samoan?"

"I don't know. I grew up in Washington Hill." Other than when he'd been hired, this was the longest conversation Tai had ever had with Sutton. And he hoped they never had another one go on this long.

"You said." Sutton hoisted the strap of an overstuffed business case to his shoulder. "Okay. That's it. Aloha, Fonoti."

"Still not Hawaiian," Tai muttered under his breath.

As Tai pulled his head out from under the shower, he heard the last of his ringtone cut off as his phone went to voicemail. He finished rinsing and hopped out, drying enough to grab his phone. Four missed calls in a six-minute shower was pretty impressive.

He played his voicemail.

DiBlasi first: "Who the fuck is this asshat you're dumping on me? I'm sticking you with both of Bob's JD girls for this. Did you fucking forget my daughter's getting married tomorrow?"

Whatever. No one liked getting stuck with the female juvenile offenders, but it was better than dealing with Beauchamp after what had happened.

His mom was next: "Hi, *la'u tama*. Phillip and I both have the Fourth off for a change. We'd love to have you out for a barbecue. You know I'd love to see Sammie, and Gina is always welcome. Or if there's someone you'd like me to meet...."

The word *boyfriend* might not be something his mom found it easy to use in connection to her only son, but she'd accepted his explanation for why he'd be supporting Sammie as his daughter but not marrying the baby's mother. He couldn't help but wonder if his mom had harbored some hope he'd have an epiphany of normal. But her hopes—and Tai's illusion of family—had all gone to hell when Josh came back in the picture. Josh and the damned paternity test. Tai couldn't wrap his brain around that. For three years Sammie'd been his. She would always feel like his, no matter what the DNA said. With that ache nice and fresh, he should have predicted the next message would be from Gina.

"Having a barbecue tomorrow if you want to stop over."

Yes, stop over and see Sammie and Gina snuggled in with Josh's family. Josh put up with Tai coming around, let him have access to the child who still called him Daddy—mostly because of Gina. Though he was glad Josh had moved them out to Overlea.

Better schools, less chance of Sammie running around with future probation clients.

The last one read out as a private number.

"Ah—um—well." The voice was barely familiar, a tease in his ears. "My lawyer—well, it's Beach, uh, David Beauchamp. My lawyer said I should call you. I'm afraid I'm going to be a bit delayed for my curfew. My car's been impounded." Then quickly, "I wasn't breaking any laws, not even speeding. But...." After he let that trail off, the message was over.

Tai pressed Callback. As soon as he heard some breath on the line, he snapped, "What happened?"

"It was a DUI trap. I wasn't drinking. You can check your little monitor thing. But they decided to run my plates. Did you know you can earn a lot of parking tickets when you're in a coma?" A pained inhalation. "Are they always so brutal with those tow trucks?"

"Generally."

"My poor baby. So I was told to let you know that there were extenuating circumstances. I suppose I should call a cab." The tone suggested a cab ride was a minor improvement over a ride in a manure truck.

"Where'd they get you?"

"I was hoping you knew. Doesn't this handy-dandy device strapped to my body keep you informed of my whereabouts?"

It did, but only sent out an alert if the client went somewhere out of bounds or triggered the ethanol detector. Tai wasn't about to give Beauchamp that information. "You have no idea where you are. And you aren't drinking?"

"I was between here and there, according to the route in my GPS. Hang on a moment." No waiting for

Tai to agree, only the assumption that he would. And then Beauchamp's voice again, tinny, muffled. "Might I inquire where on God's green earth I find myself stranded?"

The guy would be lucky if he didn't end up busted just for being an asshole.

"I'm in some wilderness known as Boston Street, east of the intersection with South Haven. Brewers Hill. Apparently they felt that an apt location for their trap."

"Beauchamp. Shut up." Tai released the punishing grip on his phone and flexed his fingers. Beauchamp would have a hell of a time getting a cab down there. But he was DiBlasi's problem now. Tai was about to tell Beauchamp to call his new PO when he remembered DiBlasi's *Did you fucking forget my daughter's getting married tomorrow?* They'd done each other favors before. And if it were anyone but Beauchamp, Tai wouldn't have hesitated to bite the bullet now. So that meant if he wanted to pretend nothing had happened, he'd be better off treating Beauchamp like a regular client. Even if nothing about Beauchamp was regular. "Yeah, I know where that is." And it wasn't far. All the more reason to pitch in and save DiBlasi from a different kind of hangover when he came in on Monday.

"How useful for you."

Before Tai could respond to the condescension, a deep exhalation whooshed over the line. "My apologies, Officer. It's one thing to face consequences for your actions while awake, quite another to have them thrown at you for something out of your control."

Maybe Beauchamp was digging for sympathy, but that sigh had acted like a balloon deflating, taking the snotty brat with it. With a sigh of his own, Tai muttered, "Fine. I'll be there in fifteen."

"Beg pardon?"

"Stay there. I'll pick you up and take you home."

Beauchamp's answer wasn't at all arrogant, and the hair on the back of Tai's neck stood on end as the man purred, "How very gallant. I'll be waiting."

THE COPS still had their checkpoint running when Tai pulled over to the side, holding out his badge for the cop who came up to his window.

"Jez, stay down." He used his sternest voice, and he heard her settle across the back seat with a grunt. He had to be honest, he hadn't brought her out of necessity. He'd walked her at lunch and taken her for their long walk after dinner. No, he'd brought her along as a big, furry chaperone.

The cop checked his badge, then scanned the interior of Tai's Focus hatchback. Tai knew the exact moment the cop saw Jez, the way he reared back, hand on his piece.

Tai had no doubt Jez was holding her stay. He might have fucked up more often than he'd care to admit, but saving her from doggie death row was the one sure good thing he'd done in his life. She was completely broken of all her bad habits.

The cop moved his hand away from his holster and tossed Tai's badge back at him. "You here on business?"

"Picking up a probie. You impounded his car."

"Yeah, the smart-assed gimp." The cop straightened and waved. "All yours. If you feed him to the dog, I wanna watch."

Beauchamp limped across the beams from Tai's headlamps, one hand on the hood, the other shielding his eyes as he peered through the window. Was he expecting a friendly wave? A thumbs-up?

Tai jerked his thumb at the passenger door. With a grin, he released Jez. "Good stay, girl."

She stood on the back seat, shaking herself as Beauchamp opened the door, then thrust her head into the space between the seats. Even Tai still startled when faced with the size of her head, the gleam of teeth closing in.

Beauchamp stood motionless as Jez loomed at him, then tilted her head. Tai kept a cautious hand near her collar, but he wanted to see how it would play out.

Beauchamp's gaze flicked over at Tai for an instant before he lowered his lids and performed what Tai could only describe as a bow—to the dog.

"The honor is mine." Beauchamp eased his hand forward in a closed fist. Jez hesitated.

"Okay, Jez."

She sniffed around Beauchamp's fist, then his wrist. In the rearview mirror, Tai spotted her stub of a tail wiggling around in Jez-speak for happy.

"You getting in?" Tai drummed on the steering wheel.

"If everyone agrees to that course of action." Again Beauchamp spoke directly to Jez.

Jez licked Beauchamp's hand, and he opened it to rest the palm on her head. She nudged for pets.

"Everyone's on board. Get in. Lie down, Jez."

Beauchamp lowered himself into the passenger seat, placing the cane between his legs. "You know, there's no difference in the way you snap commands, whether to me or your dog. Are you like this with all the people you supervise, or am I special?"

That was exactly what Tai didn't want to think about.

After Beauchamp had hooked his seat belt, Tai reversed them back onto Boston Street, grumbling, "So are you supposed to be the dog whisperer?"

Beauchamp pressed himself into the corner so he was angled toward Tai. "Isn't the dog a bit over the top? You have a badge, a gun, and a chest that could double as the deck of an aircraft carrier. Did you actually need a rottweiler?"

"She's a rescue."

Beauchamp's rigid posture softened. Jez's face popped up between the seats again, and Beauchamp stroked her forehead, rubbed behind her ears.

"If she's being a pest—"

"I love dogs."

"Should have seen her when I brought her home."

"Hardly her fault if she was abused by people who damn well ought to be neutered."

Tai grunted agreement. That would have been the least of what he'd have had in store for the assholes trying to start a dogfighting business out of Armistead Gardens. Still, not even the judge who'd initially ordered her put down or, hell, Tai's ex-boyfriend Donte could argue Jez's transformation from the unpredictable snapping animal she'd been into a model citizen.

Back when Tai thought he knew why things had gone to shit with Donte, Tai had shown Jez off, shown how docile and obedient she could be when treated the right way. And it had seemed to work, Donte kneeling to let her lick his face. But in response to the question Tai had only half been able to ask, his muttered,

"So?" with a nod around the apartment, Donte had given Jez a last rub around the ears and, with his hand on the back of his own neck as if for protection, said, "I didn't leave because I was scared of the dog, Tai. I left because I was scared of you."

One thing about Beauchamp. He didn't scare. Even when he probably should. His fancy Ferrari impounded, being driven home by his probation officer, and he took up space there in Tai's passenger seat with lazy confidence. Like he'd set the whole thing up to get chauffeured home.

Thank God it was a short trip to the address Tai remembered from the file. A short trip to Beauchamp getting the hell out of Tai's life before he did something he'd really regret.

Beauchamp's address was one of those new apartment complexes for the beautiful people coming to Fell's Point and blocking the view for the people who'd lived there through the shitty times. Tai hated the way going past the gate made him feel, so he flashed his badge before Beauchamp could offer his own ID to the guard.

When they pulled up in front of the chrome and glass and fountained entrance with the artsy iron fire pit and sculpture, he knew he couldn't get Beauchamp out of the car fast enough. Tai's palm itched with the need to wrap around Beauchamp's neck, drag him down, put his face into the footwell. And for the worst reasons. Reasons that made it hard to trust himself.

Avoiding temptation, Tai stared straight ahead at the row of birches lining the drive. "Here you go. Made your curfew."

When Beauchamp didn't move, Tai leaned across him and popped open the door.

Beauchamp put a hand on Tai's forearm.

The skin to skin contact froze him, muscles tightening under the light touch. Now he wanted his hand on the back of Beauchamp's neck for an entirely different purpose.

When Tai didn't pull away, Beauchamp gently closed his fingers. "I wonder if you'd be so kind as to take me into the parking garage, up to my floor. I'd invite you in, save you a trip for that home visit you promised." His voice was silk and sunshine, teasing the edge of open seduction. "You can check for all the illegal substances you want. Of course, Jez would be welcome too."

Tai dragged his arm back. "No, thank you."

"I'm disappointed to hear there's nothing in my apartment you might find of interest. Are you sure?" Beauchamp's self-mocking humor kept the line from being over the top.

Tai regripped the steering wheel as he imagined smooth, warm, and wet sliding down his dick instead of hinting in his ear. Not happening. Beauchamp might not be his probie anymore, but he was still in county custody.

"Get out." Tai clenched his teeth against the wave of disappointment when Beauchamp pushed open the door.

"On second thought, I hear this is the best sport-fishing season they've had in a long time off the Eastern Shore. I'd like to head out to Ocean City, see if I can't beat my record white marlin."

Tai had expected Beauchamp would have some kind of parting shot, but a ramble about fishing was hinky, even for him.

Tai stared at the guy. "You can't leave the county."

"Well, not officially…." Beauchamp looked down at his cane, shifting it from hand to hand. "But as you seem to be giving my case such *special* attention, I thought you should be able to arrange it."

The shock of understanding delivered a round of rabbit punches to the gut. Disappointment, disbelief, anger, and over it all, head-shaking amusement that bubbled into a laugh. "Shit. You're a walking disaster. You're not even good at blackmail."

"Excuse me. If you don't want to land yourself in hot water, you'll do what I tell you."

"Close the door." Tai delivered the demand in a low, steady voice so he didn't spook Jez.

The first attempt had been funny. This—Beauchamp acting full of affronted dignity—got deep under Tai's skin.

Beauchamp shut the door and looked over with a smug expression Tai would have slapped off him in any other situation.

"No, David."

Beauchamp's lips parted, but Tai kept talking, leaning over, driving Beauchamp back into the door. "No, that's not how it's going to go. And I'm going to tell you why."

Beauchamp licked his lips.

Tai smiled. "One. I'm not your PO anymore. I had your ass transferred to another officer as soon as I figured out I'd had my dick up it."

Beauchamp's breath did the hitch Tai had found so fucking sexy.

Tai watched the flush across Beauchamp's freckled cheeks, the pulse and bob in his throat, the trapped-animal stare in his eyes. "Yeah. Hungry ass too, begging, grinding on my dick in the fucking bathroom. Which brings us to point two." Tai was pretty sure Beauchamp was holding his breath. "It's not going to go like that because you were that guy, David. And you wanted to be. You don't want to tell me what to do. You're desperate to have someone tell *you* what to do and to make you do it. I could have you strip off every stitch for me and put you out of the car, and you'd thank me and call me Sir and mean it with every bit of breath in your body."

Beauchamp released a shaky exhale, but his gaze didn't stray from Tai's face.

"And we both know I'm right."

Beauchamp acknowledged that with the slightest dip of his eyelashes.

"Good. Now get the fuck out of my car."

Chapter Four

THE DREAM that jerked Beach out of sleep was dark and hot and featured his erstwhile probation officer in ways that made his dick hard and his head swim. He just didn't know if his head was swimming to or away from something. He threw off the sheet and duvet, and the air-conditioned chill dragged at least his little head back from the brink. Sprawled like a starfish across the king-sized mattress, he tried to pin down one of the dream fragments. But all the pieces were slippery, squirting away from his grasp like a handful of too much lube. Beach only knew *he* had been in them. Threat and promise in his commanding body, the growling voice.

And Beach didn't even know his name. The probation-office listing had been for T. Samuel Fonoti. He tested the name. Sam.

Call me Sir and mean it with every bit of breath in your body. The words rumbled against Beach's ears from inside his head, driving him fully awake, unable to drift back into his dream.

After rolling from bed, he staggered to the bar, a tumbler and bottle of Pappy Van Winkle in hand before he remembered the damned anklet. Treasuring a sniff of the caramel-praline scent, he put the bourbon carefully back on the bar and filled the tumbler with orange juice from the fridge. Naked but for the damned anklet, he pressed his forehead against the black glass separating him from his balcony.

I could have you strip off every stitch for me and put you out of the car. Public nudity didn't hold a great deal of shame or interest for Beach. The thrill of hearing those words in *his* voice had been from the command. The implication that by following the order he might earn that grudging praise, hear that voice telling him it was good or sweet. That was what sent warmth rushing through his veins as surely as if he'd been sipping seventeen-year-old bourbon and not orange juice. Beach slid the door open and stepped out into the hot July night.

Five floors up and at 3:00 a.m., there wasn't much potential for exhibitionism. No lighted boats prowling the harbor. But the buzz under his skin drove him back inside for his phone. Framing his nude body with the harbor at his back, he snapped a picture and keyed in the number for T. Samuel Fonoti with the text *Ready when you are, Sir.*

But his thumb hesitated over Send.

Beach knew only too well the futility of chasing a high. One perfect moment was all you got, and then things went downhill quicker than a knife fight in a phone booth.

But this, whatever this was, they'd barely scratched the surface. There were words for it, words he shied away from naming. Words he'd uttered with disdain or mockery for people who felt the need to complicate sex with silly games and costumes, when fucking was as simple and natural an act as breathing.

But what had happened, what he wanted to happen, touched more than just the happy pleasure parts, though they were certainly involved, he noted with a glance at his half-hard dick. Beach wasn't one to be counted on for deep thoughts, but standing naked on his balcony at 3:00 a.m. seemed to dredge them up. Staring at the black water of the harbor, he had to admit those dizzying moments under the thrall of the other man's authority had touched what Beach could only call his soul.

No way in hell was he going to have a bare taste and then spend the rest of his life wondering what might have been. He pressed Send as if he could reach through the phone and touch the man on the other end.

The thought tugged at his guts, then lower. If Sam—Sir?—were here now, if he sent back a hot demand…. Beach dropped the phone on the glass table and grabbed his dick, thumbing the slit to work out some precome. It wasn't the risk of getting caught driving him but the imagined presence on the phone. Faster, tighter. Even if it burned. He shivered at the idea. How much sensation, how much pain would there be in chasing this high?

The thought of pain was almost always enough to send Beach running in the other direction, but all it did right now was make his dick harder, drag his nuts up.

No.

If Officer Fonoti called back, Beach could be waiting. Aching for it. He yanked his hand away like his dick was on fire, clenching his fist in frustration as the smooth build to orgasm turned into a knotted mess in his balls.

"Now would be good," he whispered at his phone.

This was crazy. Sweating on the balcony with a chafed, aching dick when there was lube and air-conditioning on the other side of the glass. He was the only person in Baltimore awake.

His phone vibrated against the tabletop, and Beach dove for it.

Don't contact me again.

The response might have been unequivocal to some people. To Beach, the quick answer meant a lot more.

Why? Beach's finger shook when he tapped Send. *I can't.*

Beach smiled as he read the answer. The space between *I can't* and *I don't want to* held infinite possibilities.

GAVIN SMILED beatifically as he lowered the mimosa to the table. "Nothing like fresh-squeezed."

Beach's mouth watered at the thought. Miss Shirley's did them right. It wasn't the buzz he was missing. It would take more than the champagne bubbling through the orange juice to go to his head, but he wanted that taste. Could feel it at his lips, sliding over his tongue. How sensitive was the damned monitor? One little sip probably wouldn't register.

Gavin tipped his glass back again, smile going wicked. "I'm sure they could make you a virgin mimosa."

"The sweet tea is fine." Beach gripped the tall glass and glared across the table. He knew the bastard had ordered the mimosa on purpose.

"I'm sure it is."

Patronizing and smug. That prick of a cop was rubbing off on Beach's oldest friend. "How long are you going to take it out on me for that little adventure?"

"To which adventure are you referring?" Gavin's eyes and his grammar got serious. "The one where we both almost died going off the Key Bridge, or the one where you coerced me into criminal trespass out on Fort Carroll that nearly cost me my chance with—?" Gavin stopped himself as the waiter approached to take their orders.

Beach's eyebrows shot up. It was *that* kind of serious with Sergeant Boyfriend—Jamie. Beach supposed he'd better get used to the idea and the name. "Your father will be thrilled to give you away at the wedding."

For an instant the tightness in Gavin's jaw made Beach remember exactly how it had felt when the ground had given way and he'd plunged into the hole on Fort Carroll, smashing his leg in the process. Then the corner of Gavin's mouth twitched. "What a lovely photo op that would be."

"Especially if they can capture your sister's apoplexy."

Gavin's devotion to a family that treated him like a spare tire was something Beach would never understand.

"Ready?" The waiter looked expectantly at Beach.

"I'll have the crab cake and fried green tomato Benedict. With grits."

Gavin ordered the grilled salmon Florentine Benedict and handed off their menus.

"Grits for you too, hon?"

Gavin shook his head. "Hash browns."

"Heathen," Beach muttered.

Gavin smiled and sipped his mimosa. "You going to get his number or just meet him in the men's room?"

Powerful arms pinning Beach's to the window ledge while a thick cock speared him deep and hard. A gravelly *no* echoing off the bathroom tile.

"Uh?"

"Clean living is destroying your brain, Beach. The waiter."

Beach leaned around a guy shoveling in whipped cream and bananas to get a look. Tall, dark, and cute gave him a wink.

Beach turned back to Gavin and shrugged. "Not my type."

"As opposed to everyone else on the planet?"

Beach offered another shrug.

Gavin splayed his hands on the table. "So I see your face before eleven in the morning for the first time since prep school—"

"Not counting the times we never went to bed," Beach pointed out.

Gavin leaned back. "I thought being out on the town all night would violate your probation's curfew."

He'd been paying attention? Beach didn't know whether to be charmed or paranoid. He batted his eyes. "I didn't know you cared that much, sugar."

"With your epic whining, I couldn't not know every detail of your probation." Gavin gave a faint smile. "Besides, I'd rather not have to cut into my schedule to visit you in jail. Too depressing."

"I had the impression that after Fort Carroll, you'd like me to rot there."

"That would be Jamie's fervent desire. I prefer to go on having something to hold over your head."

"Thanks. I think."

The waiter was back with their food. After sliding Gavin's plate to the table, the waiter rested a warm hand on Beach's shoulder while placing the stacks of crab and fried green tomato in front of him.

"Is there anything else I can get for you?" His voice had a nice resonance, like the purr of a cat.

"Not right now, but I'll let you know," Beach offered with a promise in his smile. The hand on his shoulder squeezed lightly as the waiter departed.

"That's the Beach I know." Gavin put knife and fork to his salmon.

"Thanks. Again." Beach didn't know why it irritated him so much.

"What's causing the sudden concern for your reputation? I thought sex was still on the probation menu."

"It is."

Gavin lowered his silverware, brows arched. "Now we get to it."

"What?"

"Why I'm weeding through your obfuscatory conversation and flirtation for the second time in less than twenty-four hours."

"I invited you to breakfast. I am paying for your meal, but it's not as if I strapped you into the chair." Damn the flush that spilled from his throat up to his jaw. No way would Gavin miss that. But the echo of his words set off a string of images that had Beach shifting on his seat. Would Officer Fonoti want to do that with him? *Bind* him?

Gavin made an exasperated sound. "No. But I do have other plans today. So if you're planning on—"

"All right." Beach swallowed a forkful of perfectly seasoned heaven. "It's difficult to explain. Even to you."

Gavin's eyes widened. "You're pregnant."

Beach stabbed at a piece of crab to keep from stabbing his friend in the throat.

"If you're looking at me, the statute of limitations on that ran out almost twenty years ago."

In spite of himself, Beach started to laugh. This was Gavin. His oldest friend in the world. Without Gavin, it would have taken Beach a lot longer to learn how hard he got off with a dick up his ass. That fucking a friend was as much fun as talking a girl out of her pants.

"Just tell me if we're dealing with boy trouble or girl trouble." Gavin's voice held the smile that hadn't made it to his face. "Because I'm not really much help with girls."

"It's more me. No, everything's functioning fine, thank you," Beach added to forestall Gavin's amusement over any need for a little blue pill. "But...." Beach considered whether he'd want to do any of the things he'd looked at online with a woman being... dominant, and shook his head. "We are also talking about a man."

Gavin didn't say anything. With a nod he went back to slicing off bite-sized pieces of breakfast. The bastard.

But aside from the way he limited himself to only picking from one team, Gavin was the most sexually adventurous person Beach knew. If anyone had experience in the kind of thing Beach couldn't stop thinking about, it was Gavin.

"Your cop—Jamie. He's kind of bossy."

"Oh shit, Beach. Jamie told me what you said. About the probation officer harassing you. I am so sorry for teasing you. If I thought—"

Beach waved that off. "That was only an annoyance. It's been taken care of."

"Good." Gavin stopped with his fork on its way to his mouth. "So then what do you mean by Jamie being bossy?"

Gavin's gaze made Beach feel as if he were pinned on the end of the fork. "I—Has he—? Do you—? Is he bossy about things in a sex way?"

Gavin's eyes dipped in disappointment. "That's it? You have a sudden kink for BDSM?"

It hadn't felt like that, as easy to sum up in some initials used to label internet porn. The man's command. The way Beach wanted to be with him. It wasn't like anything he'd ever seen. And he'd seen plenty. "Not the leather and the whips. More"—Beach lowered his voice to a whisper—"about him taking charge. I mean. Of everything."

"Leather or not, that's what it is, Beach. I hear there's plenty of it around."

"Hear?"

"Sorry to disappoint. D/s isn't part of my relationship with Jamie."

"*D* is domination?"

"Did you bother to go on the computer before you dragged me out of bed?"

Beach shrugged and smiled. "You know I've always been a hands-on learner."

Gavin sighed. Again. "*D* is domination. *S* in that sense is submission." He looked up from where he was sawing through the spinach. "Really, Beach? I can't see you submitting to a firm scolding, let alone a spanking."

The flush went all the way up to Beach's hairline, and he looked around to see if anyone was staring at them. "Spanking?" he croaked.

Gavin gave him a pitying smile. "Do you have plans for dinner?"

"I would, if I weren't chained to sobriety and this tiny square of the map. Why?"

"You may have wasted a breakfast date on me, but I do know where we can find someone who has a lot of experience."

WHICH WAS how Beach found himself at a Fourth of July barbecue in Mount Washington, scrutinizing the faces of some of Gavin's new friends to see which might hold the key to information on this secret passion. Hell and hellfire, he sounded like a nineteenth-century novel. He wasn't exactly sure how he felt about disclosing his newfound curiosity to complete strangers, but Gavin's friends were at least easy enough to share a dinner with.

Kellan: tall, blond, and friendly. He would be Beach's first choice. Not only would the man be easy to talk to, but he demonstrated a quiet ability to rein in his excitable boyfriend, Nate. Though if Nate took orders, that clearly only happened at home. *So damned smart he was dumb from it*, Beach's gran would have said about Nate. An opinion about everything, and nothing in it but words. But when Kellan had a hand on Nate, he went softer and quieter in a way anybody could see.

The other couple—and that coupling was well-established when they did everything but fuck right on the patio table—was a bit trickier to get a read on. If you were going by looks, sure, Quinn was someone who could take charge and make things happen, but Beach had brought home more than one big and strong man and ended up doing more hard work than if he was with a girl. The connection between Quinn and his much younger boyfriend Eli—that took some figuring. The pale goth kid had a sweet-looking ass and a delicately featured face under long black bangs, but when he said *jump*, everyone asked how high.

Case in point, Eli had just sent Kellan and Marco—who was so innocent and childlike Beach had crossed him off the list the minute he saw the doe eyes under the brown curls—into the house to retrieve the desserts Beach had brought along.

Marco was dwarfed by a stack of two boxes, Kellan toting the other three and balancing paper plates and napkins on top. Beach supposed he had gone a bit overboard. But he'd panicked when he realized he couldn't be sure that he wouldn't set off the monitor's alarms by going into Grand Cru to pick up some wine for a gift.

"What's in them?" Nate poked open one of the boxes like it had spiders in it rather than six custard tarts.

"Whatever the good people at Le Vol au Vent had left before they closed at noon," Beach said. "Are you suffering on that gluten-free thing?" Having to give up so much might explain a lot.

"No." Kellan lifted out a chocolate mousse cake with respectful care. "He's just a vegetarian. And a pain in the ass."

"Lucky for you," Nate got out before his words were muffled. Beach couldn't quite see behind Kellan's broad shoulders when he faced Nate, but it sounded a little obscene. Beach hoped the only licking going on was from fingers.

"I've some strawberry Jell-O and Cool Whip in the fridge if you want that." Eli smirked as he sliced the cake.

"Gelatin is from animal hooves," Nate pointed out.

Kellan took the slice Eli handed him. "What he doesn't know won't hurt him."

"Oh, wait. I know." Marco jumped up and ran to the back door. He returned a moment later with a wizened, spotted banana. "Here."

"Perfect." Kellan pulled the cake away and handed off the banana. "There you go, baby. Guaranteed vegetarian."

A sense of humor to go with a controlling attitude? Beach was definitely hoping he'd been brought here to talk to Kellan.

"You brought all of this?" Marco selected a cream puff from one of the other boxes. Beach nodded.

Marco squirmed onto his lap, putting the cream puff to Beach's mouth. "Are you anyone's sugar daddy right now?"

"Uhmf." Between the custard and the kiss Marco smushed onto Beach's lips, it was difficult to answer. He looked to Gavin for help. All the bastard did was smile and shake his head. Beach had trouble picturing Jamie's sour disposition around this crew. Quinn had dragged Eli into his lap and was being fed chocolate mousse.

"Marco, honey." Beach leaned back and licked his lips. "I'm afraid you're—"

"I'm not too young. I'm eighteen."

"That's not what I was going to say." Beach put a finger to the child's lips. "I'm afraid you're too much man for me."

Marco peered at him through narrowed eyes. "Don't. No, *qué*? You aren't gay?"

"I'm flexible."

"Or as he likes to say, 'any port in a storm,'" Gavin said.

"Bi pride, dude." Kellan reached over with a fist bump.

"Oh. Both." Marco accepted that easily. "So?"

As Beach tried to think of a way to extricate himself with the kid's pride still intact, Marco wrapped his arms around Beach's neck. "Can I just pretend? For a minute?"

It was downright heartbreaking. "Sure." Beach tucked the kid against his chest.

"It's not so wrong to want to get fucked, right?"

God, Beach had never been that young. And hell, he thought Gavin had been born jaded. Where was all the conversation that had been bouncing around the table all afternoon?

"Marco." There was the firm voice Beach had suspected Quinn could bust out when he wanted to. Thank God someone was keeping track of this kid. One trip to a place like Grand Central and he'd be as cynical as the rest of them.

Marco clung a little tighter. "I'm so horny. And I'm surrounded by all this." He nodded at either end of the table.

"Gavin's alone too. What about him?" Beach murmured.

"His boyfriend is at work. He will get it later."

Beach glanced at Gavin, who was suppressing laughter with tight lips. Okay, this sure beat a stuffy Montgomery dress-up party. Beach was starting to think it had one over on anything his friends down on Riviera Beach could dream up. He tried to find another way to let the kid down gently. "Can you keep a secret?"

Marco nodded.

Beach extracted a promise, then cupped his hands to Marco's ear to whisper, "You're very sexy, but when I'm with a guy, I only like to get it, if you know what I mean." It was half true. And if he managed to overcome Officer Fonoti's reservations, Beach expected it would be true more often than not.

He felt Marco nod and lifted his hands away. Marco shielded his lips as he whispered back, "How will I learn to tell?"

Beach kept up the secrecy. "Watch. See how they stand. If they want to fuck you, they take up more room. And listen to how they talk." He pulled away. "Then you'll feel it. Here." He tapped Marco's stomach.

"Not here?" Marco grabbed Beach's hand and shoved it lower.

Beach yanked his hand free and dumped Marco off his lap, but at least the kid was grinning.

GAVIN WAS smooth, Beach had to give him that. He didn't know how his friend had managed it, but Beach was alone in the kitchen with Eli, helping him with the few remaining dishes, and didn't even know he'd been set up until Eli said, "So. Gavin said you wanted to talk to me."

Beach dried off a pair of grill tongs while he tried to figure out how to swing this subject with a guy he'd just met.

"About figuring out you're kinky."

The tongs clattered to the floor. And on the other hand, Gavin could be as smooth as a sledgehammer.

"Bastard," Beach muttered as he handed the tongs back to Eli.

Eli huffed a laugh. "He said you were a little shy about it. But if you want it, you're going to have to figure out how to ask for it. Especially as a bottom."

That sledgehammer kept right on swinging.

"Hey, it's not like I'm judging you." Eli handed over the tongs again. "I've been kinky—and queer— as long as I can remember." He rinsed off a wooden spoon and smacked it against his palm. "I'm mostly a sensation bottom." He whapped the spoon a few more times, sending water droplets flying up, misting over Beach's flushed face.

"What does that mean?" Though he guessed he knew part of it from the spoon action.

"I love to get spanked. Hard. Fucked hard. Pain like that turns me on."

"I—I don't think that's for me." If he wasn't worried about insulting Eli, Beach would have come down more firmly on the no-to-pain side. He'd been through surgery and a long recovery on his smashed leg. Pain was not a friend. He gave a side-eye to the spoon as Eli handed it to him.

"Don't freak. We don't use that one."

If Beach had been alone, he might have tested it out. All the same, he was still pretty sure about this.

His parents hadn't been spankers, but when they exited Beach's life and his uncle became his guardian, a brief period of adolescent smart-mouthing had made Beach all too familiar with the phrase, "Go cut me a switch, boy, and drop 'em."

It had been a very brief period of smart-mouthing.

Still, two days ago Beach didn't know it was worth putting up with the pain of having a dick fucking him after he'd come, worth it because someone demanded it, worth it to hear brief words of praise in a rough voice. *Good. So good.*

"Gavin said something about D/s. I've done a little of that before, and"—for the first time there was a catch in Eli's voice, but it didn't sound like shyness—"we're playing with that some too."

"I think I like the idea of being told what to do. Being controlled."

"Because he wants it, yeah." Eli's voice held a warm rush of pleasure. "When he's all focused on you and making you take more than you thought you could and you want to, for him."

"Yes." Relief sank deep, cozy as sunshine into Beach's bones. That was exactly it. He couldn't believe he hadn't known about this before.

"Of course, it all really starts when you want it to stop. When you know you can't take it, when it really does hurt, and he pushes you further."

Eli had said pain turned him on. If there were parts of this where the pain was too much for him…. That was terrifying. So why did Beach want to jump into it, ache to know what Eli was talking about now?

"What I mean is, don't safeword out too early. Not to discourage anyone from embracing their kink, but if you're going to play as a sub, a Dom is going to deal you some pain. As punishment or control. You'll probably be spanked. You should get your head around it before you play."

Nothing had felt less like playing than what had happened inside Beach when Officer Fonoti had told Beach why his blackmail wouldn't work. "And then when you two aren't playing, everything is like the way you are now?"

"Quinn still has ways of making demands." Eli grinned and handed over some silverware. "But yeah. We're not into doing it full-time. Some people do, though. They call it a discipline relationship. Is that what you're thinking of trying?"

"I—I'm not exactly sure what he wants."

"Better ask. Right away. You really should negotiate up front. Make sure if you have any hard limits— things you would never ever do—he knows about them. Safewords, safety, all that stuff. If he doesn't listen, then you need to get the hell out."

Beach had asked. Sort of. Considering some people weren't at their best in the wee hours of the morning, he'd given things another shot on the phone at the entirely respectable hour of nine. He hadn't been surprised when his call went immediately to voicemail. He'd had his message planned.

"Please accept my apologies for—well, for everything that got us off on the wrong foot. I clearly overstepped. And you called my bluff. I would never have followed through. I respect—" No need to complicate things with a lie. Authority wasn't high on Beach's list. "I just wouldn't. So I was thinking we could start things off better. Perhaps even with an apologetic blow job. My treat, of course."

Armed with Eli's information, Beach supposed his message should have been *I want to be your sub. We should negotiate what you expect. I don't know what my hard limits are because I don't know what you'd ask. A blow job is definitely not on the limits list. Spanking might be.*

"It's all theoretical at present. I'm not sure I have his attention."

"Don't worry about that. If there's one thing I can help you with, it's getting a guy's attention." Eli reached for a glass bowl, then looked at Beach. "Do you think I can trust you with something breakable now?"

NO BADGE, no gun, no Jez. Tai felt naked walking into Gina's Fourth of July barbecue. From the way the two dozen people in the yard stared, he might as well have been. He was about to check to see if his cargo shorts were still on when a guided missile hit him in the thigh.

"Hi, Daddy Tai. That rhymes."

The sweet giggle made the whole damned mess worth it. Ignoring the stares, he scooped Sammie up into a hug. "It does. You're pretty smart. How come you're so smart if school is over?"

Sammie's sigh was exactly like her mom's, and so was the patient lecture in her voice. "It doesn't go away once you learn it. That's the whole point of school."

"Good to know." He drank in the sight of her face. How could her round little cheeks already be starting to sharpen? He hoped Gina didn't have her on some crazy diet.

"Where's Jezebel?" Sammie's heels drummed his bottom ribs.

"She wanted to stay home. She doesn't like fireworks." Getting Jez to remain completely calm no matter what Sammie did to her had been Tai's top priority. Now Sammie could probably cut off an ear and Jez would simply lick her face, but the combination of random bangs and strangers wasn't something Tai was willing to test.

"Okay." Her feet kicked harder, and she squirmed.

Daddy Tai was only as interesting as his dog. He put her down, and she squeezed out a hug before running off where some kids were chasing each other around a tree.

He didn't turn as Gina came up to stand beside him. "She's still happy to see you."

Tai shoved his hands in his pockets. Being around Gina made him feel like a giant with a Barbie doll. "What's going on with her hair?"

"She wants to grow locs." Gina's tone didn't give Tai much of a hint on whether it was a good or bad development.

Tai glanced at Gina's relaxed-to-her-shoulders hair. He'd worn his own long since leaving high school, and it ran curly or straight depending on the weather. He kept it scraped back in a tight knot for work.

Gina's chin poked out. "It's her hair."

"No defense moves necessary. I'm glad she gets to do what she wants with it."

Gina relaxed. "Beats fighting her with a comb to get it into braids. She's so damned tender-headed."

"I bet."

"What would you know?" But there was laughter in her voice. "I've seen her hair after a week with you. You'd cut your heart out rather than fight with her on anything."

True. He'd been in awe of Sammie from the instant he held her. Couldn't believe the tiny little squirming ball had grown into a baby, then a toddler, now a child. That she'd been his.

Except she wasn't. Even if she looked exactly like baby pictures of his mom.

The man whose DNA profile proved he was 99.9 percent more likely to have given Sammie half her DNA than Tai strode over and offered a cold bottle of beer and an all-but-subliminal nod.

Tai took the beer.

"Glad you made it." Josh's words weren't close to a decent lie. "Got some ribs on."

"Thanks. Smells great." Which was the truth, damn it. Tai's mouth had been watering two steps from the car.

There was a rise in noise from the picnic table, and Gina slipped away. Tai knocked back some beer in the long silence. He and Josh had been friends once. Teammates. UM Terps. And Tai didn't hate Josh so much for coming back. He hated him for leaving in the first place. Leaving Gina so broken and miserable that something that had seemed like a good idea after too much rum at a party had led them here.

"You don't have to keep sending checks, man." Josh started the same conversation they'd been having for the past two years.

Tai might not be obligated for child support, but that didn't mean he didn't want Sammie to have the best. "Save it for college, then."

"Or her wedding."

Their simultaneous shudders of horror provoked an actual nod of understanding. "Tai, I'm taking care of them," Josh said in exactly the tone of voice guaranteed to make Tai want to prove he still had enough defensive tackle in him to drop Josh straight to hell before he could take another step back to his precious grill.

Where the fuck had he been when Gina had morning sickness—all day—for two months, when she needed someone to hold on to while her body pushed out the baby, when Sammie cried with colic and teething? Tai had pointed that all out to Gina when Josh came back, in the only screaming fight they'd ever had. *I know all that. But he's here now. It's my life, Tai. My decision.*

And the worst of it was, Josh *was* taking care of them. Tai couldn't argue with a solid brick detached three-bedroom in the suburbs and a yard big enough for a swing set and cousins to chase around, and grandparents and aunts and uncles at the picnic table.

"Hey."

Tai blinked and Gina was there, planted in front of him as if she knew how slippery his grip on his temper was.

"Hey." He shifted his beer to his other hand but didn't drink any.

"Want me to introduce you around?"

Tai was sure the whole fucked-up story had already made the rounds of Josh's family. "I'm good."

"Uh-huh." Gina nodded. "Anything new in your life?"

Any*one*, she meant. Gina knew, of course. Knew before the party of rum and bad decisions, knew before Tai had worked up enough nerve to confess it. But back then he'd had his head, heart, and soul set on an NFL career, and gay guys didn't get drafted, didn't get signed. Maybe a kicker someday, but not a defensive end. Two-time All-American or not.

With that question hanging between them, his phone took on a little extra weight, as if from the voicemail he hadn't listened to but hadn't deleted either. "Same old, same old."

"How's your mom?"

"She's good." Tai grabbed the escape handed to him and ran with it. "She and Phillip are doing the barbecue thing in Woodlawn. I think I'll stop up there and say hi."

"Don't forget to say goodbye to Sammie."

TAI NEVER made it out to Woodlawn to see Mom and Phillip the Pharmacist. A trip to Harris Teeter outfitted him with ribs and beer. The ribs weren't half as good as the smell from Josh's grill, but the Flying Dog Pale Ale—and the lack of certain company—made up for it. He spent the evening mindlessly clicking through the nothing on cable until a quick triple knock bounced off the apartment door.

Jez raised her head, tipped it for a couple seconds, then stood up with a stretch. That usually meant someone she knew.

Tai patted her head, set down his beer, and discovered with surprise it had four empty companions lined up across the coffee table. He wasn't lit, he noticed when he stood up, but he was feeling it.

Jez stuck to her training and sat in the living room doorway as Tai went to the door and opened it.

A completely naked David Beauchamp knelt in the hall.

Chapter Five

STARK FUCKING naked. In front of Tai's apartment. Where the nice family in 2B might find him on their way home from the fireworks. Maybe Beauchamp would be better off in the hands of Behavior Health instead of Correctional Services.

A yank, a drag, a shove, and a slam got Beauchamp behind the closed door and inside the apartment.

Tai leaned on the door for an instant, drawing in a deep breath of air-conditioning to cool his head before he turned around.

Beauchamp crouched against the wall near the kitchen door where Tai had flung him, petting Jez's head as she nuzzled his jaw and neck.

"Jez." His tone was too sharp, and she shrank into as tiny a space as she could get on the floor, head lowered. Tai took another deep breath. "Good girl." He patted her head, felt her shaking. "Good girl. Come on. Bed."

She sprang up to head for her crate. Tai shot a glare at the man in his kitchen doorway. "You. St—" *Stay* would only confuse Jez more. "Don't move."

Jez chomped on a fuzzy chew toy from her basket and carried it with her as she hopped in to curl up on her blanket, staring up at Tai out of watchful eyes that still had too much white in them.

Holding his hand near the door to the crate, he murmured, "I'm sorry, girl. You're not in trouble."

She sniffed and offered a quick lick to his wrist.

"Good girl. Bed." He thought of shutting the crate door, but she'd stay until he called her. He shut his bedroom door, though.

Beauchamp was still in the space next to the kitchen, but he'd shifted back to that kneeling pose, probably copied from something he'd seen online. It wasn't bad form, if you were grading that sort of thing. Knees apart, ass down onto his heels, palms up and open on his thighs, head down.

The only thing wrong with it was who. And where. And how fucking much Tai wanted to step forward, put a hand on Beauchamp's neck, and drag his face to meet Tai's crotch. Grind it there until he felt the hesitation, the resistance, and then the hot flood of satisfaction when David yielded, let Tai control when he got to move, got to breathe.

Instead he folded his arms across his chest and took another deep breath before he spoke. "Look at me."

David raised his head until he was staring up out of those pretty blue eyes. No wonder he'd been able to get away with so much all his life. He had a face like a model, features symmetrical and smooth, except for the bump of a healed break in the middle of his nose

and a smattering of freckles under his eyes. The blink
and half smile probably worked on almost everyone—
and his millions in the bank certainly wouldn't hurt
his chances. He looked bigger out of his clothes, maybe a little soft at the waist, but a defined chest tapered
to narrow hips, and his back was sculpted beauty.

Tai froze, realizing he'd started walking around
the kneeling man as if this really was a scene and he
really was a sub presenting himself. But he wasn't.
He was a probie. Someone else's, yes, but still in the
system and as off-limits as it got.

Tai pressed his back against the door behind David. "What the fuck do you think you're doing here?"

A thread of nervous laughter wound through
David's answer. "I was rather hoping it was
self-explanatory."

"It isn't. Explain." Tai stepped in front of him,
determined to make this as difficult as possible.

"I—I wanted to—what you said in the car." David licked his lips. His voice was shaking. Not shame,
nerves. Tai had to hand it to the guy, the bright blue
gaze never wavered from Tai's face. "Have you tell
me what to do."

The hitch in his breath. Oh fuck. "Sir," David
finished.

"And that means you show up here and pull this
shit?"

"I'm open to suggestion, Sir." That came a little
more easily to him.

Tai stepped around him, opened the apartment
door, and found a neatly folded stack of clothes. He
grabbed the pile and the cane, shut the door with
enough force to make David jump, then threw the
clothes down next to him. Standing in front of David,

Tai said, "Did it ever occur to you that you've built something out of nothing in your head? That I don't want you?"

"No."

Tai raised his brows.

David nodded. "You're hard."

Tai snorted. "You're naked. And not exactly hideous to look at."

"Thank you." This time the pause was a tease. "Sir."

"Face down." It snapped out of him. Tai put both hands behind his head as if that would help him regain his control. If David were his, even for a quick scene, Tai would have made him damned sorry for that kind of brattiness.

David had complied. His forehead rested on the industrial carpet, ass tipped up in the air.

Tai sucked in a breath through his teeth. Damn, that looked pretty. "Put your hands underneath, reach through between your legs, and grab your ankles. Don't even think about touching anything else."

He strode into his room and gripped the top of the dresser. He couldn't do this. Except he already had. As soon as he'd failed to hand Beauchamp his clothes and tell him to get the fuck out, Tai had known he was totally screwed. Didn't mean it wasn't wrong. Morally, professionally, insanely wrong. Wrong in every way but the one that pounded with his pulse, the one that urged him to see if Beauchamp really wanted this or if it was some freaky head game.

It wasn't only alcohol clouding Tai's judgment. Being with David, hell, *fighting* with David made Tai feel more alive, more energized than he had in a year.

David wasn't a patient guy. He'd probably give up after a few minutes. Tai would go out there and catch David sitting up or jacking himself, or find him and his clothes gone. Then Tai would know.

HE'D BEEN gone forever. Beach's forehead was itching and sweating from being pushed into the carpet, which smelled like chemicals and cleaner and dog, the dog being the only part of it not making him want to sneeze. His knees and forehead were so dug into the carpet that he'd be wearing the mark of them for days. *Look what curiosity got you into this time, Beach.*

It would have been easy to dismiss like that. Claim it was nothing more than his try-anything-once sense of joie de vivre, but he knew it was more. Because otherwise Beach would have been dressed and out the door. This wasn't simple curiosity. It was craving.

When he'd first been ordered into this position, after an initial shock at how immediately he'd complied, he'd been all too conscious of his butt stuck way up in the air, balls dangling, vulnerable. He'd been certain he was about to find out if getting his ass beat at thirty-four was as bad as it had been at thirteen. Except nothing touched him but the cool air. And even air felt like something ordered to torment him, to remind him of how naked and alone he was.

Would the man ever come back?

When the steps vibrated across the floor, Beach's muscles tensed. The feet moved past him, around him. It was all Beach could do to not cover the jewels. His grip on his ankles tightened, careful to avoid touching the monitor. He could take it. Show he was serious about something—for once in his life. His ears strained, everything in him more alive than he could have imagined a moment ago. He pressed his forehead more firmly down. His skin was aware of every shift in air currents, and the hunger for a touch set up a throbbing ache in his balls.

"First of all, David, you will be completely honest with me. Do you understand?"

Beach licked his lips. "Yes." Then he remembered. "Sir."

"Good."

The single word of praise washed through him like a shot of bourbon and made him all the more determined to earn another.

"Does anything hurt?" The question came from behind him, but that smoky voice seemed to wrap around him like a grip.

Beach considered. His neck and shoulders were uncomfortable, his knees protesting a little. The only thing that hurt was his shin, and that was constant anyway.

"No, Sir."

The hand in his hair might have hurt as his head was yanked up if Fonoti hadn't cupped Beach's chin to take the weight. "What did you just promise me?"

Beach stared into dark eyes that might as well have looked straight through to the back of his skull. "Not to lie. But only my leg hurts, and that always hurts."

A thumb moved across Beach's lips. "No. You promised to be completely honest. That's not the same as not lying." The thumb slipped between Beach's lips, and he licked, sucked, hungry for the salty taste of the skin and to prove he could do more given the opportunity. Fonoti released Beach's head. "Put your hands on the floor to brace yourself and sit up, slowly."

He thought he was moving slowly, but still the rush of blood from his head left him dizzy. A hard grip on his shoulders kept him steady.

"Sit comfortably."

When Beach had shifted to one hip and stretched his bad leg out in front of him, the other man said, "Tell me about your leg."

"I smashed it pretty good. Fell down onto some old brick stairs. In the surgery to repair it, I got a bone infection, then had to get a rod put in. Pretty nasty stuff. Cast just came off on Monday." *Sir* was one thing when he was facedown staring at the carpet, but in casual conversation it stuck in his mouth. "Um. I'm rather embarrassed to say I don't know your name. Your, uh, Christian name."

The brow arch was a mixture of amusement and disbelief. "Toluaotai. But most people stick to Tai."

"And most people call me Beach."

Tai stared at the knotty and thick scar on Beach's shin.

"I assure you, I've had worse." Beach rubbed at the thinner, raised line on his scalp, under the too-short hair. At least he didn't remember much about that. Comas were good for something. "The time I took a fence without my mount stands out. Lucky for me it was only my collarbone and not my neck."

Tai shook his head as if disgusted. "You need a keeper more than a Dom."

"I have one." Beach smiled and pointed to the ankle bracelet. "And apparently yet another new probation officer. Which leaves the other position… available."

With something that might have been a laugh, Tai slid down the wall to sit next to Beach. "What do you expect from this?"

Beach turned on all the self-deprecating charm at his disposal, which he had to confess was substantial. It hadn't let him down so far in life. "I'm afraid that's where my bravado ends. I throw myself on the mercy of your greater experience."

"Well, being a Dom doesn't give me mind-reading skills. Only knowledge of what I like."

"That's what I want." Beach pounced on that. It was the whole point, right? "I want to do what you like. It—I didn't expect to feel like this. In fact, it was one hell of a surprise. But I want to do that—give you what you like."

"You don't know what that is. You—Damn it, David, you can't just go offering yourself to random guys. You need to make sure it's going to be safe."

"I trust you."

"And you're right back to lying."

"No." So sometimes Beach was good at bending the truth into the shape that suited the occasion, but this wasn't a lie. He was sure of that.

"Get dressed. And get out."

"Please." Like many of Beach's reactions around this man, his cry surprised him. So did the raw feeling in it. Not like his usual voice at all. "Please don't cut me off from this." He stared down at his carpet-reddened knees. "I—Nothing has ever felt so... real before, so much a part of me brought to life. It scares me how much I find myself—I don't know that I could trust someone else with it."

Eli had told Beach to be direct about what he wanted. But Eli hadn't mentioned how horrible it could feel to have your soul exposed like that. Far more naked than skin, everything Beach kept hidden about himself lay wailing and exposed like an abandoned infant. At any moment Tai would shovel the quivering mess right out the door.

Instead Tai put both hands behind his neck and laced his fingers, letting out an explosive breath. "Put your pants on and come sit on the couch. We need to talk."

Since Beach hoped he wouldn't be back in his trousers for long, he skipped the briefs. The television was muted, some explosion-heavy action movie making flashes across Tai's face and bare arms. In contrast with the lighted hall, this part of the apartment was gloomy. Twilight couldn't compete with the tilted blinds.

After Beach sank into the opposite corner of the sofa, Tai started. From the ominous *need to talk* pronouncement, Beach was expecting a struggle, but he didn't know it would take the wind out of him so much when Tai started with, "This—us—this can't happen."

Slapping on a smile to cover the hollowness, Beach countered, "But you aren't my probation officer anymore."

"No, but you're still in county court custody, and I'm an officer of the court. Just you being here like this, now, I could lose my job. Hell, I'd fire me if I knew."

Beach looked down at his knees, picking at the still-sharp crease in his khakis. They really did deliver on their stain-wrinkle-resistant promise. He glanced up to deliver his apology. "I am truly ashamed of my earlier audacity. I'm afraid I've been known to react rather badly to limits."

In the light of a fresh explosion, Tai's eyebrows came to a peak on his forehead. "And yet?"

"Imagine my surprise," Beach agreed dryly.

"Why me?"

The orange flashes from the television made Tai appear firelit. Black hair, black eyes, unyielding jaw, broad nose and cheeks. His lips were full, but right now they held a tight line. Not the classically handsome prep-school type, but dead sexy. Beach hadn't known he wanted a man who looked like he could snap him in two until he met Tai.

"Why not?" Beach knew exactly how to inject a purr of appreciation in his voice.

"I'm not fishing for compliments. I want to know."

"Toluaotai." Beach was a pretty good mimic. He bet he had the inflection right. Glottal stops and all.

"Close enough," Tai agreed.

"What does it mean? I mean, David is *beloved*, if you can believe that. Aiken was my grandmother's maiden name; we're from Aiken too. And Beauchamp is French for—"

Tai's hand landed on Beach's knee and squeezed. "David, focus. And answer my question."

All the static went away for an instant, and Beach was nothing but the heat of the palm on his knee. Didn't need to be or do or think about anything but this.

"Because of that." He looked directly into those dark eyes under slashed brows and, with all the sincerity he possessed, tried to explain. "Because you do that, and I want to give you exactly what you asked for. I'm not saying you're not hot. You are. But I don't do this. I don't chase lovers for do-overs. You're not the first man who's ever been take-charge in bed, but you're the first one who's ever made me feel like this."

It wasn't because of what Eli had told him to do. Or because he was playing some role.

Beach went to his knees at Tai's feet because something in him had to be there.

Beach had thought he was nervous before, in the hall, exposed and waiting, but this was far worse. That could have been dismissed as a game, an experiment, curiosity. But now there was no arrogance or bravado in him. He needed Tai to understand more than Beach had ever needed anything in his life. And until that moment, everything was paralyzed. Lungs, heart, blood, nothing worked. His chest locked in a frozen burn.

Then Tai let out a breath and put his hand on Beach's head, and everything was going to be okay again. His breath came back in a shaky rush.

Tai's hand sifted through Beach's hair. "Okay, David. But we still need to talk about some things."

"I wouldn't tell anyone, of course." Beach tried not to think of how many people he'd already involved in his little quest. If Gavin knew something, chances were Jamie did. There was Eli, which meant his boyfriend Quinn. And possibly the other two, Nate and Kellan. But they only knew Beach was looking. Not who he was looking for.

"That's not what I meant."

Beach's mind strayed to the things Eli had talked about. "Oh. I understand that punishment might come up in this."

"Yes. It can be playful."

Beach had heard that from Eli but still doubted it.

"When it's not, it's uncomfortable, but it's part of the dynamic," Tai continued. "And something tells me that with you, it's going to be a really necessary part of the dynamic."

"And this punishment is... corporal." Beach had bared his soul to this man and yet tripped over the word *spanking*.

"Not always, but it can be. Is that something you don't want to do?"

"I'm afraid of pain," Beach confessed.

Tai's fingers were still drifting through Beach's hair. They paused, and a rough pad moved carefully over the thin scar on his scalp. "Yet you do all these crazy stunts that have seriously painful outcomes."

"A natural consequence is one thing. But to let someone hurt me on purpose, I don't know if I can."

Tai cupped Beach's chin. When Tai spoke gently, his deep voice buzzed in his throat like part of it was trapped there. "You realize we're not talking about anything permanent or scarring. I was only thinking of spanking you."

Beach felt his cheeks—both sets—heat up like fresh sunburn. He nodded.

"A consequence shouldn't be something you like. Especially if it keeps you out of the kind of trouble you get into. But I tell you what. We'll do different things. I won't spank you unless you ask me for it."

Since Beach was positive that would never happen, he was happy to agree.

"Good. Now get up here and kiss me."

Beach considered himself to be an average-sized man. Clothes were easy enough to come by, even if he bought them off the rack, a standard size. But as Tai pulled Beach onto his lap, he felt Eli-sized and

more aware of what Tai's dominance brought out in
Beach than when on his knees. An improbable wave
of shyness put a light tremble in his hand as he put a
palm on Tai's face.

Leaning in for the kiss, Beach realized he was out
of his element in more ways than one. Kissing was
a means to an end. Necessary and fun with women.
With men it was usually an accompaniment to the
hard slam of bodies, the rough urgency spilling into
groans pushed into each other's mouths with tongues.

But Beach was always up for a challenge. He held
Tai with both hands and put their lips together.

Soft-hard flesh and the silky prickle of Tai's goatee greeted Beach's effort. He waited, then drew back.

"I told you to kiss me," Tai said.

Beach had thought the point of being with Tai
was that Beach could take orders and coast on the
feelings, but all right, he could manage that much. He
parted his lips and pressed in again, teasing sensation
with a flick of his tongue, like he would do if he were
trying to seal the deal with a woman as they stood
outside her door.

There wasn't much reaction. Beach held Tai's
face more firmly, tilting it to be able to get in closer,
and kissed him, forgetting about anything but how he
wanted to make Tai feel, respond. Beach had to know
he'd gotten it right. No calculation, pure hunger and
need.

Tai's hand came up to hold the back of Beach's
head, and Tai kissed him back. Relief was almost as
sweet as an orgasm. Tai shared his mouth, his tongue,
texture and taste. That sent a hot jolt to Beach's dick,
an explosion of bass under his diaphragm. He drew

away for breath and realized the explosion was only the start of the fireworks down in the harbor.

"The earth moved for you too, huh?" Tai smiled, the corners of his eyes crinkling.

Beach put a hand on his chest. "I was breathless."

With a snort of laughter, Tai dragged them both into a more horizontal position. "Not yet, but you're going to be."

Holding Beach's head, Tai took the kiss from Beach. Not with the subtle give-and-take they'd been doing, but with a full assault of mouth and tongue. He was right. Beach couldn't breathe. Oxygen was overrated when a man was this focused on him, was pinning him with a hand at his neck and ass, forcing sensation into his body, building the tension with the dry hump of their hips together.

Beach let it all go, let Tai shift him, hold him, kiss him in whatever way suited making out on the couch, because Beach had no doubt about how this was going to end. His dick already associated the sounds from Tai's throat with very good things. The dizzying pulse of lust promised an epically memorable orgasm. Though the dizzy part could be from the loss of oxygen. Right when the pressure in Beach's lungs got unpleasant, Tai released him.

"Take your pants off again and kneel for me, David."

He would have resented the interruption if it wasn't for the lurch of excitement in his gut. This was what he'd come here for. Not only the sex but the rush that came from Tai telling him what to do.

"Good boy." Tai ran a thumb over Beach's mouth. "Stay right there."

His footsteps moved away behind Beach. There was a lot of this Beach liked, but the next time they had a conversation, he was going to point out how goddamned boring the waiting bits were.

JEZ LIFTED her head and huffed when Tai came into the bedroom. She was growing used to the harbor fireworks; the city found dozens of reasons to set them off between May and September. As a rapid-fire splatter of shots echoed off the humid air, she twitched her ears and settled back down, eyes still watchful.

"It's okay, Jez."

She gave him a look out of what his mom had called "high eyes." Tai had no trouble reading Jez's opinion of things. *Sez you.*

It was okay. Everything his gut had told him about David Beauchamp's hunger to surrender control had been true. The guy wasn't polished like a playmate Tai might find at Nic's, but Tai liked the rough edges; he liked the idea of shaping them to please him. Of knowing he had been the one to make David discover that need, that it was Tai David knelt for.

Tai opened his bottom dresser drawer and pulled out a set of cuffs and a link, then had to stop and press on his swelling dick with a firm palm. His head was suffering from serious lack of blood, and that was no way to start a scene. The idea of learning how to push David up to his limits until the power took them both to heaven made Tai feel like he was carrying a Taser charge in his blood. Like he was the novice, hyped up on adrenaline. He needed to get control of himself.

The gauntlets were a gift from Nic, butter-smooth dark brown leather, laced through brass gussets for an exact fit, with a zipper to make them quick to get on or off. Once Tai had found that place where the Dom came from, he'd never needed any help accessing it, but Nic had explained they weren't for that. Tai didn't need a leather vest or chaps to make things clear. The compression on his wrists was there as a reminder to keep something leashed. To remind him that it was an exchange—as the sub gave up the power, Tai's job was to control it inside their secure boundaries.

He could hear his mentor's advice. *The sub always runs the show, but the fun and the skill lies in making both of you forget that.* He'd need all the help he could get, remembering that with David. His combination of submission and stubbornness pulled on Tai's need to protect and control like the moon on the tide.

In the living room, David hadn't moved at all from where he knelt near the couch. "Good boy." Tai put a hand under David's chin to lift his head.

David's gaze lingered on the gauntlets before zeroing in on the cuffs Tai held.

"Um." David's tongue darted out to flick over his lips. "I heard something about a safeword."

"Do you have one in mind?"

"SOS?" David offered with a nervous laugh.

"Do you think that will spring easily to mind if you panic? Be easy to say?"

David shook his head.

"Let's start with something simple. *Red*, like a stoplight. You do stop at stoplights?"

That model-perfect smile lit up David's face. "Only if there's a good reason."

Tai's fingers locked on his jaw. "Well, I will stop. No matter what the reason. You understand that?"

David nodded as much as the grip allowed.

"And if your mouth is otherwise occupied"—Tai grinned—"you tap or poke me three times."

"Dot-dot-dot, dash-dash-dash, dot-dot-dot?" All the fear had vanished from David's eyes, leaving nothing but a bratty gleam. This was going to be fun.

Tai squatted down. "Boy, you better practice your Morse code, because I think your mouth is going to be occupied a lot. Give me your hands."

David lifted them from his thighs. Tai buckled on the cuffs and checked the fit.

"You law-enforcement types do like your restraints."

Tai wrapped some of David's hair in his fingers and dragged him into a hard kiss, ignoring David's efforts to kiss back or even to open his mouth to let Tai kiss him. He kept it rough, moving his head to leave the skin around David's mouth sensitive and swollen from pressure.

When Tai released him, David licked his lips again, but he didn't shift from his kneeling position. As Tai watched, David's cock swelled from firm to hard, offering definite approval of the rough treatment. Tai clipped the cuffs together and rose to stand.

David raised his hands and tugged once before lowering them to his thighs.

"How does that feel?" Tai studied David's face.

"Okay."

"I mean on the inside."

The smile was quick, almost apologetic. "Like when I'm fishing and I've hooked something big and I'm excited, but at the same time hoping it doesn't turn out to be something big enough to hurt me."

"Good." Tai unzipped his cargo shorts and pulled his cock through, giving it a few strokes as David watched, eyes widening. "I think you said something about a blow job. Your treat."

David pushed up on his knees. "That's quite a treat. I'm a bit stunned I got that up my ass without poppers."

"The flattery is stalling. Open up."

David raised his cuffed hands, and Tai moved his hips back. "I don't want a hand job. Just your mouth, David."

His eyes had been glowing an unearthly blue in the light from the TV. Now they shifted, showing his hesitation in a quick dart to the left before they lowered, dimming the reflected light. Despite his nerves, David obediently opened his mouth and leaned forward.

For the first minute, Tai let him work, savoring the wet heat of a mouth engulfing the head, the tonguing kisses down the shaft, then back up, diligent attention to the spot under the ridge where focus did the most good. When David opened his mouth wide, Tai pushed forward, driving against David's hard palate, enjoying the friction and the convulsive pressure of a frantic swallow.

After easing back until David's lips sealed around the rim, Tai drove in deeper, not stopping until he hit the back of David's throat, ready with hands on David's head when he tried to back off. He pushed deeper, first feeling, then hearing the sputter and gasp. When David struggled to free his head, Tai kept him there for another choking gasp and then released him.

"I've never—I can't—" David's hoarse stammer wasn't really necessary. Tai had already figured out deep-throating wasn't on his résumé.

"What do you do if you can't say your safeword and you want it to stop?"

David jabbed a pointed finger into Tai's quad three times.

"Right. You don't pull away or try to get free. Do you want to stop?"

David panted out a few more breaths, then squared his shoulders. "No, Sir."

"Relax." Tai softened his voice and smoothed a hand down the side of David's face before lacing both hands at the back of his skull. "Sit back a little."

Tai used his hands to angle David's head, cock sliding on his tongue. He kept the thrusts shallow. David flicked and licked at the head as Tai dragged it back and forth. As soon as the tension beneath Tai's fingers eased, he drove into that soft, tight space. The spasms around him were sweet, but although David didn't try to pull away, he went rigid.

Tai withdrew, and David clamped a bound wrist over his mouth, eyes streaming, jaw clenched.

After a few shaking breaths, David lowered his hands. Tai put a hand to a wet cheek, rubbing a tear into the skin. David leaned his face into the touch until Tai had to fight the urge to lift him up onto the couch and kiss him until he smiled again.

Cock sliding along David's other cheek, Tai whispered, "David, do you want to do this?"

David turned his head to kiss the shaft. "Yes."

Tai pulled his hips back and rested his hand over David's throat. "Then listen to me. You're mine. That's all you need to know right now. You belong to me." He moved his thumb across David's lips. "Your mouth, your throat. Mine. And if I want to fuck them, I will."

A swallow convulsed against his palm. "And you'll take it."

David nodded as much as he could.

"Tilt your head back. Let the breath out through your mouth." The hot exhale blew across the wet skin of Tai's dick, and he shivered. "Now, in through your nose."

As David inhaled, Tai started with slow, short strokes. David didn't tense, allowing Tai's hands to pull him on and off, deeper and deeper. One tight gasp and then a shudder, David's throat working him for an instant, and damn if that wasn't sweeter than if he had all that tight heat wrapped around him.

"Good boy." Tai rubbed his fingers on the back of David's neck.

It got sloppy from there, but Tai kept his hips in check, letting the tight ring of David's lips and the wild flick of his tongue send the tension snaking through his balls, waiting for that last bit of pressure, the one that would put him over the edge. He made a deeper stroke, felt David sputter, and that was it.

"Oh fuck." Tai dragged his cock out and finished the ride with the tight squeeze of his hand, painting David's face and neck and chest with long creamy strings.

Tai's body gave a couple more jerks though his balls were wrung dry, still riding out the electric jolts of pleasure from the sight of his come across David's cheeks. Tai swiped at it with his fingers, then shoved them past David's lips, onto his tongue. He sucked and then lapped the fingers clean.

Dropping to his knees in front of David, Tai kissed his swollen lips, licking the bitter salt back out of his mouth until it was just them again. One hand slid between them to unclip David's wrists, and a pained hiss made Tai rear back to check David over.

Nothing wrong he could see, except for a very hard, angry red, wet-tipped cock pressed up against David's belly.

"The leather… scratched it."

"Hmm. What should we do about that?"

David groaned. "You could kiss it and make it better."

The boy had a lot to learn. "Not happening. Spread your knees apart—if it doesn't hurt your leg."

David shook his head and put his knees wide apart.

"Looks pretty red. You should be careful not to touch it."

"Tai—"

Tai had his chin in an instant, thumb firmly on his lips. "When we're like this, it's *Sir*. Only *Sir*."

"Yes, Sir." David's voice was rough, but whether it was from a cock battering his throat or how desperate he was to get off, Tai couldn't tell.

He pulled David in close, rubbing a hand down his back and kissing his neck before murmuring, "You were very good for me, David. What would you like?"

A church organ at full throttle blared a funeral march through the apartment. "Oh shit. It's my phone. In my pants. Curfew alarm."

Ten fifteen, Tai noticed as he scooped out the phone and passed it to David. The dirge stopped after a few notes on the second go-round.

"Curfew. Better get going. Did you get your car out of impound?"

"Useless bastards won't let me do anything until Monday. I have a rental. A Lexus." David winced.

"It's a sedan." Setting his phone to the side, David resumed the position Tai had assigned him.

"Don't want you to miss curfew." Tai handed over the khaki trousers.

"Are you fu—serious?" David blinked. "Uh, Sir."

"I remember you approving of natural consequences. Welcome to the natural consequence of being on probation and having a curfew."

David looked down. "I don't need time for a shower."

"I didn't offer you one." Tai retrieved David's shirt and cane from the hall.

Dressing looked particularly painful, but David managed, then limped to the door, leaning more heavily on his cane than Tai had ever seen him do.

With one hand on the knob, Tai brushed a kiss across his lips. "I'll text you in the morning. And, David, don't jerk off. It's an order."

He closed the door on David's shocked face.

Chapter Six

BEACH HADN'T noticed he was still wearing the cuffs until he tapped in the door-lock code at his apartment. Black leather, buckled around his wrists. The blood flooded back to his aching dick so fast he had to lean on the door or go to his knees. Turning the handle meant the cuff was there again for him to see, and he staggered into his hall, catching himself against the kitchen counter. The gravelly voice. *You're mine.* The locked grip on his head, cock filling his throat, cutting off his breath. He pressed a hand to his cock to ease the throbbing back a notch, and it only made it worse.

Thank God he hadn't noticed the cuffs while he was driving, too shocked at being handed his clothes and shoved out the door while sporting a hard-on that could have done duty as a bayonet. The unfamiliar dashboard, nothing preset to his preferences, was another useful distraction. Useful because if he had noticed his leather-clad wrists, he'd now be explaining why he'd driven head-on into a light pole. He was pretty sure there was no statute about driving under the influence of a killer erection—at least not in Maryland—but he could picture a test for determining the blood ratio between cock and brain. *Sorry, sir, you're way over the limit for that.*

He stroked himself through the thin material of his trousers, twisting his wrist so the bulk of the cuff caressed him on the upstroke. It was like having Tai—Sir there. The unfamiliar touch of it. The sense of being possessed, controlled.

He wasn't disobeying. Rubbing himself through his pants wasn't jerking off, no matter how good it felt. With a little squeeze at the top, he put both hands on the counter and studied the cuffs. Tai had said he'd text tomorrow. But it was only polite to let him know Beach had unintentionally left with Tai's property.

Beach's pulse pounded high in his chest as he typed out *I believe I still have something of yours.* After snapping a picture of one of his hands with the cuff around his wrist, he sent that along.

Is that all that's mine? Tai shot back immediately.

Beach's balls tightened and throbbed. He swore they'd twist themselves into a knot in his sac if he didn't get to unload them soon. One hand on his raw throat, he sent off *No, Sir.*

Good boy.

That rush. That absolute blissful sense of right, of completeness, when Sir had whispered the phrase when Beach finally managed to control himself enough not to choke on the thick cock.

How do you feel? Tai's text came after a minute of silence when the screen had gone blank.

Beach's half smile was one of his more seductive moves. He wished there was something other than the reflective countertop to appreciate it as he sent back *Remember what I said about fishing? About hooking something big? I hooked a shark. I'm not sure I'm going to make it, but I love the ride.*

When Tai didn't respond, Beach wondered if Tai had meant the question more literally.

And I'm so hard I think it's going to fall off.

You'll live. Remember. No jerking off.

Stripping, climbing into bed, and jerking off were all Beach could think about. He suddenly realized how tired he was, but there was no way he'd fall asleep with a boner like this. He carefully peeled off his pants, then tossed his shirt away, wincing as it stuck to some of his chest hair, glued there by come.

He staggered toward his bedroom and put the phone on the nightstand. His text alert sounded. *David. I expect you to answer me.*

He wanted to tell Tai to fuck off. That it was Beach's dick and he'd jerk it until it was raw if he wanted to. But more than that, he wanted to be back there. Know what else there was to learn about how it felt to let someone take control like that. So he made sullen stabs at the letters on the screen. *Yes, Sir.*

Yes, Sir, what?

Yes, Sir. No jerking off. How the hell would Tai know whether or not he did anyway? The monitor didn't pick up semen.

Good boy.

Beach stretched out on the bed and stared at his dick.

BEACH DIDN'T know why he dreamed about getting fucked by Tai in Gavin's boathouse. Something about trying to find someplace and constant interruption from the new passel of friends Gavin had. That was where they ended up. Beach felt the rough wood of the dock under his hands and knees, but it didn't matter. All that mattered was Tai's cock filling Beach's ass, a perfect, burning stretch and then thrusts to electrify him from inside out. Tai's voice, rougher than the weathered wood. "Good. So fucking good for me. Gonna make you come so hard."

The leather gauntlet on his wrist got in the way as Tai gave Beach a reach around, but he was so close he didn't care.

"Give it to me. That's mine too." Tai poured the words into Beach's ear like smoke.

And god-fucking-dammit, Beach was awake, his own leather cuff chafing his hard cock as his hips pumped against the mattress.

Don't jerk off.

It couldn't count if Beach was asleep, right? People even got away with murder if they were found to be asleep when they did it. He shut his eyes and tried to fall back into that dream, but his body had other plans.

So close. So fucking close.

He wasn't exactly jerking off either. His hand wasn't moving. It was his hips making the friction, the rub against his open palm and the lump of leather. The edge caught him just right, hips working faster and faster and *Oh shit, I'll buy him another pair of cuffs* was the last thing that went through Beach's head as the orgasm burst out of his balls. He shook through it.

Hard, sharp, and over too damned fast. He yanked his hand away and rolled off to the side, dick more sensitive than usual. Damn, he'd needed that, but it would have been so much better if that bossy son of a bitch had actually been up his ass.

It was only ten steps to the bathroom, but the first one he tried with weight on his bad leg almost sent him to the floor. He hop-staggered the rest of the way in, wiped off his junk with a towel, and turned on the water for a shower.

When his text alert sounded, he jumped, though there was no one to actually see his guilty expression but the guy in the mirror. *What the hell?* Beach looked down at the monitor as if it had given him away. Assuming the monitor picked up the heat or his pulse, the new Officer DiPrazi or whatever wouldn't have called Tai to tell him.

He hopped back to scoop up his phone, then blinked and squinted at the time. Not that Beach was an early riser, but that was usually because he didn't get to bed before the morning. He'd been out for almost twelve hours.

Got any plans today?

Beach loved the way he could hear Tai's voice in his texts.

No—Beach hesitated for a moment—*Sir.*

Then get your ass over here.

I haven't showered.

Thought a guy who was desperate to get off would have other things on his mind, but take your time.

Beach gave a rueful look at his spent cock. *I'll be right there.*

Tai hadn't posed it as a question, so it wasn't exactly a lie. And what if he found out? Would it mean some kind of punishment? Beach's dick ached as a little spurt of blood tried to revive it.

TWO HOURS at the dog park had Jez's tongue lolling and her steps dragging. That made one of them. The burst of energy that had Tai up and at the gym by five thirty was still riding him. All he had to do was picture David on his knees, hear the surrender in his gasps, feel him give up his throat, and adrenaline exploded inside like fireworks.

Tai knew Nic would tell him to keep David waiting, that the Dom had to be the one with the self-control to set the early boundaries, but knowing didn't stop the need, the itch to find out how far this was going to go, if David's curiosity had been satisfied or if he wanted more.

Given how fast David showed up, Tai was going to go with *wanting more*.

David leaned heavily on his cane as Tai shut the door behind him. "I'm afraid I'm not—I don't know the protocol." David picked at his silky button-down shirt, made an abortive effort to shove that hand in the pocket of his navy shorts, then tucked his cuffed wrist behind his back.

Tai had seen enough of David A. Beauchamp to know unease wasn't something he was familiar with. That he was willing to let it show made Tai have to take a deep breath to find extra room in his chest for the heat spreading under his ribs.

Before he could answer, David lowered himself to one knee without any of the easy grace he'd shown yesterday. But it wasn't for Tai.

"Hey, Jez. Who's a pretty girl?"

Tai released her from her stay, and she trotted forward, accepting David's pets and rubs with wriggles and licks.

"Yes, you are a very pretty girl. Look at those eyes."

Jez tilted her head as if she were an actress mugging for the camera, then swung it back at David, catching him on the shoulder hard enough to make him wobble and have to slam a hand against the wall.

Tai stared at the leg David had stretched out in front of him, the scar and the area around it red and tight with swelling. The clench of Tai's jaw kept back a snap of anger that would have startled Jez. Disappointment kept his frustration to an icy trickle down his spine as he got a rawhide for Jez to keep her occupied. When she was happily gnawing while sprawled on her blanket under the window, Tai hauled David to his feet, steered him into the bedroom, and shut the door.

Ignoring the seductive cast the location called up on David's face, Tai kept his voice low and even.

"The first thing, the very first thing I told you was you'd have to be completely honest with me." If David couldn't manage that much, there wasn't a chance of this working.

"What are you talking about?"

"You told me your leg was fine."

"It is fine. Well, it was." David shrugged like that was an excuse.

"You can't hide pain like that. I have to trust that you'll tell me if something is hurting you."

"What about that punishment you told me about?" A deep flush stained David's throat.

"That's different. It would never be anything to put you at risk for injury. And I want you to be honest about how that makes you feel too."

The flush climbed onto David's face.

"Sit." Tai pushed him gently onto the bed. "Is there something you need to tell me?"

David shook his head. "My leg is fine. Or it was fine last night. I woke up, and it was sore and swollen. I didn't lie to you. I haven't lied to you." David looked up. "Sir."

Tai let the moment stretch, reading David's face, learning what he was willing to show in his eyes.

After a minute David looked down. "This... it's too...." He swallowed and met Tai's gaze again, this time with a regretful grin. "I don't think I *can* lie to you now."

Tai put a palm on David's face, and the stubble on his cheek prickled as David leaned into the touch.

Shifting to move a breath away from David's lips, Tai whispered, "Was that all that was swollen and bothering you when you woke up?"

"No." David's voice shook.

God, he was so open, offering himself so sweetly, Tai wanted to put David on a spreader bar and eat that tight ass until he passed out.

"You said you didn't have time for a shower." Tai peeled David's shirt off over his head. It was twice as silky as it looked, but Tai was much more interested in what was underneath.

"Join me." David pushed to his feet.

"You haven't seen my shower, but I can watch."

Tai hoped his eventual coffin was roomier than the shower stall in his apartment, but the close quarters in the rest of the bathroom weren't bothering him now. He cradled David's face and kissed him, tugging his lips apart and tickling inside them. David shifted against Tai. With a lurch of guilt, he pulled away. After lowering the toilet lid, Tai helped him sit.

"Sorry. Forgot about your leg."

"Don't let that stop you."

Tai arched his brows and bent to leave wet kisses across David's pecs, breathing in the sweat and sex smells on his skin. Trailing a palm down David's arm, Tai stopped at the cuff. He bit back a grin. It was sweet and hot that David had kept them on.

David pulled his arm back. "I can get that."

Tai held tight. "I put it on you. I'll take it off."

David shivered.

Tai reached for the buckle and noticed the crusted white stain. "Anything you want to tell me?"

"No, Sir."

He snapped off the cuff and held it under David's nose. David looked at him and blinked.

"Did you jerk off?"

Despite a guilty grimace, David tried to wriggle off. "Not exactly."

Tai leaned back. "Spontaneous combustion?"

David shook his head.

"So?"

"I was having a dream. And in the dream, I was close, and then I woke up and—" When David tried to tell the rest of the story to his toes, Tai grabbed his chin and forced him to look up. "And I humped into my hand. Does that count?" David finished.

"What do you think?"

David grinned. "There's not really a right answer for that, is there?"

"The answer is 'Yes, Sir.'" He let go of David's chin.

David swallowed. "So—uh—what happens now?"

He was pushing. No question about it. Tai hadn't ever met anyone who was more in need of consequences. But unlike most subs, David didn't understand that need in himself, and it wasn't part of the power exchange that turned him on. Yet.

"I gave you an order. You disobeyed me." Tai pulled David's other arm up and unsnapped the cuff.

David looked down at his wrists and then encircled his left one with his fingers. "I did plan to replace them. After."

"That's not what this is about." Tai slapped the cuffs against his palm. David watched, face set with a square jaw. "You can't buy off a consequence with me."

David reared back. "I didn't—"

Tai put his thumb over David's lips. "Don't interrupt me. If I ask you a question, you can answer." With David's nod, Tai lowered his hand. "You had a taste of this. Enough to know if you like it. Do you want to keep going?"

David's face became animated. "Absolutely. I—" He took a deep breath. "Yes, Sir."

"Okay. Then part of it is accepting punishment. Take off your shoes."

"What are—?" David stopped on his own.

"Go ahead."

"What are you going to do?"

"I promised you I won't spank you unless you ask me to. You're going to take a shower."

David leaned to look around Tai at the shower stall. "It might not be the spa at the Four Seasons, but I think I can handle it."

Tai smiled. "You can think it's funny now. Don't forget your safeword."

"Even in punishment?"

"Especially in punishment. Now, the next time you say something without being asked a question means more time."

David might not understand what was coming, but he sealed his mouth.

"I'll support you so you can keep weight off your leg. Put your hand on my shoulder." Tai hunched down.

As David levered himself up, Tai reached for the fly of David's shorts. His lips parted and then pinched shut again.

Tai peeled off David's shorts, then slid thumbs in the waistband of his briefs. "What's wrong?"

"It feels—Normally I enjoy being undressed by an attractive man, but this is making me feel uncomfortable."

"That's kind of the point of punishment, David." Tai stripped the briefs down to David's ankles, and he stepped out of them.

Tai put an extra towel on the floor before handing David a washcloth and liquid soap. David's glance bounced around the shower, then searched Tai's face for an explanation. "You can keep hanging on to me to keep the weight off your leg." Tai reached in, adjusted the dial, and blasted David with icy water.

"What the—?" David tried to step forward, and Tai held him inside the stall. David's eyes widened. He glanced at the temperature control and back at Tai, who nodded.

David stuck it through, Tai would give him that. Shaking and teeth chattering, David fumbled with the

soap and washcloth. He managed to get through his
face and arms, but as he rubbed down his chest and
the cloth brushed his cock, he jumped. "Jesus fucking
Christ, that's cold."

"Extra time, David. And if you swear again, that's
thirty more seconds." David looked at the washcloth
and his cock.

"Wash. It's not getting any warmer." Tai was only
getting a splatter of the cold water. It was still cold
enough to make his balls tighten, even safely hidden
under two layers.

Squinching his face, David washed between his
legs and into his crack, then down his legs, before
dropping the washcloth. His mouth opened and then
he shut it, standing with folded arms and shivering.

"Why are you being punished, David?"

David rolled his eyes.

"Another five seconds. Why are you being
punished?"

"Because I was horny and jerked off," David spat out.

"No. Keep thinking and give me the right answer."

"I can't think." He stuttered the words. "I'm too
cold."

Tai reached in and shut off the water. "Why are
you being punished?"

David's jaw was tight, eyes narrow.

"You're not getting out of there without the right
answer." Tai took the jutting jaw in his hand and
rubbed his thumb across the trembling lips. "Tell me."

The huffed sigh meant David was still fighting,
but he answered, "Because I disobeyed you."

"Yes."

Tai reached in and turned the water on again.

"I answered." David's hands moved down to cover his dick. "C'mon. I'm sorry."

"You're not sorry. You're sorry you're being punished, but that will do for now."

David shivered and shifted around the stall, trying to get different skin in and out of the icy spray.

"I'm starting your extra time now. Fifteen seconds."

"Ten. I only said something twice."

"Now it's twenty."

David looked away, but he didn't stop the squirming around. Tai shut off the spray and handed David a fresh towel.

"Oh God, that's so warm."

Tai lifted him over the lip and onto the towel on the floor, wrapping David in the terrycloth and the warmth of Tai's body.

David held himself stiffly for a minute, then relaxed. "That sucked."

"Don't disobey me."

Tai dried him off, shifting from rubbing to caressing. David leaned against him.

Yes, this boy wouldn't hold on to resentment. Tai could see how sweet a sub David would make. Brushing a kiss across his jaw and then behind his ear, Tai asked, "How do you feel?"

"Weird. It's kind of dizzying. I'm still really pissed at you, but I can't get close enough to you."

Tai yanked off his damp tank top, and David's cool arms landed around Tai's chest, face on his shoulder.

"So, do we get to fuck now?"

Tai grinned and kissed him. "Don't make me go shopping for a ball gag."

Chapter Seven

BEACH SPRAWLED on his back on Tai's bed, skin still tingling from that ice bath. As miserable as it had been, as furious as he had been at Tai for that implacable look on his face, something about it had felt right. And that was downright scary. For the first time in his life, Beach wondered if he was in way over his head.

If he had any sense, he'd be ready to leave. He'd been curious. Now he knew he liked being dominated by a guy in bed. Especially if the guy had a voice like smoke and gravel and could lift Beach up like he was a doll.

As for the other stuff....

He definitely hadn't liked it while it was happening, being undressed like a child, suffering under the brain-locking cold. No, that didn't turn him on. But waiting here for Tai to get back after taking Jez out,

Beach felt good. Better than just knowing-sex-was-coming good.

No one had ever accused Beach of having too much sense.

Keeping the towel wrapped around him, he rolled over onto his stomach, making the pillow send up a solid breath of Tai, his aftershave and sweat. Beach pressed his face in and took another whiff, his hips making a slow stroke to drive his cock against the towel. It hurt a little, skin still cold, the nubs on the cloth rough. Flattening himself on the too-firm mattress, he drew steady, deep breaths. The smell put Tai's voice in the room like he was standing there.

No, David. That's mine.

Beach made another slow rub, defying his imagination. And the sensitivity of his chilled skin. Damn it. It was like Tai could enforce his will without actually being there. Why couldn't his idea of consequences be something like his dick up Beach's ass?

With a sigh, Beach flopped onto his back. He collected his phone from his shorts and found a picture of a ball gag.

The idea of a shiny plastic—or was that rubber?—ball in his mouth had Beach's tongue practicing how he could push it out. He put a hand to his cheek like the strap was already there, feeling a great deal of sympathy for horses that curled their lips at the sight of a bit. And what the fuck was that for? He enlarged the next image of lips forced open around a circle. Why would—oh. Tai's cock forcing Beach's throat open, the eye-watering gag reflex.

Which made his distinctly perverted libido send blood zinging to his dick.

It wouldn't be the first time it had gotten him in serious trouble.

More images. Men and women hog-tied with cuffs and clips like the ones Tai had used to bind Beach's hands. Beach rolled back onto his stomach to try to copy the posture. Maybe ten years ago he could have done it.

A bar, legs cuffed at the ankle to keep the man's legs from closing. To keep Beach's legs from closing while Tai did whatever he wanted. That set the blood to throbbing slow and steady, and Beach was definitely warming up now.

Collars. Beach put his hand to his throat, squinting at the text. *For play and everyday wear.* Every day? Like so other people would know you liked to have a man tell you what to do in bed?

He glanced around the room and wondered if Tai had that stuff tucked away in here.

Maybe in the closet?

Before he'd left, Tai had done the lifting-the-chin thing that was starting to have as much of a direct line to Beach's dick as a nip on the side of his neck and said, "Be a good boy, stay on the bed, and don't poke around in my things."

Beach rolled onto his side and stared at the closet. It wasn't that he expected a Bluebeard's-wife type discovery. But curiosity was a horrible curse. He looked at his wrists and thought about those cuffs, trying to find some sort of rationalization for snooping. It would only be polite to find out what sort of things Tai liked if Beach was going to buy Tai another pair.

Beach's breath seized up like he was back under the cold shower. Until that moment he hadn't really thought about how many other men had worn those cuffs, had knelt for Tai, probably with a great deal more finesse or deference or whatever it was Tai liked. Beach had never given much thought to a lover's previous experience before, except to prefer they had some. He certainly didn't promise fidelity or expect it in return. So he couldn't understand why the thought of those more *submissive* men should hit like a punch to his gut.

The sound of Tai coming back into the apartment was soon drowned out under the click of Jez's nails as she trotted toward the bedroom and nosed open the door.

"Hi, pretty girl. Yes, I'm still here."

She approached and sniffed, then let him rub behind her ears.

"She wasn't the only one wondering." Tai leaned against the doorjamb.

Beach shrugged, hiding a confused mess of jealousy, shyness, and lust under a grin. He wished it was as easy to turn off the way those feelings tangled around each other, their roots shooting all the way down into his thighs until they ached. Maybe he should have run when he had the chance. "I'm an adventurous sort. Don't scare easy."

"I scare you?"

"No."

Beach wasn't afraid of Tai, but himself. The way he was with Tai. Like someone Beach didn't recognize, but he'd been trying to find. Someone drowning in a hunger that was satisfied with something as simple as Tai's growled *good boy*.

Tai did that stare, the one that seemed to look right through Beach's head, the slash of his brows making the look more intimidating.

"Sir," Beach added with an inviting smile.

Tai's face relaxed. He kicked off his sneakers and sat on the bed. Scratching the dog's giant head, he said, "Jez, down." To Beach, Tai said, "Does it bother you if she's in the room?"

"Is she likely to post compromising pictures online?"

"She's likely to make grumbling noises and go out into the living room."

"And what are you likely to do?" Beach drew the towel off his lap.

Tai tossed off his T-shirt. "Do you ever turn off?"

Beach eyed the breadth of that chest, the way the muscles underneath bunched and shifted like cars out on I-95. Each shoulder could easily be concealing a Volkswagen underneath the skin. "Why on earth would I want to?" He was looking forward to using his tongue to trace the intricate geometry of the tattoo covering Tai from shoulder to elbow.

From other touches, Beach knew the skin underneath was smooth, so Tai had worn the ink for years, yet the lines were clean and sharp. They spread from his shoulder to his chest, even under his arm. Did it hurt? Beach bit back the stupid question before it slipped out. Of course it had. But for some reason Tai had chosen to endure it. To prove something? A warrior-style initiation like the hazing Beach had undergone as a Citadel cadet?

The patterns were reminiscent of woven leather, like the gauntlets a now-nude Tai slid over his wrists, zipping them tight. An echo of that sound purred from Beach's belly to his balls. Straddling Beach as he lay on his back, Tai kept his weight supported on his thighs, only offering a brush of contact at Beach's hips. The ripple of abs and the cut of hips were an even more inviting place to touch and taste. Beach curled up, thumbs finding the grooves, tongue hungry for a taste of that semihard cock. He planned to start practicing with bananas, but maybe he ought to go straight for a Coke can.

Tai watched him look, but when Beach snaked a hand through to cup the velvety sac inches from his own, Tai circled Beach's wrist with a grip like the cuff had.

"David."

Beach was catching on, learning when Tai switched fully into that demanding mode that made electricity spark along every nerve in Beach's body. "Yes, Sir."

"Good boy." Tai ran a hand through David's hair. "If you behave, you can explore later. Tell me exactly what the doctor said about taking care of your leg."

Beach managed to keep the sigh and the eye roll to himself. His skin was still sensitive from the deep freeze. "Keep weight-bearing activities to a minimum, pain meds and ibuprofen as needed—though according to my probation, the pain meds are out—and start physical therapy."

"Did you start physical therapy?"

The squirm began inside, deep in the pit of Beach's stomach, rolling to his ass and legs. It was coming out of the shower all over again. A pissed-off insistence that Tai didn't get a say in things that weren't part of them having sex, battling with the shivery jolt of being the focus of Tai's attention. Beach shut his eyes and shifted his shoulders on the mattress.

"What's wrong?" Tai moved so he wasn't touching Beach at all.

"Nothing. Nothing sex won't fix, Sir."

"Answer my other question first."

"I just got the cast off."

Tai stretched out over Beach in a push-up pose, the promise of hot, hard flesh grinding against him frustratingly out of reach. He put his arms around Tai's neck to drag him down, but Tai shook his head.

"Obviously the answer is no." Beach paused. "Sir."

"Don't be a brat, or I'll send you home."

As a threat, that was particularly effective. "Sorry, Sir."

"David, I want you to call and make an appointment."

Beach tucked his hands behind his head. Measuring his tone and words carefully, he said, "I don't understand what that has to do with this."

Tai lowered himself until he was radiating prickling warmth to spark across the inches still separating them. His breath tickled Beach's lips. "You don't need to. You'll take care of your body as long as you're offering it to me."

There was that same strange shudder of pleasure without anything touching his dick. "Okay."

"Try again." Tai's brow got that look that had Beach remembering how fucking cold that shower had been.

"Yes, I will make an appointment, Sir."

"On Monday."

Damn. Beach's lips vibrated with the need to find the words that would carve him a loophole, fight this last bit of capitulation. But Tai stared down. It wasn't the threat as much as the anticipation that tipped Beach over. And not only for the physical reward hovering close enough to taste.

"On Monday, Sir."

"Good boy." Tai lowered himself, and damn he felt incredible, weight and praise all sinking into Beach with a heat that went to his bones. Tai rocked his hips so their cocks slid together, dragging a shudder and groan from Beach. That last orgasm felt a lot further away than this morning.

Beach squeezed Tai's shoulders and tried to urge him faster, harder. His dick was so hot, so heavy on Beach's. Blood raced, thickening his cock to answer the pressure. Tai took Beach's mouth, tongue driving in to remind him of the way it had felt with Tai's cock stealing his breath. Beach hung on tighter and lifted his hips. Tai pressed him down into the mattress.

Tai raised his head. "Do you have somewhere to be?"

Beach's lips felt huge, scraped. "No, Sir."

"Then slow down."

Beach groaned. Tai chuckled. The bed squeaked as he shifted his weight again, beard scraping against Beach's neck, wet kisses following. Tai repeated the action on Beach's chest, sensitizing the skin with the rub of hair and then kissing and teasing with lips and tongue.

When Tai did that to Beach's nipples, he arched off the bed, gripping Tai's head. Tai nipped the swollen flesh, then commanded, "Let go."

Beach dropped his hands to his sides. But he couldn't keep them there when Tai moved lower, the mixture of sensations on Beach's belly making him curl up around Tai.

"David, do you want the cuffs?"

"Please. Yes, Sir."

They weren't a punishment. The tight grip on his wrists, it was security and control, because Beach was going to lose his mind if Tai—Sir—touched Beach's cock. The thought that this man who could take what he wanted would give Beach that hot mouth made the tip of his dick burn with need.

Tai buckled on the cuffs and pushed Beach's arms up over his head, and the sound of clips echoed like a bass line under Beach's ribs.

"Okay?"

Beach tugged lightly. His hands were clipped to something over his head, and it felt perfect. Safe.

He started to nod, then remembered. "Yes, Sir."

There was no brush of hands, lips, or beard, but Beach felt the intent gaze on him and opened his eyes. He took a deep breath and stopped straining toward Tai. Energy flooded him, a hot rush both like and nothing like coming, because he could stay here, heartbeat after heartbeat. And despite the way his body sparked, he felt absolutely still. There. Letting Tai fill him up with that stare.

When Tai ran his hands down Beach's outstretched arms, the feeling stayed, lighting Beach up and rooting him into the mattress at the same time.

Tai moved between Beach's legs, and the feeling slipped away, chased by the shivery expectation of pleasure.

"Listen, David. This is just like last night. Your body is mine. Whatever I make it feel. Relax and take it."

Tai lifted Beach off the mattress, cradling his ass in hot, rough palms, forcing his legs apart on those broad shoulders. Beach was spread wider than he could have been with one of those bars, only it was warm, hard muscles under his thighs that ensured he wouldn't be able to close his legs unless Tai allowed it.

At least the weight was off his healing bones. Beach recognized the giddy rush of nerves and tried to tamp it down, but he couldn't stop the completely inappropriate giggle.

Eyes slitted as if that would keep him safe from any disapproval in Tai's eyes, Beach peered up. Tai didn't look pissed. He only smiled and rubbed his thumbs firmly in the crease between Beach's ass and thighs.

The urge to giggle faded as Tai's expression changed, and he leaned in to roll one of Beach's balls across a hot tongue. Tai's goatee tingled and scraped, his tongue sucked and licked, and Beach shifted, already trying to move, already forgetting he couldn't.

He was all for a lover taking care of him in bed, but he was used to participating.

Tai didn't stop but rubbed his chin against Beach's sac, lapping at the base of his rigid cock. Too much and not enough.

"Oh God."

Tai made a sound like a growl that vibrated across Beach's skin, and Beach jerked his hands.

He needed to touch his cock. Just a little. Just to take the edge off. "Please."

Tai lifted his head enough to rumble words. "You're not going to come. You're going to feel what I want you to feel."

Beach wasn't simply in over his head, he was drowning, dragged under so deep he couldn't find his way up. Tai licked up the length of Beach's dick, but too soft, the sucking pressure on the head only a tease. A giant snake took control of his spine in a twisting, undulating roll.

Tai gripped Beach's ass harder, pulled his cheeks open, and rubbed a flat, fat tongue against Beach's hole.

Slithering heat, a build of pressure, and Beach squeezed his eyes shut so tightly tears leaked from the corners.

"David." It was sharp. Harsh with demand. "Breathe."

He managed a shuddering exhale.

"That's it. I've got you." The grip on his ass shifted to a hard rub, forcing the muscles to relax or hurt.

Beach took another breath.

"Yeah. I've got you." Tai held Beach open and licked his hole, darting flicks that set off little pops of pleasure rippling out from his ass to his balls and the tip of his dick.

It built urgently, the need to move, to free his hands and take back what Tai demanded from Beach's body. Built in the burn of precome on his dick straining into the air, in the pressure of a sharp nose in his balls, in the warm wiggle of tongue in and around his rim.

But he knew the secret now. He let out a breath and rode it out because there was nothing to do but take it. Take it and let it control him, let Tai decide what Beach would feel. His legs dropped open wider, and he floated on it, more and more of him cracking open for Tai to take and hold.

Beach's breath came faster, and it was already so loud he added words to it. "Yes, Sir. Yes. God, yes."

"So good." Tai's fingers worked in, deeper than his tongue had, and Beach absorbed that new sensation, let it spread out from his ass to under his rib cage. "Mine."

"Yes, Sir."

Tai sucked Beach's balls, pulling one and then the other into a hot mouth, tension and pressure a blinding swirl of pain and pleasure. Beach found that place where he was wide-open to everything Tai gave and sucked in the hurt with the ecstasy.

He lost track of everything but sensation and the way it poured back out of him to the man pushing him, connecting them deeper than skin.

Bedcover under his ass, cock jabbing into his balls, then sliding along Beach's shaft.

Face cradled between hot palms, hips pinned under a slow, grinding weight. Thumbs warm and insistent under his jaw, and Beach tilted his head back, offering his throat to the solid grip along his windpipe.

"Fuck." Tai's grunted curse was pure praise, bursting over Beach like sweet rain.

He came back into his body to the vibrations of Tai's hand smacking around on the mattress, then the nightstand, aching from the absence of the drive of sensation. Beach jerked his hands to reach out.

"I've got you, David." The deepness of Tai's voice settled over him an instant before his physical weight pressed down and filled the hole that had opened in Beach's sternum, slick fingers pushed lube into his ass, and the sound of a condom wrapper tearing told him he wouldn't be feeling empty for long.

But he did. As the blunt head made an eye-watering stretch of his asshole, his hands tried again to reach for Tai's shoulders, to pull him closer, craving the mass of muscle and warm skin to keep that terrible emptiness away. Tai lifted Beach's hips.

"Take it, David. Open that ass and take my cock."

Beach dragged his eyes open to face the dark stare that sank into him, turned him to liquid so his body could reform around Tai as he fit inside.

It wasn't easy. It wasn't fast. But for once Beach wasn't chasing sensation. Wasn't moving on to the next high. He simply was.

He breathed and it burned, too full, but he wanted Tai deeper. No, it didn't matter what Beach wanted. He would *take* more, if Tai chose to give it.

Tai shifted his hips, small movements that were huge on the inside. But that was good because it made room for all that thickness and pressure. So the stretch went on and on.

Beach closed his eyes in concentration.

"No. Look at me." Cock, voice, eyes. Tai was finding more ways into Beach's head. He dragged his eyelids up.

Tai moved, urging Beach's legs up toward his chest, high around Tai's waist. God, so deep, pressure enough to make Beach's eyes roll back toward his hairline.

"Don't close your eyes."

The tiny part of his brain that wasn't on board with this objected *Then don't jam your cock up me until I feel it in my chest*. But that part wasn't in control. The Beach who belonged here, the Beach who was happy to belong to Tai right now, nodded.

"I'm going to fuck you now, David. You're going to stay open to me, and I don't just mean your ass."

"Yes, Sir." It burst from him on a groan, and Tai answered with one, fingers convulsing where they gripped Beach's hips.

Beach thought it was hard to keep his eyes open on the first thrust. But it was almost impossible on

the second and the third. Tai moved slowly enough
to leave Beach aware of all the different sensations.
The jar to his whole body as Tai bottomed out, the
drag that made pleasure ripple out from ass to dick,
then the screaming excitement of the nerves in muscles stretched to the limit at the rim, and then the jolt
of hot, sweet need as his cock prodded Beach's gland
on reentry.

Every stroke forced a deep breath from his lungs,
the slide out making him suck in a gasp as he willed
his eyes open to meet Tai's gaze again.

"Good. That's it."

Beach got dizzy, tried to fling his hands out for
balance, but he couldn't. Tai gripped tighter.

"I've got you. Feels good in you, David."

No one had ever called Beach David during sex.
Every time Tai did, it set off a prickle of awareness
that this was different. This was new. That Tai was
focused on this part of Beach he'd never known was
there.

But when Tai went on in his deep-as-the-ocean
voice, "So hot and tight around me, boy," Beach lost
it.

He wanted to cry, he wanted to come, but most
of all he had to touch the man who made him feel like
this. Have more than just the spot where Tai rocked
inside to mold them together.

"I'm—" Beach shook with the effort to explain it.
He wanted to be good and open, but it was hard and he
needed. "I can't—God. Please…. Sir."

Tai loomed over, fingers brushing Beach's. A
dull, heavy click and his hands were free.

He reached for Tai's arms.

"Yeah." Tai scooped him up, pressing them to-gether. "You can come for me now, David."

Beach would like that. He really would. Tai's hips pumped short and quick, cock stabbing over and over at the place inside that felt so good, so close.

Tai kissed him, openmouthed, sloppy drag of lips and beard, trailing across Beach's face to his ear.

The powerful arms squeezed him tighter. "You will come for me. You'll come just like this. From my cock in your ass." Tai's rapid breaths scorched Beach's ear. "You'll come like this because you don't have a choice."

Not having a choice was something guaranteed to send Beach fleeing as far and fast from that dead end as possible. But not David. David loved it. David didn't want a choice. He wanted this. Rough demands and the impossible challenge of getting off when he had no control over the sensations in his body.

Hotter, slicker, sweat and precome between them, and the spike of nuclear heat from where Tai jabbed with every hard slam of his hips.

Beach shook, reaching for it with everything he had, Tai deep in his ass, his chest, his head. Groans and pants in his ear. "Now, boy. Do it. Right now. Come."

The warning was a sizzle, a wisp before the force of it slammed into him, pumped out of him. Spasm after spasm yanking the hot flood from ass to balls to dick. The delicious shocks echoing into his thighs and chest and ears, until it slowed to nothing but a hum. Because this thing they were doing was still there. Even though Tai had stopped moving, had separated from Beach's body, the connection linked them, an-chored to the spot where his breath was.

Tai stripped off the condom and gave his dick a few hard jerks. Harsh grunts washed over Beach's ears, and then a gravel-scraped "So good, David. Yeah, fuck," as Tai bucked and splashed Beach's chest with warm, thick strings, sharp bleach smell in his nose.

Tai rubbed a hand over Beach's cheek while the other pushed Tai's cock next to Beach's on his belly, sliding in the slick puddles.

"You okay?"

Beach nodded. *Okay* couldn't really cover feeling like he'd come apart and shifted under his skin into something new, something better. Something that didn't fade away with the ebb of the high from sex chemicals. The sex rush was gone. What was left was like a low-level hum of arousal, a mild buzz from a couple of quick shots of liquor. But without the urgency to chase after it. He could stay here forever.

"Let me check your wrists." Tai uncuffed them, looking over the red skin, a gentle thumb on the pulse point. "Anything feel wrong? Pulled muscles? Your leg okay?"

"Well, I'm pretty sure I still have legs, but I can't really assess their condition at the moment."

Tai chuckled and lifted his weight off Beach's thighs.

"Thank you, but that wasn't really a problem. I like how—strong you are."

Tai's lips twisted. "Move your fingers, let me see them." It wasn't his Sir voice, but there was still a demand there.

Beach complied. Then he wiggled his toes. "All functional and accounted for."

"Good." Tai brought his sticky hand to Beach's other wrist, rubbing their mingled come over the redness that was already fading.

Beach caught his breath. His cock was out of commission for the foreseeable future, but his pulse ramped up. Tai kissed, then licked the inside of Beach's wrist. His skin tingled, like he'd stepped into sunshine from too long in air-conditioning.

"And how do you feel in here?" Tai made Beach's lax hand point and tap his own forehead.

Safe. Happy. And when Tai anointed Beach's other wrist and followed up with kisses, he didn't think it was unreasonable to add *worshipped*. "Pretty good," he answered and drifted to sleep with Tai's mouth still tickling a wrist.

TAI WISHED he could fall asleep like that. But no, he had to be one of the rare guys who got energized after sex. Just one more way to remember he didn't fit a category. But then, neither did David A. Beauchamp.

He was the entitled, arrogant prick Tai had pegged him for from reading the case file. But the self-deprecating charm wasn't something that came through on paper. And most of the entitled snots Tai came across would have to be a breath from dying before they'd admit the kind of vulnerability David had shared.

Tai had pushed hard last night, driven to find out if an interest in D/s was nothing more than a new adrenaline rush to Beauchamp, or if he really could give himself up to it.

And he had. Fuck, he really had.

Then today, the way he'd let Tai strip everything away with his mouth and tongue and feed it back on his cock, God. Tai rubbed his face across the sleeping man's wrist.

Leather, sweat, come. Tai's hand tightened around David's forearm. *Mine.*

With a mumbled sound, David rolled into Tai. Cradling David with an arm at his waist, Tai eased onto his back and let David settle on top, cheek prickling Tai's nipple with stubble.

Tai wanted to drag David in tighter, right under the skin, open up and pull him inside to keep him safe. Mostly from David himself. Tai had run into new subs at Nic's. Ones who had met the wrong guy and were only beginning to put themselves back together from the damage.

The way David went tearing off after things on a whim, the file full of crazy stunts, he'd been lucky so far that the worst was a coma and a busted leg.

Tai ran his hand down David's back, palm flat over the muscles, heat against the chill of David's skin exposed to the air-conditioning. At the base of the spine, Tai spread his fingers wide to cover as much skin as he could, wishing he could leave a heat signature on David's body, a warning that everyone's luck had run out.

When the Terps were in a bowl game Tai's freshman year, he'd picked up some Samoan from a player on the other team. David was *O le lima e paia le mata*, looking for trouble and bringing it on himself. If Tai remembered it right, the words were about punching yourself in the eye. Those pretty blue eyes weren't where Tai wanted to leave his message about staying out of trouble. He stroked his hand down farther, fingers grazing the top of David's ass.

That was one effective way of getting attention, but Tai knew plenty of others. If he had his way, David would start relying on self-control rather than luck. And Tai was going to make sure that, for once, things went exactly his way.

Chapter Eight

TAI FIGURED David had been out about fifteen minutes when he opened his eyes. After a deliberate rub of his cheek against Tai's pec, David lifted his head. "Hello."

Tai met David's gaze. "Hello." David smiled.

Tai hadn't realized he was anticipating disaster until that smile made relief wash through him.

"It appears I owe you an apology." David angled his chin so that stubble prickled Tai's nipple with the motion of David's jaw.

"Oh?"

"I usually have better manners than to pass out on my lovers."

"Too bad." Tai used his palm to drag David in tight. "They might have found it flattering."

David resisted, lifting his chest a bit, peeling apart skin welded by sweat and spunk. "Though if I recall correctly, I remained conscious enough to be aware of happy endings all around." He tucked his head in, peering down at where the evidence had dried.

The retreat was more than physical, the withdrawal behind that careless charm slamming a barrier between them.

Tai lifted David's chin on two fingers. "Were you happy with it?"

David met Tai's gaze steadily for a moment, then lowered his lashes. "Absolutely." He pushed down against the gentle pressure of Tai's fingers. "You seem to enjoy grabbing my chin a lot. Is it part of this thing?" David laid his hand over Tai's gauntlet. "Like leather and punishments?"

"It's a me-and-you thing. But if it bothers you—"

Before Tai could pull his hand away, David covered it, fingers urging Tai into a stronger grip. "I didn't say that. Quite the opposite. I may have discovered yet another new turn-on."

"It's good to have some spares in case your usual goes flat," Tai agreed. If David was more comfortable hiding behind banter, Tai could let him hide.

"Or flaccid." David grinned and stretched up to offer a kiss.

Tai should have held back, accepted the kiss, and let things be relaxed and easy. But his self-control evaporated around David. His push-pull of need and resistance yanked hard at the core of want inside Tai, drove him to pin David's face in a tight grip and take his mouth as if the heat and force would leave a taste of Tai behind.

After a second of it, David opened to it, absorbed the kiss with a groan that vibrated between them. His tongue stroked alongside Tai's, and damn if Tai wasn't going to be the one left with a craving instead.

He released David's mouth, eased the hold on his face, thumbs stroking his lips, his chin—which had started the whole damned thing. Even that night in the bar, the way that chin jerked out when Tai turned down the first offer had caught his interest.

David was breathing fast, eyes closed. When they opened, the look was soft, full of a need that moved them both close to that dizzy space of power offered and accepted. Tai wanted to hold him there. Cradle him in it.

David's tongue swept across his lips.

Before he could disappear again, Tai kissed him gently. "Sorry. You have this sexy hint of a dimple in your chin."

The freeze was so instant they might have been back under the shower. Tai released him.

David put his fingers to his chin. "You should have seen it in my pudgy youth. Disgusting thing. Thank God it's less noticeable now." He dropped his head, hiding his face completely. "Guess it's like a Band-Aid, right?" He ripped himself free, making them both wince as skin separated. He was hunched on the edge of the bed, feet on the floor, before Tai could recover.

"Right. So." David straightened his shoulders with an effort Tai could see in the muscles of his back. "I'm certain you have other things planned for your Saturday. Do you mind if I clean up a bit?"

Tai sat up. "What's wrong?"

"Nothing. I don't want to presume on your time. My clothes are in the bathroom, I think."

"No."

David flinched, and Tai softened his tone.

"Your clothes are in here. On this side of the bed. I brought them in before I walked Jez."

"Right." David's hand came up to his head, hesitated, then rubbed across the scar Tai had felt under thick, short hair.

"David—"

That sent him rocketing off the bed.

"I—Excuse me. I feel—" David's steps were uneven, but he still beat Tai to the bathroom and shut the door firmly.

The shower went on and the toilet flushed, a waterfall of sound, enough to mask Tai knocking.

Humidity, cheap lumber, and a settling foundation ensured the door didn't close all the way, not enough to lock, though it could be wedged tight enough to discourage Jez's curiosity.

She trotted over now and sat at his feet as he stared at the door, looking at him out of the top of her eyes again as if saying *Smooth one.*

He knew what was going on now. But David didn't. When the sound of the toilet had faded, Tai put his mouth close to the door so he didn't have to yell.

"David, listen."

"I'm fine." The quaver in David's voice made him a huge liar, but it wasn't a good time to call him on that.

"This happens sometimes. You feel shaky and sick and miserable? It's called sub drop. It's like coming off a high. A hangover." Tai listened. There was no change in the sound of the water, but at least he hadn't heard anything like a body hitting the floor.

After another minute he said, "Hey. I don't know you well enough to know what you need. So you need to convince me you're okay, or use your safeword and

I'll leave you alone." The rush of blood in Tai's ears was almost enough to drown out the water or anything David might say.

"Silence isn't very convincing." Tai took a few steps back into the bedroom to grab David's cane and his shorts. "Dav—" Hand on the doorknob, he paused. "Hey, Beach. At least take your cane."

With a squeaking jerk, the door flew open, then closed to a narrow gap with David's arm sticking through. Tai shoved the clothes and the cane at him.

"Thank you. I'll be out in a few minutes." David's voice was controlled, but the lack of emotion worried Tai more than the shakiness had. He replayed the fraction of a second when the door had come unstuck, David's hair and face dripping onto a towel around his shoulders.

Everything inside Tai demanded he force open that door and make David okay. Shield him with strength and force the understanding that it *was* okay. That the feeling was normal and would fade if David would relax and let Tai help. Three years ago, before he met Nic, Tai would have done exactly that. Letting David push him away was a lot easier in theory than in practice, though.

Hands in tight fists, he pressed them against his diaphragm, dragging calm to him and squeezing it in that grip. It might not be very Zen, but that was what worked for Tai.

When the door opened with a soft pop, he relaxed his fists.

David's hair was wet-dark, standing up unevenly from a toweling, drops still trickling down his chest and belly to the waistband of his shorts. The expression on his face was bland, a faint amusement Tai could picture David practicing in the mirror. It might have been convincing, if Tai hadn't just spent an hour watching real emotions on that face. That and the way his fingers clenched the top of his cane.

"I apologize for alarming you, but I'm fine." David started forward, and Tai moved out of the way.

David headed straight for the apartment door. Not unexpected, but it still stung, made Tai fight another urge to wrap the man up in his arms and demand they talk about what had happened.

"You might want your shirt. And your shoes. The pavement can be damned hot."

David came to an abrupt halt. "Right. Thanks." He started to turn back and caught his balance with a hand on the wall. "In the bedroom?"

"Do you want me to get them?" Tai kept his position, leaning on the wall between the bedroom and living room.

"No, thank you. I'll get them."

Tai had planned to stay right where he was until David left but went to the bedroom door. If it was the last chance, he was taking a final look at that sweet ass and sculpted back. Sue him.

David slid his shoes on and then bent down to grab his shirt. Straightening with a jerk, he swayed, overcorrected. Lips gray, features slack, eyes unfocused. Even with only the profile of his face, Tai knew what was about to happen.

Reflexes had Tai springing forward. He'd become a master at reading the signs when Gina was pregnant. In addition to the puking—or maybe because of it—she'd fainted a lot.

David sank like a rock, but Tai was already there, cushioning the drop so David landed in Tai's lap, both of them sitting.

David blinked. He wasn't out completely.

Tai waited for the blue eyes to focus. "Just so we're clear. You're not fine."

BEACH WANTED to argue, but he still felt like shit. Who knew sex that good had this at the tail end?

And he could admit to himself that Tai holding him like this made him feel better than he had since he'd woken up.

"Some of this might be your blood sugar. What did you have for breakfast?"

"Breakfast?" Beach stalled while he thought back. There'd been that text, and he hadn't stopped for food. "Toothpaste."

Tai's brows went up in thick slashes. "As in—"

"I brushed my teeth. That was all."

"How did you make it to, what are you—almost forty—?"

"I'm thirty-four." Beach's wounded pride snapped out the correction.

"Thirty-four," Tai agreed with amusement that made Beach want to turn around and level a glare, except he was really comfortable and not quite sure he wouldn't pass out. "So how did you make it this far without learning how to stay out of trouble?"

Beach leaned into the hard heat. It was different, being held like this. His experience with embraces was that they were mutual. This one wasn't. It was all Tai. This kind of difference was the good kind.

"Trouble is where all the fun is."

"Yeah?" Tai's voice rumbled against Beach's back, vibrated down his ear into his throat like a taste of something bittersweet. "I'd like to teach you different."

"So far it's been fun watching you try."

"Want another cold shower?"

Dread and desire chased themselves around deep and low in Beach's belly. "Uh, no." He didn't. That hadn't been fun at all. So why did the idea of it—of Tai making Beach do something he didn't like—why did that make his skin flush, his cock ache like it wanted to go for thirds this morning? Sucking in a breath, he added, "Sir."

Tai rasped his goatee against Beach's neck. "Food. Then we talk."

"Okay." Beach swallowed back disappointment. Over what he wasn't sure. That Tai wasn't going to punish—even that word in Beach's head made things inside go hot and tight—him, or that they couldn't stay right here a while.

Maybe it was the idea of talking. Beach liked to talk—as long as no one expected him to say anything. He was afraid this talk was going to mean making some choices, and that was something he particularly liked avoiding. *Options* he loved. *Choices* meant an option was closed.

Tai's grip shifted around as he helped Beach to his feet, never leaving his balance to chance. Which was good, because his legs felt like they were on a deck going through ten-foot swells.

"So, where's a good place for food around here?" Beach realized he was still clutching his polo shirt. He tugged it over his head, glad he'd grabbed the Loro Piana with forty-percent silk. It soothed the hot prickles on his skin.

"My kitchen."

Beach had his cane, but Tai still used a hand under Beach's arm to steer him to the couch. "Sit."

Jez had been stretching in a perfect imitation of downward dog and reversed herself instantly, rump thumping onto the floor.

"Good sit, Jez." After pushing Beach onto the couch, Tai went to pet her. "Teach him." He pointed at Beach. On his way by, Tai leaned down to rumble in Beach's ear, "You stay." As Tai straightened he muttered, "I've got to find a way to stop confusing the dog."

Tai went into his bedroom and came out in cargo shorts and a tank top, crossed the living room, and went into the kitchen. Jez trotted over and put her head on Beach's thigh. It felt like a bowling ball and was about that size and shape. But she did have the most beautiful eyes, full of her heart. Beach rubbed behind her ears, under her jaw. She tipped up her head to let him work, then twisted around to stare as Tai came back over, shoving a glass of orange juice at Beach.

"Drink this."

"Didn't your gran ever teach you the magic word?"

"Never knew either one. Drink it. You need some blood sugar." Tai opened up the fridge again. "Anything you don't eat?"

"I'm sure there's plenty of things in the world I'd rather not put in my mouth, but I'm open to trying new things, if you hadn't noticed."

Beach got a snort of laughter in answer. Jez had followed Tai into the kitchen, where she lapped at a water bowl up on a stand. The guy was sweet enough to his dog to make sure she didn't have to strain for a drink, but he couldn't manage a *please* every now and then?

At least one of them had been raised with manners. "Can I give you a hand?"

"Sure."

But before Beach could rise to his feet, Tai went on, "You can sit there and drink your orange juice so you don't pass out and get in the way."

Beach stared sharply at his feet. He'd been labeled a lot of things, but *helpless* had never been one of them.

The feelings that had sent him charging into the bathroom—where he had definitely not been crying once he got his head under the cold spray—surged back, a pull like a riptide. That infuriating chest-crushing sensation that had dropped the bottom out of the best time he could remember. He rolled his ankles around. Other people popped their knuckles, Beach popped his ankles. It always made him feel better. It didn't work as well with the weight of the monitor and scream of still-mending bone, but at last he got that satisfying snap, and a soothing relaxation pulsed up his legs.

Investigating the sound, Jez stalked over, muzzle dripping. She started to lunge forward to wipe her jowls on Beach's leg and shorts, but he diverted her to the couch.

"Ha. I'm wise to that trick, pretty girl. Don't think you're the first sweet little pup in my life." He ran his hand along her flank and stopped. There was a thick scar under the short hair, a diagonal slash across her ribs, spine to belly. He swept his hands everywhere, finding another healed wound on her opposite haunch, near the docked tail. "My God, Jez, what happened to you?"

Tai came out of the kitchen with two plates of scrambled eggs and toast. "I told you she was a rescue. Rescued her from a dogfighting ring."

"God damn them straight to hell." Beach put his orange juice down and held Jez's head. "There isn't enough punishment on earth for anyone that low." He murmured the last in a tone to soothe the anxious look in her eyes.

"Agreed. She was the only one who wasn't destroyed."

Beach might not have known Tai long, but his feelings were plain in his deep voice. He was a man of honor and kindness, and he'd fought hard to save Jez from where she'd been.

"Not only are you a pretty girl but lucky too," Beach cooed, rubbing behind her ears. "And such a sweetheart. Not even begging." He nodded at the food on the coffee table.

Jez sighed and plopped her head in Beach's lap. "She's usually more shy around strangers."

Beach leaned back against the cushions, stroking the dog's neck, and glanced over at Tai. "My charm works well on the ladies."

Tai's aborted laugh made Jez jerk up her head. She backed away and went around to Tai's side of the couch and sat. "Good girl." Tai hand-fed her a blob of egg, and after she'd gulped it and licked her muzzle, she lowered herself to the floor at Tai's feet.

"But I never thought to hand-feed them," Beach added.

"You're not feeding yourself," Tai pointed out.

Beach scooped up the plate and picked at the eggs. He missed the dog. Without her as a distraction, he was too conscious of the tug inside him. It wanted him to push Jez out of the way to kneel at Tai's feet. And every pull of it was met with disgust from Beach's brain demanding to know what kind of man wanted to grovel like a dog to another.

He took a bite of toast and forced it past the tightness in his throat, then washed it down with orange juice.

"Feeling better?" Tai said.

Fine and dandy, thank you. The lie came so fast it was almost past Beach's lips before he pinched them shut. Instead he shrugged. "What did you call it? Sub drop?"

Tai nodded.

"And it's like a sex hangover?"

Tai studied Beach in a way that made him think he was missing a big part of the answer. "Have you ever had that feeling after sex before?"

"No." Beach put his plate on the coffee table.

Tai's tone was far away from the force of his Sir voice and the bourbon-sweet urges when he had Beach spread out and moaning. It was direct, unemotional and very much like—a probation officer going over the rules.

"What you felt is a reaction from the kind of sex we had, a sharp physical and emotional drop after a scene."

"A D/s scene." The unfamiliar phrase stalled and stuttered on its way out of Beach's mouth.

"Yes." Tai's lips twisted with a hint of humor. "I don't know if anyone has done the research with electrodes and blood samples, but it's similar to the feelings athletes go through. Endorphins get released and make you feel high, then you crash."

"And that always happens?"

"Not always. It depends on the person. Doms can experience it too."

"Sounds complicated."

"But worth it."

Beach couldn't deny that. He wished he were the sort of person this sub drop didn't happen to, but he wouldn't trade away the incredible heights he'd reached. The pull was still there, wanting Tai's attention, his notice, his approval. Beach glanced at Jez, and she lifted her head and made a whistling sigh. *Poor Jez. I know just how you feel. Damn him.*

Tai had them both panting after a look or a touch. Beach certainly didn't feel the need to be the alpha male; the necessary posturing and confrontation were much too tedious, but he wasn't ready to surrender every ounce of dignity for something that felt good. He hadn't done that since he was fifteen and panting over his roommate. Then he found out it wasn't only Gavin Montgomery who could fuck him like that.

Tai went on in lecture mode. "It's usual for submissives to need contact with the Dominant after the scene, to ease—"

"Wait. I thought this was about the subm—me—meeting your needs."

"D/s meets both our needs."

With a jolt that flung him to his feet, want and shame blazed in Beach's gut. "I sure as hell didn't *need* that cold shower you shoved me into."

"David, sit down." The words, the force of Tai's voice, pushed Beach back onto the couch.

He placed his palms flat against the cushion on either side of his thighs, as surprised by the outburst that had dragged him up as the obedience that dropped him back down.

Beach didn't do anger. It was a waste of a good time. Like jealousy. If he couldn't charm it, buy it, or change it, he ignored it.

"Can you control yourself?" Tai asked.

"Of course I can control myself." Beach drew himself up straight and glared at Tai.

The slant of Tai's brows and the shift in his mouth made Beach consider the last few seconds of his behavior. "Uh, I can now." There was probably supposed to be a *Sir* tacked to the end of that, but Beach didn't feel like adding it.

"Okay." Tai's dark eyes held Beach's gaze, demanding his attention. "You did need it and you wanted it and you asked for it."

Beach opened his mouth, but Tai went on.

"You disobeyed me and you made sure I'd find out."

"I—It wouldn't have been right to leave the cuffs at my apartment." But his voice betrayed him, weak and unsure.

"You wanted to know what I'd do about it."

He did. And he wanted to know now. The want twisted around him, twisted him until he wasn't himself. "Yes." The confession was a grunt from his throat.

"And now you know. I will punish you if you lie to me. If you disobey me. If you make a bad choice."

Beach nodded, swallowing back the instinctive *no*.

"If it's something you really don't want, you can always use your safeword. Or we can talk about it."

Tai's matter-of-fact tone, the very rationality of those words, made the want turn to an ache. No. No choices. Beach would always pick wrong. He couldn't meet Tai's eyes anymore.

"Are you afraid of me?" Tai's voice had softened to the tone he used to reassure Jez. Still deep and resonant, a sound Beach could almost touch and wrap himself in.

He let out a shaky breath.

"David? I need you to tell me the truth."

Beach glanced up. A hint of hesitation flickered in Tai's eyes.

"The truth?" Beach echoed and inhaled deeply. "No. Not at all. I only need to look at Jez to know you wouldn't—" The breath deserted him. "—hurt me. It's me I'm afraid of. I want things—need things that—I don't understand how I could want this."

"Because you're a submissive."

The answer settled over Beach solid as a stone, the safe drop of an anchor, ripples spreading the knowledge through him. But how could that be when his wants had always come first? When he hated to trade the wind in his face for a harbor?

Beach bent forward, bracing the weight of his head on elbows dug into thighs.

"If you're not ready to deal with that, it's okay," Tai said in the same soft tone.

Pain shot down Beach's shin from the pressure of his elbow, and he jerked back up. "So what? That's it?" His pulse skipped and then pounded. He couldn't taste this, start to understand and feel how deep it ran in him, only to have it disappear. "Because I don't know how to do it?"

"No. I didn't say that. I don't mind that you're new to it."

"I've delivered plenty of it-was-wonderful-but-no-thanks speeches in my life. I can hear one coming from miles away. But I'd appreciate it if you give me an honest answer why."

Tai reached across the space between them on the couch, but his fingers only grazed the tips of Beach's hair. The brief contact made blood flush and burn under his skin until it felt too tight, throbbing in his fingers, his sore shin, squeezing at the stretch across his ribs, his back.

He tried to roll his ankles, but the pop wouldn't come. All he had was a stupid, cursed, impossible need, wanting another man to control him. And the truth was Beach didn't have what it took to please him, and he'd never have that feeling again, the incredible high from nothing more than Tai murmuring *Good boy* as he cupped Beach's chin.

"It's not a brush-off, Da—Beach. But you have to understand this is who I am. It's not only how I fuck. And I can't accept a game where you pretend I'm making you do things you don't want."

A light. A tiny crack. Beach could fit through that. It was what he was good at. "I don't want to pretend that." He meant it. In those moments when Tai was in control, he wanted everything Tai gave him. The problems happened when Beach had too much time to think.

"Okay. We can give it a try. You understand I expect you to obey me."

"Yes, Sir."

In any other situation, that would have come out of Beach's mouth with either sarcasm or flirtation, a wink and a salute. But there was nothing to ridicule in the way it felt to offer the respect Tai commanded.

"Will you… punish me now?" Beach still stumbled over that word. It launched a war between hunger and revulsion, fear and need inside, deep in the pit of his stomach.

Tai cupped Beach's chin, and the echo of it tingled in his balls. "What did you do to earn it?"

"I freaked out." Beach could admit it now, see how out of control he'd been.

"You get to freak out. But you need to tell me why, what you're feeling next time." Beach nodded, and Tai tightened his grip.

"Yes, Sir," Beach said out loud.

"But I did tell you to do something you didn't do." Tai released him and stood.

Beach usually had a good reason for not following a rule, so when he broke one, he knew why, but he couldn't track what Tai was talking about.

Tai lifted the plates and glasses from the coffee table. "I told you to eat and drink." Beach eyed the cold eggs on his plate. Now that the sickening drop sensation was gone, he was hungry.

Tai took the plates into the kitchen, leaving Beach to listen to the sounds of scraping and washing and the nasal hum of the microwave. Jez rolled to one side, angling her head to watch, but whatever was in the microwave didn't appeal to her since her head lolled back. With the angle of the couch and wall cutting off Beach's view, he focused on the sounds: the refrigerator door opening, the processor humming in compensation, a knife hitting wood as it sliced through something. He didn't offer to help, didn't move, reluctant to do anything in case it was something that would make Tai send him away.

After the microwave dinged, Tai came back in with the plate of newly steaming eggs, plus slices of cheese and orange and a glass of water.

He put them on the coffee table. Beach wanted to show he was following directions now, so he reached for the plate. The side with the eggs burned his fingers, and he jerked them back. Where was the fork?

"No," Tai said. "Don't anticipate." He picked up Beach's hand and brushed a kiss across the fingertips. "Just be here."

The contact made it easier, but Beach's mind was still chasing after questions, possibilities. When it was sex, there was a direction in mind, however they got there. But with their clothes on, Beach was lost.

Tai kissed Beach's fingers again and released his hand. "Now. When we're together, there are consequences for your behavior. Not for your feelings. There are good consequences and bad consequences."

"Punishment," Beach blurted, his eyes shooting a glance at the plate of food.

"And rewards. But you need to understand both come directly from your actions. What are we addressing now?"

"You told me to eat and drink, and I didn't."

"You will take better care of your body, David."

"Yes, Sir." Beach shifted on the couch. His dick wasn't ready for another round, but the electricity he had always associated with impending wood was shimmering through him, heating his skin like a quick shot of bourbon.

Tai lifted the plate from the coffee table. "Take off your shirt and sit in front of me." He tapped the coffee table.

Beach stripped the cool silk and cotton off and folded it over the couch back. He was adventurous in food and sex, but combining the two wasn't for him. He wasn't interested in hiding the taste of his lover behind a flavored syrup, and the resulting mess wasn't worth it.

"Don't anticipate. Just do what I tell you." Tai's voice went deeper, and Beach dropped his ass on the warm spot on the coffee table. "Put your hands under your thighs."

Beach tucked his hands away, swallowing back reluctance. He didn't know what to expect, but this didn't seem like Tai, humiliating Beach by putting the food he didn't eat on his body.

Pain stung his ear. He jerked out of his thoughts. Tai had flicked his nail against the cartilage at the top.

"Focus on me. Turn off your head." Tai picked up a slice of cheese. "Open your mouth."

"Like the dog?" Beach asked.

"Do you feel like a dog?"

"No." The cheese had come close enough to smell. Sweet and nutty, like a Gouda. Beach's mouth watered, and he opened it. God, he was hungry.

Tai arched his brow, the cheese still between his fingers. Waiting.

Beach licked his lips and forced another swallow down his throat. "No, Sir."

"Good."

Beach opened his mouth, and Tai put the bite-sized piece on his tongue.

Beach had been to a Dutch dairy farm, and this surpassed the best piece of Gouda he'd ever had. He chewed, taste and texture incredibly strong.

After Beach swallowed, Tai said, "Open."

Beach didn't feel at all like a dog or a child. His senses were alive, sharp. He could see tiny variations of the dark brown of Tai's irises, the hair-thin lines at the corners of his eyes as he leaned in. A sigh from the sleeping dog filled Beach's ears before fading to let in the sounds from the street under the window. Every bite of cheese exploded with rich flavor on his tongue.

Beach loved parties. There was always that one perfect moment, the right mix of people who had come and gone, the right level of alcohol, the right song, one moment of absolute perfection. Beach always knew when it hit, knew nothing would match it and it was time to go.

There had already been so many of those moments with Tai. A sharp conviction that this was the moment he'd remember but could never recapture. And then it went on. Building. Dizzying.

"I'll hold the orange slice for you. You suck the flesh off."

It was awkward, and he'd pulled a hand free for an instant before he tucked it back. Tai feeding him the cheese had been sensual. This was control.

Beach bit into the membrane, felt the individual pockets of juice burst into his mouth, sucked and tugged. Sticky juice ran from his lips and over his chin as Tai pulled the rind away.

He wiped Beach's jaw with a thumb before following with a warm kiss. "Very good." Tai picked up some of the eggs.

When Beach opened his mouth, Tai said, "No. You're anticipating again." He held the eggs on his palm, chin level. "Take it out of my hand."

Beach wasn't sure he was still in control of his own movements. He was aware of every sensation, but it was like someone else had slipped into his skin. *This must be what it's like under hypnosis.* His head dropped enough for his mouth to reach Tai's palm, for his tongue and lips and teeth to nuzzle up the bits of scrambled egg from among the calluses, the valleys between his fingers. The egg was gone, but Beach kept licking the skin.

"God, David. That's…." Tai's hand moved to cup Beach's cheek. "So good."

The kiss that followed was hard at first, shocking Beach out of his daze. He wasn't sure if it was allowed, but his hands slipped free and grabbed Tai's shoulders for balance as he opened his mouth to Tai's tongue.

Beach had been entirely mistaken about mixing food and sex. Or maybe he'd gone about it the wrong way. Even a two-hundred-dollar mouthful of white winter truffles couldn't be as amazing as this.

Tai pulled back, still stroking Beach's face.

"If that was punishment, I think I will be very naughty."

Tai pressed his forehead into Beach's. "From what I've seen, that's your default setting."

Chapter Nine

THE KEY to having a good time was knowing when to leave the party. Beach knew all the signs. And they were there. He just didn't want to go.

There hadn't been any of that sub drop after Tai fed him eggs and cheese and fruit from his hand. They kissed, Tai pulling Beach toward him until he was straddling Tai's knee. The making out became more about holding each other, and when Jez nudged at Tai's leg, the last sign lit up. Not just neon. Tai went for a billboard-sized LCD display. No way to misunderstand.

With a sigh, he eased Beach off his lap. "David. I want you to go home now."

Beach wasn't unfamiliar with an abrupt end to an interlude. He'd been given the number to call a cab, sent out for coffee to find no one there when he got back, and once been handed his clothes while he was standing on the front step. Though that one was his fault. He had gotten the sisters' names mixed up.

Those dismissals had been easy to shrug off. Not this. He stared down at the silk weave of his shirt and rubbed it between his fingers. Nothing. He'd gone numb from the neck down. Full weight on his bad leg didn't bother him at all, as he didn't really know the floor was there. Still, the muscles all took signals from the brain, put him on his two feet, pulled the shirt over his head, got his shoes back on.

When Tai caught Beach's chin, he didn't feel that either. Numb all over, then. "Listen. You didn't do anything wrong."

Beach understood the words, but they didn't seem to fit inside his head.

Tai brushed his thumb across Beach's lips. "You were perfect." The soft voice threatened to melt the numbness in a way Beach didn't want to stick around to deal with.

"Thanks."

"You need to spend some time away from me to think about this."

This? What was *this*? "Being submissive?"

Tai's fingers tightened on Beach's jaw, and for an instant he thought Tai would kiss him again.

"Being *my* submissive."

"Oh."

"There are things we should have talked about, limits, expectations, but—" Tai tapped Beach's lips, then released him. "—we seem to be more about doing than talking. There's a checklist."

Now that Beach's body appeared to have shaken off the numbness, his brain was going. "A checklist?"

"About things you might want to try or that are absolutely off-limits. I'll email it. I want you to fill it out at home so I don't influence you."

"How delightful. Homework. Though I must say that sort of assignment would have done wonders for my grade point average back in school."

Tai's eyebrows came to a sharp point on his forehead. "Don't be a brat." He reached into his back pocket. "Here."

Instinctively Beach held out his hand, and the cuffs slapped into his palm with a light sting. He closed his fingers around the pain and the leather.

"In case you get bored," Tai added. "I'll call you Monday."

"Monday?" Surprise forced a humiliating supplication out of him.

Tai nodded. "Don't forget to set up a physical therapy appointment. And stay out of trouble."

THE HEAVY, hot air bounced off the water, reeking of marine diesel and decaying seagrass as Beach left the pavement for the dock at the marina. The shift in his footing made him lean on the cane for a step or two, and then he was able to move with the bounce and sway. Saturday afternoon of a holiday weekend, most of the slips were empty, except for the one with his sport cruiser the *Fancy Nancy*.

The judge and the damned all-seeing monitor might keep him from taking the *Nancy* out, but he could at least stand on the deck and pretend to be bouncing over the waves on his way to anyplace but here.

Damn his leg and caution and probation. He vaulted over the gunwale.

The shock of landing sent a steel blade through his shinbone, pain to make him sweat and almost drop to the deck. *Hell.* What if he'd rebroken it? He squeezed his eyes tight, fighting the waves of nausea. He slapped his hands on the aft bench, the cane clattering onto the fiberglass before spinning out onto the swim deck.

One wave, one wrong shift of weight, would send it rolling into the bay. And that would be a hellish crawl back to the car, assuming he hadn't snapped the damned bone again. His eyes were still slits, focused on the gleaming black cane against the teak, his breath shallow, whistling between clenched teeth.

How the holy hell did these things happen to him? A curse on the Beauchamp line? The sins of the father being visited on the son? He shuddered through another stabbing bout of pain. The longer he waited, the more likely it was a wake or wave would tip the cane into the water. The polished wood should float, but the steel finishing might drag it down, and Beach didn't fancy a swim in the brackish water.

As the sweat dripped off the end of his nose, Tai's voice, his Sir voice, rumbled in Beach's mind. *Breathe, David.*

Picturing Tai standing there, wishing for a touch to make it easier, Beach forced his jaw to relax and drew in a long, deep breath. It didn't move the cane any closer or stop his leg from feeling like a demonic version of Jez was chewing on the bone, but after a second slow breath, the tight panicky edge faded. Imagining Tai watching, aching to show he could do something as basic as stand on his own damned boat without disaster, Beach blew the air back out and balanced on his good leg while stretching over the bench and bow. His fingers brushed, then latched on to the shaft. He snatched it up, straightening and brandishing it over his head.

"Aha!"

Imaginary Tai only folded his arms. Perhaps if Beach had been a little more impressive—

You were very good, David.

—he'd still be there at Tai's apartment, discovering what else it meant to be… a submissive. Tai's submissive.

"Ahoy, the *Fancy Nancy*."

Beach swung the cane tip down to the deck and looked starboard. A thirty-foot Sea Ray at idle approached. Shading his eyes and squinting, he made out the waving figure from the flybridge. Clayton Earnshaw. Beach supposed it was too late to take that dive overboard.

"Ahoy."

"Need a hand?" Clayton dropped the idle lower.

"No. Everything's fine."

"Okay. You were waving like you were sinking."

"No." Just waving at an imaginary Dominant. "Saw you coming."

"Has been awhile. Let me tie her up. Unless you were headed out."

"No." Definitely not as long as he was shackled to Baltimore County.

"Right."

Beach calculated the time necessary for his long hobble out to the car versus Clayton berthing his boat and came up with a dead heat. Hardly worth the effort. Especially when there was nothing to run to.

Not with Tai making Beach wait until Monday. What was wrong with tonight, or tomorrow?

Beach took advantage of the few minutes to make his awkward way off the *Nancy* without Earnshaw's questions or feigned concern. Feeling like a feeble geriatric, Beach used the ladders to climb back onto the main dock.

When Clayton came striding up a moment later, Beach was ready with a distraction. "What are you doing up from Charleston? Figured you'd be doing the holiday with the clan."

"Had enough holidaying with the clan on Carolina Day."

Beach did a mental head scratch and came up with the name of Clayton's fiancée. "Iris turning up the pressure on a date?"

Clayton looked as morose as a hound in a cartoon, mouth drooping with his frown. "Iris. Mama. Grandmother. Iris's mother. Iris's aunt. My aunts. If it's female and I've seen it in the past month, it's demanded a schedule. Thank God for these ladies." Clayton nodded at the *Nancy*. "No demands and always good for a quick escape. Surprised you're not out chasing marlin or someplace else chasing tail."

"Can't." Beach tapped the ankle monitor with the cane.

"The other kind of ball and chain. Heard you ran into trouble." To Beach's ear there was a satisfied suggestion of *about damned time* in Clayton's tone.

Beach shrugged. "A bit."

"Rumor is you threw an illegal party out on Fort Carroll." Clayton jerked his thumb east-southeast toward the harbor. The island was far enough away to be hidden by the hazy sky.

Beach clapped Clayton on the shoulder. "Not without inviting you. No, I got wind of a family heirloom going missing there at a party back in the seventies. The authorities took a dim view of my trespass on the bird sanctuary or something. The lawyers will all hash it out in fines. No worries."

"Busted your leg, though."

Beach suspected Clayton was sifting for the best story. The Earnshaws were gossips and tightwads, every last one. Clayton was lucky Iris would have him, since he'd have trouble finding anyone else who wasn't a cousin to marry.

"It's healing. Make a good story in a month or two. Are you staying on your boat?"

"Soon as I realized the way the wind was blowing, I lit out like my ass was on fire. Christ, I only proposed at Christmas to get them out of my hair."

Beach clenched his back teeth together. "Be glad to have you stay with me."

"Thanks. Knobs together—"

"Always together." There was something to be said for enduring the misery of hazing together as knobs, otherwise known as Citadel freshmen.

"I'll grab my bag."

CLAYTON GAVE a thorough dental examination to the gift horse when they arrived at Beach's apartment. "Just the one bedroom."

Beach hadn't taken the apartment with an eye to acquiring a roommate. Still, Southern hospitality had its demands. "You're the guest. I'll sleep on the couch."

"I couldn't let you do that," Clayton protested.

They went on through rounds of escalating demurrals, covering the rules of hospitality, Clayton's long trip up from Charleston, and Beach's four additional inches of height, until Clayton played a trump card. "And you really should take care of your leg. I'll be fine on the couch."

You'll take care of your body as long as you're offering it to me.

It took every bit of control Beach possessed not to shiver. And since Tai wasn't here, Beach could damn well answer back as he pleased. *Since you threw me out of your apartment, I'll thank you to stay out of my goddamned head. Sir.*

"Please help yourself to anything in the kitchen."

"Wouldn't say no to a beer."

"Ah. Sorry. The only alcohol is what was already opened at the bar. This"—Beach pointed with his cane—"ball and chain monitors me for alcohol intake. I removed the more obvious temptations."

Clayton ran a hand through what hair he had left. "David Beauchamp condemned to sobriety? Thought you said it wasn't a party that got you in trouble."

"It wasn't."

Clayton went right for the seventeen-year-old Pappy Van Winkle, of course. A generous pour sloshed into the tumbler. "Find what you were looking for? Your heirloom?"

Not so much an heirloom as proof that the charges keeping Beach's father out of the country were a lie, that the accusing girl's ring was a fake. "No."

"Did you think of looking sober?"

For a man knocking back Beach's three-hundred-dollar bourbon, Clayton was a fine one to talk.

"I was sober. I'd just gotten out of the hospital."

"Heard about the bridge." Clayton moved the drape in front of the glass balcony doors. The balcony five stories up. "You never seemed the type."

"I'm not the type. I wasn't trying to kill myself." Hell, Beach wished he could remember that night. But everything after leaving Ruben's party was a blank until he woke up in the hospital.

And why the hell was Clayton Earnshaw grilling him about it in the living room of Beach's own damned apartment? His leg ached. If he couldn't be with Tai right now, Beach could at least be asleep and dreaming about it.

In answer to Beach's glare, Clayton shrugged. "My Aunt Bobbie Lynn and your mama went to Sweet Briar together. Guess she's worried."

"Your aunt?" Because he sure wasn't referring to Beach's mother. She'd never shown up at the hospital, despite the large window of opportunity afforded her by his coma.

Clayton turned away and looked out of the window toward the harbor and Dundalk. Beach rested his ass on one of the barstools at the kitchen counter. *See? Taking care of my leg*, he told no one in the room at the time.

"So you can't even have a beer with dinner?" Clayton said with another sip of the finest bourbon ever to grace a man's lips.

"When they arrested me for trespassing, the police report from the bridge got a good looking into. I wasn't sober then," Beach admitted. "So no. I can't. Or go into a bar or liquor store or leave Baltimore County. I can get called in for drug tests." And that wasn't the worst part of being on probation. Because if the terms of his release didn't include the GPS tracker proving he'd been in this apartment from 11:00 p.m. to 7:00 a.m., maybe he could have spent the night— Never mind. "Worst thing is, I have a curfew."

Not only did Clayton do grief like a cartoon dog, he tipped back his head and howled with laughter. "Sweet Mary, Beach. The whole damned Corps of Cadets at school couldn't keep you in your room all night. This is too much. Like the opposite of catching the Pope in a whorehouse." He finished off his drink. "Well. That's one smooth bourbon. Too good for me."

If that wasn't an understatement.

"Let's go get something cheaper. I feel a bender coming on, and my designated driver's got a curfew." That set Clayton off again, and he howled all the way to Beach's rented Lexus.

TAI STABBED the intercom button at the front door of Nic's town house.

"Come in and come up. You know the way." Despite the scratchy sound from the speaker, Nic's dry humor came through in the last part. The lock buzzed, and Tai went into the hall. He leaned against a solid, brightly polished table to unlace his running shoes and slip on the sandals Nic kept at the door.

Tai wouldn't ever be able to tell Stickley from sticks, but he knew nice when he saw it, a comfortable home when he was in one. Which he supposed was good for Nic's sake, because Tai had never seen the man outside of it.

He might not know furniture, but he knew enough about Baltimore to ballpark a property. He'd done lots of looking for a place for him and his mom and Gina and Sammie when he first came home from school before discovering it was way the hell out of his reach. Nic's place was an easy one point five. In David Beauchamp's budget, one and a half million was probably what he spent getting high in six months.

Tai wished he knew which one of the two versions he'd met was the real one. David, choking as much on his need to surrender as his resistance to it, or the party boy who'd swaggered into Tai's office two days ago. Only two days ago. And already Tai wanted David owned. Collared. Marked as his.

Sense and self-control had gone flying the minute he had opened his door and seen David kneeling in the hall. Everything Tai had worked so hard to keep leashed had torn free to meet that challenge. Maybe Nic could help him get it back.

Tai knew Nic well enough to expect some kind of show. Nic didn't disappoint.

When Tai stepped into the long second-floor room, he found Nic with his dick down another guy's throat. Not that there was much to see. Nic was fully dressed, long-sleeved dress shirt, cuffs rolled over his forearms, trousers not even unbelted. And Tai would bet there was a superthin sheath on Nic's cock as well.

The guy on his knees was only missing a shirt. Baggy jeans, ball cap with brim sideways. The sub's hands were cuffed behind him, chain looped around the floor-to-ceiling pole in the corner.

Nic glanced up and waved, as if they were meeting in a restaurant. "I'll only be"—he checked his watch—"two and a half more minutes." He rocked his hips forward, pushing a groan out of the man on his knees. "That's all the time left this little bitch has to work for my load if he wants to get that chastity cage off this week."

Another groan and the acceleration in the frantic bob of the sub's head indicated he'd gotten the message. Tai knew it wouldn't matter. Nic wouldn't come if he didn't want to. And from his voice, he might as well be ordering a pizza instead of fucking a desperately willing mouth.

"Help yourself to a drink." Nic tipped his head toward the bar and minifridge along the inside wall.

Two minutes was a long time to not stare, and Tai hated to give Nic the satisfaction of knowing Tai enjoyed the well-timed show. He crossed the floor to the fridge. Next to two stainless-steel butt plugs were minibottles of water, juice, and club soda. Tai grabbed a water.

He could manage casual too. He'd certainly seen—and been part of—enough playtime in this room. "You want anything?" he called back.

"Club soda, thank you."

Tai reached in for one. The guy was getting somewhere; Nic's voice wavered on the *you.* As Tai eased into one of the swivel chairs at the bar, Nic's breathing started to echo under the high ceiling. Either the sub had stepped up his game, or Nic had decided to reward him. From this angle, Tai couldn't see Nic's face.

A thin beep cut through the room, followed by a deep sigh. Tai couldn't tell if it came from Nic or the sub.

"Guess you get to wait longer." Nic cupped the wet face, then turned the cap around, pulling it down over the sub's eyes. "And don't think that's your only punishment. You should have begun like that."

The man sagged. Tai could see if his hands weren't bound to the pole, he'd have put his forehead on Nic's foot.

"I should let my friend see if you've learned anything." Nic glanced at Tai, who shook his head. "But I don't want to waste his time. You will think about how you can do better." Nic reached into his pocket and took out a mini MP3 player and headphones, which he fitted on the sub.

Nic stripped off the condom and tucked himself away before joining Tai at the bar, chair turned to keep an eye on the man who slumped in a rejected heap against the pole.

Tai raised his eyebrows.

Nic shrugged. "Humiliation kink. Service sub." He lowered his voice. "Been seeing him a couple times a month."

"You should have told me. It could have waited."

It was Nic's turn to arch his brows, except he had a skill that had always eluded Tai: the ability to raise just one. Maybe because it had a thin diagonal scar slicing through it. "Your email was ominous." Nic's faint Greek accent only came through on the *r*'s, *t*'s, and *s*'s. The sounds, combined with sharp features and a compact, hard body, made Tai think of a jaguar. Nic's eyes had that look too, predatory. It had subs dropping at his feet. "All I said is I wanted to talk. Face-to-face."

"Please tell me you did not take Donte back."

"No."

Nic relaxed into his chair and opened his club soda, gaze darting from Tai's face to the sub kneeling, head bowed.

"You have eighteen minutes before I go back and let him have some success. You can spend it staring at me or tell me about"—Nic's dark eyes lasered in on Tai's face—"your new submissive."

Tai had been trying to fend off Nic's too-perceptive stare with his water bottle as a barrier. At Nic's successful pronouncement, Tai crushed the plastic, sending a spurt of water into his own face and neck.

"If you wanted a facial, I'm sure Bobby would have obliged." Nic's chin jutted toward the guy in cuffs.

Tai wiped his face with his arm. "It's freaky when you do that."

"It's not that difficult to pay attention, Toluaotai. Seventeen minutes."

"He's—I shouldn't have—I met him through work." It wasn't entirely true, but it was a big part of the problem. "I shouldn't be having sex with him."

"It's already happened. So let's move on from there. What is the problem?"

The problem was too big for seventeen minutes, but it was also too big to keep chewing on alone. Learning about himself with Nic's help had given Tai the control he'd thought he had to fight for all his life. A way to manage his anger and desire. Now David's bottomless appetite had Tai on the edge with him. And damn if he didn't want to take that fall. "He's new. Never experienced D/s before."

"So he has no bad habits to break." Nic drained half of his soda in one gulp.

"He's pushy. Not bratty so much as challenging."

Nic's brow went up, but there was a smile on his face. "All things guaranteed to intrigue you. I'm waiting to hear the problem."

"He won't—"

"Not your submissive's problems, Tai. Yours."

He crumpled the bottle and tossed it away. "It's been two scenes. In two days. And I want him." Even now Tai's palm itched as if it could call up the memory of David's skin, his hair, some tangible proof of that obedience in the quiet moments when David surrendered. "When we're in that space—"

"You love him."

"I never said—"

"Falling in love is easy. That connection and that focus mean for the moments when you're in D/s space, you love every submissive for what he offers you. Staying that way when it's over, that's what takes effort." Nic spun the cap back onto his bottle and placed it on the bar. "I read somewhere that attraction registers in less than a second. That in thirty seconds you make up your mind whether or not to have feelings for someone."

"Love at first sight. Really?"

"Leave the hearts and flowers of romance out of it." Nic's gaze softened as he looked beyond Tai to where Bobby waited. "There are people you can easily walk away from and people you can't. And if you both can't, you see what you're willing to do to make it work."

"You make it all sound easy."

"Of course it isn't. Who he is and who you are, those are things neither of you can change. Whatever you feel for him now, what attracts and repels you, none of that can be erased or hidden by reciprocal orgasms once the endorphins fade."

Which meant what? Beauchamp was a careless, manipulative shit, and David was everything Tai wanted with a big red bow around his neck. Once the endorphins faded today, David had taken to being hand-fed as if he'd been waiting for it his whole life.

Nic sighed into Tai's thoughts. "I wonder if you're aware what you're looking for," Nic said.

"But you know. What I'm looking for, I mean." When Nic didn't answer, Tai said, "Are you going to tell me or just sit there being all superior about it?"

"Yes."

"Asshole."

"One of the things D/s offers is a crucible to reveal the essence of a person."

"What does that mean?"

Nic slid off the barstool. "It means you've had two scenes with him. If you found a reason to walk away, you would have already done so. Instead you're here, looking for advice."

"Fuck." Why had Tai thought coming to Nic was a good idea?

"I believe the expression is *screwed*. Best of luck staying on the right side of the leash."

Tai stood.

"Don't bother wiping that up." Nic indicated the water splattered on the polished wooden floor. "Bobby will enjoy the task."

Chapter Ten

TALKING TO Nic was supposed to make things clear, not drag up more questions. Tai didn't like questions. He liked knowing the play. Everyone on the same page. His page.

He burned through an hour of leg work Sunday morning. With the throb of blood pounding under tight, sweat-soaked skin and the acid streaking in his muscles, Tai felt like himself again. He'd never been one for living in his head. He knew what he wanted.

After his shower, he still had two hours before it was time to pick up Sammie. He called David.

After four rings, a strange man drawled, "Hello."

A shock of rage, white-cold then black-hot, blasted behind Tai's squeezed-shut eyes. He hadn't told David anything about fucking other guys. Hadn't thought he'd need to after yesterday. Tai dragged the phone away from his jaw and let out an explosion of breath. It didn't help. Everything stayed tight and hard and furious.

"David Beauchamp."

"Uh, I'll get him. He's in the shower." The accent got thicker as the *r* on shower completely vanished.

Tai's hands clenched. The right one into a fist, the left squeezing the phone until it made a creak of protest. There went any hope there was some reason other than the obvious for why this man had picked up David's phone. Tai could hang up, but David would realize why, and that was unacceptable. The idea that David's curiosity, his wide-eyed hunger for submission, had led to him going out to find it put Tai's phone's structural integrity at serious risk.

After a few moments of silence, there was a knock and the drawl again. "Beach. Phone." The man hadn't bothered to mute the microphone.

Another knock, then a door opening, and the hiss of water got louder. "Sorry, Beach. Phone."

"Christ, Clayton, I'm in the shower. It'll go to voicemail."

Tai's fist relaxed. Phone-answering close but not shower-sharing? Brother? Cousin? "No, it won't. I, uh, answered."

"You answered my phone? Why in the hell would you do that?" The water was still running, but David's voice was loud with frustration.

"ID said Officer Fonoti, and you did say something about being called in for drug testing. Called you David. Figured it to be important."

"I didn't change the entry for—Fuckgoddamn." The water shut off. "Give it to me and get out."

"Makes sounds like one righteously pissed-off bull," Clayton said.

"Out." The door closed, and there was silence except for David's breathing. Tai pictured him staring at the phone, considering what to say.

At last David's voice came through clearly, though sullen enough to have sprung from pouting lips. "It's not Monday."

"It's not," Tai agreed. "Is there some reason I shouldn't have called?"

"No." That was his David, the response quick but the hitch in his voice obvious on the single syllable. Almost as quickly, his cockiness came bouncing back. "You mean Clayton?"

As much as he hated to admit it, Tai supposed the jealousy was already obvious. "Who is he?"

"An old college friend. Seems to have run away from home at the ripe old age of thirty-three." David had to be drawing out this pause on purpose. "He's sleeping on the couch."

Tai's jaw relaxed. "Glad to hear it."

"If you weren't—I mean, is that the kind of thing that would lead to more punishment?"

The shift back was so sharp it gave Tai whiplash. The sudden hesitation, underlying yearning laid bare in David's voice.

"For someone who says he doesn't want to be punished, you seem focused on it."

"I don't—It confuses the hell out of me too." David's laugh was tight, as if trapped in a thick throat.

"David, does thinking about it make you hard?"

"Um, I could be... headed in that direction."

"Stroke yourself for me. Don't say anything. I want to hear it in your breathing." It didn't take long for the first hitch, followed by a gasp.

"Good boy. Now." A harsher sound bounced back in answer to that word. "Stop."

A bitten-off grunt.

"You're going to save that for me."

As David's breathing slowed, Tai felt resistance like static on the line. At last there was a sigh. "All right."

"Excuse me?"

"Yes, Sir."

"I want you to know there is only one reason you're not spending today in my bed, learning how to please me."

A much less resentful David asked, "What?"

"I already had plans."

"Oh." Surprise, hurt, and embarrassment colored that single sound.

"With my daughter."

A DAUGHTER.

Beach sat on the toilet lid and stared down at the phone. He knew people had them, of course. It had simply never occurred to him that Tai had one. Had a life, connections outside of his job, outside of making guys like Beach beg to be cuffed to Tai's bed. Beach supposed he'd been lucky so far not to have such an entanglement himself, though he was equally as careful when he had sex with women as with men. In fact, he wasn't sure the idea of fatherhood didn't terrify him more than the prospect of contracting HIV.

Tai had a child.

Beach barely had the sense to keep himself dry and fed. And most of his friends considered even those skills beyond him. To be responsible for another human? One utterly dependent on you? He shuddered. He didn't even want to suffer another day with his houseguest. He'd never realized how much the warmth of a buzz smoothed away the rougher edges of his companions. Sober, all Beach could focus on was the way Clayton omitted the first half of ninety percent of his sentences, which had him thinking there must be untraceable poisons for sale on the internet.

Clayton certainly wouldn't have noticed what was mixed with the liquor he kept pouring down his throat. After Beach had dumped him on the couch last night, he'd hoped for a few minutes of peace in the morning, forgetting that the bastard never suffered a hangover. Screw Clayton and his metabolism and his syntax. Beach needed to get out of there.

In his bedroom, he dragged on a shirt and slacks and grabbed his cane.

"Hey." Clayton greeted him at the counter with a frying pan in his hand. "Made breakfast."

I made breakfast. Beach wanted to throttle him with the dish towel Clayton had dropped on the counter. *I. I. I.*

Completely unaware of his imminent death at the hands of an alleged felon, Clayton went on. "Had to repay your hospitality. Not much in the fridge to work with. Egg whites? Couldn't find any bacon or grits."

Only an Earnshaw would repay hospitality by raiding the larder and complaining about its contents.

"Haven't been to the store lately." Christ, now Clayton had Beach doing it. He ground his back teeth and slid onto one of the stools at the counter.

Clayton scattered scrambled whites onto a plate and added toast from under the towel. "Was that your probation officer?"

"No. He's not." The denial sprang to Beach's lips so fast he missed his chance at a decent lie. Clayton would have had to believe a sudden departure was due to being summoned for a probationary review. He wished he had been summoned. The things they'd done yesterday, the way that it had felt to be controlled and then praised for it....

"Oh." Then, "Oh."

Clayton's exclamation derailed that perfectly lovely train of thought. Beach hated whatever was showing on his face.

"So, your gate's swinging the other way at the moment?"

Beach jabbed at his eggs with a fork. It felt like such a mundane way to eat them after yesterday. "It doesn't work like that." Every time Beach swore off trying to explain his sexuality to straight—or gay— friends, he found himself back at it, like some kind of earnest conspiracy theorist. And he made about as much headway. "Hell, you ought to know as much."

"It—Nothing really happened." Clayton went redder than sunset. "We were only eighteen, and there was only one female in the whole school."

"Relax, Clay. The fact that you and I enjoyed the occasional Princeton rub didn't change you any more than it changed me. You like what you like. And I like what I like."

"Which is?"

"Variety. God, don't you ever stand at the registers and think of getting a different candy bar? A new flavor of gum?"

"Of course I do. Oh fuck." The color faded from Clayton's face, and he dropped his elbows on the counter, then buried his face in his hands. "I can't marry Iris."

"Yes, you can. I've stood there with you a hundred times, stood there last night when you were three sheets to the wind and letting out the jib, and I have never seen you walk out with anything but a Snickers bar." *Usually with me buying.*

Clayton looked up, his hands clasped together like a man who'd been praying intently.

"And that's it. Whatever flavor you're in the mood for?"

Beach followed the gaze to his phone. Tai. It wasn't only a new taste. It wasn't even the same hunger. The feelings ran so much deeper than what made Beach's dick hard. He shrugged. "You go prix fixe. I go à la carte."

"That way is always more expensive."

"Yeah." Beach smiled. "But it's so worth it."

WHAT LITTLE hair Clayton had left would have been standing on end if he had seen the à la carte menu Beach was examining on Monday afternoon. Fortunately Clayton had found another poor sucker to mooch dinner from tonight.

First up on the alphabetical checklist Beach had printed out: Age Play.

Beach hadn't expected any of this to light his fire, so he was determined to consider each item for a potential new source of that incredible rush. The idea of a daddy and a boy didn't turn him on, but it didn't revolt him. The directions at the top—and it really was like homework—said to put a check mark if that was the case. Stars were for yes, please. *X*s for no way.

He handed out stars for the various anal-play options.

Animal Roles? Beneath that was Puppy Play and Pony Play. A quick peek online had him giving that an *X*. Not saying he couldn't change his mind, but he liked the use of his opposable thumbs.

Ball Torture.

After a protective shift and wince, Beach gave it a check. If it was as bad as it sounded, that was what a safeword was for.

Biting. He was putting a star on that when he decided it needed a comment. *Not to the point of needing a bandage*, he printed at the side.

Blindfolds. His heart rate kicked up, that feeling of flying out on the waves in his boat, the risk. The high. *Gold star for you.*

Blood Play. He really didn't want to enter that into the browser. He didn't even like to get a tetanus shot. *X*.

Bondage. He reached into his pocket and ran a finger over the leather cuffs. It was pretty damned safe to say that being tied up was on the cock-hardening list.

Breath Play. Tai's hand sliding from Beach's jaw to his throat. Tai's thick cock cutting off his air. Beach's lungs aching with it while the rest of him felt that buzz of hooking something big, something scary. He shifted his trousers again and drew in a careful star.

He'd made it to Medical Scenes, which, given his opinion on shots and doctors in general, was getting the big old *X*, when his phone rang.

Not a number he knew, but the Baltimore area code didn't show the pesky signs of someone looking for money.

It took a few moments to recognize the voice. It wasn't until the lilting "I called to see how my advice went. Did you get his attention?" that Beach was able to place the caller.

"Eli?"

"Yup. So…?"

"It was"—what the hell—"yes, your advice came in handy."

"Glad to hear it." Eli chuckled in his ear. "Gavin gave me your number, but don't be pissed at him. I'm irresistible."

"I see." Beach put a check next to Nipple Play and an *X* next to spanking, then realized he had a much better source than any search engine on the phone.

"Eli, what's shibari?"

"Oh, it's beautiful. It's this elaborate bondage with ropes. Takes a bit of time, and it's really restricting. But it's gorgeous to see." That chuckle again. "Have you heard of Google, hon?"

"I prefer hands-on learning. Or primary sources."

"Sorry. Wish I could say I'd tried it. It looks really cool. So, you guys are going to make it a thing?"

Whether or not it was a thing—did saying *You need time to think about this* make it a thing?—wasn't included anywhere on the checklist. Maybe Eli had insight on that too.

"Not sure." Damn Clayton's contagious speech pattern. "I'm going through this list right now to give back."

"Yeah? I've seen those. Fetish checklists."

Beach doodled some waves and then a marlin in the corner of the page. *Fetish* was a creepy word. When they were doing it, it didn't feel creepy. Just right. Almost like their hearts and breathing got in sync, and there was all this energy.

That blend of dread and want curled in his stomach as he scanned the rest of the list, and he wanted to be done as soon as possible.

Eli was still going on. "Not doing one with Quinn, though. Don't want to freak him out. Though I gotta say, the guy is seriously inventive with stuff around the house. It's nice to have someone else kinky to talk to."

Maybe it would be, once Beach got used to having that word applied to him. For now he'd take anything that would get this over faster. "What's sounding?"

"Ah, it's these rods that go down your piss slit—"

"Ah, gotcha." Big dark *X* there. "Violet wand?"

"That's pretty hard-core. It's an electric shock, a toy, but depends on where the shock is hitting you."

"I bet."

"But there's a TENS unit thing some people use. It makes muscles contract. They use it in physical therapy."

Ah hell. He'd never called for a physical therapy appointment. He snuck a look at the time on his phone. Four thirty. The text he'd gotten at one had been as direct as it had been arousing. He didn't have to fake the urgency in his voice. "Eli, I'm sorry. I have to go."

"Okay." Eli's voice had a smug smile in it. "I hope he's the one to put that panic in your voice."

Eli clicked off, leaving Beach sputtering for an answer.

He put the phone facedown on the counter and finished off the list. What the hell was this at the bottom? Essay questions? And he had something else he needed to do—

Fuck all, he'd forgotten the PT appointment again. His doctor had recommended someone, some place. Beach scanned the options a search on his phone turned up. Something with—ah. Sports Science and Rehabilitation. When he dialed, the pleasant man's recorded voice informed him regular office hours were between the hours of seven thirty and four thirty. *Regular* his ass. There was nothing regular about a business that opened at seven thirty.

A cold weight dragged at Beach's gut as he considered *his ass* might be all too apt an expression. He'd been considering a little push, showing up a hair past his five thirty deadline. Wondering how Tai would react to the challenge had given Beach a sweet prickle in his balls, spreading out under his skin.

But not this. He'd honestly meant to make the appointment. He was sick of the limitations forced by the cane and his leg, and if a bunch of exercises would help, he was ready for it. He had honored his promise and called for an appointment; he simply hadn't gotten one. For once the rationalization didn't offer any comfort. In the meantime he decided he wouldn't be late.

Chapter Eleven

THE KNOCK came at exactly five thirty, and Tai rode a rush of power all the way to the door, opened it, and found himself holding David's face in a kiss before becoming aware of deciding to do it. After a startled breath onto Tai's lips, David kissed back, instant hunger in the slide of his tongue, the open welcome of his mouth. Tai kicked the door shut with his heel.

Tai didn't know how long he'd have kept them standing there if Jez hadn't pushed between them to demand her own greeting. David lost his balance, one palm slapping the wall.

Jez jumped.

"Sorry, girl," David said as Tai was telling her she was all right.

"Sorry to keep you on that leg."

"Maybe I just swoon from your kisses, Sir." David's words rolled with a thick accent, hands rubbing behind Jez's ears. His cane clattered to the floor as he went down on one knee to let her nuzzle his hair and neck.

Tai scooped up the cane. Jez dropped to her haunches to watch him, eyes bright like she thought it was a new game. When Tai put the cane on his desk, though, she lowered herself with a sigh.

"Did you think about whether you want to keep doing this?" Tai turned to watch David answer.

Without the dog to play with, David's hands dangled at his sides, but he didn't get to his feet. With his gaze somewhere between Jez and the bedroom door, David nodded.

"That's not an acceptable answer, David."

David flicked his tongue over his lips, head lifting until he met Tai's stare. "Yes, Sir. I do."

"Okay. Did you bring the checklist?"

David started to nod again, then said, "Yes, Sir. Here." He slid a folded paper out of the pocket of his cargo shorts.

Tai took it from him, drinking in the obedience on offer, the hunger in David's eyes as he tracked Tai's every move.

"When I ask you to come here, you will always be on time. After you say hi to Jez, you will remove all of your clothes and put them on this chair, folded neatly." Tai turned his desk chair out to face the couch. "Then you will put on your cuffs and"—he couldn't have David kneeling with that bad leg—"sit on the floor until I am ready for you."

"Yes, Sir." David climbed to his feet and stripped off his shirt.

Under his husky breaths of arousal, there was something of a pushback. "What?" Tai asked.

David swallowed. "It wasn't on the sheet. But I don't like waiting. I get bored."

Tai watched him, drawing the tension out, feeling it stretch like a wire between them. David didn't look away, not even as he unfastened his shorts, dropped them to the floor, and then peeled away the briefs underneath. As he folded them between his hands, Tai stepped forward.

"Too bad. You'll wait if I want you to. But as for you being bored, I'll take care of that." Tai took the shorts from David and fished the cuffs from his front pocket. "Give me your hands."

The light from the blinds could have been the reason, but David's pupils widened as the leather was buckled over the tender inside of his wrists. Only a hair's width of blue iris showed as Tai leaned forward to breathe the order across David's mouth. "Go sit on my bed and wait for me."

David didn't answer, but he went, disappearing around the corner. Jez had gone off to stretch out under the air conditioner when she realized it wasn't her kind of play date. Her ears barely twitched as Tai unfolded the checklist to scan it.

He was relieved to see David wasn't looking for anything Tai didn't feel able to deliver.

In fact, with the exception of impact play, they were well matched.

Tai wouldn't say he was a sadist in the way he understood it from Nic's point of view. If Tai marked a sub, the satisfaction was in the proof of ownership, not the hurting. To him, impact play was about a submissive surrendering to what Tai wanted, demanded. That pleasure and pain came from him. And the sight of a guy over Tai's lap, upturned ass waiting for the smack of his hand, got him hard enough to cut diamonds.

He tucked the list in his back pocket and went into his bedroom.

David had followed orders—insolently. He was sitting on the bed, barely. His legs were wide apart, and he leaned on one arm as his other hand made a lazy stroke on his half-hard dick, as if he wouldn't mind waiting until August to get off.

Tai leaned back against his closet door and folded his arms. It would serve the brat right to make him wait that long. "Are you challenging me, David?"

David's hand stuttered in its stroke, his voice husky and low as he answered, "No, Sir. I get bored." He looked away. "I'd rather you put me in the shower again than make me wait."

"Better negative attention than none? I think you should learn patience, boy. Get up on the bed. On your back. And get your hand off your dick."

"Yes, Sir."

"Spread your legs. Wider." Tai buckled on ankle cuffs and attached them to the restraints he had under the bed. Kneeling at David's side, Tai studied David's face. There was the quick slide of his tongue he did when he was nervous but no fear in his eyes. "You will tell me if your leg hurts from this."

"Yes, Sir."

After licking a kiss across David's palm, Tai attached the left hand to the corner restraint.

David's breath came faster. His head turned to look at his wrist. "I can take a picture for you," Tai offered.

He wouldn't mind having that picture. David with his Abercrombie looks, spread out and pinned down with dark leather and steel clips. Held open for anything Tai wanted to do.

David's eyes widened. "Um, I—Not this time."

"You trust me to tie you up but not with a picture." Tai smiled. "Ah, well…."

Tai ran his finger along the forearm of David's unbound hand, drawing a shiver. "What's your safeword?"

"Red. Or—" He flexed his fingers. "I don't think I could reach anything to tap."

"I won't gag you." Tai used his teeth and lips on each fingertip, then clipped the restraint onto the cuff. "Because we're going to talk."

"Talk?" David arched up, and the cuffs pulled him down again.

"Yes. About patience. Lie flat. You challenged me, and I will punish you, David. When I tell you to wait, that is part of you submitting to me. Concentrate on that. You're not only waiting. You're giving me obedience. And in waiting you have my attention."

Tai pushed off the bed, backing away. "Tai—Sir?"

"Yes?"

"Are you leaving me like this?"

"Close your eyes."

The soft lids were almost convincing.

"All the way, David." Tai moved around the bed. "I'm still here."

Eyes still shut, David nodded then stammered, "Yes, Sir."

"Is your leg okay?"

"As much as it ever is."

"When is your physical therapy appointment?"

This time David's tongue made a full sweep of his lips. "Ah. I called." When Tai didn't answer, David kept rolling. "But they'd left for the day so I didn't get an appointment. But I did call, and I'll call them back tomorrow."

Tai moved to the window and peered behind the blinds. "You had time to go get your car from the impound but not to call for an appointment."

"I forgot." For the first time, David's voice held genuine regret. "I meant to." Tai turned back to watch his throat bob with a swallow.

At last in the silence, David whispered, "I'm sorry, Sir."

"Why?"

David blinked, his eyes unfocused for a minute, and then he looked at Tai.

"Why are you sorry?"

"Because I—" The apologetic tone vanished, replaced with something stronger. "I made a promise. And I like to think I'm a man of my word."

Tai leaned down and brushed a thumb across David's lips. "Think about that, David. Do you like displeasing me?"

Tai watched understanding crash over David like a bucket of ice water. Shock, a sharp intake of breath, the strain in his immobilized muscles to protect himself from the knowledge. Then the relaxation of acceptance.

"No." David's voice was as hoarse as if he'd been under a cold shower.

Tai bent to kiss him. "Good boy."

Damn. If he'd known, he'd have started there. It would have been a perfect time to pull David onto his lap, reinforce that yielding, the recognition of his desire to please.

David shifted, squaring his shoulders against the mattress, and the moment, along with his vulnerability, slipped away.

"How do you feel?" Tai asked.

"Comfy. I could sleep like this." David closed his eyes again.

"I want you to practice patience, not fall asleep, so I have something special for you." Tai had made a quick stop on his way home from work. Even without the checklist, he'd been pretty sure David would take to light cock-and-ball torture. He'd nodded at the clerk at Studs and Satin and gone right past the bachelor and bachelorette party stuff and into the back room where the serious stuff was. He'd eyed a triple crown of metal rings, but then remembering how David had loved the leather cuffs, Tai had bought a five-stud leather band with a ball separator.

Now he took the band out and trailed it down David's chest, watching the skin prickle in reaction. David lifted his head to peer down.

"Everything's already cuffed."

As the edge approached David's cock, Tai flicked it up and then let it lightly snap against the inside of David's thigh, provoking a flinch and a hiss.

"Not everything." Tai dragged it up from thigh to groin.

"Oh. Oh shit." David's dick filled as Tai watched, lengthening and thickening.

"Relax. It's easier if you're not fully hard."

Tai's words had the opposite effect. He grabbed David's shaft. "Don't make me jerk you off."

David laughed. "That is the most peculiar threat I've ever heard."

"Trust me." Tai breathed the words into David's ear. "You won't enjoy what I've planned if you've already come."

"Damn. You telling me that is not likely to make me less—ah—tumescent." David's voice leapt from baritone to tenor as Tai fastened the leather tight around the shaft and behind his balls.

Tai chuckled as he checked the fit.

"Ah—I think it's too tight," David complained around a high, fast breath.

"It's going to get tighter as you get more *tumescent*."

"You told me to—Even saying hard is—shit—making me harder."

"Are you bored?"

"No, Sir."

"Good." Tai smiled. He lifted the T-strap and drew David's balls up close, carefully checking the snaps to avoid pinching hair or skin.

"Oh sweet Jesus." David shuddered. "I—Don't—I—" Tai ran his finger up the throbbing vein on the underside. "T-Tai, Sir, please."

"What do you want, David?" Tai crawled up from the foot of the bed to crouch between David's shivering legs.

"I—don't know." Desperation grated through David's clenched jaw.

"Good. Don't think. Don't anticipate. Take what I give you."

"Yes, Sir."

Tai flattened himself, dropping his legs off the mattress to reach David's balls with tongue and lips. One long lick of the velvety skin stretched tight by the straps, and then he gently tugged one side of the sac in to cradle the soft roundness in his mouth, nose buried in the sweat and sex pouring from David's skin.

The body around him jumped and twitched, harsh groans following David's breathing. A little harder on the other side, a firmer tug of lips, more pressure as Tai traced the shape with his tongue. After a row of wet kisses along the underside of David's dick, Tai slid backward off the bed.

David's panting got shallow and fast to the point where Tai stopped stripping his clothes to put a palm on David's chest.

"Shhh."

David's eyes had been screwed shut. They popped open, and he twisted his head back and forth for an instant.

"Still with me?"

David nodded then blew out a long, steady breath. "Yes, Sir."

"Good boy. If you hyperventilate, you'll pass out, and I have plans." The tightness under Tai's palm eased. "That's it."

Tai stepped out of his shorts and dropped them on the chair, watching David's breathing even out. He leaned to brush his lips across David's neck. "I'm proud of you."

David turned his head, and the surprise in his eyes made Tai have to kiss him. At first David tried to push frantic hunger into it, but when Tai's hand landed on his cheek, the stroke of tongues became slow and deep.

Right then it wasn't a scene, didn't feel anything like playing. It was more than an eager sub, obedience on offer. The familiar buzz was there, connecting them in this space, but it was different. A dizzying pull that

kept him matching his breaths with David's as they
kissed, kept Tai stroking the cheeks and rough jaw
under his fingers, kept him there, forehead pressed
against David's when the kiss ended.

"I've got you."

"Yes, Sir."

"I want you to remember this when I ask you to
wait. Remember it's for me. It's being good for me
like this. Taking what I give you."

"Yes."

Tai stared down into David's eyes and wasn't sure
which of them was deeper in.

Dragging himself away, Tai took out the checklist and gathered other supplies from the nightstand
drawer.

"You skipped the last two questions." Tai held up
the lube and the curved steel wand, slicking the heavy
ball at the end.

David licked his lips. "I did answer them."

"Hmm." Tai moved around to the foot of his bed
again and knelt on the mattress. "Lift your hips a
little."

When David did, Tai slipped the bulb on the wand
up against David's asshole and pushed, barely enough
to let him feel the pressure. With the other hand, he
held the checklist out for David to see.

"Are those really answers?" He rocked the tip of
the wand, stretching the rim of muscle. David's thighs
started shaking. "*How were you punished as a child?*
Answer: *Same as everyone.*" Tai studied David's face.

He groaned, jaw and lips tight. "If I answer, what
do I get?"

"It doesn't work like that, David. You answer because I ask. But we'll come back to that one. *What*

nonphysical elements of D/s do you like the most? Answer: *Can't I just tell you?* Yes. You can tell me now." Tai nudged the heavy steel ball deeper, so the full width of it stretched David's hole.

"This," David managed on a gasp.

Tai rocked the toy back and forth by fractions. "What about this?"

David's shoulders rolled, his chest undulating like a snake, hands into fists as his muscles pulled at the restraints, his words a raw whisper. "When I don't have a choice. When you tell me I don't have a choice." He kept his eyes tightly closed. "Please tell me I don't have a choice."

The power of David's surrender hit like a helmet to the chin, the force snapping down Tai's spine, rattling in his skull. But unlike suffering a stinger and having to be carted off the field, after the dazzle of impact faded, he could move. He pushed the wand in deep, then dove forward, braced over David's body on fists.

He dragged his mouth, then his teeth through the sweaty-sweet taste of David's neck, his jaw. "That's right. And right now you don't have a choice about coming. Your dick is mine to use how I want."

David's head cranked back against the mattress, opening more skin to Tai's teeth. Drunk with it, Tai sucked a mark up under David's ear, and another, sharper, faster, along his jawbone.

Tai might as well have been socking away liquor for all the coordination in his fingers as he dug out a condom, tore open the wrapper, and got the tip over David's dick.

"What are you do—?" David's words cut off as Tai put his mouth over the latex-covered head and rolled the edge down with a rough stroke of his hand.

"You don't need to know. Because I'm making the choices."

David groaned, but his gaze was steady on Tai as he slicked the condom, then reached back to lube himself. It was fast, rough, and nowhere near enough stretch to make this easy, but that slur of dazed heat inside him wouldn't let him slow down.

"Yeah, David," Tai said to the blue eyes wide with the question. "I'm going to ride you. And you're going to stay hard for me."

A protest started in closed lips and tighter eyes, then faded on a moan as Tai gripped the base of David's cock to angle the entry.

It burned, too much and too fast, but Tai only gave himself a few seconds to recover before sliding down over the head again.

The sound that burst out from behind David's bared teeth made Tai want to go faster. A strangled scream, tearing, gurgling like David was drowning as Tai sank all the way down. He slid his palms up David's chest, thumbs coming to rest at the notch in his collarbone.

"Tell me what I'm making you feel."

David whispered the answer without hesitation. "It's good. Tight. So tight. And that thing inside, God, so heavy, and it's pushing right. It's heavy and pushing—"

Tai rocked forward.

"Jesus." David's body jerked.

"Yeah, boy. Your dick is in me, and I'm still fucking you." Tai started a slow grind, David's dick shifting and touching all the right places inside. "Gonna have to wait for it. Wait for me."

"Yes, Sir."

Tai moved faster, shoving David's cock in deeper, pushing them both further into a place where everything was raw and hot to the touch. Strength and power unleashed between them.

Tai trailed his thumbs gently alongside David's windpipe, the absolute trust in David lifting his chin to give Tai access to every inch of that fragile stretch of flesh. The perfect submission sending another druglike wave to cloud Tai's brain. Even if they'd done breath play before, practiced it, if he knew every cue from David's face, he couldn't risk that now. Not with Tai's head high on this buzz.

He spread his palms wide on David's shoulders, the deltoids solid and hot as the muscles flexed and strained, and took a grip to anchor them for the fuck.

David's eyes came back into focus, zeroing in on Tai's with the first thrust. Tai moved his hips in hard, shallow strokes, keeping David's cock angled to rub Tai's gland over and over. The quick burn of friction didn't take long to put him right up on the edge. Despite Tai's weight and the spread of his thighs, David did his best to meet the thrusts, his hips slapping up against Tai's ass.

"Please, Sir. Please, God, please." The words might have begged, but David's voice was a raspy growl.

"Wait. For. Me." Tai timed with his thrusts.

"Yes, Sir."

Tai slowed and released David's shoulders, bringing a hand to his mouth. "Make it wet for me."

David sucked in Tai's fingers and licked over Tai's palm as if lapping up honey. "Good. You're doing good."

Even with Tai's body pulsing from the pressure in his ass and the urge to come drawing his balls up tight, his own hand on his dick felt like a stranger's. He was so focused on David and his reactions, on the way David had melted into pliancy, that Tai had pushed back the demands from his own body.

He tightened his ass around David's cock, drinking in the moans, the strangled breaths and the pleas as he started moving again. It was good and sweet, the slide of his hand and the stab of pleasure from being fucked. A long, steady rise and fall of sensation on the climb, until it wasn't. Until something switched inside him and it was there, a violent shock, jolting bright and hot from his balls, the first shot flying past David's shoulder. Instead of a drop, the next wave was sharper, then harder, spasms from deep inside as he painted David's jaw, his lips, his chest with endless streams until Tai was wrung dry and aching.

"Fuck." The word shuddered out of him with a last, rough gasp, and he hung there, staring down into David's face, cock giving a desperate final twitch as David licked the come from his lips.

Tai pulled the edge of the sheet from the mattress and wiped David's eyes. The body under Tai trembled, the cock in his ass swelling and throbbing.

He eased forward, letting David slide out of him, then rolled to one side.

With one hand on David's jaw to keep his face turned to Tai, he reached down first to unsnap the strap on his balls, which produced a bone-deep whimper, and then freed his cock.

There might have been curses or only sounds from David's lips, but Tai kissed them away, pulling off the condom and working David's dick with firm strokes.

"You were a good boy. Now you're gonna come for me, David." Tai breathed in David's gasp through another kiss and jacked him faster.

David tore his head free, and his body convulsed into jerks as his cock spilled thick and warm and creamy across Tai's arm and fingers.

"God, David." Tai breathed in the smell of his hair and skin and the faint bleach of spunk. "So good. So sweet, baby."

David smiled. "I waited so long I was afraid I forgot how to do it. And then it was the best one of my life."

"Patience can be rewarding." Tai swept his hand up through the trails of come on David's chest.

"Yes, Sir." But there was a hint of a brat in the hoarse voice.

"I'll be happy to convince you some more."

"I'm looking forward to you topping that."

"Oh, I plan to." Tai nodded.

"Mmm." David let out a long breath and sank onto the mattress, then flinched.

"Right. Let me get that for you." Tai reached between David's legs and gripped the curve of the wand. "Breathe out."

"Appreciate it. Hard to relax with a stick up your ass."

Tai chuckled as he eased it out of David's body and tossed it on the mattress at their feet. If David needed teasing and humor to come down from sub space, Tai was happy to go along with it. It beat the hell out of pounding on the bathroom door.

"Damn, that was good." David turned his head to look over at Tai.

He'd never actually seen eyes sparkle before. But there it was. Happiness and good humor and the late-afternoon sun made David's eyes clear and bright.

So when it hit, it was as sudden a shift as the last time. Tai had just decided to start unhooking David from the restraints when he jerked his arms. Hard. And again. His face went slack with panic.

"Red. Okay? Red."

Tai blessed Nic for teaching him to always have quick releases on restraints. Both David's hands were free before he'd safeworded a third time. But he repeated the word over and over as Tai released the clips on his ankle cuffs.

"It's okay. You're okay," he whispered as David curled into a silent ball. Tai reached for David's shoulder but hovered an inch above his skin. "I'll leave you alone if that's what you want, but don't try to get up until you feel steady."

"I hate this."

David's mood had shifted fast enough to give Tai whiplash, but those words spread something cold and hollow through him, until he wondered which of them would end up in the bathroom hiding a reaction under running water.

David uncurled enough to roll his shoulders and head to look to where Tai stood at the foot of the bed. "It's so damned stupid." David's laugh echoed the hollowness in Tai's chest.

"What is?"

"I want it so much. I fucking love it. What you do, everything." David paused. Swallowed. "And then." He shook his head. "First time I ever got drunk enough to puke, Chip Montgomery slapped my back as I was hanging on to the toilet for dear life and said, 'If you run with the big dogs, you've gotta learn to piss in the tall grass.' Guess I'm still learning."

Tai stood silent, waiting.

"I'd rather—Don't go. Please."

"Okay." Tai sat on the bed next to him.

When David moved closer, Tai stroked a hand down David's spine. "I've never been much of a backslapper."

"Really? Would have figured you for a sports guy."

"Figured right. But that's all ass slapping and chest bumps."

"I think I'll pass on both right now."

Tai's phone launched into Gina's ringtone.

David followed Tai's gaze to his shorts. "Do you need to get that?"

Tai leaned back on his hands. "No. Not unless it rings again."

"Your... daughter?"

He hadn't given David time to ask any questions on the phone yesterday. Hadn't ever expected to mention Sammie to—

The phone went off. "Sorry." He fished it out.

"She's all right," Gina said immediately, though from that opening and the strain in her voice, his baby girl was anything but all right.

"What happened?"

"There was an accident. But she's okay. Might have broken her wrists."

"Wrists? Gina, what happened?"

"She got hit by a car. She's okay." How did hit by a car equal okay?

"I want to talk to Daddy Tai." Sammie's voice, thank God her voice, sounded from somewhere. And then a lot of other voices, indistinct, and one saying, "How about a ride, princess?"

"We're going for X-rays now."

"Where are you? Johns Hopkins?"

"Mercy."

"What the hell for?" Gina worked at Johns Hopkins. His mother worked at Johns.

"It was closer. I have to go. She wants you to come."

"On my way."

He pressed End, though disconnecting by throwing the phone through the nearest wall felt like a better plan, then turned back to David. Who was gone.

Tai yanked up boxers and shorts and was reaching for a T-shirt when David appeared in the doorway, dressed and leaning on his cane.

"I have to—" Tai started.

"I know you have to go," David interrupted. "I'll see myself out." His voice was firm, and if the windows weren't toward the sun, Tai might not have noticed how pale David's face was. But after what had happened, there was no way Tai could miss the flatness of his eyes or the faint vibrations in the hand that held the cane.

"No. You'll get in my car."

Chapter Twelve

ONE OF the reasons Beach was used to getting his way was that he could predict the argument against him and be a few steps ahead.

At that moment, he ran the projected conversation like this.

Me: I'm all right.

Him: Like you were last time. (A snort for emphasis.)

Me: I've had practice now. I promise to drink some juice and make no sudden movements.

Him: I don't have time to argue with you. (Accompanying growl.)

Me: So don't. Your daughter needs you.

Yes, that should work. But before the words left his mouth, Tai stood in front of him. Next time Beach would have to take into account the way sub drop also slowed down his brain.

"David. Let's go."

A hand on the back of his neck, warm thumb rubbing behind his ear, made Beach as docile as Jez when Tai told her to stay.

His well-used muscles protested the uncomfortable passenger seat in Tai's cramped Focus. Beach's Spider waited across the street, gleaming like the ocean where it touched the sky. He couldn't believe he was leaving it there among the jetsam of indifferent crossover wagons, battered trucks, and faded minivans. He should be cradled in the Spider's Daytona-style seat, driving away from all the thoughts that asked him what the hell he was doing, what kind of man was he to let another man use him like that. The gruff, explicit demands from Tai that made Beach's knees give way like rusted hinges would have made Beach offer to punch the shit out of a man who spoke like that to a woman.

There was one piece of bondage that his safeword couldn't get rid of. The damned monitor kept him trapped here, where one text would send him crawling back, hungry to learn how much further, how much higher Tai could take him.

The seat belt jabbed into his neck, too tight across his chest, and he clawed it away from his skin.

Tai covered Beach's hand and lowered it. "You passed out last time." It was that soft, sexy rumble that had hooked Beach from the first.

"I hadn't eaten." Beach slid his hand away, but Tai's palm rested warm and heavy on Beach's thigh, heat sinking through the khaki, solid as an anchor.

"I need to go see Sammie."

Beach filed away Tai's daughter's name.

"And I need to take care of you," Tai continued. "That means you come with me."

It was high-handed. Insufferably arrogant. And possibly the only time anyone had ever said that to him.

He'd had to chase his mother to London after his father split for Venezuela. Even Gavin, as good and loyal a friend as he was, seemed more inclined to put up with Beach than to encourage his presence.

Tai's words might be part of the formula of kneeling and leather and checklists. But a lifetime of sifting through platitudes and polishing them to sparkle with sincerity made Beach keenly aware of when someone was only mouthing the expected.

Tai meant it.

All Beach had to do was accept it. "Yes, Sir."

Tai brushed a thumb along Beach's jaw, fingers light on the top of his spine.

That horrible, clenching emptiness left Beach's gut on the next breath. Maybe the key to not having sub drop was to keep subbing. Hair of the dog? He barely smothered a laugh at the thought.

Tai's hand landed back on Beach's knee. "Better?"

Beach considered what advantage there was in denying it. But he didn't want what Tai was offering to come out of manipulation. It wouldn't feel this good. Besides, it wasn't as if Tai would stop the car and leave Beach there in Little Italy to walk home.

"Yes."

"Good." Tai squeezed Beach's leg.

WHY DID hospitals all have the same smell? Beach must have inhaled so much of it during his coma that he went cold from the first breath. As soon as the emergency room doors slid shut behind them, Beach worked to tune out the rest of the waiting room.

Pacers, bleeders, people doubled over in pain, and one woman sobbing uncontrollably. A woman in wine-colored nurse's scrubs came up to them. Beach winced. If a nurse was coming to meet them, it must be very bad. And Tai had wasted time on Beach?

"Toluaotai."

"*Tina.*" Tai bent and kissed the nurse's cheek as she reached up to pat his.

"She'll be fine, *la'u tama*." The nurse hugged Tai. "She's just a baby."

"All the better. She'll heal fast." The nurse kept a hand on Tai's arm and gave Beach a solid appraisal that made him all too conscious of the fact he'd barely had a chance to towel the come off him. And he was sure his hair was styled à la just-fucked.

"*Tina*, this is David Beauchamp. David, this is my mother, Kara Mosely."

"Your mother?" Beach tried to keep the shock out of his voice. The middle-aged black woman in nurse's scrubs was Tai's mother. Beach snuck a comparative glance at the man he was... dating? Fucking? Submitting to? Beach recovered and offered his hand. "—Is a very beautiful woman. And I am honored to meet you, ma'am."

"Nice save," Tai murmured with a hint of amusement in his voice. "I'm going to go see Sammie." He tromped off toward the triage desk, leaving Beach to draw on every skill he'd perfected over years of social fencing.

"How do you know my son, David?" Her glance lingered first on Beach's cane, then on the ankle monitor.

"Everyone calls me Beach, ma'am. Ah, socially."

"Boyfriend?"

That might have freed him from the fear of accidentally outing Tai, but he still didn't know how to answer. He supposed his being brought along on an urgent errand made them seem longer acquainted.

"We haven't—"

A roar from Tai spared Beach from answering.

"She's asking for me! Her mother called. For God's sake, would it kill you to go ask? There's two of you in there."

Behind the glass partition, the nurse facing Tai said, "I can't release any information. If a parent wants you, they'll come get you, but only two people are allowed with a minor patient."

"I heard you the first time. Jesus Christ. Go ask them."

"Sir—"

"Toluaotai." Kara Mosely's voice wasn't that loud, but the authority in it cut through the protests of the nurse and Tai. "Boy, you need to take all of the seats. Right. Now."

Tai pushed away from the partition and strode toward the entrance doors and then through them.

"He'll cool down. Boy has always had a temper. I'm sure you've noticed."

But Beach hadn't. Tai's rumbling voice demanded obedience, but never with anger.

Always steady, in control. Solid. Even when he spoke of punishing, there was never a hint of the rage Beach had just seen.

"He's told you about Sammie?" Despite her reassurance, Kara watched the doors for her son's return.

"Yes."

"We were so sure she was his. Even after Josh came back. Don't think he's quite adjusted to that. But how could he? She's his baby."

Beach filled in the few gaps. No matter what had happened with Sammie's mother and Josh, Tai obviously still considered Sammie his daughter. And he damned well deserved to be with her.

Mercy Hospital took no chances with security. The nurses behind the glass controlled access to the doors leading from the waiting room. One came out to take the patient with a blood-soaked towel around his hand through to the back.

It was good from an insurance and business model perspective, but hell on waiting.

Beach hated waiting.

"Please excuse me for a moment, ma'am," he told Kara and stepped away, pulling out his phone.

It only took two calls. Midland-South Health was a name that got people moving if they knew where their bread was buttered.

Tai came back in as Beach tucked his phone away. With an explosive breath, Tai said, "I can't get Gina on the phone." He paced around. "How did she get hit by a car? She knows better than to play in the street." Tai paced and muttered before looking up. "David, sit down." It wasn't the frustrated snarl he'd been using, but softer, a mildly exasperated concern. As Beach sat, he wondered how long there had been between Tai learning of Sammie's paternity and Jez coming to live in the apartment on South Streeper Street. Now there was Beach to order around in that fond but stern voice.

Doctor Stevenson cleared the doors to the emergency room in just under five minutes from the time

Beach had hung up. The white coat and ID might have labeled him a doctor, but the tie and crisp blue dress shirt said he hadn't seen an ER patient all day. He combed a hand through the thin wisps of hair at the apex of a frowning brow.

"Mr. Fonoti?"

Tai started toward him, and Doctor Stevenson's eyes widened behind his glasses.

"I'm Doctor Stevenson, the director of the emergency department." He offered a handshake, then continued with a trace of a grimace. Whether the expression was from the force of Tai's grip or the doctor's attempt at looking contrite was hard to determine at a distance. "I'm so sorry you were kept waiting, sir. Things can get a little cramped back there. I hope you'll understand. If you'll follow me, I'll take you to—back."

Tai glanced over his shoulder, and Beach found himself nodding encouragement along with Tai's mom.

The doors buzzed, and Doctor Stevenson led Tai through. Beach leaned back and rolled his cane across his thighs until Tai's mother pinned him with a sharp look.

"Don't you just look like the cat that ate the cream and both of the canaries."

Beach sat up straight. "Excuse me, ma'am?"

"Don't 'excuse me, ma'am' when you've got feathers all over your lips. How did you do that?"

Beach put his cane against the floor and studied the tip. "I simply knew the right person to call."

Kara didn't have her son's thick brows or his intimidating muscles. But she did have a look that had

Beach ready to confess sins he hadn't even thought of committing.

"Are you a drug dealer?"

Beach dropped his cane. "Ma'am?"

"Mafia of some kind?"

"I—No. Not at all."

Kara's eyes lasered in on his anklet and then back up to his face. "You going to try to tell me that you got your anklet at a craft fair at the county jail?"

"No, ma'am. I got myself into some trouble. But Tai didn't know about this"—he pointed at the monitor with his cane—"until after we'd—ah—met."

"What kind of trouble?"

"The kind I'm ashamed to admit. Though it seemed like it was the right thing at the time. If I had to do it again—"

"You'd do the same damned thing." Their voices were nothing alike, but Kara sounded exactly like her son.

"Probably," Beach conceded with a rueful smile. "But I wouldn't have made the mistake of involving a friend the way I did."

Beach didn't know what he'd expected of Tai's family. He hadn't actually given it any thought, though he'd known the man hadn't randomly appeared on the planet. Now seeing Kara's perception, her obvious force of will, it was clear where Tai had come by some of his personality. Certainly Kara would have needed that kind of strength to deal with Tai as a child—and adult.

"And what happened to your friend?" There was a warning in her voice. A maternal protectiveness Beach had only encountered from a distance before.

"He's all right. Unscathed in body and in terms of his relations with the police."

"But you weren't."

"I wasn't as lucky, no, ma'am."

Kara glanced toward the nurse-guarded inner sanctum of the ER and then back for another slow once-over of Beach. "You're not the sort of man I would have expected Tai to bring around."

Again Beach tried to picture what sort of man— submissive—Tai had been with before.

He didn't tell his mother about that part, did he?

"Though you must be important, or you wouldn't be here right now."

Beach hurried to clear that up. "My being here is only a matter of timing. I—There wasn't a way for Tai to get here without me tagging along."

"I'm sure you know well enough Tai would have found another way if he wanted to."

Beach smiled to concede her point. "He is direct."

"That's one way to put it." Kara's demeanor softened from her inquisitor role, leaving Beach feeling like he'd cleared the most difficult stretch of the course.

Noting the gold band on her left ring finger, Beach asked, "Is his father the same?"

"Tai's father passed away when he was only a baby."

"I'm sorry." And he was. His own parents might not be ideals, but at least they'd been present awhile.

"So am I. I think he'd have been pleased."

"Tai is a son to be proud of," Beach said quickly. As the words left his mouth, he realized it wasn't only polite conversation. A man who was still devoted to the child he'd learned wasn't his, a man who saved a poor dog destined for euthanasia, anyone could recognize how Tai protected and took care of others.

And I need to take care of you.

Beach twirled his cane between his palms. He wasn't a child or a dog to need rescuing. And that was Gavin's schtick, ending up screwing the cop who'd found them when Beach and Gavin went off the Key Bridge.

"What about your family, Beach?"

"Ma'am?"

Kara wasn't one to be put off by a delaying tactic. "What does your family think about your *trouble*?" Her emphasis covered everything from his scarred shin to the cane to his ankle monitor.

"We aren't that close. My parents prefer to live outside the country." Beach shuddered to think of what Uncle Sinclair would say about his adventure on Fort Carroll. At least Beach was out of range of his uncle's peach tree full of switches.

Kara shook her head. "I've never heard of a South Carolina mafia, but you do make me wonder."

"Honest, ma'am. The business interests of the Beauchamps are firmly on the right side of the law."

"Just not the personal interests?" Kara had him there.

Beach wondered if she'd had time to do an internet search on her phone while he was slicing through bureaucracy. To find out about why his parents preferred to live outside the country.

He was saved from having to answer when Tai returned, carrying a dimpled girl with a neon-green cast on one slender arm and a purple one on the other.

Kara rose to greet them, and Beach's manners had him scrambling up after her. As she approached her son and granddaughter, Beach studied the couple in their wake. A petite woman in a purple sleeveless dress—whose similarity to Kara made some of the confusion over Sammie's paternity clear—was accompanied by a solidly built but shorter-than-Tai-by-several-inches man with light brown skin wearing a golfing shirt and tan slacks. He kept a possessive arm around Sammie's mother's waist.

"Gooma, you have to sign my cast next," Sammie called out to Kara. As the child started wriggling, Tai lowered her as if she were made of glass. "Then we're going for ice cream and everyone gets to feed it to me." She held up both plaster-encased forearms.

Poor kid. Beach's tendency to seek out higher and more interesting places meant that by Sammie's age, he already knew the fun attention from sporting a cast turned to stale inconvenience after three days. Even he'd never needed two at once. Though he was discovering that broken bones healed much more easily under the age of fourteen than they did at thirty-four, medical advances notwithstanding.

After a careful hug, Kara examined Sammie's casts, Tai hovering over her as if he would lift the kid to safety if she so much as frowned. Beach eased himself away from the group, pulling out his phone again.

"What now?" Gavin sighed without a greeting.

"I need another ride."

"What the hell, Beach? I just drove you to get your goddamned car."

Beach wondered if Gavin's speech patterns would continue to devolve into those of his policeman. "Yes, and I thank you for it. But it's some distance away at the moment. I'm at the emergency room at Mercy Hospital."

"Please tell me this is some unfortunate attempt at humor." There was the Gavin Beach knew. "If the next words involve something stuck up your ass, I'm hanging up."

There'd been something sharper than teasing to Gavin's voice. Something that made an unfamiliar shame oil through Beach's stomach before settling with the greasy weight of deep-fried butter. Which may have had something to do with the indignation giving him a sensation akin to heartburn as he snapped back, "I came along as moral support for a friend."

"I'm finding it hard to place you and 'moral' in the same sentence. You're lucky they aren't monitoring bullshit levels along with alcohol."

"Does Sergeant Boyfriend have his hand so far up your ass you're his puppet now? Forget it. I'll call a cab."

"Beach, wait. I was teasing."

"Did I interrupt your boyfriend time?"

"No. I'm working."

"Well, bless your heart." Beach wasn't sure he bought the just-teasing excuse. "On what?"

"The shelter."

Right. Gavin's dusty building with the guard tower/solarium on top. "Did you buy that"—he opted for tact—"property?"

"That's what I'm working on. To see if we can get the right kind of permits there. And fuck you too, by the way."

Beach relaxed. That kind of frustration was probably why Gavin was acting like such a prick. "Sounds like a pain where you wish your boyfriend was. I'll call a cab and leave you to soldier on."

"What about the person your alleged morals were supposedly supporting?"

Beach glanced over at the cast-signing party. "It's complicated."

"Of course it is. It's you."

Which was possibly the most insulting thing Gavin had said to him in twenty years. Beach was utterly laid-back and a complete joy to get along with. It was other people who got all tight-assed about rules and relationships.

Before Beach could lay out some of what Gavin had coming about complications, Mr. Dating a Freaking Cop went on, "Mercy, right? I'll be there in about fifteen."

Using a cane made it hard to be unobtrusive. And Beach was leaning on it more than he normally did as his shinbone protested the unusual activity earlier in the evening, but he thought he'd managed to slip away and into the men's room without Kara's or Tai's notice. *Take that, Gavin Montgomery.* Beach was anything but a complication to be solved.

He'd give them a few minutes to roll on to their ice cream destination and then go out to wait for Gavin.

He ducked into the stall when he heard the door open, but the heavy tread and the athletic footwear alerted him before the intruder came to a stop in front of the stall door.

Beach opened it. "Do you ever get tired of following me into men's rooms?"

Tai stepped away to let Beach out. "Not so far."

For an unaccountable reason, Beach couldn't look Tai in the face and seized on the distraction of some compulsive hand-washing. But he made the water too hot and flinched, jerking his hand back and sending giant gobs of foamy soap flying. He'd been so good at distracting himself he hadn't noticed the water temp until it was blistering. Now he blinked at his reddened, throbbing hand.

Tai lunged forward and turned on a neighboring faucet. "David. Come here."

The order soothed more than the cool water Tai shoved Beach's hand toward. Until he heard Gavin's voice. *What the hell, Beach? Cut the Southern-belle routine.*

"Do we count this as part of a scene? A little pain and punishment?"

Tai released Beach so fast he had to grab on to the sink or risk falling. "What? Where did that come from?"

Beach stared down into the sink at his hands gripping the porcelain rim.

"David. Do you think you deserve to be punished?"

His smartass remark had come after he burned himself. And it had been an accident. He didn't answer.

"I'll decide if you need to be punished."

Yes. That was what Beach wanted. Everything out of his hands. No need to decide what was worth a risk or reward.

Funny. He'd never considered consequences— the good or the bad—before. So maybe it was no surprise he wanted to turn that burden over to someone else. A simple *Yes, Sir* and he'd be caught up in Tai's control. In the tingling buzz, the aching rightness of it.

But when Beach's mouth opened, what came out was "Or if I deserve a dog biscuit or ice cream?" He watched Tai's reaction in the mirror.

He'd been leaning against the door. Now he straightened but folded his arms across his chest. "If you think you've been treated like a pet or a child, you're the one with a problem. You're not comfortable being my submissive, then tell me. I made it clear I wasn't interested in dragging you into something you pretend you don't like."

"And how long has that all been clear to you?" Beach couldn't stop digging, needed to see that he was worth some of the temper Tai's mother claimed he had such a problem with. "That bossing around your bedmates was a way to make up for losing your daughter?"

Beach had spent twenty-five years smoothing and cajoling. Nothing harshed a buzz faster than a blast of temper. It was better to be comfortable than right. Now he was throwing dynamite into the bear's cave and blocking the exit.

He'd wanted a hot explosion. He got a slow, hard freeze.

"Certainly a lot longer than your experiment in curing your poor-little-rich-boy boredom." Tai opened the door. "I'm sure your money will get you off, and you can go back to chasing a high the good old-fashioned way. Go on." He nodded at the door. "I'll take you back to your oversized toy car."

As sweet as every piece of praise Tai had fed him was, the disgust was bile sour, burning in the back of Beach's throat.

"That won't be necessary," he drawled. "I've arranged to find my own way back. Thank you."

A quick inhalation gave a lie to the slow arch of Tai's brow. "Whatever you want."

Damned if he'd get the last word, if something that had shaken Beach to the soul could be dissolved so easily.

He'd burn it to the ground first. Pouring every bit of disdain he'd learned in a lifetime surrounded by people who knew they were better than everyone else, he gestured with his cane. "After you." The pause was deliciously bitter. "Sir."

Chapter Thirteen

DAVID INJECTED the word with so much sarcasm it rang in Tai's ears until understanding lit up his brain. He dragged the door shut, sealing them in.

If David had used any other word, Tai would have let him go. Been too stupid, too hopped up on the roller coaster of panic and anger from what had happened with Sammie to see, to hear, what was going on with David.

David took to D/s so readily, it was hard to remember it was all new to him. Everything David had said and done from the moment Tai tracked him here had been a demand for reassurance, a need to know that Tai was still in control.

And Tai wasn't going to fail him.

He pulled David off balance and then pressed him against the door, using size and weight rather than a grip to keep him there.

David didn't fight but held his body rigid. "If you get this turned-on by industrial tiling and the smell of urinal cakes, it should be easy enough to recreate it at home." His voice was flat, but the tightness in his eyes and mouth showed it was anger, not fear.

"I'm sorry."

David tilted his head. "That doesn't sound very dominant of you. Aren't you breaking the rules?"

"I already broke them. I brought you here with me because we hadn't really ended the scene. I shouldn't have left you like that."

"I assure you I am able to function without constant supervision. Even if you and the county believe otherwise." David shifted his foot to press the band against Tai's ankle.

"And yet there's still a problem."

"No. There isn't. At least there won't be if you get out of my way. I have a ride waiting. You have a daughter waiting to be fed ice cream." David didn't try to move.

"You're still acting like a brat."

"If you aren't enjoying my company, you have only yourself to blame."

That was true. Tai was to blame. Talking wasn't what David needed. It wasn't what either of them needed right now.

"But you're my brat, aren't you, David?" Tai put his hand on David's jaw.

The shiver ran through both of them. An electric arc of connection, the knowledge that this was exactly where they were supposed to be. David's head dropped back against the door, and Tai accepted the offer of David's throat, stretched and waiting. Thumb and fingers spread wide, Tai slid his hand over the prickle of jaw to rest at the open V just above David's larynx. Staring into eyes with only a hint of blue left around the flared pupil, Tai let the weight of his bones do the work, owning, accepting what David offered.

David sucked in a breath, one Tai felt fight its way past his fingers.

"Aren't you?" he demanded, though the proof was there, blood and air struggling, throbbing under his fingers.

David kept his head tilted up in surrender, his choked whisper vibrating into Tai's fingers. "Yes, Sir." His body shuddered. "Bastard."

Tai brushed his mouth over David's. "We'll talk about your behavior later." As Tai withdrew his hand, David strained to follow it for an instant, then fell back against the door.

David took a deep breath and blew it out with a rush of sound before relaxing into Tai's body.

Tai wrapped his arms around David's waist. "Good boy. I've got you." The closer Tai held him, the more tension ebbed away.

"Is this supposed to feel like this? Every time?"

"Tell me what *this* is." Tai pressed his forehead to David's, sharing his breath.

"Like I swallowed a bottle rocket. I should be afraid, but the explosion is too amazing." He held out a hand as if he expected to see a spray of sparks from his fingertips.

It sounded about right. But Tai wanted to absorb that burst, soak it up, and keep them both from coming apart with the strength of it. Tai didn't know what it was supposed to feel like, but he wanted more. "It can be." *If you stay mine.*

David's phone emitted a blast of music about party people. Weight still against Tai's, David took it from his pocket, glanced down, and tucked it away.

"Your ride?" Tai asked. David nodded.

Tai kissed him. He'd meant it to be a quick check-in, to be sure David was ready to leave, but that wasn't the reason for the second kiss. Or the third. The way he tried to leave a print on David's mouth he'd feel all day if he had any doubts.

The phone repeated its tune.

"Is it your run-away-from-home-at-thirty-three friend?"

"No. It's Gavin." David said the name as if it held a defining label that fit into no other category, catching Tai off balance, trapped between jealousy and want.

David only shifted his weight, but Tai felt the separation pull them much farther than a centimeter apart. "I should get going. I've already pissed him off. Though he's put up with me for twenty years, as he likes to remind me, I probably shouldn't risk it. He's the only one who's managed."

David smiled, retreating in a way Tai couldn't follow after. No shaking or bratting or freaking out. Tai had no good reason to keep him there.

"And I'm sure Sammie's looking for you," David added.

Tai stepped away. "I would have driven you back."

"I know." The surety in David's voice echoed the trust he offered when he put his throat in Tai's hand.

Tai took a deep breath. "I can smell us fucking on your skin. And I want it again. Want—"

Another eruption from David's phone saved Tai from going too far while dazed by hunger.

I want to mark you up. Leave the bruises on your skin that prove you're mine. So you know you're mine.

Those were the kinds of things that freaked people out. Had freaked Tai out too until he got to understand things better. It would send David running, especially with his limits around impact play.

David looked up from his phone. "I should—"

"Come with me." Tai was careful not to use his Dom voice, kept it soft and husky.

"For ice cream?" David raised his brows.

"If you want." Tai had no problem introducing David to Gina and Sammie. And as far as Josh was concerned, he could suck it.

"I don't know. Ice cream is a good exercise for limbering up the tongue, but I have to keep my sublimations in check." David patted his waist.

The exaggeratedly coy protest wreaked havoc with Tai's resolve not to turn the invitation into a power play. "Okay. I'll take you back, and I'll use your throat until you need ice cream for it."

David's eyes widened, but his tone still teased. "What kind of man would I be to come between a father and daughter? Weren't you just telling me to learn to be patient?"

Tai's text alert chimed, and while he was busy checking it, David eased away, tugging at the door. Tai pressed it shut with his hand as he read the text aloud. "She fell asleep three blocks away from the hospital."

"Poor kid."

"She's pretty tough. But she's upset about not being able to swim." That had been the only thing to make her lip quiver when they were in the ER. A piece of his heart chipped away every time she looked at

him with the conviction that Daddy Tai could fix anything and he had to tell her he couldn't.

"Ugh. Wet casts are no one's friend," David said
with authority.

"The voice of experience?" The introduction of
a six-year-old, even if only by conversation, made it
impossible to keep other things in focus. Tai stepped
back from the door as David opened it.

"Far too much of it. You played sports, what
about you?"

"Two fingers and my nose and bruises that lasted
all season."

"Sounds colorful."

"It was."

A convertible glided toward them as soon as
they stepped outside. Matte black, smooth shape, like
something out of a Bond movie. One rim probably
cost more than Tai's rent for the next two years. And
the driver…. If David could model for Abercrombie,
this guy could be on the *GQ* cover.

Tai's hand automatically came to rest on the small
of David's back as he approached the car. They hadn't
decided—well, David hadn't decided—where he was
headed.

"Sorry to keep you waiting." David went up to
the driver's side.

"No problem. I live to keep hauling your ass out
of trouble." Gavin took a long look at Tai, who felt the
urge to bare his teeth and growl.

David leaned on the driver's door. "See, I knew I
brought meaning to your life. So when I called, I thought
Tai was going to be tied—held—up longer. But—"

"Things got less complicated?" Gavin suggested
through a thin smile.

"Exactly."

"Meaning you're going to get laid, and I drove here for no reason."

"And everyone thinks Chip's the smart Montgomery."

Gavin stared at Tai again.

"Just think," David continued, "you can get to Sergeant Boyfriend that much sooner."

"Beach," Gavin began in a low voice, but whatever he was going to try to say, he abandoned in favor of finishing with "you're lucky you're such an asshole you make me look good by comparison."

"Come on. When have you ever known me to turn down a good time?"

Gavin shook his head. "Never. Especially if it's wearing pants. Or a skirt. And for all I know, a clown costume."

Tai's ears throbbed, then flushed with a steady heat. He knew the dig was for him more than David but couldn't figure out exactly what Gavin was aiming for. Tai brought his fingers up to graze the back of David's neck.

The result was sweet. David straightened, body shifting under that touch. His energy turned toward Tai, away from Gavin.

"Ooo, baby. Those red noses. Big and shiny, pushing forward. Mmmm. I get a boner every time." David slapped a hand on the top of the doorframe. "Say hi to your—to Jamie."

"I'll call you tomorrow." It sounded more like a threat than a promise, but David only waved as Gavin drove away.

"Sorry." David turned to Tai. "He's usually less of a prick. It's not like I haven't done the same for him."

"Gone out of your way to be blown off?"

"Exactly."

But in the car, David retreated again, off somewhere in his head. Tai replayed the conversation with Gavin, and his hands tightened on the steering wheel. "Do you have sex with women?"

"Yes."

Always looking for a good time and the fuck with anyone else. Gavin had been offering Tai a warning. *Today it's you, tomorrow it's... who knows.*

"What about clowns?" His question didn't come out as light as he'd meant it to.

"No. Not really my thing. Is it yours? I didn't see it on the checklist." David abandoned the bantering tone. "I haven't had sex with anyone else since we started this thing. Is that what you want to know?"

What Tai wanted—needed—to know right now was whether *this thing* was like any other in a long line of fascinations for David.

When Tai didn't answer, David went on, "I realize that as"—he let out a long breath—"your submissive, it isn't my business to set rules for you. But I want to tell you I wouldn't expect you to only confine yourself to me. I mean, to have me as your only submissive."

"What if I wanted that from you?"

"You want me to tell you not to be with other people?"

"No."

"Oh." The word was clipped. Sharp. "Well, you're the only Dominant I know."

Tai summed it up. "In other words, you want to keep your options open."

Silence poured into the space between them like morning fog off the harbor.

Tai backed the car into a spot a few houses down from his door and was reaching for the ignition when David said, "I want this. It isn't anything I ever spent time thinking of before, so excuse me if I screw it up sometimes." More softly he added, "Or a lot. If you remember, I told you one of the things I like best is when you take away the responsibility of having to make choices."

Tai turned off the car. With the summer heat still pulsing around them, this conversation would be over soon one way or another. Neither of them could stay in the car long. "I can't order you not to fuck around."

"Why not? You can order me to make an appointment. I'm not saying—I don't mind that you do."

Tai pressed himself back against the seat. "I think you should want to not fuck around."

"I don't know that I do." David put his hand over Tai's shoulder. Was that the first time he'd initiated a touch? "What I do know is that I want things with you, want you to do things with me, to me, I don't even have the words for. And I don't want that with anyone else. I like… submitting to you." There was less of a hesitation on the word this time. "If that means only having sex with you, then I can do that. Hell, I'm hoping you keep me too worn-out for anything else."

Tai opened his door. "Before that, I'm going to have to take Jez out. Do you want to stay in my apartment?"

David climbed out and tried a couple of steps. "My leg feels pretty good right now. Mind if I walk with you?" David's phone went off with a generic ringtone. The uncharacteristic blandness was a brief warning for the tension that came into his face. "I have to take this." He turned away before pulling the phone from his pocket. "Dad?"

Tai wrestled with a desire to stay and find out the cause of that sudden tight jaw, but David's back and the way he had dropped his voice to almost a murmur made it clear he wanted privacy. Tai left him to it and went upstairs, taking a quick sweep of the apartment after greeting Jez, then, leash in hand, peered through the blinds at the front of the apartment to see David still on the sidewalk, shoulders hunched, unmoving. Keeping Jez to her usual routine, Tai walked her to the door and had her sit to get her focused. And to get himself focused.

It should be as easy to control the environment out there as the one in here, but as he knew from training Jez, things never went that smoothly. One moment when his attention shifted and she felt it. One phone call from outside and then another and then it was back to the endless push and pull.

He went down the stairs first, Jez following as she'd been trained, sitting again at the front door as Tai clipped the leash to her collar.

David's conversation was over by the time they approached, the phone gone. David crouched as he always did to greet Jez face-to-face, but she sensed the absence of something in him as Tai did, her tail stub twitching in concern rather than wriggling with joy. After a minute she looked back at him, as if in accusation.

"Bad news?" Tai asked as they started down South Streeper. Might as well bring it up since even the dog knew.

"Just news."

It was almost full dark. Tai decided they'd only do the block. David would have to leave to make his curfew soon enough.

"Your daughter is very cute."

"She is. Though I guess my mother told you I didn't have anything to do with that."

David shrugged. "I think personality plays a lot into a person's attractiveness. And that is nurture, not nature. She lights up a room because she knows she has a lot of people who love her. That happiness makes her beautiful."

All the things he told himself, that his mother and Gina had said about him still being part of Sammie's life, none of it had the impact of David's words. Sammie was who she was because Tai was there, not because he was her real father.

David went on, "Broken wrists aside, she's a lucky kid. Three parents. Security to spare."

"I guess. Though as she gets older, I'm sure she'll be sick of it. I don't think Josh and I will ever be ready to consider her old enough to date."

"She'll need help from her mom and your mom when she gets there, then."

For a second there was a pause in the street noise of cars and stereos and TVs, enough for Tai to hear the tapping of David's cane. He eased back on the pace. Both Sammie and Jez were energetic walking companions, and Tai had managed to forget about David's scarred leg.

The moment of quiet was swallowed up by an SUV with a sound system that echoed from pavement to skull. When the echoes died away, David said, "So why do you call your mom Tina if her name is Kara?"

"It means *mother* in Samoan. She said my father called her *tina la'ititi*—little mother—all the time when she was pregnant with me. And he called me *la'u tama* when I was a baby. He died before I was one, so we use the words to remember him."

"Not a lot of security." David's voice was barely audible over the whine of car brakes from a sudden stop at the corner. They rounded the block.

"No. But Mom was awesome. And I had my mom's dad for a bit, until he died."

"Your father was from Samoa? Have you ever been there?"

"American Samoa. And no." After what had happened with Sammie, he understood now why his mom had cut them off from his father's relatives, could relate to her fears about the pressure of losing him to his father's huge, tight-knit family. But it still felt like half his identity was a shadow, waiting to come to light. "Maybe someday." If he found which of the twelve hundred Tau Fonoti records he'd turned up would lead him to the right family.

"And your mom—"

Tai felt the corner of his lip curl in a smile. He'd take David's hedging over people's blunt *What are you*s any day.

"Is black. You can say it. It's not an insult."

"No, of course not."

"If you were curious, why didn't you ask?"

"Where I grew up, who you're related to is the most important thing about you. I've only ever considered lineage a factor in picking a racehorse."

"So who are you related to?"

"No one worth mentioning." David's voice was flat. They turned back onto South Streeper in silence.

"And I thought the conversation in the car was awkward. Who do you think will win the Davis Cup this year?"

"Tennis isn't really my sport."

"Damn." David's laugh was all air and no joy. "I'll have you know I actually have a reputation for being good at this."

"At what?"

"Small talk. Charm. I've been known to sweep people off their feet."

Tai didn't know why delving into family history—which was apparently painful for both of them—would be considered small talk. But charm? David had that to spare. Thick hair and sun-creased eyes and dimpled chin and an ability to laugh at himself. Not to mention the sweet, yielding submissive under it all. They reached Tai's door. "There's plenty you're damned good at, David."

Good wasn't necessarily the word Tai would have chosen to describe things upstairs. Jez grabbed a nylon bone to chew on in her corner under the AC, but David bounced from hall to living room to kitchen.

"Come here." Tai sat on the couch and looked back at where David was scrutinizing the cabinet over the stove.

"For?"

"Because I asked you to."

"Oh. Are we—?" David's tone shifted from uncertainty to lilting and sly. "What if I don't?"

Not *What if I don't want to*, Tai noticed. He'd see how David intended to play this out. "Your curfew is in two hours, and I want to spend some time with my submissive."

David shrugged and leaned back against the kitchen counter.

Another time, Tai might have enjoyed the challenge or even encouraged it with a teasing response, but after everything that had happened, he'd wanted to lose himself in the way David opened to him, let Tai reach in to take them both out of their heads and back into that space where the connection burned away everything else.

Real resistance is always purposeful. And never convenient. Nic had had plenty to say on that subject. But for the subs Tai had played with for a few hours, it had only ever been part of the scene, a make-me attitude part of what got them off.

Tai deepened his voice. "David, you will go into the bedroom, take off all your clothes, and wait for me." After a moment of staring David down, Tai turned away, taking out his phone to stare blankly at the home screen.

The air behind him was alive, full, swelling with the pressure of whatever was driving David so hard. The minute Tai had decided to wait ticked by, stretching, growing heavier. Then it crashed as David's sandal flew to land in Tai's range of vision, rolling to a stop under the coffee table. Jez jerked up her head. David's other sandal landed sole down and skated under the couch.

Jez shook her head until her ears flopped, then got stiffly to her feet and stalked into the bedroom, carrying her bone.

In the silence that followed, Tai heard her settle in her crate.

David's shorts came next. Balled up, they sailed over Tai's head to hit the coffee table and tumble off

the end. The guy had excellent aim. His shirt landed
on Tai's shoulder, soft, rich with the smell of David's
body. Sweat and sex and the faint rain-sweet echo of
his aftershave.

Tai awaited the next move. David took the long
way around, to the kitchen end of the sofa, and then
strolled between the coffee table and the TV, around
the side where Tai was sitting. Just as David was
past him, Tai stood, snatched a wrist, and jerked him
back. He was about to flip him over the couch arm
and spank the brat out of him when he remembered.
He sat back down, dragging David close, pinning him
against chest and thighs so he sat on Tai's lap.

"Tell me what's going on."

"You said get naked. I got naked." David didn't
struggle, but he held himself tense.

"I told you to go into the bedroom first."

"Same result."

With one arm keeping David tight and close, Tai
grabbed David's chin, turning his head so their eyes
met. "You are being disrespectful and challenging me."

"Yes."

At least it was clear David knew what he was doing. "Tell me why."

David shrugged as much as Tai's hold permitted.
"What are you going to do about it?" David yanked
his chin out of Tai's grip.

If he knew David better, the punishment would
be to deny him the punishment he was so sullenly demanding. But there was something different working
here.

An intensity inside him as still and weighted as
the eye of a hurricane, breath held for the next explosion. It wasn't difficult to track where the storm had

started. Would the mention of his father drive David deeper inward or shatter the potential for them to get somewhere?

"It sounds like you're asking me to punish you."

"You keep talking about it. But you never do anything."

"And I told you I would decide when. Now I want you to tell me why you are acting like this."

David gave him a look, eyes half-lidded with boredom, mouth and nose pinched in contempt, as if it was all too difficult for Tai to understand. He dumped David onto the cushion. "Do you have any allergies? Anything your skin reacts to?"

"No."

Tai went into his closet. Impact was out, but there were other sensations.

He came back and put the empty burlap bag on the seat of his desk chair. David hadn't moved, except to right himself into a slouch. Pulling a few sheets from the printer, Tai moved his keyboard out of the way and set up paper and pen on the desk. Rather than turn this part into a battle, he tugged David to his feet and led him to the chair.

"You understand you still—"

David cut him off with a sneered, "Have a safe-word. I get it."

"Good. Sit down." Tai pushed him onto the burlap. "We'll start with one hundred."

"One hundred what?"

Tai leaned over, picked up the pen, and wrote *I trust and respect you, Sir*. "One hundred times. The whole sentence at once. Both of your hands stay on the desk." He took David's wrists and lifted both onto the desk. "Start now."

David picked up the pen and moved it slowly through the first repetition. He looked up as if expecting something from Tai, but he only watched until David started the next one. As he wrote, Tai went into the kitchen and found the spray bottle he'd used to get Jez's attention when he was training her, refilled it from the tap, and came back in.

David twisted his head around to look.

"Focus on your work."

David pressed the pen harder through the third line.

"Spread your legs," Tai said as he reached for the edge of the rough cloth on the seat. After David complied, Tai tucked the material over David's balls and dick, then sprayed it with water to give it weight enough to stick. David jumped as the first round of drops hit. The cold and clammy part was a bonus. It should encourage him to complete his task in a hurry. And maybe help him think before asking for this again.

Tai sat back on the couch. "Keep going. If you don't finish before you have to leave, we'll do this tomorrow. And we'll start at number one."

Chapter Fourteen

BEACH TRACED over the *I* in his next line, carving deeper into the paper. This was stupid. Uncomfortable, childish and stupid. Which was pretty much punishment in a nutshell. Wasn't that the whole penal system too? You were naughty, you got caught, publicly scolded, and made to suffer in uncomfortable situations with fewer rights than a child.

The penal system that Beach would be extremely familiar with if the DA was able to make the felony charge stick.

Exactly how much fucking help do you think you'll be able to give me from jail? his father had said on the phone. *For once, I thought I could depend on you. That you could be the son I needed.*

Beach dashed off the rest of the pointless phrase. He should have known from the homework of a checklist that all this D/s stuff was too much like school.

With the addition of a damp, *itchy* diaper. He knew exactly what he'd been doing, poking at Tai. Begging for something to stop the maddening urge to do the first thing Beach could think of that would violate the damned probation. Not that he needed the high from risk or drugs; he needed to know he was still who he'd always been. The life of the party, the man people wanted to be around. Not the complicated problem, a freak who showed up at the emergency room with a light bulb up his ass, the way he saw himself reflected in Gavin's eyes. Or as incompetent and useless as his father saw him, until the man needed something.

Just call your uncle. Is that too much fucking responsibility for you, David?

He tilted his hips to press his balls harder against the scratchy fibers. If he ground down enough, focused on that unpleasant prickle, maybe he could stop feeling like his skin was on wrong. Tai was supposed to give Beach that. Hold him here. Shove him into a cold shower, force pain and pleasure into him with his hands, his cock, his mouth, and his strength.

Even the wadded burlap, with the burn that spread from taint to ass to dick, would have been okay, good even, if he knew it was something for Tai. Beach could deal with the itch that had him squeezing his left hand hard against the desk to keep from digging and shoving the cloth away. Hell, maybe it would turn him on if he knew Tai was paying attention. If he seemed to care.

But he moved around the apartment silently, as if he were alone. Puttering in the kitchen, bathroom, bedroom. How long had Beach been staring at the pointless words on the paper?

He threw down the pen.

"Finished?" Tai was immediately at Beach's shoulder.

"I can't."

Tai looked down at him. "You already made your choice when you threw your shoes. You added to it by refusing to explain why. This is what you asked for."

Unless you ask for it. "No. It isn't." Beach moistened his suddenly dry lips and then said the words in a rush. "I want you to spank me."

The words hung there long enough for Beach's lips to dry out. Tai studied him, as if waiting for Beach to take it back with a *just kidding*.

When Beach licked his lips again, Tai lifted him out of the chair and the burlap and sat on the couch with Beach standing next to him.

"Get over my lap."

Beach wasn't sure how he'd expected it would go down when his brain seized on something that would guarantee Tai couldn't ignore him. It wasn't as if Beach had never been spanked. There had been a few bruising encounters with fraternity paddles during hazing, but the alcohol blurred the edges of those memories. Probably more familiar was the occasional swat on the ass during sex. Women had done it from a missionary position, and men from doggy style. He hadn't minded the sting, the spread of warmth. But this was different from either. First, there was the whole idea of punishment versus sex, emphasized by Tai being dressed and Beach naked. But there was a huge gap between sex slaps and his other understanding of corporal punishment, which involved a peach tree and bending over a back-porch railing.

Staring at the dark green material of Tai's cargo shorts, Beach tried to will himself to comply with Tai's demand. This would be much easier if Tai dragged Beach where he was supposed to be. He glanced up at Tai's face. No anger there, no distance either, his eyes alight with whatever it was that made Beach yearn toward him, want to get back to that place where being open and ready was easy. Not this gut-knotting tangle of fear and frustration.

"You need to show me this is what you want. That you accept what's going to happen."

When Beach didn't move, Tai's deep, dominant voice solved the problem. "Now, David."

It was more awkward than Beach could have imagined, leaning down and climbing across Tai's lap. Beach's junk was in the way until he got it dangling in the space between Tai's concrete-hard thighs. Beach's feet stayed on the floor, his torso and sweaty hands stretched across the seat cushions, pulse loud as the bass of a club speaker in his ears, heart so high and swollen in his chest he was surprised he could still breathe. "What about sound? Neighbors?" he had to ask.

Over Beach's shoulder, the television buzzed to life. A few clicks and it landed on something with a laugh track rolling every few seconds.

Beach strained to hear the dialogue, to figure out what it was, but the blood in his ears was too loud. No matter how he tried to distract himself, all his senses kept focusing on his ass. On the way Tai had raised his knee so Beach's ass was tilted up higher for whatever Tai was about to do.

Spank him. *Get your head around that, Beach. He's going to hit you. And you asked him to do it.*

Hyperawareness warned him, a shift in air currents across his ass had him tensing, but all Tai did was place a warm palm on Beach's cheeks and start rubbing. The massage went down under the curve that met his thighs, fingers dipping lightly into the crack, and Beach's dick woke up to notice the friction of a fold in the cotton of Tai's shorts.

"Do you feel secure?"

For an instant Beach had thought Tai was going to ask if he was comfortable, and a nervous laugh blew past his lips. Comfortable, no. Secure? Tai's non-ass-massaging hand held Beach tight at the waist, close to Tai's hips. He didn't feel like he was going to fall, so he guessed secure was the right answer.

"Yes."

A smack landed hard and sharp, the imprint of Tai's hand written in sizzling nerve endings. "Yes what?"

"Yes, Sir."

Tai's hand rubbed the site of impact, turning the burn pleasant.

But that wasn't what Beach was here for, though he could see what Eli had been talking about. Under the right circumstances it wouldn't be a bad warm-up for sex. The way Tai's hand spread out the sensation made Beach's dick strain for more friction.

But as his body started to shift into arousal, shame coiled around his guts. What was wrong with him that something that scared him as much as this did made him want to get off? And sex, even as amazing as it was with Tai, wasn't going to be enough to fix this crazy urge rising in his chest. The need to tear free of everything holding him here.

"So is this foreplay or punishment? Sir."

The sound from Tai might have been a laugh or a growl. Beach felt the vibration more than heard it. Then Tai's grip tightened around Beach's waist, and it started.

No rhythm or pattern, only the slam of Tai's palm into Beach's ass. Some slaps stung, some thudded, and always more. Heat spreading into his skin, aching deep underneath.

It hurt, but not in a way Beach couldn't handle. Every so often Tai would nail the same spot three or four times with enough force to make Beach wince, but right when Beach felt like he had to jerk away from it, Tai would leave that spot alone. All the tension in Beach's stomach melted. This was nothing like slices of skin being stripped away by the switch, his silent, disgusted uncle behind him. It was Tai. His strength everywhere, pushing the sensation Beach craved into him while keeping him safe and anchored.

Much better than the stupid burlap diaper and the dull repetition of words on a page. "Good," Tai murmured, barely audible over the background noise of one-liners and laugh tracks. He pressed his forearm against the small of Beach's back. "That's it." Beach let the pressure tip his hips, his ass lifting toward Tai's hand.

"Yes," Tai encouraged, landing a few smacks near the tops of Beach's thighs, a new kind of sting, but also one that made his dick fill.

Tai stopped spanking and rubbed. It made the burn and sting spread out, the flesh absorbing the pain until it didn't hurt anymore, leaving a tingle like arousal over tight, hot skin. Beach would love to get fucked now, transfer that ache into the scrape and stretch of Tai's dick driving in, his hips smacking into Beach's ass. He wouldn't even mind a few more cracks of Tai's hand to keep the warmth lasting longer.

"That's the warm-up, David."

Beach had gotten lost in a fantasy of being fucked and smacked until he came, so Tai's words didn't make a lot of sense. *Huh* didn't seem to be the right answer, so he went with something safer. "Yes, Sir."

"What are you being punished for?"

"Throwing my shoes and clothes?"

"We'll start there. One minute." Tai handed his phone to Beach with the timer function set to a minute. "Press Start when you're ready."

All the tension and dread came rushing back as Beach stared at the screen with the 1:00 blinking back at him. He didn't want to press Start. He was pretty sure he wanted to press End.

"Do you have something to add?" Tai said.

Beach had known he was asking for punishment when he kicked his sandal into the living room. And he'd very specifically asked to be spanked. He'd said he liked having his choices taken away. Tai had given him all that. There wasn't anything to say.

"No, Sir." Beach pressed Start.

Tai spanked. His hand thudded on Beach's already sensitive skin, like boiling water on a sunburn. At least he thought it was Tai's hand. It was hard enough, dense enough to be a canoe paddle, but Beach hadn't seen him get a weapon. His breath rushed out of his lungs, eyes squeezing shut at the explosion of pain from the solid, rapid slaps. He sucked in a breath and opened his eyes. Fifty seconds left. Fifty? He couldn't lie here and take this for fifty more seconds.

He didn't make a conscious decision about it. His body did. One hand reached back to protect his ass while his hips tried to flop him out of the way of the blows that kept ratcheting the pain higher and higher. Tai caught Beach's hand and pinned it to his back, and all the flopping did was get the swats to land on the more sensitive sides of his hips where there was no cushioning. And there were still thirty seconds to go.

"I can't." His voice sounded like he'd run up twenty stories.

Tai kept Beach's hand clamped against his back but shifted them so Beach was folded over one leg, the other trapping him in place, and all the time that heavy hand kept crashing into his skin. Tai attacked the spot at the crease of Beach's thighs now. Hard and steady, the same spot until his eyes watered and his teeth ground together.

"Please," he hissed out, but he might as well have been begging the seconds to suddenly tick by because Tai didn't stop, didn't ease up. Fifteen. How could there still be time left?

The smacks came and the pain built and his breath rasped against his ears. When the alarm buzzed, Beach yelled, "Time," but Tai was already rubbing, much more gently now.

"Okay. It's okay." Tai kept repeating it, but it was almost impossible to hear over the force of Beach's breathing. The hand on his back was free, but he was too tired to move it.

Tai's hand slid down Beach's back, making him aware of how slick with sweat he was. "How are you?"

His ass was hot and swollen, and his throat ached from panting so hard. But the pain that had been impossible to think of enduring for another second was gone. "I'll live. Sir."

Tai chuckled, fingers tickling across Beach's ass. His dick had gone soft, but the teasing touch made blood throb at the base again.

"Why were you spanked, David?"

Beach remembered the shower. How he didn't get out until he found the right answer. "For challenging you, Sir."

"Good." Tai took his phone back. "There's another behavior we have to address. Your disrespect."

"I take it back. I'm sorry, Sir." It wasn't only to avoid what he already knew was coming.

He was sorry. Sorry that he'd been so absorbed in his bad mood that he'd been rude.

"Thank you, David." Tai's finger stroked through Beach's hair. But when Tai handed back the phone, there was another minute on the timer.

"I don't think I can take it." A tremble vibrated through Beach's body. He knew the pain didn't last long, as bad as it seemed while it was going on. It was hardly unbearable torture. Most days, his leg hurt worse than his ass did now.

"You don't have a choice."

But in the way back of his mind he knew he did. One simple word would stop it.

Everything about what Tai was going to do right now was Beach's choice.

"I'll hold your hands for you again," Tai said, "but I need you to press Start to show me you accept this."

Beach nodded and tapped the screen. The pain was different this time. Sharp stings, like Tai was finding new nerve endings to send the screaming message to Beach's brain to make it stop. Like it had last time, his hand obeyed the instinct and shot back, and Tai caught it.

Fifty-five seconds left and already Beach's eyes were watering. What the hell had he been thinking? It was much worse. He was insane. His body went into a full-on rebellion, bucking and shifting away from the relentless smack of Tai's hand.

Red. That one single word grew huge at the back of his brain. All the promise in it. No more pain. Get out of jail free. Skip over the consequences.

Tai adjusted his grip, taking away even an ability to squirm, and then his hand fell on Beach's ass with enough force that everything up to now had been a love tap. Beach couldn't think. Couldn't watch the timer. Couldn't do anything but feel pain bursting again and again on his skin. His body tensed like he was heading into an orgasm, and then he collapsed onto Tai and just took it.

The pain had stopped, the timer was buzzing, and Tai was whispering "I know" over and over. Beach realized it was because he kept whispering "I'm sorry" into the cushion.

Tai lifted Beach to place him on his lap. It was more childish than being across Tai's knee, and Beach's ass wasn't at all happy about the pressure from Tai's quads, but the hard arms around Beach made everything else bullshit.

"Feel better?"

It should have been an incredibly stupid question. But he did. He felt calm, light, energized, like standing on the flybridge and opening the throttle on a perfect day at sea.

No destination, open space all around him.

"Yes. Thank you, Sir." Beach couldn't help a smile as he added, "How's your hand?"

Tai brushed a soft laugh into Beach's ear. "Sore, thank you." After a quick kiss, Tai took Beach's chin in his hand. "We're not done yet."

Beach's ass throbbed in time with his heart, but the rest of him felt so good he didn't care. "Okay."

"Tell me why we needed to do this."

"I challenged you and was disrespectful."

"That's not what I asked you, David."

A hard spanking must be better than sodium pentothal because Beach blurted "My father" before he had time to think about what he was going to say. The doubts slithered back in, filling him with the need to push it all someplace where he didn't have to think about it.

He shifted his ass on Tai's legs, settling more weight on it so pain echoed along his nerves. It gave him some of that floating feeling back.

Tai didn't rush him.

"It's complicated and boring. But my father is in some trouble. And he reminded me that since I may be in jail soon, I won't be in a position to help him. I have to do him a favor."

"What kind of favor?"

"My uncle isn't returning my father's calls. He wants me to call him."

"Okay."

Beach knew on the surface it sounded like an incredibly minor thing to have thrown a tantrum over. And it was obvious now that was what he'd done. It really wouldn't be that awful to have to call Uncle Sinclair and find out why he'd stopped sending money to Dad. Not his favorite thing in the world, but not worth acting like an asshole over.

"So tomorrow, you need to make the appointment for your physical therapy and call your uncle."

"Yes, Sir."

"Good." Tai kissed him.

Beach let out a long breath. "I'm ready."

Tai tipped his head.

"You said we weren't done. And you, uh, spanked me for challenging you and being disrespectful. And now for"—he remembered the words Tai had given him to write out—"not trusting you with why I was being such a dick."

Tai held Beach's face and kissed him hard. "I'm proud of you, David."

"But you're going to spank me more." Beach had to grin when he said it.

Tai eased Beach to his feet then led him to the back of the couch. "Bend over it until your feet come off the floor."

A sensation like when the bottom dropped out of a wave hit Beach's stomach as he hung suspended, ass burning from nothing but the flow of air.

"It's going to be one spank at a time. And after each you need to tell me why you're here."

Beach nodded and bit his tongue to keep from asking how many. It was probably easier if he didn't know.

He flinched when Tai rested his hand lightly just above Beach's ass, then the stroke hit, reigniting every single inch of pain on his skin. As he blew out his air, he remembered he was supposed to say something. "I will trust you, Sir."

He'd barely finished the words when the next blow forced the air out of his lungs. "I will trust you, Sir."

"Good." Tai's hand on his back soothed and petted, but he still slammed the message into and out of

Beach eight more times. It got harder and harder to put the words in the right order, and the requirement kept him coming back to process the pain every time.

Tai turned Beach around and hugged him, hands stroking his back and squeezing his ass. "Good boy. I'm so proud of you."

Beach sagged against him, muscles shaking with exhaustion.

"Sit, or stand if you want, while I get you some juice."

Using the couch for balance, Beach made his way around and planted himself on the cushion, wincing as his weight pressed him down but still liking the way the echo of heat made him feel. Quiet. Free.

Tai sat next to him and handed over the juice. Beach raised his eyebrows at the cherry-bright reddened palm.

"Yes," Tai said. "That's about what color your ass is. But I don't think it will bruise. I was going for more of a sting, so I didn't hit you that hard until the last few."

Beach didn't want to think about what *hard* would mean. But after sucking down half the glass, curiosity got the better of him. "And was that as hard as you—I mean, full strength?"

There was a quirk, barely a twitch at the corner of Tai's mouth and almost hidden by his goatee. "No."

Not even close was the implicit end to that statement. Beach shifted on the couch as he tried to find a comfortable spot. That corner of Tai's mouth threatened a smile.

"Sadist." Beach knocked back the rest of the juice with only a minor regret that there wasn't any vodka in it. It was all he could do to handle himself with Tai sober. Who knew what kind of trouble he'd get into with a little fermented lubrication?

"Actually, no." Tai spread his hands at his hips.

Beach looked over, down. Other than the usual ample evidence of Tai's equipment, there was no bulge of arousal. Tai took the glass from Beach's hand and then pulled Beach back onto those hard thighs. Beach winced, and Tai buried a chuckle in the skin of Beach's neck.

"It turns me on that you let me. That you accept me being in charge. And yeah, handling your ass, looking at it getting red, that definitely lights a fire. But not the idea of dealing pain just as pain."

"So pain with a purpose?" Beach shifted so he straddled Tai's lap, and the ache from the shuddering down his shinbone was far worse than the heavy, hot feeling in his ass.

"Yes. And doing that to yourself doesn't have a purpose." Tai lifted Beach and spun him, dropping his ass back down over Tai's lap, legs dangling to the sides. Tai tucked his chin over Beach's shoulder as the strong arms wrapped around his waist, the hard chest pressed into his back, and his ass throbbed and prickled from the solid weight of them together.

"You earned a sore butt, David."

"Yes, Sir." He wasn't agreeing to avoid an argument. The echo of the pain, the promise in the strength holding him here, the strength that could make him take more, feel more. It was exactly why Dav—Beach felt so content to simply be here. He wasn't anticipating anything, wishing he was anywhere else. He sank deeper into Tai's hold, aware of every sensation and perfectly at peace with them.

He shut his eyes to block out the television, to concentrate more on the beat of Tai's heart against Beach's back.

The organ dirge of Beach's curfew alarm made panic shoot through him. He jumped, mouth full of a sour, metallic taste, body shivering. Tai squeezed him and then slid him onto the couch.

"I'll get it."

As full and content as Beach had been a second ago, it was gone. He was hanging, stretched thin and empty across space, heart racing above a rolling stomach, pounding like the one time he'd tried one of Westie's "study aids" and learned that speed and Beach were a bad match.

The funeral chords cut off.

"David, what's wrong? Are you dropping?"

"No." Not unless you counted being wrapped up by those muscular, inked arms an addiction and this as a withdrawal. "But…." He was terrified to get through the rest of that sentence. He'd hit on more people than he wanted to count and had more than his fair share of polite or rude rejections. Yet pushing this simple request past his lips seemed like the biggest risk of his life. He rolled his ankles, staring down at them, then looked up to face Tai. "Would you spend the night with me?"

Chapter Fifteen

DAVID EXPECTED a no. Tai read it in the dip of David's shoulders, the flicker at the corners of his eyes, the flatness of his smile.

Tai had been about to suggest David take a shower and slide into Tai's bed where he could show how much he appreciated what David had given when the phone went off. The funeral music was a fitting choice.

Until the alarm sounded, it had been easy for Tai to forget about David's curfew. Forget anything but how amazing it had been for David to offer himself, to push past his fear. Something had shifted in him, and Tai didn't want to do anything but wrap himself around David, taste and touch every bit of this new connection between them. He didn't know how he could possibly go to work the next day and not have David filling his head and his dick. The chance to have him in bed all night wasn't something Tai was going to turn down.

David sweetened the offer before Tai could respond. "Jez is welcome too, of course."

Tai stepped forward and kissed him. "Then I guess I'll come along to keep her company."

IN THE semidark of David's bedroom, Tai opened his throat and took David's cock deeper, squeezing his ass, while David tried desperately to stay as quiet and still against his mattress as Tai had ordered him to be.

A ragged moan slipped past the fist David had crammed in his mouth, and Tai let David slide free with a last lick on the head. This groan was louder, provoking a sigh from Jez, who had finally stopped pacing around her new surroundings and fallen asleep on the blanket David had put down for her.

Tai climbed up and straddled David's waist. "Shhh. If she wakes up, she'll need to go out and water the tires of the Mercedes that stole your spot again."

David's smothered laugh shook against Tai's muscles. Jez wasn't the only one they were trying to stay quiet for. David's houseguest had slammed his way around the kitchen and living area twenty minutes ago. It wasn't until the fourth hoarse whisper of "Beach, you still up?" went unanswered that Clayton gave up.

Rocking against David, cock enjoying the friction of the hair trail below his sternum, Tai murmured, "She'll wake up and he'll wake up and I'll never finish what I was doing."

"Please." David breathed it out.

Tai leaned down. "Please what?"

"Please don't stop."

Tai pinched one of David's nipples, hard.

"Sir," David added quickly, a soft smile on his face.

God, he was so beautiful like that. Not only in the way he'd lucked out in the genetic lottery, but here, like this. Every time he got that blissed-out look of submission on his face. The harbor lights shone through the balcony doors, streaming across the bed, bands of brightness across David's face and chest. He fought hard to keep his eyes open.

Because Tai had told David to watch.

The constant battle with his eyelids, focus fading and coming back into his eyes as Tai reached behind to stroke David's cock, was such a small piece of surrender. Each time David's eyes fixed on Tai's, heat bloomed under his skin, flowing out from his chest like lava to catch heavy and thick in his throat. Until he was the one who wanted to look away, hide that he'd been stripped to nothing but the need to bury that heat inside David. To find belonging in the acceptance David's obedience offered.

He yielded to it, dropping his full weight onto David, sucking a bite into his shoulder, working their dicks together with hard snaps from hips and thighs. David's hands had stayed up by his head where Tai put them, but now they clenched into fists, tendons popping on the wrists. Tai circled his fingers around those bones and veins and muscles, tighter than a cuff. He wanted inside, but he couldn't stop, couldn't wait for condom and lube, couldn't stand all that time not touching, owning. He took David's mouth, hard, deep tongue thrusts. David gave it, hips open, tilting and arching for more friction, a frantic, eager lick into Tai's mouth, wrists jerking in Tai's grip.

Tai lifted his head.

"Please, Sir. Please let me touch you."

David's fingers, his hands sliding all over Tai's back, gripping his ass to drag up more pleasure from the grind. Yeah, he'd like that. But they both wanted this more.

"You'll take what I give you."

More than the whispered agreement, Tai felt the answer in the hot pulse of fluid from David's dick as they moved together. David's neck arched back, skull a bare inch from the wooden headboard. Tai licked up the exposed throat, teeth closing on the stubble-rough jaw still tasting of soap from their quick shower.

"Don't close your eyes."

David looked back at him, eyelids pinned open.

"That's it. You want to be good for me, right, David?"

"Yes, Sir. Fuck me. Please." David rocked up into the rut of Tai's hips.

"No. You're mine. You don't get to decide. If I want to suck your cock or fuck your ass or grind off on you and leave you hungry, I will."

David's answer was a long hissed *s*, between tight teeth.

"Watch." Tai humped, letting the heat and friction and power of it build.

David's eyes flickered and then opened, mouth slack, panting. He had that look again.

Absolute surrender, like he was drunk with it. It pushed Tai over the edge.

"God, yes." He sprang to his knees. "Watch me come all over you, boy." He took his cock in his hand to finish it, not needing much. A tight, hot pressure in his balls and then he went up and over, coating David's chest with ropy shots. Long, shuddering blasts that emptied him and left him hunched and shaking.

David's eyes stayed on him, tongue wetting his lips until they shone like the streaks on his chest in the light from the window, his dick hard, straining up against his stomach.

Tai squeezed out an aftershock, rubbing the head of his dick in a pool of come on David's belly. "Good boy. So good."

David's tongue flickered back over his lips. Tai smiled and bent to lap come off one of David's nipples. Licking and sucking up to his ear, Tai murmured, "You should get a reward."

David's mouth stayed closed, but a whine escaped his lips.

"And I'll decide what that is." Tai sucked another bite right behind David's ear, earning an answering pant and tremble. After dropping a kiss on each of David's wrists, Tai stroked his beard across them and kissed them again, teasing the throbbing vein with his tongue. "Leave your hands right there."

Crouching between David's legs, Tai palmed David's ass and lifted him, shoulders keeping his legs open wide, fingers pulling his cheeks apart for a flick of tongue on his hole. David's muscles jumped, squeezing, and then he relaxed. Oh yeah, Tai had to put a spreader bar on the schedule, watch David's face as he gave in to that helplessness. Tai swept his tongue along the crack, tasting the mix of shower damp and sex sweat. He teased the rim, over and over, until David's legs shook, and then traced the shape of his balls, leaving his poor cock straining into the air.

Tai went back to the rough-edged hole, kissing and sucking, tiny stabs of his tongue that made David buck into Tai's grip. He dug his fingers into David's glutes and pushed harder against the ring of muscle. There was no sound in the room but the harsh grate of their breath and the wet noise from spit and flesh. Tai added a hum into David's tight skin, and he bucked and jerked.

"I can't take it." David's hoarse whisper curled low in Tai's gut. He drank it in with more pressure, thumbs spreading David wide enough to let Tai barely scrape with his teeth.

The strangled sound in response made him raise his head to see David cram his fist into his mouth.

"You don't have a choice, boy." Tai lowered his head, losing himself in texture and taste and every attempt David made to control his body's reactions to Tai's mouth.

David's muscles kept convulsing, even after Tai lowered him to the mattress. "Open your eyes." Tai demanded, pressing into David's ass with one finger.

David managed for an instant, but it turned to a blink as Tai found the point inside he was looking for and started rubbing.

David's hands went to his hair and tugged it, fingers twisting to hang on to something. "You can come now, David."

"I can't."

"You will." Tai leaned in and swallowed David's dick, pulled off and then down again to the root, working him between tongue and palate.

"Fuck. Shit. God." The groan was loud, but David was coming and Tai wasn't stopping until he'd sucked him dry.

David's ass crushed Tai's finger, then pulsed as the first spurt hit Tai's throat, filling his mouth and spilling past his lips faster than he could drink it down. As soon as he released him, David curled into a little ball on his side and Tai wrapped himself around him. "Okay, baby?"

"Jesus, yes." David grabbed Tai's arm, dragging him closer. A shiver had Tai raising his head to look into David's face.

"An aftershock." David patted his cheek. "But I wouldn't mind…."

"Go ahead." Tai kissed David's ear.

"Can we stay like this till I fall asleep?"

"Sure." Every fucking night would be just fine with Tai.

TAI STILL had an hour to sleep when his bladder forced him awake, out of David's bed and into the bathroom. He was going to crawl back into that warm, sleepy space when a human yelp and confused woof hit his ears at the same time.

"Holy shit. What the—Beach?"

Tai slid into the living area right as Jez skidded into his shins. Tai had to slap his hands onto the coffee table to keep from falling into David's houseguest, who was clutching a blanket around his chest like a terrified virgin.

"Who the hell—Beach?" Clayton gripped the blanket tighter. His thin, dirty-blond hair stuck out from his scalp, but whether that was fear or just really obnoxious bedhead was hard to say.

Jez came back to butt Tai's knees with her head with an anxious whine. "What did you do to my dog?"

Clayton gathered the blanket tighter, eyes growing wider, the whites glowing in the dawn light. "N-nothing. I—He—stuck his nose in my face and—I would never hurt a dog." He managed to sound indignant and frightened in the same breath. "Beach?" Clayton's gaze shifted to scan Tai from head to foot, forcing the realization that he was towering over the man, tackle swinging in the breeze.

Tai straightened, but that only put his equipment at eye level, and damned if he was going to cover up like he'd done something wrong. He looked back at Jez. With Tai between her and the stranger, she was sitting, stub wriggling, jaw open. "It's not funny," Tai told her.

"Yeah. It kind of is." David strolled out of his bedroom, and apparently he didn't see the need to cover up either.

"Beach," Clayton muttered and then stared down at his blanket-covered knees. "For Christ's sake."

"Clayton." David put a hand on Tai's back. "I see you've met Tai. And Jezebel."

David's matter-of-fact introduction made Tai feel he should offer his hand, but they'd kind of moved past that moment.

Clayton reached around to rub the back of his neck, adding more chaos to his hair. "You, uh, didn't mention you'd be having another guest."

"I didn't know I would be." David looked at Tai and grinned, and if they didn't get back to the bedroom, Clayton was going to get more of an eyeful than he'd already had.

Clayton rooted around on the floor and came up with a T-shirt, which he jerked over his head, finally letting the blanket fall away. "So, is he—that is—is this your—?"

Was it possible Clayton didn't know David was bisexual? Assuming that was what David meant when he said he had sex with women.

David's grin got impossibly wide. "He's my Dominant."

Chapter Sixteen

IN THE doorway of his apartment, Beach bent down to give Jez a good rub behind the ears in good-bye before standing to offer a different sort of rub to her human. He wished he hadn't conceded a pair of boxers and a shirt to Clayton's modesty, or the contact would have been far more interesting.

When Beach reached for Tai's face to kiss him, Tai caught Beach's hands before they landed on his jaw, lacing their fingers together, arms outstretched.

"I'm not so easily had for an ear rub," Tai murmured, his gaze flicking over Beach's shoulder to where Clayton puttered around the kitchen like some demented duenna.

"That's because you've never had one of mine. Tell him, Jez." At the mention of her name, she bumped their legs.

"Sit."

Beach knew that was aimed at the dog, but the strong voice made him want to crawl right inside the man in front of him.

"And you behave." Tai's demand rumbled along Beach's bones.

Beach adopted a hypnotized monotone. "Yessir." He didn't know the last time he'd felt this kind of happy, free. Before the trip off the bridge he still couldn't remember, and possibly before that.

Tai stared down. "Call for your PT appointment. And call your uncle."

Not even the reminder of that duty could chase away the feeling that kept making Beach smile, that made a laugh threaten to burst out of his throat for no reason than that it felt so damned good.

"Sore anywhere?" Tai breathed the words close to Beach's ear.

"Some beard burn." Beach grinned, then leaned away so Tai could see the accompanying wink.

"Sorry about this." Tai swung one pair of their linked hands between them and lifted Beach's bruised wrist for a delicate kiss.

"Didn't mind at the time." Though, when Beach had noticed the dark imprints as he dressed, he'd opted for something with long sleeves.

Tai brought the opposite wrist to his mouth. The soft pressure from his lips and the trace of his tongue made Beach shiver, and not only because of the tingle on an overlooked erogenous zone. Tai was hard enough, strong enough to make those marks, and gentle enough to soothe them the next day. Like when he'd been… spanking Beach.

"Hmm." Tai made the skin vibrate, prickle under the hair of his beard. "If you don't want to find out how long two minutes can be"—he released Beach's hand, stepped back, and clipped the leash to Jez's collar—"you won't forget to make those phone calls."

He was gone, but Beach's good mood wasn't. Even with the face Clayton pulled as the door closed behind Tai.

"Acts god-awfully like a policeman."

"No. Gavin's the one dating a cop."

Clayton's gape put fresh-caught carp to shame. "Montgomery?"

"That's the one."

"Something in the water?"

Beach turned away from the fridge. "What?"

"Really? Him? That's your type?"

"I thought we established I don't have a type. I enjoy variety."

"Like in having a Dominant. Do y'all get in the leather stuff for that?"

God bless internet search engines. But Clayton's question only provoked a smile and a shrug, unlike the discomfort from Gavin's overbearing scrutiny. Clayton's curiosity came across as if Beach had ordered something bizarre in a restaurant that Clayton was trying to be brave enough to try.

"Costumes are optional."

"But he—ah—bosses you around?" Clayton tugged on an ear.

"With my permission."

"So just theatrical, then." Clayton nodded, looking as satisfied as if someone had offered to pick up the tab. Again.

It was easier to let him think it. Easier to think of it that way himself. What happened between Beach and Tai was like a play. Unscripted, but still for pretend. Except when it was happening, Beach wasn't faking giving up everything because Tai asked him. And feeling like this now. Like he'd thrown all the ballast overboard and was riding so high in the water he could fly. This was real. It wasn't alcohol or some other chemical shift in his brain. Hell, he hadn't even had coffee.

"Well then." Clayton slung his ass onto one of the barstools as if he'd been having a tough time standing and thinking at the same time. "Meant to tell you last night. Talked to Iris."

"Oh?" Beach tried not to spook him. He'd heard from a cousin about an Earnshaw who had stopped by for a drink and didn't leave for three years.

"Yeah. Calmed down some. So, figure to shove off today. 'Bout eleven." Beach nodded and concealed his relief in a big glass of orange juice. "Unless, that is…?"

Beach would have been happy to supply Clayton with the rest of his sentence and an answer but didn't have any idea where it was headed. He put down his glass and opened his hands in encouragement.

"You need the company?"

"Not at all." Damn, he'd said that a little fast for civility. In compensation, and to ensure a swift departure, he added, "It's fine. I'm fine. Thank you, though. I can drop you by the marina."

DOWN AT the Harbor Lights Marina, the thick summer heat cooked the familiar brackish and oily reek of the water into something powerful, with a side of fishiness that had Tai wrinkling his nose. David was exactly where his text had said he was, Dock G, Slip 17, though Tai wondered how David managed to keep his balance walking with a cane on the bobbing slats of wood. But he was doing fine. Looking fine. Every bit of him glowing in the solid, hot noon sun bouncing off the water.

"So he's gone?" Tai asked as he got closer, wishing he could lose the rest of the smells in a deep breath of David's neck.

David pointed at a shining spot dancing along with other shining spots out in the harbor, then placed a hand over his heart to clutch his shirt and sighed in exaggerated relief. "It was touch and go for a bit. Had to send him for some dutch courage in the lounge over there." He nodded at the hotel and bar that lent their names to the wharf.

Tai gripped the dock post against a blast of anger. "And then you sent him out driving a boat?"

David went still. Not that he'd been fidgeting. But the energy that had seemed to bounce off him like the July heat shrank down. As Tai blinked in the too-bright light, he got an afterimage against his lids, a negative imprint of the man in front of him, dark and light in the wrong places.

"I didn't put a gun to his head. He had a drink. I didn't. You have a problem with that, call the harbor police." David turned and climbed down into the boat in Slip 17, the *Fancy Nancy* according to the cursive across her stern.

Overheated fiberglass added a plastic smell to the rest of the noxious scents as Tai followed, eyes squeezed to slits as the light bounced off all the white surfaces of David's boat. Blinded or not, Tai found David easily. Not a lot of space to run on thirty-five feet of deck. He was in the cockpit, where it was shaded but oven-hot and close, his back against the wheel, legs and arms crossed.

"Doesn't much seem like you passed me off to another officer." In that instant David's drawl could have put Clayton's to shame. "What with you checking up on me from work."

"I did. I wasn't." Tai snapped his jaw shut. Defending his actions was an entirely unfamiliar feeling, and he wasn't going to make a fool of himself by sputtering.

"So this is the other kind of checking up on me?" David's stare was challenging. Not by being bold, but in that half-lidded indolence he'd perfected that made Tai itch to give that almost pouting mouth something better to do.

"What's the penalty for buying a friend lunch and watching him have a drink? Dunk me in the harbor? How long do I hold my breath?" David spun around and gripped the wheel, staring out over the bow. All that faked laziness was gone, his whole body drawn up tight enough to shatter. "I fucking hate this."

No air. God, it was stifling. And then David yanked away what little oxygen there was. Light-headed, Tai latched on to the back of the captain's chair before his knees buckled. Every time he thought he had something real to hold, it slipped through his fingers because he'd tightened his grip.

David went on, his voice as lifeless as the air. "He's going back to a life duller than an endless economics lecture, and I still want to trade places with him. I'm trapped here. The only time I don't feel like I'm suffocating is when I'm with you." He spun around, and his eyes widened, like he didn't expect Tai to be that close. There was no place left for David to back up, and Tai wasn't moving. "And then you come around and make me feel like shit for making sure we had the place to ourselves." David shoved past him.

Tai almost let him go. Then his hands shot out. Wrapped around David's biceps. Forced him to stay. "To use your own words, I didn't put a gun to your head. But hey, middle age is high time to grow up and show some responsibility."

"Fuck. You." David used his forearms to break Tai's hold and then shoved him away. "Who the hell are you to come preach about being responsible? You're all for it when it's something you can slap a proud label on, my dog, my kid, but when the law might keep your dick out of someone on probation, that one's flexible."

"You came to me."

"Damned right I did. I'm not the one spouting moral judgments like I've got all the answers. I know it's all Tai's road or no road with you, and I'm fine with that. Hell, I had no idea how fine I would be with that." David paused for breath and rocked on his feet. The boat shifted underfoot, reminding Tai they weren't on solid ground, and out at Slip 17, land was a good fifty yards away.

David huffed out a sigh. "We're clear on the me liking you telling me what to do. More than just in bed. But I also like being me. And I simply don't see me ever measuring up to your ideal of responsibility and good judgment."

Tai put out an arm as a barrier when David headed for the stern and the dock again. "I didn't say you had to."

"Yes, you did." David made a noisy exhale, like Jez would if she were shaking her head. "But let's forget it." He peered out the side window. "It's hot, huh? Think it's going to storm later. I can feel it in my leg."

This was completely different from his deliberate provocation last night. No hint of wanting Tai to take control, but David was definitely asking for something. Tai dug through the load of words David had dumped between them before scurrying away.

"David, stop."

"What for?"

Tai lunged, gut instinct making him reach for David, to stop him, force him to listen. But Tai's gut instincts hadn't spent any time in a boat and were useless at predicting a shear of wind that slammed into them and started everything rocking. David shoved free, Tai regrabbed, and they were both headed to the deck. The best thing Tai could say about it was that he managed to turn enough to take most of the impact with David on top of him. David wasn't a tiny guy, and Tai was still fighting to get his wind back when David reared over him, pinning Tai's shoulders flat.

"Well, if this was what you wanted, you could have just said so." David's eyes glittered, bright and hard. He worked the belt on Tai's jeans, popped his fly. "It's a lot to measure up to, but I don't mind trying."

David yanked down the zipper, hand diving in to palm the shaft through Tai's Jockeys before Tai remembered what he'd figured out before they hit the deck. "Were you asking me if I *like* you?"

"Well, I know part of you does." David reached through the slit, a gliding touch on bare skin.

"That's an understatement." Tai grunted and then choked off a gasp as David's grip turned firm. Tai stuck his own hand between them and caught David's forearm, careful to avoid the bruises on his wrist. Hauling him forward then wrapping him in a hug, Tai said, "Do you think I do this with just anybody?"

"I'm the guy from the bathroom at Grand Central, remember?"

"I do. And yeah. But that's not what I'm talking about. I would never ask someone I didn't like to be my submissive."

"My, aren't you a friendly guy to amass all that experience."

"I didn't say *a* submissive. Any more than I mean *a* fuck. I said *my* submissive." Tai let a little of his Dom voice roll into that. Another gust sent the boat bumping back and forth in its berth.

David turned the motion to his advantage, grinding against Tai's dick.

"And if you ask me what the difference is, I might not show you." Tai moved his hands down to David's ass.

He was smiling, but the hint of his tongue at the corner of his mouth suggested he wasn't as cocksure as his throaty "So?"

Tai held tight to stop David's motion, but that didn't keep the boat from continuing to rock, a dissonance that made Tai's stomach lurch. "Yes. My dick likes you. More importantly, I like you. And I want you to be my submissive."

David's body jerked, his breath sucked in fast and tight. "Okay."

Tai squeezed David's ass until he winced. "That's not how you answer me."

David bucked again, driving his cock against Tai's. A good kind of rub to keep the pulse of arousal lasting forever. But they needed to get things clear first. David wanted boundaries, and Tai loved drawing them for him. He swatted David's ass, mostly palm, but with enough force to make an impression through his deck shorts.

"Yes, Sir." David rocked against him harder.

"*Yes, Sir* what?"

"Yes, Sir. I want to be your submissive."

"No."

David's breath was short, ragged, his brow wrinkling under his hair.

"Yes, Sir. I am your submissive," Tai clarified for him.

David repeated it, and the raw yearning in his voice frayed the hold Tai had on himself. He tried to roll them, but they were wedged in a space between benches. Whoever thought boats were romantic settings had never tried to fuck on one.

"Ah hell," he muttered and gave up on a better location, reaching between them to get David's fly undone. "Get these off."

"Yes, Sir."

While David was busy with the tangle around his anklet, Tai pushed and hauled them out of the tight space, gaining a little maneuvering room but keeping them shielded by the canopy over the cockpit. He sat up, dragging David up until his thighs opened across Tai's, settling into his lap.

"Mine." He took David's mouth, fingers gripping his ass.

"Yes." David hung on, tilting his hips so their cocks rubbed together.

The first rumble of thunder shook the boat. Somewhere in Tai's head he knew that water and thunderstorms were a bad combination, but that head wasn't driving. His senses were locked on to David's groans, the hot, silky rub of his cock, then God, the way their own electricity jumped between them when Tai's finger worked into the damp heat of David's crack to press on the satiny-hard muscle around his hole.

"Yes. Please. Fuck me."

David's words seemed to come from inside Tai's head.

He grabbed David's face and stuffed a finger into his mouth, feeling the wet pull and rub traveling straight down to Tai's dick.

"I decide."

David managed a nod, steady suction on Tai's fingers as he shoved a second one inside. The blue eyes had gone soft, hungry. When Tai let go, David's head dropped back, exposing the line of his throat, so close Tai could see the swirl pattern in the stubble under his jaw.

"Oh no, boy. I want you to work for it. Grab our dicks. Jack them together."

Tai watched David pull himself into coordination, hand shaky, then firm, thumb spreading precome.

"You got more spit. Use it."

David's mouth was open, but the sound got swallowed in a bigger rumble and a hard knock of the boat against the wood pilings.

Tai watched, hands back to spreading David wide open, finger circling and pressing, dipping and testing the yield of his hole.

Just as David brought his hand back to their dicks, Tai shoved both fingers in, reading the reaction in David's face, in the way his body fought and then opened to take it. After a few harsh sounds, David's face shifted from pain to hunger, ass relaxing the crush around Tai's fingers so he could move.

Oh God, so hot and soft. Squeezing. Pulsing. Like David was already coming. Tai's hips snapped him forward. He wanted it. Wanted all that heat and texture on the bare skin of his dick.

He knew he could have it. David would let him. David was barely able to focus on stroking their cocks, his grip uneven, going slack as Tai twisted his fingers deeper.

He could have it.

The knowledge made Tai dizzy. Hot prickles under his skin, the rush of complete power. Dominance. It wouldn't take much. He could lift David, then drive up into him, keep his ass open, then fill him with cock. Watch him struggle to take it on nothing but spit.

The boat shook under another blast of wind. Power.

David panted, voice scraped raw. "It's enough, Sir. You could—"

"Shh."

The rain started then, sheets of it slashing against the hull, spraying in from the stern. Power was nothing without control.

"You want my cock, David?"

"Yes, Sir."

"You think you can take me on just spit?"

"God, yes."

"You'd take me raw? My bare skin in you?"

"Yes." David's voice shuddered through that.

"I'll lift you up and slam you down on my dick, and you'll have to take it like that. Hard and deep. And then I'll make you work. Make you fuck yourself."

"Yes, Sir."

"Did I tell you to stop jerking us off?"

"No, Sir. But—"

Tai leaned in and kissed the edge of David's jaw. "But what, boy?"

"I'll come." It was a desperate whine.

"What makes you think that will matter? That I wouldn't fuck you even after you're all soft. You're mine. Aren't you?"

David's eyes shot open, his fingers tightening around their shafts. "Stroke faster, David. Just you. You're going to come."

His eyes were wild. Not that drugged look of submission, but a flare of want and fear.

"Come, David."

Tai fucked his fingers in and out, scissored them, not sure he could get the right angle like this.

David's knuckles brushed against Tai's cock, the slide of his fist a whisper of sound above the storm outside.

Tai felt it in David's ass first, the start of his orgasm, and then his groans, his pleas. "Fuck, please. Please."

The wind blasted rain onto Tai's back as David shot warmth between them, his ass clenching and pulsing and then locking around Tai's fingers.

David's head hung heavy on his shoulders, and Tai urged him closer, letting him rest his forehead on Tai's shoulder.

He ran his free hand down David's back, over the soft cotton of his shirt. "Good boy. I've got you. Relax."

David shuddered, a ripple starting at his shoulders before moving to his hips, his muscles finally easing enough to let Tai slide his fingers free.

David turned his face into Tai's neck, kissing every bit of skin he could reach. "Yeah." Tai leaned back, inviting more. "You want a taste? Clean me off, baby."

David went to work, shoving Tai's shirt up, lapping at his skin, wet, soft kisses moving down into his groin. As David wriggled his legs and hips behind him, he used a hand to lift Tai's sac toward warm lips and the hungry flick of tongue. David put a stroke on the skin behind Tai's balls, making him jolt, then moved back to mouth up along his shaft.

The combination of gentle pressure and eager attention was maddening. David's light licks didn't have enough pressure or focus, but they were everywhere, constant sensation on Tai's balls, his dick, belly and groin. He let it build, ignoring the chill of wet wind behind him in favor of the heat from David's mouth until it was too much.

Sliding one hand deep into his hair, Tai held David's head steady and pushed up between his lips into wet suction. David kept up those fast flicks of his tongue, dipping into the slit, wrapping around the head. Tai drove up until David had to hold him between his tongue and palate, soft squeeze, the flutter of his throat closing making a hot flood build, spill over in his balls.

He pumped into David's mouth, the first shot of come coating his throat and tongue to make those last few jerks sweeter. Letting go of David's hair, he fell back as the pleasure receded.

"Damn," David said from where his head was pillowed on Tai's thigh. "We're a mess." There was no arguing that.

David went on, "I know there are some towels below, but I don't think I have anything you could wear."

"Below?" Tai glanced around the boat. "In storage?"

"A shower too, but no hot water right now." David wobbled to his feet, turned, and unlocked what Tai had thought was an engine cabinet to reveal a small doorway and steps leading down.

"You have a downstairs." Tai stared, hoisting himself up. "That's out of view and dry?" He peered around David through the hatch. "And that has a bed?"

"Yes. Oh. Well. It was…." David trailed off and looked down. Tai caught David's chin and tipped his head up. "Yeah. It was."

Stripped to his boxers, Tai glanced around the downstairs of David's boat. They were in a small living room kind of space, with kitchen stuff and a bathroom to one side of the wall opposite the sofa, and a flat-screen TV took up the rest of the wall.

"I don't bother to keep the cable hooked up," David said through the door that opened into a bedroom, sounding like he was making an apology. He held up a T-shirt, looking between the cotton stretched to its limit in his hands and Tai. "Yeah, I don't think that'll work. Now I'm wishing I'd gotten the washer-dryer instead of worrying about cabinet space." David had barely paused for breath since they came down those stairs, issuing a combination tour and commentary on the amenities as if he were a desperate used-yacht salesman. Because this wasn't a fishing boat. It was a yacht. Knowing David was part of the one percent was different from standing here, surrounded by the kind of luxury that belonged on TV. This was in-his-face unavoidable. Like the phone call from Tai's mom telling him what David had done to get Tai in to see Sammie, it was a 3-D, surround-sound experience reminding him how they might as well have been from different planets.

David trailed off under one of the storm's departing rumbles. Rain still splatted on the deck overhead.

"I didn't come down here for this," Tai said.

David put on his too-pleasant smile and spoke faster. "For laundry service? I guess not. Though there is a laundry room available at the hotel, access included as part of my docking fees. I could run over and do a quick wash and dry while you wait. Do you need another towel?"

"I need you to come here." Tai let his Dom come through in his voice.

David tossed the T-shirt behind him and stepped out of the bedroom. His face and his steps showed too much hesitance.

Tai pulled David down onto the sofa and held him, his back to Tai's chest.

"I'm not dropping. I feel fine."

"Okay. But you listen better like this."

"I listen just—" David's sigh was rueful. "Yes, Sir. I do."

"I wasn't saying that I didn't enjoy what we did. Only that I got sidetracked." David tipped his head to one side to show off a grin. "Glad I could help."

"And you're trying to do it again."

David straightened, not resisting Tai's hold but no longer relaxing into it.

"My mom called and told me what you did. At the hospital."

"What did I do?" David's surprise was genuine, a flinch throughout his body. "I was a perfect gentleman."

Tai shifted them so that he could tip up David's chin. "You made them let me see Sammie. Thank you."

David lowered his eyes. "Yes. Well, I'm not particularly fond of stupid bureaucracies."

"My mom thinks you're in some kind of mafia."

"She mentioned that." David fidgeted, rolling his foot in a circle until the ankle joint popped audibly over the slap of rain. "Beauchamp is a name healthcare administrators are familiar with. I went over the nurse's head."

Tai had expected smug. Not an almost apology. "Well, I appreciate it."

"No trouble. It was a simple phone call." But there was more deflection than courtesy in David's answer.

Tai went fishing. "Did you make those calls you were supposed to?"

David slid free and turned to face him. "I did. I have a physical therapy appointment at three forty-five."

"And?" Tai prompted.

"And my uncle said he couldn't talk at that moment, but he'd call me back."

"Good."

The praise didn't shift David's eyes from their focus on his knees. The luxury around them might have made Tai aware of the gap between them, but right now he could only see David's need.

Tai lifted David's chin. "Tell me."

David blinked, then let his cheek lean into Tai's hold. "My father—I haven't seen him since I was ten. Something happened—a girl accused him of having sex with her when she was underage. I don't remember it very well. There was a lot of money involved and lawyers and then my father left the country. He's in Venezuela, and if he comes back, they'll arrest him." David licked his lips. "My mother…." David paused and shrugged. "I guess she was so embarrassed by it all, she went to Europe, and I went to live with my aunt and uncle."

"The same uncle you called."

David nodded. Tai tugged David into an embrace, keeping his back pressed tight against Tai's chest. This time David relaxed.

"The thing I remember is that the girl claimed she had a ring because my father gave it to her. A family-heirloom thing. We had a painting of my great-great-grandfather wearing it. I was fascinated by it because according to my grandfather, you could spin the gem and underneath was the family seal. But I don't remember my dad having it."

David twirled his foot again, but the ankle didn't pop. He flexed the ankle with the band back and forth.

"So that's how I ended up with this. I ran into a cousin who told me the ring didn't make it to my dad because his grandfather swiped it and then his uncle lost it on Fort Carroll during some party in the '90s. If I found it, her case would be shot and my dad could come home."

From everything Tai knew about evidence and indictments in general, it seemed like there had to be much more on the side of the accusing girl than her say-so and a ring to keep a man with the kind of power Beauchamp money could buy out of the country. But Tai had promised David trust, not a legal briefing.

"How did you plan to find a ring on an island, even one that size?"

David stopped swinging his foot. "I admit I wasn't too clear on it. I thought I had a good fix from what

Beau had told me, about a gun port that faced due east, but that night…." He shook his head. "It seemed like a simple plan."

"And now?"

"Now I know I'd need a metal detector at least. The place is a mess."

Despite his best intentions to work the kind of supportive-reflective-de-escalating-listening crap the state forced POs to go to in-services on, Tai couldn't keep a half grunt, half growl from escaping his throat.

"And a permit. Or whatever." David pulled away. "I really don't want to go to jail. I'm not going to do something stupid." He rolled his eyes. "This time. I wish I hadn't dragged Gavin into it that night. Maybe he and his—"

David's phone chirped with that bland ringtone, and he sprang off the sofa, winced, and then hobbled to where his deck shorts were hanging off a cabinet knob.

After retrieving the phone, he mouthed *My uncle* at Tai before tapping it and bringing it to his ear.

Either David's cell phone had impressive reception or his uncle had a particularly loud voice, because there weren't many words from either side of the conversation that Tai didn't catch.

He might not have been familiar with the uncle's voice, but there was no mistaking the tone for anything but a sneer of disgust as he said, "What kind of trouble are you in now, David?"

So much for everyone calling him Beach.

"None. Well, nothing new." David's attempt at charm faded fast. "It's only that Da—my father has been unable to reach you, and he asked me to call in his stead."

"Yes." But there was nothing else forthcoming from the man on the other end of the phone.

After a moment of impatient tapping on the counter, David faced Tai and made a dramatically exasperated face that did nothing to hide the real tension underneath.

"Well, sir"—David capitulated to the silence—"he's concerned."

"I'm sure he is."

"About money, sir. About his dividend check." Into the continuing unhelpful silence, David blurted, "I offered a wire transfer from my account, but he said it wouldn't be enough."

"Small mercy that you never got the full shares."

"I don't understand."

"That's not much of a surprise. What do you know about your father's financial situation?"

David turned back to the counter, hiding his expressions from Tai. "Nothing."

After that whisper, the uncle's voice was jarring. "Precisely. And you've chosen to remain unaware. So don't pretend you're going to tax your brain with it now. Might get frown lines on that pretty face of yours."

David's voice deepened but held a note of appeal. "I managed a business degree from a fairly respected institution of higher learning. If you could explain it to me, Uncle Sinclair, I'm sure I could—"

"And you've done what with that exactly? Don't trouble yourself. Just stay out of it."

"It's no trouble at all, sir. I can't come down home at present, but—"

"I'm all too aware of your situation."

"But if you could send someone, or I could meet with someone—"

"It's a bit late for that, my boy."

"I don't understand."

"And you should be on your knees thanking God for that."

David went to stare out of a rectangular porthole in the wall, his forehead against the glass. "What am I supposed to tell him when he calls again?"

"Tell him he damned well knows why."

David pulled the phone away from his ear, staring down at the screen, but it was obvious his uncle had disconnected.

"Well." David leaned on the counter and smiled. "At least I can cross that off the to-do list. Now, can I buy you lunch?"

Chapter Seventeen

TAI'S CLOTHES had progressed from soaked to damp by the time he pulled them back on.

David continued to talk about anything but his conversation with his uncle.

"The restaurant here specializes in seafood, unsurprisingly, but it's quite good, which is surprising."

The air had gone muggy after the storm, and the damp clothes might be a nice buffer, but Tai had to change into something less jizzed on before going to work, and his dog was waiting to go out.

"I'm going to run home before I go back to work."

"Right. Probably isn't the best for a probation officer to be seen hanging with an alleged felon in public."

Contact with criminals was dead-on for Tai's job description, but he cut through David's defensive bullshit. "I'm sorry your uncle wasn't much help." Though if the charges were serious enough that

David's father was hiding out in Venezuela, the guy deserved a little inconvenience. Statutory-rape laws existed for good reason.

David gathered up the damp towels and his long-sleeved shirt, stuffed them into a canvas drawstring bag, and tossed it back up through the hatch. "Dad should have expected it. Uncle Sinclair's self-righteousness is a lot to live up to. You may have noticed, the rest of us Beauchamps are a bunch of scalawags. Right on back to my carpetbagger great-great-grandfather who got us slung out of Charleston after the war."

"David." Tai could see the name and tone alone couldn't break through. Something sure needed to. He blocked the hatch, hands braced to either side.

"I know you have to get back to work. And I need to wash these. Mold is a bitch on a boat. And once it digs in, you might as well forget about ever getting rid of it."

Tai got tired of waiting for David's effort at charming bravado to run down. One step forward and Tai locked him up in a hug.

"Um. Thanks." David returned the hug for an instant and then pulled away as much as Tai's hold let him. Patting Tai's back a couple of times, David said, "I appreciate it. But it's no big deal. My family's shortcomings are not exactly a surprise."

When Tai didn't let go, David pushed. "Really. I'm fine."

Tai kissed him, then propped one foot up on the small steps leading to the deck, dragged David forward, and pushed him over Tai's elevated thigh. "What the hell are you—?"

Tai swatted his ass, not hard, but enough to make his intention obvious.

"Let me rephrase that. Why are you doing that? Sir," David ground out through clenched teeth.

Tai smacked him three more times, dusting his palm across the top curve, aiming for sting rather than impact. "First, let's be clear about what I'm doing." He rested his hand on David's ass and waited.

"From what I can tell, you're blocking the way out and hitting me." That was his boy, not going down without some fight.

Tai rubbed David's back, then swung hard, wrist flicking to make sure there was a good, long sting.

David jolted forward. "Ow."

"We can do this on the sofa with your pants off, or we can do it faster. What am I doing?"

"Spanking me."

Tai squeezed a handful of cheek. "Who am I spanking?"

"Your submissive, Sir." David's voice was rough, but not with suppressed anger anymore.

"Good. When you were in a similar position last night, what did you tell me?" Tai smoothed the material of David's shorts over his ass.

After a long, steady breath, David said, "I will trust you, Sir."

"Yes, David." Tai spanked him fast until he could see the reaction in his lifted head and feet. "You don't have to talk about what's going on, but you do not run from me or lie to me."

"Yes, Sir."

Tai finished with a few hard swats. "Stand up." He held David's arm as he got his balance.

With his head down, David unbuttoned his shorts and shoved them and his briefs off his hips before leaning forward over Tai's leg again.

The rush of heat under Tai's skin made him want to kiss David, not spank him. But rejecting David's need, failing the trust in that waiting surrender, would destroy everything they were creating.

Tai stroked a hand down David's spine. His David. So resentful of restrictions while craving to be held down, have accountability forced on him. That he shared it with Tai, had confidence in what Tai offered, electrified the air more sharply than the storm, pulsing between them. No. He would not let his boy down.

Hitching his leg up higher, Tai held David tight at the waist to keep him secure. His ass was barely pink, though following so close after last night's spanking, it was probably more tender than it looked. Tai wanted to make sure David got the release he was looking for. "Five more. Hang on to my leg. If you reach back, we start over."

David latched on to Tai's calf, muscles tensing as Tai rubbed the hot flesh. "Relax. I'm not going to start until you relax."

David let out a long breath and stopped clenching.

"Good boy." Tai slammed his hand down under the curve, one swat turning the pink much darker. "What do you need to tell me?"

"I'm sorry, Sir."

"Good."

Tai aimed for the same spot, getting a sharp hiss in response before David repeated his apology. Three more and Tai's palm was stinging, and there was a faint hand outline in the middle of David's ass.

"Stand up." Tai helped David balance, then led him to the couch, sat, and pulled him down, holding him steady as his breathing slowed. When he shifted on Tai's lap, arms going around his neck, Tai kissed him.

"Okay?" Tai whispered against his lips.

"Yes, Sir."

"I got you something." Remembering David's marked wrists and long-sleeved shirt on a day headed for triple-digit temps, Tai had stopped at the leather store before heading for the marina. He pulled a dressier pair of cuffs from his pocket. "I got these for you. They snap and there's no clip. They're for decoration, not play." They were woven from strips of two different shades of brown leather, softer and smoother than a braid, suede against the skin. "Not a collar," Tai said, wondering if David understood what that would mean, and got a quick nod. "But I want you to wear them for me."

David brushed a finger across the pattern, then smiled, offering his wrist, palm up.

The cuffs were on the decorative side. Not Beach's usual style, but then everything about Tai was pretty far from Beach's usual style.

He didn't care what they looked like. Could have been made out of neon-green plastic, and they would have still felt good. It wasn't as if he wanted to try to explain the bruises on his wrists to people with more curiosity than manners, but he liked the dark circle of smudges. All morning he'd snuck glances at them. Accidentally-on-purpose being sure his shirt cuff rode up so he could see them there, the ring a perfect reminder of the dizzying freedom of surrendering to Tai's dominance.

Now he had the cuffs and a throbbing burn in his ass. It wasn't like the pleasure Eli had described. Isolated pain like that was still something to try to avoid as far as Beach was concerned. But after? It was like every bit of stress and frustration and all those endless, unsatisfied wants got flushed out of him, leaving nothing but a peaceful, solid sensation. Being here. Belonging. Not only to Tai but to this moment. Free of the need to go chasing a distraction.

Funny how something he still didn't like thinking about and that also hurt more than he thought he could stand made him feel so good afterward. It was the reverse of sex, when things were great in the moment but the letdown after made everything awkward.

He kept touching the cuffs and sinking into the ache of his sore ass meeting Tai's hard thighs. Tai rubbed Beach's back, then kissed him.

"I'm glad you like them."

"Yes. Thank you, Sir." The *Sir* came out edged with a shy breath. Beach wished he knew exactly when they were supposed to be Beach and Tai or Sir and David. He knew he had a safeword as a signal for needing to end the scene, but what was a word for saying you were fine with it lasting longer?

Tai brushed his beard back and forth across Beach's chin. Soft, then prickly when a hair caught in the wrong direction. "I can stay a bit longer if you want."

Beach wanted. Wanted to tell Tai to pack up Jez and they'd fly right out of the harbor. Out to Bermuda or down to the Keys. Away from jobs and pending court dates. Turn this week of discovering each other into a life of it. Beach pictured them on the porch of one of those pretty pastel houses on Key West.

Seagrass whispering around them. The Tai in his fantasy never wore a shirt, skin tanning darker in the Florida sun. No ankle monitor. Hell, not even shoes, their bare feet propped up on the porch rail as they watched the sunset.

Fantasy David and stuck-in-Baltimore Beach rolled an ankle. The pop was satisfying, but the monitor was still there.

"I know you're supposed to be out checking on the rest of the miscreants." Beach smiled and stroked Tai's beard with his thumb.

"I'm thinking more of Jez with her legs crossed and a giant pile of files that need updating."

Beach leaned in for a kiss, and Tai gave it, holding Beach's head and pushing that wonderful sensation of being owned into him with lips and tongue. Beach was still high from it as they stepped off the *Nancy* onto the dock.

"Who's Nancy?" Tai asked.

Beach imagined a hint of jealousy in the deep voice, but he told the truth with a wry smile. "Me, actually."

At Tai's stunned look, Beach explained as they strolled down the dock. "It was the first spring break home from Deerfield. I brought Gavin home—well, to Uncle Sinclair's to visit. We were fourteen or fifteen, and we kept acting out some skit from school that amused us every time we did it." He remembered Gavin's laugh, the way a cowlick made his hair flop up and then down into one eye. "My uncle had a different opinion. 'Look like a couple of damned nancy boys.'" Beach sneered in imitation. "Gavin got all tense."

Poor Gavin. Beach had pretty much picked up on that vibe from his friend, though he hadn't considered for himself if he was interested in more than some rubbing or touching with another boy.

"So." Beach shot a look over at Tai and cleared himself some space for a proper reenactment. "I did this grand bow to my uncle"—he demonstrated—"and said, 'I think that should be *fancy* nancy boys, sir.'"

That sexy-sweet smile teased the corner of Tai's mouth. He glanced back at Beach's boat then huffed a single-breath laugh. "What did your uncle say to that?"

Beach had hoped they'd skip this part of the story. He stepped off onto the shore and tried to keep his tone light. "Oh, the usual. A big sigh followed by a 'Cut me a switch and drop 'em, boy.'" Beach smiled. "I assume he sighed because peeling the skin off my ass was a giant inconvenience."

"God, I'm sorry." Tai stopped walking.

Beach felt the sympathy and regret come at him in a smothering wave.

He shook his head forcefully and tapped his cane against the side of Tai's running shoe. "Don't. I am keenly aware of the difference."

Tai had that look where his brows made a tent over his eyes.

Beach took a deep breath and settled the laundry bag over his shoulder, the cuffs cradling his wrists, suede rubbing on the ring of bruises. "You ask me to trust you. Can you trust that about me?"

The return of the sun and blazing heat made all the wet pavement shimmer and steam, creating ripples behind Tai. Jaw tight, he nodded.

Beach smiled and gripped Tai's forearm before starting toward the hotel and the parking lot beyond. "Turned out to be the last time. And the last time I went back to Uncle Sinclair's. There was always an invitation to go to Gavin's. Plus"—Beach waggled his eyebrows—"Gavin felt obliged to put ointment on my butt, and that led to some interesting rubbing and exploration. I always tell Gavin he owes me for helping him figure stuff out."

"He was your first boyfriend?"

However much fifteen-year-old Beach might have wanted some kind of acknowledgment from Gavin, that hadn't ever been forthcoming. "Not quite that. Though he was the first in other ways. We fumbled around together."

The grunt from Tai might have been annoyance or acceptance. It was hard to say.

The happy sensation Tai gave Beach, the certainty from giving up everything to Sir, spread out from Beach's chest. "As it happens, that position is still open."

Tai's stare—Sir's stare—fixed Beach to the spot and made him lick his lips in nervous habit. "What position?"

"My first boyfriend."

Beach wished he were standing close enough to touch Tai because the growl that accompanied his words would have made an electric vibration.

"Consider it filled."

THE POSITION was well filled. Jesus, it was well filled. Beach had no complaints. He'd always thought answering to someone in a relationship would be like wearing the ankle monitor times ten. Not only blinking lights and a weight, a nagging human would make Beach feel guilty about how he spent his time. Instead he found himself checking his phone constantly for a random text from Tai. Some were funny, some echoed with Tai's frustration about work, and some made Beach's balls tingle and throb until it was hard to follow Tai's order to keep hands off unless taking a piss.

That's mine, boy.

Yes, Sir.

The anticipation of seeing Tai at the end of the day didn't make time drag. The charge of excitement rushed time forward, until it had been over a week of having a Dominant boyfriend and physical therapy, and Beach was getting the hang of both. His leg was tired, but the bone seemed to ache less. And Tai had a way of making the extra exercises very rewarding.

The returning strength in his muscles meant Beach could kneel at Tai's feet. Being there made Beach's head quiet. No worrying about the court date for his sentencing looming in two weeks. No need to think about anything but being there, being David for Sir.

Beach reached for the baklava after finishing off the moussaka from the Greek takeout Tai had brought with him, and Tai put his big hand over the plastic covering the pastries. Beach quirked a smile. "I cleaned my plate, so to speak." He tilted the empty container.

"After."

Beach was a little full for sex. Burping up spiced beef could put a damper on the mood. "After what?"

"Didn't the physical therapist say you should start daily walks to strengthen the muscles?"

Damn him for paying attention. "Yes, Sir."

"Jez could use the walk too."

Beach cleared the remains of the meal off his counter, gazing wistfully at the flaky honey-soaked triangles under plastic.

"One taste?"

"Don't be a brat." That particular warning from Tai came in two different tones. One affectionate and teasing, which meant the consequence of ignoring him was likely to be the same. This was the deeper, gruff warning. Ignoring this could escalate into unpleasant consequences. The least of which would probably be Tai departing with his baklava, so Beach left the lid on. There was a bit of sticky sweetness on his thumb from moving the container though, so he sucked it clean.

"David."

That one word could do so many things to Beach's insides, stirring that now-familiar tangle of want and dread at the idea of punishment. The way his heart expanded under the narrow focus of Tai's attention. Beach didn't think he'd ever be getting off on pain, but the idea of surrendering to it, taking it because it was what Tai wanted, that felt amazing.

"I didn't open it, Sir."

Tai came around the counter to stand in front of Beach, hand closing over the leather cuffs Beach wore everywhere but the shower. Tai drew Beach's hand up until the soft beard tickled his knuckles as Tai licked Beach's thumb.

"My job, boy."

"Yes, Sir." They needed to do that walk. Now.

His father's call dropped into that sweet anticipation like an acid bomb.

Chapter Eighteen

BEACH STARED at the number. He never bothered to put caller ID in for the number, because it
changed often. But he recognized the country code,
the moussaka congealing into a cold lump in his belly.

Tai released his hand. "Your dad?"

Beach nodded and picked up the phone.

His father didn't bother with a greeting. "Where
the hell is the money? Why didn't you call me back?"

"You told me never to try to contact you through
my cell phone."

"That doesn't answer the question about the money, David."

Tai put his hands on Beach's shoulders, a comfortable weight urging him down. Remembering what
the therapist had said about squaring off joints, Beach
carefully lowered himself to his knees, sinking into
the security of being Tai's. His hand rested on Beach's
head as he leaned into Tai's leg. Funny, *David* sounded

so different when his dad said it. To say nothing of
how hearing it felt inside. From Tai, a solid, steady
warmth. From his father, a curl of shame and regret.

"Did you call Sinclair as I asked?"

"Yes, sir." The *sir* to his father was as automatic
as a *God bless you* to a sneeze. Instinct rather than the
respect weighting his voice when he spoke the same
words to Tai. When they were deep in that space together, Tai *was* Sir, guiding, controlling everything so
all Beach had to do was take and feel.

"When did you call?"

"Right away."

His father made a disgusted sound. "We all know
that could mean anything with you." Beach did prefer
to put off anything unpleasant. It only seemed reasonable. Why do something distasteful if there was
a chance that ignoring it would make it go away? But
he hadn't put it off this time. If calling the very next
morning was in any way lacking, he knew Tai would
have pointed it out.

"I called the next morning."

"And?"

At that moment Beach envied Tai his unknown
dead father. The deceased couldn't hang a millstone
of disappointment and disgust around your neck the
way the living could. From Dad's perspective, it probably appeared an easy task: convince Uncle Sinclair to
loosen whatever hold he'd placed on Dad's cash flow.
From Beach's point of view, it was like arguing with
the tide. It would flow when it flowed.

He swallowed, then took a deep breath, leaning
into Tai's leg, wrapping himself in the comfort of
Tai's dominance.

"Uncle Sinclair—I asked him. I asked him to ex-plain, or to let me handle things. He said, 'Tell him he knows why.'"

"Sanctimonious fucking bastard."

"Sir, I would be happy to wire money directly—"

"It's far too late for that."

Which was what his uncle had said. How could it suddenly be too late? As his father so often com-plained, he'd been living in exile for twenty-five years. Dad continued, "If you hadn't gotten yourself into this mess, maybe you could have been some help. But with you tethered to the state of Maryland, there's nothing you can do."

Beach knew better than to suggest his mother or Beau's side of the family. Beach might have been young, but he knew how wide the gulf was between his parents, and between his father and his cousins.

"I was trying to find the ring. Beau said—"

"Forget the goddamned ring, David. I need help, not some trinket."

"Yes, sir. If you tell me your account details—"

"Forget the whole damned thing, me included. That shouldn't be hard for you, after all."

"Da—Father, I want—"

His father hung up. Beach pressed Redial, but there was no answer, no voice mailbox. He stabbed at Redial harder. The phone stopped ringing almost immediately. Before he could make another attempt, Tai took the phone.

"Walk now. Try again later."

The surety and calmness spread out from Beach's belly, radiating into his legs and feet and tingling into his fingers and hair. "Yes, Sir."

Tai didn't say anything as they walked along the edge of the infinity pool, then along the birches screening the property from glimpses of anything not upcycled from the area's former life as a working wharf. Jez was on her best behavior, keeping pace right at Tai's knee, her leash loose but arranged so Tai could check her if she started to wander. Tai and Jez were exemplary citizens. Beach, on the other hand, was a complete failure.

Though he had less need of his cane now than he had even three days ago, he stabbed it viciously into the ground as they walked. What was he supposed to do? What else could he possibly offer his father? Beach lashed out to the side with his cane, and Tai put out a hand to stop it before a row of innocent petunias suffered a premature beheading.

"David." Tai yanked the cane out of Beach's hands.

As if his grip on the cane had been a breakwater, anger spilled over, then bled away.

Beach shook his head in disgust. "Stupid, I know."

"Don't put words in my mouth."

"What would you call it, then? Why do I even care that they all think I'm an utter waste of skin?"

"You care because it's your father."

"One I haven't seen in twenty-five years." He wondered at that. Maybe if he'd tried to visit?

"That is a long time." Tai tossed the cane back. "Did you ever ask—maybe there's another reason he can't come back?"

Beach poked at a clump of green leaves torn from a birch in the storm last night. "No. I've never asked. I suspect I don't want to know. He's not much of a father, but he's the only one I have."

Tai took Jez off the pavement and onto the grassy verge for a spot of business. "Leaving the country and not being able to return for this length of time suggests something pretty serious. There are probably things that were kept from you when you were younger."

"And you're saying I should go digging up skeletons?"

"It makes more sense than digging for buried treasure on a forbidden island."

"Now I'm both feckless and frivolous?"

"I told you before not to put words in my mouth." There was no heat in Tai's voice, just that calm dominance he used on Jez. Beach was tired of it.

"And probably not ones you haven't heard before."

"Check your assumptions, David. I took the SATs. I wouldn't call you completely hopeless, though right now you're sliding into careless."

Shame soured on the back of Beach's tongue. He'd never been the kind of person to put down others, been the kind of snob his cousins were. But being unable to get under Tai's skin was infuriating. "And I suppose you have all this advice because of your vast experience with a male parent?"

If it hadn't been for Jez, Beach might not have known how deep he'd struck. She pinned herself to Tai's side, ears flattening, nose curled as she swung her head toward Beach with her lip lifted. It was barely audible over the slap of water, but the air vibrated with her growl.

"Enough."

Beach was pretty sure that was more for him than the dog, but Jez lowered her threat level, bristling but not growling.

Tai stroked her head, and she sat. "I'm not going to play stand-in for your father." At last exasperation colored his voice.

"Of course not. Because you putting me over your knee to spank me isn't remotely paternal."

"I'm your Dominant." Tai was back to the reasonable tone. "You're my submissive, not a child. And each time, you were very clear in what you were asking for."

Beach dropped his gaze to stare at where he dragged his cane tip across the pavement. "And if I'm asking you to punish me now?" He hated his own diffidence, but he hated the way his insides felt—like everything was out of place and hard and hurting and would never be fixed—more.

"No."

Beach thought things were hurting before, but that rejection was sharp enough to take his breath away. He started walking again, moving as far and fast as he could to outrace the burning ache inside. But he couldn't outpace it. Or Tai.

"David, I'm not going to punish you because you're upset about a conversation with your father. The D/s should only be about us. Not drag anyone else in."

But Tai had done that before, hadn't he? When this feeling got too big and Beach couldn't take the *Nancy* somewhere to avoid it. Couldn't chase it away with bourbon or X. Couldn't lose it in a random body. Tai had given him that. Why couldn't he do it now?

Beach gave a tight nod and kept walking as fast as he could. So much for feeling like he'd found something that gave him all he needed. Something that promised there was enough right here. No need to chase it.

Tai caught up and grabbed Beach's arm. "I've told you not to run from me."

"I thought this wasn't about us. That it was about my daddy issues."

"When you run from me or hide your feelings from me, that makes it about us."

"So what the fuck do you want from me?"

"I want you to control yourself and think about what's really going on. You're angry, but you don't get to lash out at everyone."

"At you, you mean." And he wasn't angry. A little frustrated, but not angry.

"And at yourself." Tai released Beach's arm and took a familiar grip on his chin. "You need to think about what you really want, what you're feeling. So you will not speak again until I give you permission."

Beach opened his mouth to protest and then closed it.

"You have fifteen seconds to argue."

It burned high up in his throat, like a shot of rot-gut moonshine. The reasons why not. An explanation that talking was how Beach figured out what he was feeling. The flat-out denial of accepting Tai's demand. It choked him, and he didn't say anything at all.

"Good." Tai caressed Beach's jaw and pressed a gentle thumb against his lips. "Don't forget."

The sternness of that warning made adrenaline leap in Beach's veins. So he could have what he'd been looking for, submit to that brief pain to get that release.

Tai must have read the intention in Beach's face, because the dark eyes narrowed under the slash of brows. "If you speak before I give you permission, your ass is going to be more than sore. Three solid minutes. And it won't be my hand. It will hurt like hell."

Beach's pulse still raced with excitement. It would be awful. Tai was deadly serious. But after….

"Be a good boy for me, David." Tai brushed his thumb across Beach's lips and resumed walking.

Beach blew out a breath as he followed. Damn him. Tai had handed the choice neatly off to Beach. If he really wanted the risk, to chance the pain for the release that followed, all he had to do was open his mouth. Bastard. Worse, Beach really hated displeasing Tai. In a completely different way, enduring the inability to speak because Tai demanded it gave Beach a prickle of warmth all over his body, like summer sunshine after too much air-conditioning. He wanted to luxuriate in Tai's authority like a cat in that sunbeam. At the same time Beach wanted the out-of-control rush from Tai's power and strength forcing pain into Beach's body.

He didn't want to have that option. For once, freedom weighed on him like an anchor.

Why couldn't Tai make the choice for him? For them?

Beach had never realized how often he started a conversation to avoid being stuck in his own head until this restriction sealed his lips. Once he barely caught himself before snapping his jaw shut. *Shit.* This was harder than he'd thought. It was one thing to deliberately court punishment, but another to fail in control.

Tai pressed Beach into the sidewall of the elevator as they rode up to the fifth floor. "Remember you're supposed to be thinking about what you feel, not avoiding it."

Tai's warm, hard body felt damned good against Beach. Faint spicy aftershave, the rumble of his voice, tang of sweat. Beach wanted a great big gulp of that kind of avoidance. He licked his lips.

The corner of Tai's mouth twitched, and he shook his head. "Not that either. Focus." Beach sighed and then tightened his jaw against a more verbal complaint or persuasion. Right as they crossed the apartment threshold, Gavin texted.

Beach glanced at Tai, not sure how far the prohibition went. Tai nodded, and Beach opened the message.

What are you doing?

Beach considered his answer for a second. *My boyfriend.* Let Gavin chew on that.

I wasn't aware you knew the meaning of the word. Gavin was a fine one to talk. *Pardon my interruption. What are you doing on Saturday?*

I devoutly hope more of the same.

Sunday was Tai's day with his daughter, and their time on weekday evenings seemed so short. Like now. This wasn't helping with the focus Beach was supposed to be doing. A focus he planned to show so they could get on with dessert and sweeter things.

Catch you later. He turned off the phone and left it on the counter. After a wistful look at the waiting baklava, he glanced back at Tai.

"Sit."

Jez went over to her blanket, and Beach dropped on the couch. When Tai knelt in front of Beach, his breath whistled between his teeth, but Tai only checked Beach's shin for signs of swelling.

Beach sucked back the protest that it was fine and then enjoyed a quick massage from Tai's hands, pressure stretching and loosening the muscles again. He lifted Beach's ankle to rest it on the coffee table before turning the TV on to the last three innings of the Orioles game, muting the sound, then settling next to Beach to watch.

Beach found baseball stupefyingly tedious. With the sound off, he couldn't even devote some mental energy to mocking the announcers. No. Nothing but him in his head. Hadn't he shown that he was in control now? He was over it. Like he got over everything. All he needed was an idea to replace the problem thoughts, some sweet anticipation, and everything would be back to happy.

They'd have the honey-flaky treat and then lick it off each other's lips. Yes. Beach would show off his recent practice with frozen bananas and earn the praise of Tai's hands, heavy caresses through Beach's hair. He shifted a little, making room for the swell of his cock as he pictured it.

Tai glanced over. "I don't think you're focused on the right thing." His voice was a little annoyed and a little amused.

What was the point of dwelling on Beach's failings with his father? His uncle? Entire months of his life went by without any contact from his family. He hadn't heard from his mother since her Christmas card.

He'd been frustrated after the phone call. And now that was gone. The end.

Tai had said Beach couldn't talk, but not that he had to stay on the couch. He slipped off, kneeling next to Tai's legs, foot flexed to avoid strain to that healing shin. Tai's hands sifted through Beach's hair.

"Very nice, boy. But it's not going to get you out of what you're supposed to be doing." Beach was supposed to be thinking about how he felt. What he felt was that tug that made him want to be here. Kneeling at Tai's feet. Obedient. And horny. There was also that. So that was what Beach concentrated on. How it felt. He shut his eyes, because the pictures on the TV were distracting. They took away from how right it felt to be there, to belong to Sir. He started to float on that connection, his chest full of heat and light, breaths even and slow. Time never mattered when he got there, so it might have been a few minutes or an hour when he was aware of Tai moving, his voice settling into Beach's head. "Keep your eyes closed. Open your mouth."

Sweet and sticky, airy fragments of buttery phyllo and rich filling flooded his mouth. After he chewed and swallowed, Tai urged him to open for another bite. Baklava should always be eaten like this. His senses swam with texture and smell, the dizziness that came with that absolute surrender. Tai held a glass to Beach's lips.

"Tip your head back."

Water. Had it ever tasted better? Beach swallowed. Then swallowed the swell of feeling in his throat that made his eyes prickle with moisture. As amazing as submitting to Tai felt, yielding this made Beach feel the most cared for, the most grateful for the caring. The simple act of food from Tai's hand fed parts of Beach that had always gone hungry before, filled him and took away that endless desire to anticipate the next distraction. The completion found every hollow, left him full and sated but alive with energy.

When Tai said, "Open your eyes," and urged Beach to eat the rest of the pastry from a cupped palm, it felt natural to lick all the traces of flavor from Tai's skin, then kiss the pads of his fingers in gratitude. Beach smiled into Tai's hand, remembering the husky whisper of *My job, boy* when Beach had licked his fingers earlier.

"What? You can speak." Tai's voice was as breathless now as it had been then.

Now that he could, Beach found he didn't want to, didn't want his usual bland banter to come between them. He shook his head.

Tai grabbed Beach's chin. "Are you being a brat?"

Instead of his default reaction to push back, Beach opened his eyes wide and shook his head again.

"Hmm." Tai leaned down to kiss him, beard a tingling rasp against Beach's evening stubble. "I'll take that as a challenge then."

He tested Beach's control, kissing him into the bedroom, examining the strength of it in a steady stroke of his cock before pushing him onto the bed.

Beach held out as long as he could, sounds and pleas confined by a tight jaw, until Tai swallowed and groaned, lips brushing the base of Beach's shaft, that pulsing, hot, wet throat so tight, drawing his cock deeper.

"Please. God, please, Sir. Can I come?"

More perfect agony, Tai drawing off and then sinking back, slick pressure on every inch and the rough texture of throat on the head. Beach's muscles cramped as he fought to hold back the fiery flood in his balls.

Tai pulled off all the way, abandoning Beach's dick to the chill of the room. "Not yet."

Beach didn't care. He needed, God, how he needed. His wrists were locked together over his head, legs pinned open by Tai's weight. "Anything. I'll take anything, do anything. Please, Sir."

"No bargaining. You will take whatever I give you."

"Yes." It was true. The knowledge wound more tightly through his balls. He would take whatever Sir gave him, craved that control, and for the first time the knowledge came free of any shame. What did it matter what other people thought if he had this?

Tai took him back to the edge, making Beach frantic with the added sensation of a spit-wet finger rubbing around his hole.

Beach wasn't sure what he was saying now. Like in all that silence he'd forgotten words, but when Tai stopped again and the tension rebounded inside, tears squeezed out from the corners of Beach's eyes.

"This, David." Tai loomed, brows in a deep, serious V on his face, but his kiss was silky soft. "This is what I want you to take. What I want you to feel for me. You can do this for me, boy."

"Yes, Sir." The answer came out on a sob, but Beach tried to relax while still holding on to the orgasm burning in his balls and dick, all the way through to his shaking thighs.

Tai scraped his beard down Beach's chest, teasing his cock with the soft prickle of it. Oh, he could come from that, couldn't he? If it was just a little harder. Higher.

The finger teasing his hole became two, slicker, a rough push in that went right to Beach's dick.

"When I tell you to come, you do it right then or you won't get another chance tonight."

Fuck. Beach's head fell back, throat, stomach, legs, balls, everything straining, caught on the knife-edge where Sir kept him.

Tai's fingers fucked fast, hard, and the burn helped Beach hold on until the friction turned to stroking stabs of pleasure against his gland and his legs shook. Though his eyes were squinched shut, he could feel Tai watching, and he tried to find a place where the tension wasn't so terrible, where he wasn't need but was surrender. He spread his legs wider, tipped up his hips, opened his ass.

"You are so fucking beautiful like this." Tai's voice sounded like he still had a cock in his throat. He pressed a kiss to Beach's belly, then demanded, "Now," before swallowing Beach's cock again.

It should have been easy, he'd been waiting so damned long. But it wasn't. He bucked up against Tai's shoulders, trying to get the rhythm, the pressure to meet the need.

He shuddered, mind frantic. Tai would leave him hanging here, but even worse, David would disappoint Sir.

Another twist of fingers, along with the slide of a hard hand on his shaft, brought him closer. Exquisite suction and Tai's tongue flicking over the head had the rush taking over, a flood of it, endless spasms of pleasure, blasting into Tai's mouth. Muscles cramped and ached as the shocks rang through him until it ended in a bone-melting lassitude.

"So good." Tai freed Beach's hands. "That's it. Good boy. Roll over for me now."

Beach's body wasn't exactly cooperating, so Tai twisted and shoved, and Beach ended up with his ass up, hips tilted over the wadded-up sheet, dick protesting even the contact of the satiny thousand-thread-count percale.

It would hurt to be fucked, but Beach really didn't care. In fact now would be a perfect time to be branded, or tattooed, or for another round of surgery on his tibia.

Tai's cock slipped along Beach's ass crack. Beach shoved back toward him, squeezing. "Yeah, just like that." The voice was more gravelly, abraded from— God, from having *Beach's* dick in so deep, so long. Tai's voice, rasped and shaky with want.

I gave him that. Me.

Beach shuddered, then pushed back harder, shifting to try to line them up. Satisfaction pulsed hot in his belly. *I can give him this too.*

Tai pressed him down, full weight pinning Beach to the mattress. "Not gonna fuck you. Keep it tight for me."

Beach did, clenching his muscles and rocking against Tai's thrusts. The pressure on Beach's hole sent a painful throb of blood to try to fill his dick. The desperate, hoarse groans from Tai only made it worse, like the pleasure spilling out from where Tai sucked a bite into the back of Beach's neck. But the unbroken chant of his name before warm, slick come sprayed between them made the ache worth it.

Tai didn't move off, arms wrapping through and around Beach's, the anchor holding back any threat of a drop as they drifted off.

When Beach woke up with an urgent bladder and the need to stretch a cramp out of his hip, Tai peeled away with a sigh.

"Y'okay?"

"Everything's good. Be right back." Beach swung his feet onto the floor.

Jez was sprawled on her side, not even giving a twitch of an ear as he passed. After he pissed, he executed some contorted maneuvers with a washcloth to despunk his back and decided he could do with a glass of water.

His phone sat on the counter in silent rebuke. After eyeing it through his emptying glass, he resigned himself to seeing if he had a message. Three texts from Gavin, and a voicemail from his father. He chose the lesser evil first. *Be sure you have something to wear to charm some donations out of grande dames on Saturday. Garden party at the Manor.*

Why the hell would Beach willingly subject himself to that when he could be subject to Sir?

There was a follow up. *You. Owe. Me.*

And finally. *Wear blue. The ladies like it when it matches your eyes.*

Beach rolled the orbs in question, though he knew guilt would win and he'd be there.

Guilt also had him gingerly bringing the phone to his ear to listen to the voicemail.

"Might have a way out of this shit. Be ready to wire two point five to an offshore account. I'll call back with the information."

Two point five million would pretty much empty Beach's accounts. The *Fancy Nancy* was his, free and clear, and the town house in Charleston. This apartment, docking fees here and at other favorite spots along the coast, the place he kept in Juno Beach, all that drained from his account. He earned it back in dividends—the trust fund had a steady stream of investment income—but he wasn't like Gavin. He couldn't sneeze a million dollars into his hand. He'd barely cover the next two months if he wired that to his dad. And he certainly wouldn't be able to make a splash at Gavin's fundraiser.

Though if Beach did... if he cut that check to his father, handed it over, maybe he'd finally feel free of it. Finished. Done with the expectations of what family should be.

He pressed the button to call back. A computer voice answered, *"El número que usted ha marcado no está en servicio. Por favor revise el número y trate de nuevo."* Beach had taken French and German, but he got enough to know the number was out of service.

It stiffened his spine with a jolt of alarm.

No real reason. Beach might believe in ghosts, but he sure as hell wasn't a psychic.

There was nothing unusual about his father dropping one burner phone for another.

The unease came from all those things. A sudden demand for cash after refusing it. The desperation in the voicemail. The promise to call back to get the money and now the out-of-service answer.

Beach left the phone on the counter and padded into the bedroom, stopping for a moment to peer out through the windows.

He loved predawn light. The first shift from black to deep indigo. All the promise in a new day—though he much preferred to catch dawn from an all-night-out perspective rather than needing to be up at a crazy hour. He slipped back into bed and stared at the shadowy block that made up Tai. In Beach's absence, Tai had clutched onto a pillow, face relaxed as he curled around it. Tenderness rolled through Beach, and he stroked a hand through the long black curls. So satiny

and scented with a sweet oil, almost almondy. Tai
curled closer.

It was like having a sleeping tiger in his bed.
Lethal power with a deceptive feline softness. And
somehow, Tai chose to share that with Beach. Gave
him the gift of the terrifying and tender places they
went to.

Beach wanted that now. Wanted Tai's solid, emphatic control poured over the tangle of fear and confusion in Beach's mind. He stared at Tai's face, willing him to wake up.

Couldn't he feel it? Didn't that connection, David
to Sir, still vibrate between them? Beach felt it all the
time, like something rooted right under the bottom of
his sternum, a cord that pulled him to Tai.

Beach made another stroke through Tai's hair,
contemplating a tug, an accidentally purposeful kick
to his shin.

I'm not going to play stand-in for your father.

That wasn't what this was. Beach was completely
over the desire for any parental guidance in navigating
life. And he certainly didn't want Tai to be—what had
Eli called Quinn when they were joking around the
grill?—Daddy. Beach didn't want any kind of a stand-
in. Not for Gavin off focused on Sergeant Boyfriend,
or their other friend Lee, who was caught up in his
wife's Machiavellian manipulations. He wanted this.
Brand-new. And all Tai.

But maybe that was all Tai saw it as. Why he listened patiently when Beach whined about the family
disaster. Why he urged Beach to take care of himself,
to go to physical therapy for his leg. It was Tai's job,
straightening out the miscreants so they could go on
to be good little members of society. He'd just found

a better than usual way to help out Beach. When his probation was over, when Beach was trained to good behavior, Tai would find a new cause. Beach wished he had enough courage to be bad enough to keep that from happening.

Chapter Nineteen

9:23 A.M. *Last night was sweet, boy.*

10:08 a.m. *Did you unstick yourself from the sheets yet?*

10:42 a.m. *Didn't wake you when I left. Too much temptation when you're conscious.*

11:18 a.m. *What dessert should we try next?*

Work went by both faster and slower spiked with anticipation created by exchanging flirting texts with David. Which was why the silence of four unanswered texts was damned distracting. Tai jabbed at the screen again, trying to force it to answer. Sub drop? It had been a while since David had had a bad drop, and never this far removed from a scene.

If something was going on with him, Tai wanted to know. When he got back from letting Jez out at lunch, he called. It rang until he thought it would roll to voicemail, but David answered.

"Hi. I'm kind of busy. I'll call you back."

Tai was left frowning at the call-ended screen until he shoved away from his desk and vented some frustration with forceful filing. It bugged him more than he wanted to admit. He was used to David hiding with some humor or pushing at him with a what-are-you-going-to-do-about-it brattiness, but not to him sounding flat, brittle.

It was this shit with his dad, that Tai was sure of. He could easily run a background check, find all the skeletons David was reluctant to dig for. Tension seized the back of his neck and squeezed. He'd done that for Gina—for *Sammie*—when Josh had come back, and Gina hadn't been grateful. The exact opposite. The memory of being compared to a psycho stalker still stung.

Tai retrieved his lineup of drug-test packages for the afternoon. He'd suggest running a check to David. When he wasn't in sub space. If David wanted, then Tai could do it.

The endless stream of afternoon check-ins and drug tests weren't enough to keep Tai from checking his silent phone. Every whined excuse from a probie cranked the vise at the base of Tai's skull tighter. And because that wasn't fun enough, one of the teen girls he'd inherited from Bob Meade got out of summer school and went home to hold a knife at her mother's throat.

By the time the Violation of Probation had been signed off on and filed and Lizzie Borden Junior was safely locked up, it was seven thirty. Even after Tai collected Jez for her much-needed walk and fed her, David still hadn't called back, and a double dose of extra-strength painkillers hadn't scraped away any of Tai's headache.

Tai wasn't going to get another uninformative brush-off. He'd go over and find out for himself what was going on.

His phone rang in the car, and he snatched it up instantly. It wasn't David.

It was DiBlasi.

"How's that trade working out for ya, ya big bastard?"

"What the fuck?"

"You were all bent on dumping that rich twat on me. You like your ride up to Towson tonight? Having fun filing the VOP? Sutton ream you out?"

Tai put a hand on the back of his neck and tried to flatten out the pain, or at least spread it out. "Actually, Sutton was glad I was the one on it, so shit got done faster than the newsfeed could pick it up. As opposed to dicks who leave an hour early and stay on the clock."

DiBlasi faltered a little on that. "You try and say no to your wife and baby girl when they're planning a wedding. Just thought you oughta know what you traded."

David. A chance to get to know his boy. Who was today hell-bent on making Tai crazy by ignoring him. "Oh?"

"For a one-percent motherfucker, he's been all right. Shows up for his meetings, tests clean. Today he calls, all polite and proper, asking about how he files a change of address."

The headache turned into red-hot spikes being driven into the back of his brain. Where the fuck was David going?

"He can't leave the county."

"Don't snarl at me, Fonoti. I ain't your probie. Yeah. He knows. Says he's been having problems with his lease and landlord. Thought those rich bastards were the landlords. But the point being, he called me. How many addresses you been to, chasing Meade's other girl juvie around the fucking county?"

"Fuck. You."

Tai shut off the phone and threw it in the footwell. Jez nudged at his armpit with a whimper, and he reached back to reassure her. David was going to be goddamned lucky Jez was there. She was the only thing making him keep control of his temper.

DAVID ANSWERED the door, then folded his arms and leaned against the frame, lashes dropping in that lazy way he used to piss Tai off. "Did we have an appointment, Sir?"

There was nothing remotely respectful about his tone.

"Do I need one to come over?" Tai swallowed back the *boy* he wanted to use to finish his question. Safer to keep this way out of D/s space.

Jez was looking anxiously between David's kitchen and back over her shoulder to plan a retreat.

David bent to her. "Hi, sweetheart. I'm very pleased to see you." He rubbed her head. "I got you a special toy today." He grabbed a long, furry squirrel-shaped chew toy off the counter.

Jez sat as she'd been taught, her eyes bright and fixed on the toy.

"Catch." He tossed it up in front of her, and she lunged, jaws snapping on it and head violently shaking any remaining life from her prey. She flipped it in the air, then caught it, delighting in the squeak from inside, and trotted off to rend it to pieces.

Tai let out a frustrated breath. "You could have run it by me."

David stepped up to him. "Is there an approved-toys list? I need your permission for that?"

"You need my hand on your ass." Tai squeezed the back of his neck. "What the fuck is going on, David? When were you going to tell me you were moving?"

David's shock and surprise was the worst kind of answer. He retreated to the other side of the counter. "Do you check up on me at work?"

"No." And thank God he hadn't run that background check. "Your PO said something to me."

"He knows about us? I thought that would be very bad."

"No. He—Never mind. I think the point is you planning to move and keeping it from me. Christ, it's the only thing I've asked you for. To be honest with me."

"And when the hell have I lied?"

"Running and hiding isn't very honest."

"For your fucking information, you opinionated asshole, me moving was all about you."

"What?" The headache spread into Tai's jaw. He interlocked his fingers behind his head and tried to stretch the agony out. He'd never seen—heard David so angry. Never had it directed completely Tai's way.

David stomped over to the small bar near the balcony, ran his fingers over one of the bottles, and then came back and poured himself an orange juice. "Want something?" As quick as the explosion began, it was over, David's voice mild as he held up a glass.

"An explanation." Tai planted himself on one of the stools at the counter.

David paced on the other side, his orange juice untouched. "The management company here has a very selective policy regarding pets."

"You said they were allowed."

"They are. Except those that become a nuisance or are perceived as a threat, which means"—David made air quotes—"such dog breeds with a reputation for violence, including but not limited to American pit bulls, German shepherds, Doberman pinschers, and rottweilers, are not permitted." He sighed and stopped to wrap his fingers around his glass. "Nothing about that rabid dachshund on the third floor who goes berserk in the elevator and tries to make off with my Achilles tendon."

"So it's about Jez?" The headache eased back from a ten to a nine and a half.

"Apparently if you both continue to visit, I'm facing a sheriff eviction in fourteen days. That probably won't look good to the court."

"They can't evict you with just one notice."

David took a sudden interest in his orange juice, his words half swallowed by the glass as he drank. "Ah, they can when it's the third notice."

"What?" The skull pressure ratcheted back up to eleven.

"I had an email. And a voicemail message. The certified mail today was a bit more peremptory. I guess we shouldn't have let her piss all over the tires of that prick's Mercedes."

Tai's fingers itched to grab David and haul him across the counter, but he slammed an open palm against the sealed granite as his next best option. "You ignored the first two notices?"

"I suppose that's one way of looking at it. Another is that their policy is asinine and prejudicial."

"That was irresponsible. Now you have to—"

"How is it irresponsible? I know I have to keep an address on file with the probation office, and I damned well knew it couldn't be yours."

"You should have—"

"I found a hotel that will, for an exorbitant deposit, allow Jez as a guest. Your Officer DiBlasi didn't think highly of my plan to take up residence on the *Nancy*." David turned to the sink and began washing out his glass.

"David—"

"If you're going to say my name with that amount of disgust in your voice, call me Beach," he said to the running water. "I thought you'd—I wanted to present it as a done deal. Something I took care of the right way. On my own. Something you'd approve of."

Tai wanted to wrap his arms around David, ease the protective hunch in those shoulders. But Tai had come over here furious, and that wasn't a good time to start a scene. Telling himself that didn't do a damned thing to ease the need to get his hands on his—David. Tai stepped around the counter.

David spun the faucet off but spoke with his back to Tai. "I like you spending the night. The evenings are short. And even on the weekends, well, I know you have Sammie this Sunday, and that is really important, and I have to do this thing for Gavin. I owe him. I really do. He may be milking it for all it's worth, but he saved my life and—"

Tai lost the fight with his better nature and reached out to drag David against him. "Take a breath." He brushed a kiss behind David's ear. "I already have a headache."

David pulled free, moving to the end of the counter. "Wow. That's a new one. I'm usually much too incompetent to inflict anything more serious than fleeting frustration."

"That's a pretty big jump from what I said."

"At least you won't have to come in after me."

Tai rubbed his forehead. "Exactly what are we talking about now?"

David shrugged. "I'd just as soon forget about it all."

The pressure inside Tai's skull was nothing compared to the boulder slamming into his diaphragm. His nuts hiked up tight and hard. Over. Like that.

"I think there's an Orioles game on again, if you want to watch it." David started toward the couch.

Tai's lungs stopped seizing and a bit of oxygen reached his brain. Forget the *conversation*.

Okay. That was fine. It didn't seem to be doing them much good anyway. "Baseball's like that. Pretty much every night for six months."

David nodded, picking up the remote. "What channel is it, then?"

"You pick something."

David arched a brow, blue eyes wide, then nodded, flicking around to some kind of mysteries-of-the-supernatural documentary, if you could call that bullshit documented. He didn't join Tai on the couch but bounced around, filling the water bowl he had for Jez, playing with her and her new squirrel toy.

"Do you want to watch this?"

David threw the toy for Jez and then came over to the couch. "I'm fine with baseball."

"C'mere."

David walked around to Tai's side, lowering himself to kneel on the floor.

Tai stopped himself from the instinctive stroke of David's hair. Things were too unsettled to go there right now. "No. I meant sit here with me." He patted the couch.

"Are you tired of us doing that?"

"No." Tai's voice had so much force Jez stopped shaking the soggy strip of fur. He softened his tone. "I'm not tired of it. Or of you, if that's what you're asking."

David sat next to him but still felt miles away. "The hotel is right downtown. You can park in the garage for free."

"Do you need help moving?"

"No, I'll take a suitcase. My stuff can stay here since I still have a lease. That is, if you want to see me there."

"David—" Tai pulled him in against his side. "—yes. I want to see you there." After running a hand down David's arm, Tai closed his fingers around the cuff on David's wrist. "You're my boy."

As they settled on the couch to watch, Tai tried not to mock the overly serious tone the narrator was taking about the dramatized events that took place in the Richardson home over the course of "one mysterious summer," confining himself to a deriding snort when the word *mysterious* was also applied to a figure, a sound, a room, and a clock. The program might have been stupid, but the company wasn't. His fingers wandered around on David's arm, rubbing the cuff, stroking his fingers, massaging the hard, muscled shoulder. Tai rolled his head on his neck, the tension melting into the comfortable cradle of David's sofa.

By the time wild theories were being flung around in summary, Tai's headache had faded to a faint pulse, though the muscles of the arm and back resting against him were still rigid with tension. Tai would see what a little making out on the couch could do about that, but before he got started, David pushed to his feet and went into the bathroom.

Tai switched the channel over to check the score of the O's game and then stared as David came back out with a bath brush that he put in Tai's lap.

The internet could be a hell of a dangerous place for information, especially on D/s.

That was one serious escalation, from a limit forbidding spanking to an implement that easily bruised even toughened, hard-to-mark sub asses. Had David discovered a masochistic kink? No, the crotch of his cargo shorts was untented, though his eyes were dark and his breath came fast.

"Sit down."

David folded stiffly onto the couch.

Tai turned the brush over in his hand, feeling the weight in the flat-backed wooden head. "Tell me what's going on."

"Last night you said if I broke silent mode, it wouldn't be your hand. I wondered what—then I saw this."

Tai had meant his belt, maybe a ruler if he could find one, something short where he could control the impact.

"You said I'd be sore, and when I looked, this seemed pretty serious." David's eyes tracked the motion of the brush as Tai swung it and tapped it lightly against his palm.

"That doesn't explain why you brought it to me now. You didn't break your silence last night."

"You told me I needed to trust you enough to ask for what I needed."

Point for David there. "Did something happen you haven't told me about?"

David shook his head.

If he got off on it, if he needed it to calm down, it would be one thing. Yes, Tai was pissed David hadn't come to him about the problem with the lease, that David had ignored the first two warnings, but after a shitty day, how much frustration would Tai be venting on David's poor ass? Tai let the brush rest across his knees again and made his voice as soft as he could get it. "I don't feel in the space for this."

"Oh." David got up and walked to the balcony, slid the door open, and stepped outside.

Tai dropped the brush on the couch and followed.

After the cool of the apartment, stepping through the hot night air felt like moving through soup, a soup of marine diesel and dead fish given the smells from the harbor. Then a breeze came, chasing it all away, and it was only the sparkling lights out on the water, summer air moving over them, lifting the hair from Tai's neck like a kiss. And David was ready to give this up so Tai and Jez could spend the night with him.

David had one hand on the rail as he turned to face Tai. "Is there some kind of safeword for Doms?"

Tai let out an amused breath. "Not usually necessary. Though some people do switch between the roles."

David nodded. "It's just—I don't—It's how I know to be around you. It feels like I've done something wrong, that you don't want it. You told me it was who you are."

Christ, Tai had been one epic asshole tonight. He dragged David close, wrapping him in a hug until David let out a long, shaky breath. "You're right. I've been giving you some majorly fucked-up signals since I got here, and that's wrong. Maybe you should try out the brush on me. Did you go buy it today?" The nod rubbed against Tai's chest. "How did that feel?"

"Terrifying. But—" David turned his head so that his mouth was aimed near Tai's ear. "Right and exciting. I felt so stupid when I opened that letter. Then pissed-off enough to stomp into the management office and tell them where to shove their bigoted ideas about dog breeds. Getting a matched pair of Dobermans as a fuck-you didn't seem fair to the dogs, so I ended up buying the brush. I felt somewhat less crazy after, so then I found a hotel and called Officer DiBlasi."

Tai lifted David's chin. "And how do you feel now?"

David's gaze flicked away until Tai tightened his grip. Barely meeting Tai's gaze, David blurted, "Like there's a thing hanging over me. I need to do something. Go somewhere. Try something."

David needed. Tai wanted. A connection deep and satisfying and as certain as when Sammie first focused on his face and closed her tiny fist around his finger.

A gentle suggestion in Tai's grip, and David sank to his knees on the balcony with a shudder that echoed through them both. David rubbed his face against Tai's groin. He knew, deep down in his gut, not only would David kneel for him out here, yield under the sky, with the risk of eyes watching from neighboring balconies or the dark windows on the next wharf, but with the slightest encouragement, David would suck him off. Power surged under Tai's skin. He could light up the harbor with it.

He dragged David to his feet. "Inside, now."

Once the balcony door was closed behind them, Tai tipped David's face up and kissed him hard. With a groan, David opened his mouth and took it, answering the rough thrust of Tai's tongue, pushing to flatten their lips against teeth and bone. Hand tight in David's hair, Tai yanked David's head back and licked a line up his throat.

"If you think you need to be punished, go get that brush and bring it to me." Tai released him, letting David find his balance, letting him decide.

After a few shaky breaths, David walked over to the couch and picked up the brush.

Then—damn, but he was perfect—he knelt and offered the brush, resting on open palms.

Tai ran his fingers over David's hot, swollen lips before grabbing the handle. "Take a piss first. Then go into the bedroom. Take off your clothes and wait for me."

"Yes, Sir," David whispered.

Tai caught his breath as David walked away. When he was out of sight, Tai checked over the brush. The back was varnished, sealing away any rough spots that could drive in a sliver or break the skin. The heft of it, concentrated in a six-inch-diameter-circle head, would be a lethal enough impact. Tai never used an implement he hadn't tried on himself first—or with a single tail, let Nic try on him. Tai took a few practice swings on the top of the sofa, wincing at the dent, then choked up on the long handle to shorten the swing. He smacked the side of his thigh, sucked in a pained breath, then aimed for his ass and jumped a little at the impact. *Christ.* David was going to get more than he bargained for. Tai had topped for heavy-sensation bottoms and pain sluts, learning from Nic how to dole out the impacts, timing, and placement. He'd punished service subs who craved the correction and brats who couldn't stop themselves from pushing. David might go the brat route sometimes, but that wasn't what he was asking for now. He wanted this—he'd made the choice clear—but what drove him wasn't like anything Tai had seen.

David had taken to D/s like he'd been waiting for it his whole life. There were bumps and adjustments, but he was always straining for more with a half-frightened, half-hungry look in his eyes. Tai started to smooth his gauntlets only to realize they were still at home, that he hadn't planned on any of this. Now David was waiting for Tai to give him the release he needed. Tai remembered his own eagerness, wanting to discover everything, try everything. Taking a firm grip on the brush, he locked down the fear that he couldn't, wouldn't be enough for David. At least not enough to keep him.

As Tai came into the bedroom, David looked up from his seat on the bed. Anticipation had him licking his lips and rubbing his hands over the bedcover while his feet circled in opposite directions. Tai switched on the lamp and drew the curtain over the balcony.

"Stand up."

David bounced to his feet, and Tai selected a seat where he could angle David across his lap.

"Come here."

David stood in front of him. There was a jump in his muscles, a fine vibration like a tremble. It reminded Tai of the horses headed for the gate he'd seen when he worked summers at Pimlico. The sharp edge of expectation, an explosion waiting beneath the surface. David's body might have been excited, but his cock was soft, balls loose and heavy, though a deep breath brought Tai the smell of sex in the sweat from David's crotch. "Did you jerk off today?"

"No, Sir."

"It's all right if this turns you on."

"It doesn't when it's happening. It hurts too much. It's after. Because—it's like the cuffs. I can still feel you. And it doesn't hurt for long."

"You might not say that this time, boy. Let's go." Tai pulled David's wrist and settled him across Tai's quads. The bed supported David's torso, while his feet were on the floor.

Tai warmed him up with brisk slaps, catching David's hand as soon as he reached for his ass, pinning it to his back. He alternated the slaps with rubbing and squeezing, sensitizing the skin while easing David into the sensation. As soon as his ass started to color, Tai stepped up the force of his swats until he heard grunts spill out along with David's pants.

When Tai stopped, David's body went slack against him. The room was suddenly quiet, David's breath the only sound. Even the air-conditioner fan had shut down. Tai ran a hand down David's spine, then felt the heat of his skin.

David's breath turned to a hiss. "Shit. I forgot how much it hurts."

Tai smacked him hard. "Why are you being spanked?"

"Because I asked you to punish me. Because I know I shouldn't have ignored the first two notices, and I guess I should have told you what I was planning. Sir."

Tai picked up the brush. "You guess?" He placed the smooth wooden back on David's ass and rubbed it in a circle. "Did it affect us both?"

"Yes, Sir."

Tai tapped lightly, bouncing it off one cheek and then the other. David squeezed his ass tight.

"Don't clench like that, boy. You'll take what you asked for." And there'd be less bruising, less ache to-morrow if he stayed relaxed.

"Yes, Sir."

Tai had considered starting over David's cargo shorts. The material wasn't heavy like denim, but it would still let him get a feel for the impact of the wood before it stung and slammed deep into his skin. But Tai needed to see what effect he was having so he could stop before he went too far.

He gave him a solid spank, turning his wrist so the weight of the brush and not Tai's strength was what David felt. The result was electric. David reared off the bed.

"Back down, right now."

Just as quickly, David got back into position. Tai shifted to pin David's legs under one of his own. "Give me your hands." He didn't want to chance hitting David's wrist or fingers. Hitching David closer, Tai gripped both wrists in his free hand.

"H-how long?"

"I'll decide that, boy. You take it."

The sag of David's weight told Tai he was on the right track. His own heart hammering high and hard in his throat, he laid on the brush. No force, but the weight and the jerk of his wrist delivered a bruising thud and sharp, echoing sting. David flinched at every

stroke, breaths sounding trapped. Tai checked to make
sure his mouth wasn't covered.

"Don't hold your breath."

"I'm sorry," David spat out.

Tai nailed him three times on the same spot, low
on the cheek.

"Sir. I'm sorry, Sir." David's gasp was full of
desperation.

Tai stopped, leaving the brush on the bed while he
rubbed David's ass, taking in the reaction, the ragged
breathing, screwed-shut eyes, fingers and toes clenching as his body absorbed the pain.

Tai picked up the brush again, resting it on the top
curve. David didn't have much room, but he shrank
away. Tai tightened his grip on David's wrists. "Fight
it if you want to, boy. I've got you."

Tai dropped the smacks faster, concentrating on
one spot at a time until David jerked. Tai drove him
harder, felt the rebellion rise up in a push from David's legs, and held on as he tried to buck off.

"Please, Sir. Please. I can't."

The rush of power Tai had felt when David knelt
on the balcony was nothing compared to this. It was
dizzying, hot, strong. He was enough. He could make
a man as jaded as David feel something he craved so
badly. And Tai would keep him safe through it all.

"No choice, boy." Tai aimed for the top of David's thighs, and he struggled harder. "You're mine."

"Please." There was an edge of surrender in that
plea.

"Get your ass up for me."

David stopped bucking and tipped his ass as
much as he could with Tai pinning his chest and legs.
Tai flipped the brush and dragged the bristles over

the cherry-bright skin. David shuddered but kept his ass tilted up. There were some darker spots, a hint of a bruise where Tai had focused on the crease of David's thighs. He'd feel it a little tomorrow, maybe. Tai scraped with the brush, back and forth over the sore skin.

David groaned. "Please, Sir. I don't think I can—"

"Almost done." Because they were almost there. "Trust me to give you what you need."

"Yes, Sir."

"Don't think, just feel, David."

Tai started laying down smacks in a rhythm, following a pattern like the five spots on dice. Slow at first, listening to David's breath, then faster. David pushed up to meet the brush, body there even if his head wasn't yet. He was almost relaxed, a steady exhale.

Tai didn't give him a warning but increased the force and speed, laying it all on the spots that were already darkest. David made one more attempt to fling himself off Tai's lap, then collapsed like he'd come, surrender in every inch of him, limp and vulnerable to the smack of the brush on his ass.

His voice was thick as he slurred "Yessir," over and over.

Tai tossed the brush on the mattress and helped David to sit up. His nose was running, his eyes a bit wet, but his breathing got under control fast.

"Good boy." Tai kissed him gently. "Tell me how you feel."

"Sore, damn." David leaned his head into Tai's shoulder. "Sweet Lord, that hurt. But that feeling of something I had to do—it's better. Thank you."

Tai studied David's face. "You know how we end this, David."

David's breath came sharp against Tai's skin. "Sir…." He looked up from under spiky lashes.

If things were going to work between them, Tai couldn't fail them because of the appeal in those wet blue eyes. "You needed that, yes, but this is something you earned." He stood and dragged a pillow to the center of the bed. "Over it." Tai didn't give David time to think about it, tugging him so that the pillow put his ass up.

"Fuck me, please, Sir."

That decided it. Tai picked up the brush and dealt out a good swing. "Fuck. Oh fuck. Tai—Sir."

Tai lowered his chest onto David's back, breathing in his ear. "This isn't just about you, is it, boy?"

"No, Sir."

"It wouldn't have been hard to call me. To answer a text and let me know what was going on."

"No, Sir." Now David did sound sorry. Probably more because of what he was dreading.

"This is so you remember." Tai pushed himself away. "Ten. If you kick, reach back, or swear, there will be extra. After each one, you will tell me what you're going to do better." Tai shifted his grip to shorten the swing, though from how dark the bottom half of David's ass was, even that would be enough to make his point.

The brush connected with David's ass, pushing deep into his reddened skin. "One. Let's hear it."

"I won't ignore things, Sir."

David's fingers grabbed up fistfuls of bedding on the second stroke. "I will not ignore your texts, Sir."

By seven, David's feet were flexing rapidly, toes curling and uncurling, but they stayed on the bed. His answers had become repetitive, but sincere. "I won't ignore problems, I promise, Sir, please."

Tai wasn't sadistic in the sense of just the idea of causing pain turning him on, but the sight of his David suffering so beautifully, holding himself there obediently, made heat prickle in Tai's nuts, pump blood to stiffen his dick. But his boy still had to push. On ten, his feet kicked, drumming into the mattress.

"Don't move. Two more." Tai slid the grip down. Two full swings, even without muscle behind them, should take care of that.

"I'm sorry, Sir," David said immediately, but Tai gave him the two extra spanks, and David held himself perfectly still.

"Stay right there."

Tai found some kind of lotion in the bathroom and soaked a washcloth in cool water. David wiped his face on the washcloth as Tai smoothed lotion over the superheated skin. David arched into the touch.

"Good boy." Tai stripped off his clothes and climbed on the bed. He licked a drop of sweat from David's neck. "Very good."

David came willingly as Tai pulled him onto his side, spooning up against him, though he flinched when his ass came into contact with Tai's dick. Shifting slightly, David eased back and pushed his ass into Tai.

"Can we fuck now, Sir?"

"No."

"But—"

"I want you to be quiet and feel that for a bit." Tai moved the arm under them to place his hand over David's heart, while pinning his hips with the other.

"Yes, Sir," David sighed out, but his heart thudded against Tai's palm.

TAI'S BREATH was steady in Beach's ear. Even in sleep, Tai held Beach firmly. He'd gotten used to falling asleep like that, wrapped up in or pinned under Tai's strength. On the occasions when Beach had shared a bed with a sex partner, Beach had preferred sleeping face-to-face, not touching. It was more convenient for talking, or to see if anyone was up for another round, or to make an excuse for departure. No matter how he and Tai fell asleep, Tai kept some body part on top of Beach, as if to keep him from slipping away. Usually he found it charming, flattering to be significant enough to merit a portion of unconscious attention. *Charming* wasn't what Beach would call it tonight. Consuming, maybe. Like he'd dived into the heart of a fire and somehow was safe, but he couldn't escape, wasn't sure he wanted to.

It wasn't merely figurative. Tai radiated a good deal of body heat, but the biggest factor was Beach's ass feeling like he was sitting on hot coals. The—*say it, Beach, you asked for it*—spanking had calmed the feeling that he was coming out of his skin but left him with another problem. The more sensation faded from fuck-that-hurts to a glow, the more Beach's dick wanted to party. Somewhere between that eye-watering pain and the dread that he couldn't take it was a warm flood of pride that he could offer Sir that much surrender. The more the simmer faded, the more pride and belonging built.

But right now his ass was hot and itchy from Tai's pubes, the breath across Beach's ear a furnace blast, Tai's whole body blazing like sand on an August beach at noon. The cool glass of the balcony door was only a few steps away. Incremental shifts moved Beach far enough to risk lifting Tai's arm so Beach could slide out from under it.

Tai yanked Beach back. "No."

Despite how much Beach had been craving the respite in a body length of cold glass, that one word moved through him like a complete reset. All levels back to normal.

A second later Tai's voice rumbled, "Need to piss?"

"No." Beach tried to find a cooler spot on the sheet for one of his legs. "Just hot."

Tai chuckled. "I can feel where you're hot, boy." He ground his crotch into Beach's ass and slid a hand down his chest before grazing Beach's dick. "Oh." The hand cupped Beach's balls, fingers light, stroking. A harder pulse pumped in Beach's cock. "If I jerk you off, do you think you could sleep?"

"Yes."

Tai tugged on the sac. "And if I jerked you off with my dick up your ass, what about then?"

"Yes." Beach rocked his hips back. "Please."

Tai's voice softened to a whisper. "I wouldn't want you to be confused about punishment. Sex isn't always going to happen after." His hand slipped between Beach's legs, squeezing the sore curve of his ass.

"I understand."

"Good boy."

Tai put him flat on his stomach, fucking into him at an angle that made Beach feel too tight, the friction more fire on his nerves.

"So fucking good, David." Tai poured the praise into Beach's ear with kisses and licks and sweet, sharp bites on his neck. It made Beach clench his muscles around Tai's dick, the scrape of his thrusts making them both pant. "God, baby. Feel so sweet. Don't move."

Arms wrapped around Beach's chest, Tai rolled them until Beach was on top, his own weight forcing Tai's dick deeper, sweat cooling everywhere on skin suddenly exposed to the air-conditioned room, the shock taking the edge off the need in his cock as it waved in space instead of grinding against the sheet.

Tai held Beach pinned there with an arm on his chest and a hand on his hip, rocking them enough to keep his dick moving.

In twenty years of as much sex as he could get, Beach thought he'd tried every position. But this was new. Everything about it. The angle of the cock inside him, the motion like rocking in the *Nancy* anchored for the night, and that prickling, throbbing fire from his paddled ass dragging against Tai.

"Gonna stay inside you like this all night."

"Yes." Beach wanted that too. He pushed down to take in more. More cock. More soreness in his ass. More Tai. This was where he was supposed to be. Just here. Sir's boy. Nothing else.

But as much as Beach wanted to freeze time, ride this perfect moment forever, his dick had its own plans. The urgency drove him up and down on Tai's cock. Dick bobbing, balls tightening as a shift made Tai drive steadily across Beach's gland.

"Work your cock, boy. Come for me."

"Yes." Beach's cock leapt to meet his hand like it had been years instead of hours since he'd last come. Tai's palm drifted up Beach's chest until it rested over his larynx. Thumb and fingers stretched out to circle Beach's throat.

"Put your other hand on my thigh," Tai whispered. "Three taps, remember?"

Beach nodded as much as he could, precome dribbling from his slit at the thought of what Tai was going to do.

The pressure started slow, nothing more than a tight-collared shirt, until it wasn't. Until Tai's hand held Beach's life in the squeeze of his fingers. Heat, so much heat. Cock, ass, head. Dizzy from it. Blood aching as Beach stripped his cock faster, harder, grinding down. His hand gripped Tai's leg, the lifeline there if he needed it. The edge felt just out of reach with the puffs of darkness flooding his head, the strangeness he felt in his blood as it tried to feed his body. He strained for it.

"Mine. God, David. Mine."

Beach couldn't answer with his voice, but he could with his body. He stopped pushing for the orgasm and let Sir force it into him. Loose and tight, white-hot and icy-black, he gave into it, spilled over and through it. Cock shooting off fireworks to match the explosions of color behind his eyes.

He was more than wrung out, more than dizzy. The rush didn't fade back to normal after coming like usual. Even though Tai released Beach's throat, sensation kept pulsing into his toes.

Tai rolled Beach back underneath. In the roar of rich, sweet oxygen in his blood, he was only barely aware of Tai stripping off the condom, the quick sounds of his hand on his cock, a gut-deep groan and the heat of come splashing across skin. Tai rubbed his cock into Beach, spread the slick puddle, painted it on the sore spots on Beach's ass, dragged it in a pattern across his back.

The last thought Beach had was wishing come could glow so he could read what Tai was writing.

Chapter Twenty

BEACH GLANCED at his watch and pushed back from the table, the iron legs of the chair in the little outdoor seating area grating hard enough to make his teeth ache. "I should leave to get dressed. I really am sorry about this."

Tai folded his arms across his chest. The French-cafe-style furniture at Le Vol au Vent already looked doll-sized with Tai around. With both his upper arms in view, the table shrank further. He took up a hell of a lot of room, but after two days of him absent from Beach's apartment and bed, Beach had decided that space was widely overrated.

"You're only going to a friend's party as a favor. Not to Europe."

"Right." Beach glanced at his ankle monitor. "Not anytime in the foreseeable future."

"So the apology isn't necessary. Neither was the fancy bakery for breakfast. Though thanks anyway."

"You're welcome. Things are just taking longer than I expected with the hotel and the address-change approval, but I'll be in on Monday." Beach's leg was feeling stronger than ever, so he'd left the cane in Tai's car for the walk down the block. He knelt to pet Jez behind her ears, and she leaned against him.

"David." But Tai didn't add anything to that. As Beach looked at him expectantly, Tai took an unusual amount of time choosing his words. "Is there something else to this?"

Beach raised his brows.

"Feelings for Gavin," Tai suggested.

"No." Beach shook his head for emphasis. "He's just my oldest friend. Nothing like that."

"His feelings for you?"

"I would imagine any feelings would come as a surprise to his boyfriend." Beach smiled. "There hasn't been anything like that between us for twenty years."

"Okay." Tai dragged his chair away from the table, and Beach noticed a few glances directed at Tai.

Beach had appreciated admiring, envious glances when he'd had a lovely woman on his arm. But these were from other men and women, aimed at his Sir. He felt like preening in a completely different way. *Yes. He is that incredibly strong and beautiful. And I belong to him.* The thought made the layers of the mille-feuille he'd consumed tip like the Tower of Pisa in his stomach, as a line of sweat broke on his forehead. He reached for his cane to distract himself and remembered he'd left it in the car.

"So what is going on?" Tai asked as they headed up the block.

"Aside from not wanting to go? I guess I resent the demand on my time when there are other things I want to do." Beach offered his most charming leer.

"I'm sure you'll survive."

Beach heaved a sigh as he slung himself into the passenger seat of the Focus. "Contrary to medical belief, you can die of boredom."

Tai grabbed Beach's jaw and pulled him across the console for a kiss. "Can't have that. We'll stop to get your clothes and car, then you're getting dressed at my place."

MEDITATING ON what Tai might have in mind provided the distraction of shivering temptation. Beach couldn't say what had thrown him when he'd read the looks aimed at Tai—and by extension himself—in the small cluster of pastry fans. Beach had never hidden his enjoyment of both men and women, but public functions being what they were, he'd never been out, so to speak, among the general public. And Tai's body language had been exceedingly proprietary. Or was the exposure of his submissive side what made Beach's breakfast lurch around? Either way, he wanted that moment of confusion out of his head. He double-checked that he had everything from his socks to his sunglasses to his black card, and draped his seersucker suit over the passenger seat like he was riding with the invisible man. As he drove, he imagined a conversation with Tai.

I forgot my tie, Sir. I'm sorry.

How late are you going to be, boy?

In Beach's fantasy, Tai was tapping the bath brush against his palm.

Beach shuddered. He hated that thing. Should have broken it after what it did to his ass. He never wanted to do that again. Except he wanted the after. The feelings that came after, in his body, in his head. His fingers went up to brush the fading bruise where Tai's thumb had been on Beach's throat. Would that have happened, been so intense… could Beach have let himself give in like that if Tai hadn't first driven home how much Beach craved that intensity? Right on up to the pain that terrified him.

Tai and Jez were waiting on their front stoop when Beach arrived with his suit. "What time do you need to leave?" Tai rose.

"Gavin said the party was one to five. So around four?" Beach grinned.

Tai leveled a glare that had Beach's dick testing the roominess of his shorts.

He tugged at them. "Fine. Ten of one. No one ever gets to these things on time. Not even the host. He would get a beautiful day too, the bastard." Beach looked up at the fluffy clouds in the bright sky.

"I gather this isn't the sort of thing you need to help him set up for?"

Beach laughed. "No. Not exactly. It's a silent auction, thank goodness. A bunch of rare rose and azalea cultivars along with other garden delights to tempt the good charitable ladies of Charm City into supporting Gavin's cause. I'm just eye candy."

Tai let them into his apartment. "And what's his cause?"

"This one? He's started a foundation to fund a shelter for teens, focused on the ones who get kicked out for being gay."

Tai stopped, and Beach banged into him, dropping his suit. "What?" Beach asked.

"And you can't imagine why that's worthwhile?" Tai's face had turned to sharp lines, his voice disdainful and not like Sir's at all.

The pleasant tingles from anticipating Tai's plans evaporated into the hot air. Real dread, real panic about where they might be headed was nothing like what they did as Sir and David. Tai's anger, his disgust, slammed the breath from Beach much harder than any bath brush. The weight of it made his knees wobble, and he had to put his hand on the wall. "Of course it is." Beach tried to find a way back into that light, fizzy energy. "I much prefer this to saving the dwarf wedge mussel, however important it is to the Chesapeake ecosystem." He picked up his suit. "And I do love the Bay."

Tai stared at him, then turned and walked away. After standing at his desk for a minute, he came back with a check and handed it off. "Give this to Gavin. Tell him—if he needs help or runs into any kind of problems with law enforcement or corrections, he can contact me."

Beach folded it without looking at the amount and tucked it in his wallet. "I don't think that will be an issue, but I'll tell him." Maybe there was a reason behind Tai's reaction to the shelter idea.

"Your mom didn't seem to mind, I mean, she knew I was with you." Beach had never bothered to say a word about his sexuality to anyone in his family. Gossip carried the news without any effort on his part. Had Tai and his mom had a conflict?

"I don't have to personally experience an injustice to want to correct it, David."

"I never said it wasn't a good cause, just that fundraisers are boring as hell."

"So is a lot of work. Filing, making phone calls, running drug tests. But it can help people."

"Yes. Of course." Beach's easy agreement had no impact on Tai's expression. "Well, maybe I should head out. I can get dressed at Gavin's."

"Yeah, you could."

Cold. Had it been hot in here? Beach's ears buzzed, and he put a hand on the wall again, staring down at his feet as if he wasn't sure they were still there. He couldn't feel them.

Tai went on, "Sure. Walk away. Hide behind that smile and pretend everything is good." Every word made Beach feel less and less attached to his body. Yes. He was smiling.

What was he supposed to do? Admit that Tai's opinion of him mattered more than anyone's ever had?

"Apparently I've come off as some sort of selfish, unfeeling asshole in your eyes. And since I'm so un-likable, I think I'll leave you to your own company." Damn it. He'd left the cane in the Spider. It would have helped with the whole not-being-able-to-feel-his-feet thing.

Tai charged him, body held away, but his palms slapped into the wall on either side of Beach's head, boxing him in. "I know you're no coward. Christ, I know you're not afraid of anything. So what's so god-damned difficult about standing still and talking about this?"

Beach started to raise his hands to push Tai away, then stopped, leaning back against the warm plaster. "I don't see the point. You're angry. I'll be angry. Things will be said to make people feel bad."

"People? You and me, David. We're the only people here."

"Right." He looked past Tai to Jez, who was
watching them with a tilted head and barely audible
whine. "Well, Jez doesn't like it either."

Tai glanced over his shoulder, then slapped the
wall hard enough to make her skitter off to the bedroom. "For fuck's sake."

Beach took a deep breath. "I think perhaps you
misunderstood me. I think what Gavin is doing is
wonderful. He has my support, personal and financial.
The reason why I didn't want to go today is because I
wanted to spend the time with you. I know you have
another important date tomorrow."

Tai's face relaxed at the thought of his daughter.
"Maybe you should meet her."

"If you want. But you both should have time to
yourselves. I don't want to arouse jealousy."

"Usually she's more interested in the dog."

"I meant me. I am terrible at sharing. I had to repeat kindergarten."

Tai pushed away from the wall. "But a fucking
genius at getting me off track." Beach raised his palms
and shrugged. Tai shook his head.

"I promise I will take my job of helping Gavin
nail down donations very seriously."

"Hm." Tai narrowed his eyes, but everything was
all right again. The threat of a permanent break—of
options reduced to a goodbye—faded behind them,
thunderclouds racing away on the horizon. "You're
damned right you will. You're going to sell the hell
out of those heirloom roses culti-whatevers, and I'm
going to help you with a reminder."

Tai went into his bedroom and came out with a small box, which he placed in Beach's hand. "Don't open it yet."

The box was black, covered with a faux-velvet finish. Not Tiffany's, that was certain. It had a solid feel, though, heavy for its size. He was turning it around when Tai reclaimed the box.

"Strip."

Beach complied, a buzz in his nuts as he slid under Tai's authority. When he stood in nothing but his cuffs, he waited.

Tai took one wrist in his hand. "Are you keeping these on?"

"I want to."

Tai growled and grabbed Beach's face, kissing him. Everything—heart-lungs-cock—ramped up, zero to eighty, faster than his Spider, and then it was over too fast. Tai stepped away.

"Gotta get you ready to go."

Beach glanced down at his dick, and he'd swear it winked back. "Oh, I am, Sir."

"No, but you will be. You can open the box now."

Beach knew what the bulb of shining heavy steel was immediately. But his brain took longer to connect a butt plug displayed on blue silk like it belonged in a museum with getting dressed for Gavin's garden party.

"That should help inspire you." Tai put the box on the desk.

Tai hadn't said Beach couldn't speak, but for once he had nothing to say. Tai was going to send Beach off to mingle with the cream of Baltimore society with a plum-sized piece of steel up his ass. The thought left

Beach without a drop of blood anywhere but his hard, aching, dripping cock.

"Gonna need to get that under control, boy." Tai picked up Beach's shirt from the couch and guided his arms into it as he stared at the plug in the box. Tai had the buttons done up to Beach's nipples before he noticed.

"Ah-uh-I—"

"I'll take care of you." Tai fastened all the buttons, the collar brushing, hiding that faint bruise. "Tie?"

Beach shook his head, and Tai unfastened the top button before rubbing his thumb over the bruise. He'd touched it, kissed it, licked it dozens of times since it appeared. Beach was sorry it was fading so fast.

Tai helped Beach into his jacket like a master tailor, settling it across his shoulders with tugs on the sleeves. "Your eyes are so blue and sexy in that."

The heat in Beach's cheeks shocked him. He couldn't remember the last time he'd blushed.

Tai held up Beach's ocean-blue briefs. "Matched to the skin. Step in."

The blush burned hotter. "But—"

"We'll get there." Tai held the shorts out.

Beach wasn't sure why he didn't feel infantile, being helped into his clothes. All he knew was the warm bubble of excitement and contentment that came from Tai's control. He stopped with the elastic waistband under Beach's balls.

"Hmm. I bet some ice would help you there, make it easier to tuck inside."

"Fuck." Beach breathed the word. The throb in his dick faded at the threat.

"Better." Tai jerked the briefs up, and Beach winced.

Slacks and his belt followed, Tai fastening everything.

It had only been a tease, then. Beach looked at the gleam peeking out of the box. He supposed that was good, since he'd had no idea how he could sweet-talk Mrs. Dougherty into competing for a new azalea variety when his attention was on his ass. But he couldn't prevent a sigh of disappointment.

"You look like you oughta be in a magazine." Tai checked him over.

"Thank you."

"Now go grab the lube and bring me the plug."

Beach startled into obedience. The steel was heavier than it looked. Not too large or thick, but with the curve and weight, there was no way Beach would be unaware of it. The illicit thrill of it made the hair on his body stand up, mind locked into a refrain of *This is happening*.

Tai unbuckled Beach's belt, unzipped his trousers. "You're my submissive, aren't you?"

"Yes, Sir."

"You wear my cuffs, and now you're going to wear this. Every time you move, you'll know who you belong to. Bend over the back of the couch."

Beach would have traded the *Nancy* for one minute of attention to his aching dick, but all Tai did was drag the elastic of the briefs over it again as he exposed Beach's ass and spread the cheeks.

"This stays in until I take it out, except for a call of nature. If you disobey, you won't come for a week."

The tip pushed, making Beach push back to fit it in. "Yes, Sir." He tried to spread his legs, but they were pinned by his slacks.

Tai shoved it in with an eye-watering stretch that subsided quickly into a sweet burn. Despite taking Tai's dick up his ass a couple of nights a week, there was always that first resistance, the shock and scrape as his body adjusted. The plug was smaller, and the narrow neck meant his muscles could relax. The loop that made up the base settled smoothly against Beach's skin, tucked close to his body. Tai tugged and shifted the plug, sending pleasure rippling out from where the smooth ball rolled across Beach's gland, then stepped back.

Beach straightened, ass closing, clenching, sending off another wave inside. He closed his eyes. Fully dressed for a party and fucked at the same time. Not just fucked. Owned. Tai would be in him no matter where Beach went or who he talked to. He wanted to drop to his knees, but whether he would thank Tai or beg him to take it out, Beach didn't know.

Even in silence, with every breath, every move, Tai demanded and Beach—David gave. "You make that face when I'm in you." Tai put a hand on Beach's cheek.

"You are, Sir."

"Good boy. Go make me proud."

MONTGOMERY MANOR fronted the water, and today that brought breezes that kept the July sun from being brutal as it gleamed on the guests and the flowers and the caterers. Everything was the height of elegance. Even the breeze displayed enough etiquette to flutter the table linens while refraining from disruptive force. Beach tried to maintain equal standards by not emitting moans and keeping his program or jacket angled to hide the constant interest his dick had in the sensations from his ass.

He escorted Mrs. Dougherty along the table where the cultivars were displayed, either in picture or in person. "Just think of how this shade will draw attention to the veranda. It complements your hydrangeas perfectly."

"They don't bloom at the same time, dear. But I'm flattered you remember the hydrangeas."

Since he'd hidden in them when he was sneaking out of their house one night—he hadn't known the Doughertys' daughter Julia had gotten married in London—they were rather prominent in his memory.

"Your gardens have always been a special part of any visit, ma'am."

"Your Southern charm will be the death of me, and call me Lydia."

Beach flipped open the cream-colored leather auction folder. "Perhaps I should put a bid on them. My aunt would like them." Knowing which levers to push, Beach drew his finger down the list of bids so Lydia's eyes would follow.

Her gasp was as predictable as it was satisfying. "If that... that *arriviste* Sierra thinks she'll buy her way into the Francis Scott Key Azalea Society with that, she is sadly mistaken." Lydia wrote an impressive figure on the next line and signed with a flourish.

Gavin had definitely known what he was doing, not providing numbers to the bidders.

The competition was only enhanced by seeing the names of the competitors.

"It is a striking color." Someone brushed by, jostling him, and his muscles gripped, awakening a fresh round of heat to flush his face.

"Beach, I have never seen you so passionate." She pulled him down to buss his cheek. "Your mother would be thrilled to see you taking an interest. She loved her gardens."

Beach tried to politely point out that his mother was not dead, just in France—well, the last he knew. "I'm sure she's quite busy with her lilies in Lille."

"That was dreadful, Beach." She laughed and shoved lightly at his upper arm, creating a new shift inside him. Following the torture of the car ride, after which he had needed to hold a cup of ice against his lap to make himself decent, he'd adjusted to the feeling of the smooth weight resting at such an intriguingly pleasant angle inside. In fact, he'd almost convinced himself he was in control, that he could ignore it as long as he wasn't moving, but then he'd catch himself clenching because he missed it. Missed the mark of Tai's possession, his presence. It wasn't only the thrill of getting away with all but having sex under everyone's nose; it was having Tai here, so close that Beach expected to feel the rumble of Tai's voice or the solid brace of his hands at any moment.

Like the leather bands Beach kept tugging his cuffs down to conceal, the constant prod and shift inside reminded him that he belonged to Tai. Yielding that much control gave Beach more freedom than he'd ever had, even steering the *Nancy* out to sea.

He wanted to give something to Tai in exchange. "Lydia, I wonder if I might ask your opinion of this particular breeder."

One item at auction was the opportunity to work with a breeder for exclusive rights to a rose cultivar, including the choice of name to appear on the official registry. Not that Beach had noticed Tai having any particular appreciation for flowers, but he might enjoy giving that to Sammie, or his mother. Beach would claim Tai had purchased it with the donation check Beach still needed to turn over to Gavin. Beach tightened his ass again and bit back a sigh. He was looking forward to that conversation.

Lydia read over the details. "The breeder is new, but his work is getting good attention. I heard he's light in the loafers himself, which would explain the generous donation."

I don't have to personally experience an injustice to want to correct it, David.

"Not that it isn't a wonderful thing Gavin is doing for those children," Lydia amended.

"Of course not."

Lydia lifted the bidding folder and opened it. Her razor-thin brows rose. "Apparently the rest of the bidders think highly of his work."

Beach looked at the last number. He didn't recognize the name of the bidder, but the number made a salient impression. Still, it was for a good cause, and his father hadn't contacted him about the money. He raised the bid to six hundred thousand and signed off, thinking of Tai's expression when he realized he could have a flower named after his daughter.

"Thank you kindly, ma'am."

"I can never resist that drawl of yours." She tapped him with her purse. "Now, be a good boy and bring me some champagne."

The trip to the bar along the graveled path was almost equal to the level of torture produced by the vibrations in the Spider. Beach was chewing his lip by the time he arrived. A vaguely familiar platinum blond was turning away as Beach stepped up. One close look and Beach placed him. Baby-faced with seductively old eyes and a fuck-off attitude.

Beach had been intrigued, but Gavin had declared Silver completely off-limits.

Silver had two glasses of something that smelled sweet.

"What are you drinking?" Beach eyed the creamy head on the fizzy liquid.

"KZ cream soda."

"Champagne and a KZ cream soda."

Silver raised his brows. "The soda's for me. I'm on my best behavior today." The plug shifted as Beach reached for his order.

"How boring for you," Silver answered.

"It can have its own rewards." Beach considered what he'd earn later for all his good deeds.

"Hmpf." Silver either didn't understand or understood too much.

They moved back down the path. Silver was in lightweight trousers and a linen shirt, but if his slacks had been black instead of gray, he might have been mistaken for a server.

"How did you get roped into this?" Beach asked.

"I'm the horrible example."

Beach stopped. "Of what?"

"The need for the shelter."

Beach still couldn't follow. "You—"

"Parents tossed me out, I hit the streets, turned to prostitution to survive." Silver uttered the last in a dramatic-documentary tone.

"I didn't know any of that." His voice sounded strangled, even to him.

"Jeez, Beach, 'fraid you might have been a customer?"

"No. Not at all, but—where are you living now?"

"Right now, with my boyfriend, till I move into an apartment on the first."

"Didn't think of you as the boyfriend type when we met at the gallery with Gavin."

"You either." Silver jerked his chin at Beach, then looked pointedly at his wrists. "But someone's holding your leash now."

Sir's hand around David's throat. His collar tight there. Beach's body locked around the plug, driving it in, his hips shifting as it tapped his gland.

"Yeah." Silver had a knowing half smile, but he shook his head. "Guess you never can tell."

Why hadn't it bothered Beach to name Tai his Dominant in front of Clayton, but he froze under the knowing smirk from someone barely an adult?

"I—have to deliver this champagne to a lady. It was nice to see you again, Silver." Beach downed his soda and went to bump up his donation to seven-fifty.

TAI LOOKED up from where he'd been staring at his toes to explain, "Everything we do, he's ready for more."

"Well, that sounds dire indeed." Nic's face was more sharply angled than usual given the bars of light from the crossbeams over his deck, a pergola he called it, when Tai couldn't figure out why no one had bothered to finish the roof. By mid-August, it would be overgrown by climbing vines offering complete shade, but now the top was still open to the sun.

"How do I know if I can be enough? Or when to stop?"

"Has he ever used his safeword?"

"Yes."

"Then he knows how to stop if he needs to. I sense you're not talking just about scenes, though." Nic poured himself another glass of wine, but Tai waved the offer away.

"He said he didn't know how to be around me when he wasn't my sub."

Nic settled back in his chair, stretching out his denim-clad legs to cross them at bare ankles. "That is a lot of pressure, expecting you to maintain control."

Embarrassed by Nic's sympathy, Tai dropped his face into his hands. "I want it too. It's hard to make myself back off when it's a real-life situation and not simply play."

"Now I see the problem. You both enjoy a 24/7 consensual D/s relationship."

"Yes."

Nic started to laugh, and it stung.

"C'mon. I'm serious. How long can we keep that up?"

"With the right sort of cock ring, I imagine pretty long."

"Thanks a fucking lot." Tai rose in frustration, then stepped down from the deck and peered into the vibrant blue of the rectangular pool. "I'm serious."

"Toluaotai, I've seen you with all kind of subs. You make them fly, and it feeds you, but you walk away without a backward glance. Did it never occur to you that a fully D/s relationship is what you've been after?"

"But how will I know I'm doing it right?"

"Like every other relationship. You figure it out as it goes. From what you've said, your boy has no trouble asking for boundaries."

"He craves them." A burst of heat flooded Tai's chest as he thought of David wearing the plug, enduring the discomfort, the endless sensation, because Tai demanded it. "He knows how much he needs them, even as he pushes."

"I look forward to meeting him."

"I hear the *but* in your tone."

Nic sighed. "I can't give you permission to do this. I'm not your Master, I'm your mentor."

"I didn't ask you for permission. Just advice." Tai sat back on the deck and leaned against a support beam for the pergola, back pressed against the climbing vines.

"Very well. One, stop crushing my grapevines. Two, stop looking for reasons to walk away."

"Me? Are you saying I have commitment issues?" But he did straighten from his lean.

Nic's voice was soft. "You could have fought for Samantha."

"I did. I insisted on DNA rather than just a blood type."

"You were the sole financial support for almost three years."

"I didn't want her to go through that, to feel like a prize in some tug-of-war over who stayed."

"And will you be stoic and noble and let your boy go for his own good?"

"I wouldn't make him stay."

"Not even if it was as easy as asking him to?"

Tai stood and walked to the pool again. "I'm not the one with commitment issues. He can't even commit to a gender to fuck."

"That's grim. I thought Samoans were the happy people of Polynesia."

"What the fuck—" Tai bit off the rant as he caught on to Nic's point. "So it's a generalization. Doesn't mean it's not true."

"Or that it is. Has he been pining for feminine company?"

"Not that he's mentioned." Tai played back their breakfast outing. David's eyes hadn't strayed much from Tai's face.

"Then it appears the only thing standing in your way is you. Stop thinking about what could go wrong and enjoy what's going right."

BEACH WAS unable to find Lydia Dougherty anywhere, so of course he had to be holding the flute of rapidly warming champagne when Gavin walked up.

"It's not mine," Beach explained and placed the glass on the nearest table under the tent. "I was delivering it to Mrs. Dougherty."

Gavin blinked. "I never said it was. What's the bug up your ass?"

Beach tried to control it, but he snorted and was afraid the ending sound was too close to a giggle for comfort. "I'm fine. Where's Sergeant Boyfriend?"

Gavin's half smile was rueful. "He doesn't play well with others. Plus he had to work."

"For which we are all supremely grateful. And by that I meant we appreciate his sacrifices as he does his duty to keep us safe."

Gavin shoved Beach's shoulder. The motion sent off a chain reaction that left Beach gasping as his staggered steps moved the plug hard and fast against his gland. His dick swelled, and he had to drop into a chair to hide it under the table linen. Next time Sir sent David off with something up his ass, he was dressing in something more concealing than lightweight cotton.

Gavin surveyed the party for a moment and must have decided it was fine without him, because he joined Beach at the table. "Sorry, Beach. I forgot. I know you must be sick of the cane, but should you really be going without so soon? You've been walking funny all day."

Beach gulped in air to forestall his laugh but only succeeded in choking until his eyes watered. "The physical therapy has been helping a lot," he gasped when he could speak.

"What the hell is going on with you?"

"Nothing. So really, how are things with Jamie?"

"I'm shocked you admit to knowing his name. Things are fine."

"Speaking of boyfriends—" Beach reached into his breast pocket and took out Tai's check. "—this is from him, for the shelter."

Gavin glanced at it before tucking it away. "Thank him for me." His hand smoothed the surface of the table. "So, is this the one I met at the hospital, the one you're trying out your kinks with?"

Beach leaned back, shifting the plug, and smiled at Gavin. "Exactly how many boyfriends have you known me to have?"

"Point taken." Gavin's sudden attention made Beach flush, as if his friend could see what was putting the grin on Beach's face. "He's... big."

Beach rolled his eyes.

"So that's what you do? All you do? Leather and bondage?"

Beach looked down at Gavin's fingers splayed on the cream-colored linen. For twenty years, Beach had told Gavin everything and listened to his complaints about his father and his siblings. Gavin had been with him on every adventure of Beach's life. But he froze at the thought of trying to explain that kneeling at Tai's feet made Beach feel more content than anything ever had, that the only thing that scared him now was not having that again.

"Seems like more than you and Sergeant Boyfriend have in common."

Gavin shrugged infuriatingly.

"No. That's not all." Today they'd sat and talked for two hours outside Le Vol au Vent. Beach couldn't remember what they'd discussed, only that he hadn't been bored for an instant. That he would have sat there longer.

It was easier to control the movement of the plug sitting down. Damn, he could work it pretty sweetly like this. Though that wasn't going to make it easier to stand up, and he wanted to check on his bid for the cultivar.

"Goddamn it, Beach."

He jerked his attention back to Gavin. "What?"

"You're high. What are you on?"

"Nothing. I swear."

"I know you." Gavin reached forward and pulled Beach's sunglasses from his face. "Jesus. Look at your eyes. Your pupils are huge."

"It's dark in here."

"Bullshit. I can't believe this. Do you want to go to jail?"

"Of course not. Gavin, I'm not—I swear, I haven't had anything stronger than orange juice in two months."

"I wish I could believe it. I hope they don't call you in for a test before you get it out of your system."

Beach tried to keep a straight face. He really did. But he felt so damned good, and *Get it out of your system* was just too funny to ignore. He clenched his jaw, but that only clenched all his other muscles, including the ones reminding him exactly what was still *in his system*. Laughter erupted from his chest.

"God, Beach, do you need to go somewhere and sleep it off?"

Going somewhere to jerk off wouldn't be bad, if only Sir would allow it. Beach shook his head, pinching his lips together so the laughter made its way out of his nose.

"I'll get you some coffee."

When Gavin left, Beach took out his phone. The sight of the message from Tai set off a fresh round of his ass clenching around the plug. He had to grind the heel of his hand against his dick to settle himself down.

Find a quiet place and text me.

Beach rocked in the chair before he realized that wasn't going to help get him in any state to walk through the party. He thought of cold and shriveling things and then strode off to the house, easily finding his way to Gavin's room and his private bath.

He pressed Tai's number as soon as he shut the door. "I told you to text."

"This is better." Beach put the phone on video.

"Don't push, brat." Tai glared back at him.

"Yes, Sir."

"Where are you?"

Beach explained.

"Kneel."

"Yes, Sir." Beach lowered himself, propping the phone on a shelf.

"I gave you an order, and you didn't follow it."

The argument came and went in Beach's mind, then regret left his mouth dry. "I'm sorry, Sir."

"You will be." The rumbled threat turned the regret to anticipation. "Lower your trousers and briefs. Then show me."

Beach had been hard since he made the call, but exposing his cock made everything tighten more. The skin stretched, the precome welled from his slit.

"Tell me how that plug feels," Sir demanded.

"It's heavy. And every time I think I'm used to it, it moves and God, Sir, I need to come. I'm so hard it hurts."

"Tell me how it feels in your head."

Beach lowered his eyes. "Like you're here. When it moves, you…. It's like you're making me feel it, and I want to show you."

"Show me now. Reach back and work it in your hole. Let me watch your face."

It was exquisite and impossible like this. The waves of sensation rippling out from the friction drove him mad, but at least the suffering had a point. Sir could see it.

"Stop."

Beach whimpered and forced his hand away with a jerk. "Please, Sir, please let me come. I'll be good."

"I know you will be, David. But you still have to wear the plug, and it will be uncomfortable if you come now."

"I don't care."

"Do you need a lesson about who's in charge?"

"No, Sir."

"Good. How's the party? Food good?"

God, he couldn't be like this and talk about the quality of the duck tartare with roasted hazelnuts and orange-blossom-scented crème fraîche.

"David." Tai said it softly, and Beach met his eyes on the tiny screen. They were shadowed but focused on him. "I've got you."

Beach slowed his breathing, concentrating on letting Sir lead him instead of pushing. The scrape and burn on that desperate edge of need softened, Sir's authority cushioning him from the worst of it. "Yes, Sir. I think the foundation is going to make a lot of money. Gavin knows what he's doing."

"Good. Now behave, and I'll see you in an hour."

"Yes, Sir." Only an hour. Beach tried to hold on to that as Tai disconnected.

"What the fuck is going on with you, Beach?"

Beach tried to spin around to face the door, but he was tangled in his undone pants, and his shin felt like he cracked it again as he dropped back down on the tiles. Dignity was hell and gone from where Beach flopped around like a gaffed tuna in front of the shower, but he gave faking it a shot.

"Sweet Jesus, Gavin, don't you knock?"

"It's my own goddamned bathroom. What the hell are you doing here?"

"Taking a piss."

"Bullshit, Beach. I've been standing here for five minutes."

Beach wanted to curl up and hide. At the moment he'd gladly trade places with the tuna. "If you enjoyed

the show, I'd appreciate a tip. Leave it on the sink."
He managed to wriggle back into his pants.

"I didn't."

"Well, it wouldn't be the first time we've had sex
in front of each other. Guess that can get old."

"Is that what that was? Sex?"

It was so much more. It was his fucking soul on
the line there in those moments when he surrendered,
and he wished his best friend could understand.

"Look, Beach, I'm not judging the kink."

"Really? Because it sure as sweet, spicy hell
sounds like it."

"This stuff getting you off in bed is one thing, but—"

"Right, because you've never been bored enough
to sneak off at a party for a little fun in a bathroom."

Gavin acknowledged that with a bland nod that
pissed Beach off more. "So, did you?"

"Did I what?" Beach crawled to his feet. The plug
was still making itself felt, but now his leg was throbbing enough to make him forget everything else.

"Get off."

"You said you stood there and watched, you perv.
So you must know the answer."

"I know you get fascinated by new things." Gavin
was doing that thing where he chose his words carefully, pretending diffidence when he really was looking for a way to make you feel like an idiot.

"What am I now, a kitten with a ball of yarn?"

"No. But you're pretty damned defensive."

"You spied on me."

"Beach—or should I be calling you David now?"

"God no." Beach shuddered.

"You were acting weird. Giddy. I thought you were
high, so when you came up here, I followed you."

"Bet you wish I was up here having a sniff instead."

"I don't want you to go to jail."

"Me either. That is so not on my bucket list." Beach started washing his hands for something to do. Now he got why Eli had called him twice. You got a little hungry to talk to someone who didn't look at you like you belonged in a zoo.

"I don't really care what—or who—you do for fun. But you're different. It's like this thing is changing you."

"This *thing* is my relationship. With my boyfriend. Did I tell you how to conduct yourself with that squat pile of attitude you've started dragging around?"

"Yes."

"Well, then I was wrong." Beach limped past Gavin into the bedroom. "Sorry."

"I'm in love with him." Gavin's words made Beach freeze.

He'd known that, of course. Had to be love to put up with Mr. Short, Ginger, and Surly. It would be easy enough to say he was in love with Tai, except that love didn't seem to be enough to cover it. He loved the *Nancy*. And Pappy Van Winkle bourbon. And Gavin.

Beach worshipped Sir. As difficult as it was to separate them in Beach's brain, Tai was more than Sir.

Tai had given Beach a piece of himself he didn't know was missing. Made him not only complete, but more. It wasn't only the moments when Beach gave everything he was over to Tai to hold. It was that Tai had held all of him and wanted to again. That was so much more than love.

"Mazel tov. Have you set a date?"

Gavin caught Beach's arm. "I'm trying here, Beach. Is this BDSM all you do?"

"Jesus, Gavin, you sound like your father. And for the record, it's mostly the *D* and the *s* parts. But we also talk and we eat and we watch TV and go for walks—"

Gavin choked and let go of Beach's arm. "For walks? You go for walks?"

"He has a dog. So, what do you do with Jamie when your cocks aren't hard? You ride along on cop stuff?"

"We… hang out. With his friends."

"Did you really say 'hang out'?" Though the *with friends* part went a long way toward explaining why Beach had seen so little of Gavin lately.

Gavin shrugged. "We went to the movies."

"We're going next week," Beach threw out. "See? No leather or whips involved."

"What are you going to see?" Gavin's eyes narrowed.

"We haven't decided yet." Blithe conviction was the key to a successful lie.

"I'll find out when Jamie's working. We can go together."

"Absolutely. It's a date."

Chapter Twenty-One

DESPITE BEING the sort of bastard who spied in bathrooms, Gavin would never be so ungenerous a host as to make people walk to their cars, a gallantry for which Beach was profoundly grateful as he made his way to the front of the manor. As the valet went to get his Spider, Beach took stock. He was three-quarters of a million poorer, but for good reason. He was in possession of the rights to a rose cultivar for Tai's daughter, a no longer intriguingly erotic ball of steel in his ass, and what he was pretty sure was his first case of sub drop in weeks. And without the comfort of a mind-blowing orgasm to soften the blow.

The man who crawled into the molded, Daytona-style seat behind the wheel of the Ferrari wasn't the one who'd swiveled out of it with a gleam in his eye a few hours earlier. He handed a fifty to the valet and managed to get to the end of the drive before the shakes and nausea got so bad he had to pull off on the side of the road.

The things he'd come to rely on at moments like this—orange juice, Tai, a safe place to crash, and Tai—weren't easily found in the dashboard of Beach's Spider, despite his having the full range of upgraded options. Beach shivered under the hot afternoon sun, his nuts drawn up so tight and small they were trying to crawl back into his body. A spasm knotted his guts, and he popped open the door, hunched over to heave, but only managed a pathetic shot of spit.

You really have your shit together, Beach. He drew himself back up into the driver's seat and punched the radio dials. He needed to get out of here, find something to distract his brain enough to—*crawl to Tai and tell him you couldn't manage an afternoon alone with your oldest friend? Who the fuck are you?* Maybe Gavin was right. Beach wasn't himself.

He tuned the satellite radio to an aggressively cheerful pop station, cranked the volume, and put the car in gear.

He pulled off the verge, tapping the wheel in time to the beat. As he glanced in his mirror, he realized he didn't have his seat belt on. For some reason, buckling his seat belt seemed like the height of responsibility at that moment. If he could buckle his seat belt, he'd prove capable of handling everything else. A simple action he'd performed thousands of times, and under far greater impairment than some damned endorphin crash.

Fuck. His hands were shaking. Stupid. Irrational. He could do this. It was just a goddamned seat belt. A simple buckle in a latch. A two-year-old could do it. So a thirty-four-year-old man damned well ought to be able.

He glanced down at his hip, fumbled, and finally shoved the tongue into the latch when a horn blared over the peppy chorus.

He jerked his gaze back to the road.

A gigantic black SUV loomed over him, barreling down. He yanked the wheel, went off the road, overcorrected, and crossed behind the SUV, plowing deep into thick brush. The belt burned against his neck, but at twenty-five miles an hour, he hadn't hit anything with force enough to set off the airbags. What hurt most was his heart, hammering high and sharp into his sternum. He put a hand over it to make sure it was still inside.

Through the adrenaline-spiked panic of swerves and squealing brakes, the fear that had reached deepest into Beach wasn't for his own safety, nor that an accident could revoke his probation. But God, he'd looked into that windshield and seen two frightened people and a curly-haired toddler in a car seat, and oh shit, he really was going to throw up now.

But he didn't. Assuming he could get the Spider back on the road, which didn't seem likely, he was obviously in no shape to drive.

He pulled out his phone. There were other people he could call. Gavin, less than a mile away. Ruben, down in Riviera Beach. A tow truck. But he was going to need to explain this to Tai sooner or later, and for once, Beach picked sooner.

When Tai picked up, Beach strove for a casual tone, though his heart was still hammering in his ears.

"Hi, I'm sorry about the unscheduled call, but—"

"What happened? Are you okay?"

The sudden concern that softened Tai's voice almost sent Beach over the edge into babbling. He bit the inside of his cheek to stop the flow of words.

"I'm fine."

"David, skip the bullshit and tell me. I can hear it in your voice. No hiding, no running, remember?"

"Yes, Sir." So much easier like this. No worrying about whether he should be able to handle it alone. Surrender.

"I wasn't feeling good when I left the party. I pulled off and waited until it passed—"

"Just tell me where you are and what you need." Tai's voice dropped to the purring rumble Beach loved to feel against his back.

He took a deep breath. "The GPS says 2799 Holly Neck Road in Essex. And I think I need a tow truck."

A THIRTY-MINUTE drive was a long time to discover exactly how deep into a pit of guilt Tai could dive. He should have brought David off. Had him take out the plug. Then he wouldn't have been distracted while driving, wouldn't have run himself off the road. Obviously a twenty-four-seven D/s relationship had way more potential for disaster than Nic could handwave into unimportance.

As Tai slowed at the scene, he saw flares and lights flashing from an unmarked cop car.

A uniform was talking with David as he leaned against the Spider, but it wasn't the usual county uniform. His windbreaker said Harbor Police.

Tai pulled off behind the cop car, turning on his hazards, and ordered Jez to stay as he climbed out. He couldn't override a cop with his badge, but it might help make sure David didn't get caught up in proving he wasn't violating probation. David was lucky he'd already cleaned up his tickets.

Approaching, Tai said, "Tow truck is already on the way."

The cop had bright red hair and a pissant attitude to match. "Yeah. And you would be?"

"Officer Fonoti, Department of Corrections. Reaching for my badge." Tai pulled the shield out and offered it to the cop, who gave it a glance before he snorted.

"You called your probation officer?" That disgusted sneer was aimed at David.

David opened his mouth but only ran his tongue over his teeth, glancing helplessly at Tai and then back to the cop. "Not exactly," David said finally. "This is Officer Donnigan." He made the introduction like he was still at his garden party.

Tai fell back on acting like a probation officer. "Any property damage, Officer?"

"Other than to his piece of Eurotrash here?" Donnigan jerked his chin toward the Ferrari. "Nope. Ran over some saplings. There's a preserve that way." He jerked his thumb behind him. "But this much belongs to the county."

"Who called you?" Tai asked.

"And how the fuck is that your business?" Donnigan tipped his cap back to glare up at Tai.

David started to explain, "Officer Donnigan has a friend in the area, and he was just—"

"And what are you trying to pull with that, asshole?" Donnigan's aggressive attention shifted back to David. "You think you can make me clear up your shit for your PO?"

Tai had his body between David and Donnigan faster than a thought. When Tai went on a warrant with a cop, they were on the same side, disgusted by the assholes who thought the rules didn't apply to them. Now he was protecting David—his boy—against a bully with a badge.

David tapped Tai's shoulder, three deliberate taps. "Officer Donnigan and I are previously acquainted."

Tai brought his red alert back to amber but didn't move out of the way. An engine sounded from the road, wrong direction and too low in decibels for the tow truck.

A familiar sleek black car rounded the corner. Donnigan threw up his hands in disgust and pointed behind Tai's car. "Fucking party now. You happy, Beach?" He stomped off toward the new arrival.

David put a hand on Tai's arm. "Jamie is Gavin's boyfriend. He was on his way to Gavin's, and he stopped to see what had happened."

The scene made a lot more sense with that bit of information. "Then why was he being such a dick to you?"

"In Jamie's defense, he's a dick to everyone."

"Not much of a defense."

David pulled Tai to face him. "I didn't know what to say when you showed your badge. I don't want you to get into trouble."

Tai reared back. "Is he that much of a dick?"

"No. At least I don't think he is. Anyway, you aren't my PO, and Jamie doesn't have a lot of stones to throw, considering how he and Gavin met."

Gavin and Donnigan came into view, the swagger of the cop making Tai want to punch him in the face.

"You're Beach's probation officer?" Gavin asked, eyes narrowed. "I don't think I knew that when we met outside the hospital."

"Because it's not true." David straightened from his lean. "Tai is not my probation officer. My probation officer's name is DiBlasi."

"Same office, though?" Donnigan's insinuating tone had Tai's fingers curling into a fist.

"Tell us again how you and Gavin met?" David stepped forward.

"Sure. Since Fonoti isn't your PO, he probably doesn't have the details. That would be the night you slipped liquid X into Gavin's drink, and after driving while you were both high, you decided to stop and take a swim in the bay—while you were on top of the fucking Key Bridge."

David's smile was brittle, though his tone was lazy, heavy on the accent. "I'm sure you'd know plenty about those sudden urges to cool off. Since y'all got pissed enough to drive your truck off the end of a pier and all."

"I didn't drag Gavin in with me."

"He got wet just the same, though."

Gavin gave Tai a look and a nod he'd seen often on other dog owners. A concise version of *I'll hold mine and you hold yours.*

"David." He said it quietly, but David's rigid pose relaxed instantly.

"Have we had a chance to talk about what movie we'd like to see?" Gavin's brow wasn't the only thing arched.

David laughed and gave a little bow to Gavin. "*La Commedia è finita.*"

Gavin chuckled and bowed back, making Tai wonder if it had something to do with the school skits David had mentioned.

As the tow truck arrived, slowed, and got into position, Tai asked David about it.

"No. It means 'the farce has ended,' but it's used kind of darkly. It's from an opera where everyone dies."

"As opposed to the operas where everyone lives happily ever after?"

"Exactly." David laughed again and then gasped. "Making me laugh is mean, Sir."

Tai tightened his jaw at the reminder, though David's flushed cheeks and dark eyes didn't make it seem like he was suffering. Maybe they could do this. Draw the boundaries where they wanted them—needed them to be.

David frowned. "I wasn't—I didn't have anything to drink. Today, I mean."

Tai put a hand on David's hip, shielding it from the view of the tow-truck driver where he stood talking to Donnigan. "We'll talk about it later." Tai pushed him at the driver.

"Yes, Sir."

As David settled up with the driver, Tai became aware of Gavin's appraising stare and returned it with a caught-you nod.

Gavin gave a faint smile and drifted closer to Donnigan.

The winch lifted the front end of the Ferrari, and David winced and cringed as the brush scraped and pinged off the undercarriage and frame.

"I told him to take it to the body shop. A vine got wrapped around the front axle," David said as he rejoined them. "I hope I can get a ride." He smiled at Tai.

Jamie rolled his eyes. "Sure you can fit him in your car, Fonoti? Saw your dog."

"We're fine." Tai put his hand on the back of David's waist.

"Thank you kindly for your assistance, Officer."

"Christ." Jamie turned and reached for his car door. "Hey, Fonoti. You're a pretty big guy. You really need a dog like that for protection?"

"Does walking poor Annabelle really challenge your masculinity that much, Jamie?" David threw back.

"If you don't mind—" Gavin started.

"Not at all. We're done." Hand on David's lower back, Tai headed for his car.

DAVID WAS quiet on the drive back, and Tai snuck a glance over to see him drift asleep, jerking awake when Tai pulled into a parking place on South Streeper. Tai watched him drag himself awake, putting on his usual dimpled smile with effort.

"Sorry to nod off."

"No problem. Stay here for a minute. I'll be right back."

Tai left the car running for the AC and took Jez up to the apartment. He fed her and did his best to ignore her devastated expression as he went back to the door without her leash. "I'm sorry, sweetheart, but he needs me more right now."

David was dozing again when Tai opened the car door. This time David shook himself awake, then gave Tai a leer as familiar as it was feigned. "Usually if I'm going to fall asleep in the middle of the day, it's because I've gotten off. Must be this feeling of having you inside me. Where's Jez?"

"At my place. Thought we'd have some just-you-and-me time."

"I could be up for that." David waggled his brows.

Tai shook his head. "I mean you and me, boy. No distractions. No games."

"Yes, Sir."

In David's apartment, Tai steered him into the bathroom. "Strip for me."

As the jacket and trousers came off, Tai hung them in David's closet. Coming back into the bathroom, Tai wrapped his arms around David from behind. "You were so good for me, wearing this." Keeping one arm across David's chest, Tai brought his other hand down to grab the base of the plug and fuck it gently back and forth.

David gasped, the strangeness Tai had felt coming from him washing away.

Tai worked the plug faster, drawing it out enough to stretch David's hole, driving it back in across his gland until he clutched Tai's arm for balance.

"That's it. I want you to feel good. Want you to come for me. Do you want to come for me, boy?"

"Yes, Sir, please."

Tai got David steady on his feet and turned on the shower. Holding David's hand, Tai unsnapped one of the cuffs.

At the startled, wide-eyed look on David's face, Tai said, "You're getting them back. Don't want to get them wet."

"Right." David flushed and looked down.

Tai pulled David into the shower and settled behind him, squirted some shower gel into his hand, and washed David's chest, his neck, his back. Whether it was because he was tired or because the plug had kept him close to it, David yielded immediately, no resistance, no questions as Tai soaped David's sac, then stroked his cock to full attention.

Curling a finger through the loop at the base of the plug, Tai started working it, guiding David between the steel filling his ass and the hand gliding on his cock.

"Is it good, baby? Still enough lube?" Tai kissed and licked the water from David's neck.

"Yes. But…."

"What? Tell me. It's okay."

"I don't think I can hold it for long."

"Good. Come when you're ready, boy. I've got you."

David drove faster into Tai's fist, and he tightened his grip, angling the plug to pull the loudest moans, the sharpest breaths from David's throat.

"That's it. So damned good for me, boy."

David's fingers locked with bruising force on Tai's forearm, hips jerking and snapping, dick spilling thick, creamy spunk over Tai's fingers.

"Yeah." Tai held on until David shuddered to a stop, then turned him under the spray to rinse them off. Tai's dick throbbed, nuts heavy, full and needy. David was loose and pliant and counting on Tai to take care of him. He clenched his muscles and told himself to ignore the ache.

"Relax now. Breathe out." Tai pulled the plug from David's body, rinsed it, and leaned out to put it in the sink.

His boy was drained, hanging on wherever he could get a grip, swaying on his feet. "Few more minutes." Tai shut off the water and dried them off. He thought about heading right for the bed, but he needed to know what had happened. After wrapping them in fresh towels, he pulled David out of the bathroom and onto the couch. With David between Tai's legs, he settled against an arm, David's back to Tai's chest. He tucked David under his chin.

"How did the party go?"

"Good. Raked in a ton of donations, and between your contribution and mine, we got Sammie a rose." The excitement in David's voice made it sound like it was better than a florist delivery.

"That was nice."

David turned. "I mean, she gets to—or you get to—design it. The species is set, but you can specify color and shade and name it after her. It will go in an official registry of rose cultivars. Latinus somethingus 'Samantha'. Or 'Sammie' if she wants that."

Tai knew he should be saying something, but his jaw was locked, aching as his throat swelled. He knew David wasn't ungenerous. He'd hosted a friend who could have obviously afforded a hotel. But this was different. It was for Tai's baby girl.

"Between your contribution and my five hundred dollars, we managed that, huh?" David went still. Tai squeezed him in a hug. "Thank you. It was incredibly thoughtful. She'll be ecstatic."

David relaxed again. "Well, I figured if she wasn't a flower fan, you could give it to your mom."

"I suppose I should be glad it wasn't a horse auction."

David laughed.

"So, between buying a rose and driving off the road trying to put your seat belt on, what happened?"

David shifted. "It's kind of funny."

Tai had his doubts about that. "Really."

"I was feeling—well, a steel ball up my ass, and Gavin decided that my bright eyes and warm cheeks meant I was on something."

"And you told him it was more that something was in you?"

"Not exactly. But he figured it out."

"Uh-huh." Tai tucked David back under his chin.

"I—It felt like sub drop. After that. Even though I hadn't come." Tai waited, guilt slithering sticky and hot under his ribs.

"So when I felt it, I pulled over. I was going to call you, but it faded."

"Just like that." Tai couldn't keep his tone even.

David started to shrug, then sat up. "I did stop and wait until I felt better. When I started driving again, I realized I hadn't put my seat belt on. The other car was speeding." David met Tai's gaze and then shook his head. "Listen. That, whatever it was, that is not because of you. Not because of the butt plug or the conversation we had in Gavin's bathroom."

Tai narrowed his eyes, feeling his brows pinch together. "Excuse me?"

"You like to take control and God, I love—it, but it doesn't mean that you can control everything."

"Where is that coming from?"

"Gavin made me feel weird about us and the D/s. I let that get to me. Then I made the choice to start driving. And to try to put on my seat belt at the same time." David tipped his head and looked steadily at Tai. "Not my best choices, though definitely not my worst. But they were mine. If you think...." David started to look away but checked himself. "If you think I let you down and I should be punished, then I accept that. But I don't accept you feeling guilty."

The sticky feeling was annihilated by a blast of warmth. Damn. His boy was figuring it out. "C'mere." David let Tai pull him back down. "I'm proud of you. That was some pretty good stuff."

"Thanks. So...." David picked at the nap of his towel. "Are you going to punish me?"

"No."

David gulped and nodded. "Why not?"

"Because you got there without it."

AFTER THE show on the side of the road, Tai didn't figure they'd be seeing Gavin and his overbearing dick of a cop friend anytime soon. So David saying Gavin had invited them to dinner and to tour the building his foundation was buying came as a surprise.

Gavin must've tightened Jamie's leash quite a bit, because aside from general complaints about asshole boaters, asshole drivers, and asshole red tape as it applied to Gavin's shelter, he could pass for civil if you graded on a curve.

For the most part, Gavin and David carried the conversation, David telling exaggerated—or at least Tai hoped they were exaggerated—stories about past adventures. Jamie, the cop, rolled his eyes a lot, but when he glanced at Gavin, the sneer on his face softened to a patient almost-smile. Watching David work to draw a laugh from Gavin—and whatever passed for humor on Jamie—made Tai wonder why David hadn't become aware of his submissive nature before this. He'd been the leader, especially in the riskier of the exploits he related, but a desire to please shone through all his interactions. When they were deciding over dessert, he shot Tai a glance, a request for permission that brought a spark of heat to Tai's balls and electric power to his spine.

He put his hand on David's menu, pressing it onto the table as he lowered his own and told the waiter, "We'll split the mousse trio."

Jamie rolled his eyes for at least the sixth time, but David grinned, making Tai wish they were enjoying room service in David's hotel room, where Tai could take his time licking the chocolate and salted caramel off David's lips. Under the table Tai rested a hand on David's thigh. There was a twitch as David's fidgeting stopped.

Gavin ordered a brandied coffee, and Jamie added, "Make it two."

After the waiter left, David said, "I'm looking forward to being an adult again soon."

Jamie muttered, "Didn't know you ever were," as Gavin arched his brow and said, "Really?"

David laughed. "I've never eaten so much dessert as I have with digestifs off the menu. I may have to be rolled in for my court date."

"You think you'll just stroll back out with a fine? Get right back to partying like nothing happened?"

David's smile didn't dim, though tension snapped into the muscle of his thigh under Tai's hand. "Gavin paid a fine."

"He didn't drag his best friend off the Key Bridge and then out to Fort Carroll."

"Plus the having sex with a cop at the time probably helped."

"Like your PO doesn't ha—" Jamie cut off midsyllable and glanced at Gavin, though the other man hadn't moved or made a sound.

Tai suspected it was something similar to the squeeze he'd applied to David's leg, but both Gavin's hands were visible.

The waiter returned with their desserts.

Into the silence that followed, David said, "Jamie, I admit I wasn't thinking clearly, either night."

"Yeah, GHB will do that to you," Jamie grumbled into his coffee.

David didn't fight back. "It was stupid. Not our—my—usual kind of stupid either. I was fixed on this ridiculous idea that there was some proof of my father's innocence on the island. If I'd stopped to think, I'd never have put Gavin at risk."

Jamie's cup clattered into its saucer, but Gavin answered, "It's fine, Beach."

"Jamie?" David ducked his head and flashed his dimples.

It was decent of David to include him, especially as he wasn't the wronged party, and if the bristling little prick turned him down, Tai would—

"Fine, whatever." Jamie spared Tai the necessity of deciding how far the testosterone battle would go. "Is this like a twelve-step thing?"

"No." David dug his spoon into the dark chocolate mousse but didn't bring it to his mouth. "It's only an apology. And a truce." David shook his napkin as a white flag.

Jamie stared at Tai instead of the napkin, like he was trying to figure out if someone else could be blamed instead.

"Okay."

Gavin shifted the conversation onto the building he'd invited them to tour, thanking Tai again for his donation and interest.

The building was downtown, on the east edge of Mount Vernon, which made sense if they hoped to provide beds and other options to the teenaged hustlers who worked a few blocks away.

There were two parking spots on the alley side, and Gavin led them around to the front door, which he unlocked.

"So you bought it?" David asked.

"We did," Gavin answered, though who the *we* involved wasn't clear.

The door led into a hall with two arched openings. "It's important that it not look too institutional." Gavin switched on the lights. Bare bulbs flared up immediately, chasing away the twilight. "We need to avoid any association with the kind of places they've learned not to trust."

"The Gospel according to Blondie. I'm going to see if the exterminator fixed your rat problem in the kitchen." Jamie stomped off down the hall.

As they followed, Gavin explained, "I'm lucky enough to get insight from someone who could have benefited from the shelter if it was in place at the time."

"Ah." David sounded as if he'd just worked out the identity of the killer in a mystery.

"That should help," Tai said, over the sounds of metal scraping against concrete, which he chalked up to Jamie's inspection of the exterminator's work.

"I was thinking the office could be back here." Gavin indicated a door.

"Fuck," Jamie barked from the kitchen.

"If he's locked himself in a refrigerator, I want to see it." David ducked through the kitchen door.

"I wonder if you'd give me your opinion on this, Tai." Gavin pushed open the door. "We're bound to get some residents who are working with Corrections."

Tai's finely tuned bullshit detector red-lined, but he followed Gavin into the storeroom.

What was it going to be? Tai was betting on something about the D/s. Didn't figure it to be about boundaries or "our kind of people" with Jamie in the picture.

Tai leaned against a shelf. "Spit it out."

Gavin smiled and held his hands in a pose of surrender. "Of course you'd see through that. Though I'd hope I could rely on you to steer potential residents our way."

"You could." Tai waited for Gavin's complaint. David's friend's expression was hard to read, a pleasant mask. It reminded Tai of the banter and humor David used when he was pushing away anything unpleasant, but it was far less animated.

"You're good for him."

That wasn't what Tai was expecting. He straightened.

"God, he was even on time for dinner tonight," Gavin continued. "I don't know if it's the particular kind of relationship you have, but it's good for him."

There was no disgusted emphasis to Gavin's description, but Tai knew he hadn't been singled out just for ego stroking.

Gavin met Tai's stare. "He's calmer, for want of a better word. When I heard the restrictions for his

pretrial release, I worried he'd do something crazy—
or take off like his father."

"Do you know the whole story there?"

Gavin gave a curt nod, jaw tight.

"And you've never told him?"

"I'd heard things, but Jamie pulled up the record
after Beach and I were on Fort Carroll."

"So why not tell him, even what little you knew,
to keep him off Fort Carroll? Or from doing 'something crazy' now?"

Gavin didn't step back, but his face became more
of a mask. "If Beach wanted to know the truth, he
would."

"You think you're protecting him."

"Did you look into it?"

"No. It's his call."

"Or you're protecting him too," Gavin said.

"The difference is I trust him to know what he
wants. What he needs. Whether it's protecting or
ass-kicking." Tai folded his arms and resumed his
lean. "So what did you drag me in here to tell me?"

"It's difficult." Gavin tucked his hands in his trou-
ser pockets. "I'm very fond of Beach. And I can tell
you have feelings for him too."

Feelings. What a way to describe the surge of lust
and pride and owning and belonging and power and
need that ripped through Tai every time he looked at
David.

Mine.

"There's no way to say this that doesn't sound as
if I'm running him down, but that's not my intention.
It's simply who Beach is. He gets… fascinated. In-
tensely so. It isn't that he's insincere. But his passion
burns up, and then he's bored. If it weren't for the

monitor, he'd have taken the *Nancy* and been gone at the start of the summer. He never stays long in one place."

Gavin's words introduced a surprising shock. In this hot, dusty room, icy shrapnel sliced strips of sensation away until numbness buzzed at the base of Tai's skull.

He shook it off, dragging feeling back with the heat of anger, though his voice still sounded far away. "If his friends act like this, why the fuck would he bother to stick around?"

Gavin's half smile was infuriating. "I'm glad you're on his side." Over Tai's growled, "Someone should be," Gavin went on, "But I am too."

"Funny way of showing it. And you're telling me this because you want to protect me from him? I think I can take care of myself."

"I wouldn't wish a broken... relationship on anyone. But I'm telling you this for Beach's sake."

Tai clenched his jaw and nodded, the buzzing starting behind his ears again.

"Beach is fond of grand gestures. As I guess his record shows. I'm afraid that when he feels he needs a fresh start, he'll do something extreme to justify it. So when he decides to move on, what I'm saying is, please, let him go."

"Let him go? You think I—" But didn't Tai want him collared, cuffed, want a fucking tattoo on David to let the world know he belonged to Tai? "You've known him a long time, right?"

"More than twenty years."

"And the *Nancy*. How long has he had that boat?"

"Ten years." Gavin's eyes widened, a tilt to his head as he acknowledged Tai's point.

"If *David* wants a fresh start, I won't be hanging on to him. But maybe you don't know him as well as you think you do."

Chapter Twenty-Two

TAI MIGHT have gotten the last word, but that didn't stop the questions tumbling through his head as he drove them back to pick up Jez before heading to David's hotel.

Just how well do you know David? Exactly how do your three and a half weeks stack up to twenty years?

They spent as much time together as their schedules—Tai's schedule—allowed, eating, talking, fucking. He had a change of clothes and a toothbrush at the hotel. Was that an example of how David avoided permanence?

Tai wondered which would bore David first. Having a boyfriend? Not fucking women?

The D/s?

Tai could—he did—have vanilla sex. And he could have it with David. But Tai couldn't turn off the part of him that demanded submission, wouldn't stop wanting that surrender from David, drinking in the high of watching him control himself and then give it to Tai.

Trying to cut off that part now would take a tourniquet, but one around his chest to cut off the blood flow to who he was. He'd tried to push it back before, with Donte, and made them both miserable. Maybe that was what being tied down would feel like to David. Vitality choked off, withering.

"Okay, I know Jamie's a total prick and it rubs off on Gavin sometimes. What did he say to you? It's about the D/s, isn't it? He's been a little freaked about it, which is weird because he's always been kind of adventurous when—"

If Tai hadn't been so preoccupied, he'd have noticed David wriggling in his seat before the word vomit. "He said I was good for you."

David went as still as Jez when Tai checked her on the leash. "Huh." David settled back in his seat. "Then it must be true."

THERE WAS no reason on earth why Jez's insistent nudges for Beach to reach back and pet her should trigger any connection with the acquisitions list of Midland-South Health, but that was when David remembered his plan.

"Shit. Sorry." At least they were still on the east side of the harbor. "I need to stop at the apartment for a suit. I forgot I had a meeting."

"With your lawyer?"

Usually Beach liked Tai asking questions like that. It had always seemed like the worst part of relationships for his friends, that endless prying and accountability. The truth was no one had ever had the

vaguest interest in where Beach was going before—
unless it was to a party. But this question made the
tiny clock ticking away to his sentencing date next
week chime like Big Ben. He tried to muffle it.

"No. I decided I wanted to take a closer look at
where the company was heading. Do more than show
up at stockholder meetings and terrify administrators
keeping you from your daughter." Being more active-
ly involved in the business—once he figured out exactly what it would entail—was something else he'd
meant to present to Tai as a fait accompli.

Arranging the meeting, Beach had pictured Tai's
lips curving, a rumble of praise from his throat. That
went a ways to explaining why Jez's demand for af-
fection had triggered a reminder.

We aren't so very different, are we, girl? Beach
rubbed under her chin.

"Is this what you've been doing on your laptop?"

"Yes." Beach shouldn't have been surprised that
Tai had noticed, but it rushed heat under his skin. Not
quite arousal, but still tingling pleasure.

Tai reached over and squeezed the back of
Beach's neck. The rush got sweeter, better than any
high modern chemistry could dream up. *Nope, Jez. We
really aren't.*

As they turned onto the wharf, Beach said, "You
can drop me off in front. The elevator's faster than the
garage, and I only need the top half of a suit."

Tai's brows came to a sharp peak. "Excuse me?"

Beach grinned as he climbed out. "It's a video
conference. They'll never see my legs."

"Hmm. Maybe we should test your concentration
and preparation."

The flush of blood went straight to his balls. Leaning in the open door, he said, "If y'all get your walk in now, we can have lots of time for practice."

IN EVERY real-estate purchase, Beach insisted on a clause that guaranteed no one had reported the property haunted. Even before he'd rented here, he'd checked into the history with the diligence he usually reserved for searching out the best bourbon distilleries. No one had died in the old warehouse that had been razed to make room for the apartment building. But as soon as Beach stepped off the elevator, he felt he wasn't alone in the empty hall. Technically the house back in Aiken belonged to him, but he had never felt comfortable in it. Always felt watched, even when he was in it alone.

He wished he had keys to jangle as he walked along the hall, but the door was coded rather than keyed. For an instant he thought he saw something out of the corner of his eye, but when he spun, there was nothing there. An attempt at a jaunty whistle failed him, but it was okay because he reached his door, punched in the code, and shut it safely behind him.

His deep breath of relief ended in a gagging cough. *Christ.* He'd only been away for three days, but the General Tso's chicken leftovers had turned the garbage into rancidly hazardous waste. Five minutes of exposure to that stench and Tai wouldn't want to be in the same room with Beach, let alone make being pantsless interesting.

Holding his breath, he tied off the garbage bag and held it as far from his body as possible as he went back out into the hall.

The smell was almost enough to make him forget the crawling sensation on his back, but not quite. Driven by a need to get rid of the stink and return to his apartment, Beach quick-stepped down the hall and around the corner to the utility room with the garbage chute.

As soon as General Tso had taken the long plunge, Beach spun back toward the door and jumped out of his skin, or at least his heart gave a damned good try at it, slamming up against his teeth as he bit the edge of his tongue.

A man stood there. Blocking the door. But it was a man, not a ghost. That is, he was solid. And the last Beach knew, alive.

"Dad?"

Chapter Twenty-Three

TWENTY-FIVE YEARS was a hell of a long time. Despite pictures and a rare Skype appearance, Beach thought his father should have been harder to recognize. But he was instantly familiar in a dozen ways. Voice, posture, even the way he held his hands, arms braced on his knees as he sat on Beach's sofa.

Dad.

"I need your help, son."

"Of course, sir."

With that automatic response, reality came flooding back. This wasn't some happy reunion, his long-lost father home at last. They were two alleged felons.

And a probation officer was waiting for Beach to come back downstairs.

Tai was waiting.

Even if Tai weren't a law officer of some kind, asking someone to help hide your fugitive parent was a big burden. Distilled to its purest essence, involving

Tai in anything to do with the presence of Stephen Thaddeus Beauchamp asked Tai to make a choice between his job and Beach. And he wasn't ready to come out on the losing end of that.

"What do you need?" It came out of Beach sharper than he wanted.

His father set his glass of bourbon on the coffee table with a thunk. "Something more urgent waiting than helping your only father?"

"No, sir. But I, ah, do have someone waiting, and the fewer questions there are…."

"Hell, women and questions. Worst combination in the world. Don't you have enough trouble already?"

"Apparently not, sir."

Call Beach an abject coward for it, but discussing his bisexuality with his father—let alone his recently discovered passion for submission—wasn't going to get Beach out the door any faster.

He had to laugh at himself. He'd pictured his father at graduations, christening the *Nancy*, simply being at the end of a phone call when Beach had a tale to tell, but now all he wanted was to put as much distance between them as possible.

"Venezuela is a hell of a country, son. Anything you want comes your way if you have enough money, but once it runs out?" His father spread his hands.

"I still don't understand what happened with Uncle Sinclair."

His father pushed away and strode to the bar, poured out another bourbon, and offered a glass to Beach. "Have your first drink with your old man."

"I can't."

"Why in the hell not?"

Beach tugged on the knee of his trousers enough to reveal the ankle monitor. "Detects ethyl alcohol from my skin pores. As well as my whereabouts at all times."

"Jesus fucking Christ!" His father dropped the glass. Beach jumped out of the way, hoping the fumes wouldn't trigger the monitor.

Stabbing a finger wildly around the room, Dad demanded, "This place? Is it monitored too?"

"No." At least Beach was reasonably sure it wasn't. Thinking of all the things he'd done with Tai—well, something about it was bound to be illegal, even if he wasn't on probation.

"Thank God. So it's safe here?" His father ignored the glass on the floor and grabbed a clean one.

"Do you need a place to stay?"

"Don't be an idiot, boy. Why the hell else would I have spent six days on a cargo freighter if I didn't need to hole up here?" A double shot of bourbon disappeared down his father's throat.

"What happened?"

"The less you know about it the better. All you need to understand is I couldn't stay in Venezuela anymore. What I need from you is a safe place to sleep and that two point five million I told you to get me."

Beach had heard his father's voice on the phone before, disgusted, angry, but never seen that sneer twisting his face from handsome to grotesque.

Backing up toward the couch, Beach said, "You're welcome to stay here, of course. I won't even be in your way. I've been staying elsewhere."

"I don't give a shit where you've been getting your dick waxed, boy. What about the money?"

Even if his father had sounded like the desperate man on the phone instead of an angry drunk, Beach could never have explained how three-quarters of a million dollars had disappeared into the idea of a worthy cause, a smile on an adorable child wearing two brightly colored casts, and the warmth of one man's approval. With the length of the sofa between them, Beach swallowed. "Until the dividends deposit at the end of the month, I only have access to half of that."

"Half?" His father sloshed out more bourbon into the glass. Beach was wondering at what point the glass would become superfluous. At least it was the Woodford Reserve and not the Pappy Van Winkle.

"What about cash?"

"I can withdraw some in the morning. But anything over ten thousand, the bank—"

"Reports. Yes, I know. Damn it. Didn't your uncle teach you anything? Safety deposit boxes?"

"I've never needed—"

"Of course not." His father turned away, staring out into the dark harbor. "David, I'm sorry. I never meant to involve you." The voice was husky, but whether it was the bourbon or emotion, Beach couldn't tell. His father put down the glass and came over, resting his hands on Beach's shoulders. "It's not easy for a man to be brought low enough to ask for help from his son. It should be the other way around."

"I don't mind, sir."

His father leaned his forehead against Beach's briefly and then straightened. "Of course not. You're a good boy." Dad patted Beach's cheek with a hand that smelled like marine diesel and brackish water. "Here are the account details for the wire transfer. I know I shouldn't have to ask, but give me everything you can and as much cash as you can get without making it a federal case." Another cheek pat and his father stepped back.

The defeated posture wasn't any better than the drunken bluster. Beach wanted to be anywhere else.

"I will. Make yourself at home."

"That's right. Got plans. Don't give her a reason to bust your balls."

Beach almost sprinted for the door, but then he remembered his suit. As he ducked back into his bedroom and opened the closet, he felt queasy, like he was out of place, digging through someone else's closet rather than his own. As beautiful as the balcony was, and all the reclaimed distressed fixtures, he'd be glad to leave it. He tossed the suit over his arm and went back out to find his father leaning against the dark glass door to the balcony.

"I'll write down the door code for you, but you should probably stay inside. There are security cameras in the halls."

His father made a noncommittal grunt, and Beach made his escape.

Though it might be more of a leap into the fire from the frying pan, considering that Tai was waiting and Beach hadn't managed to conceal anything from him so far.

But either he hadn't been gone as long as it had felt like or Tai had been enjoying his walk, because when Beach got into the car, Tai only said, "All set?" as he pulled out of the circular drive.

Beach held the folded dry-cleaning bag on his lap and rolled his ankles. After a few minutes, Tai had almost broken Beach with the silence. He was ready to confess.

Sliding his hand up along the inside of Tai's denim-covered thigh seemed the better plan. Tai didn't move to grant easier access. Far more familiar with using sex to distract himself rather than someone else, Beach abandoned the preliminary round and went right for the prize.

The heat under his palm and the answering pressure were reassuring, but then Tai tossed Beach's hand back to his own lap.

"I'm driving, David."

Not playfully stern. And not his behave-or-else Dom voice. Just flat.

Tai must have had Jez jogging on their walk. Her head hung down, steps soft and slow as they made their way through the hotel garage to the elevator.

In the suite, Beach hung up his suit and stripped. "I think I have a pound of asbestos on me from Gavin's building." Not to mention the potential of spilled bourbon and whatever had been clinging to Dad. "I'm going to shower. Coming in?"

The suite had one of those giant stalls with multiple heads. The first night, they were in it until 2:00 a.m.

"In a minute." Tai glanced up from his phone.

He couldn't know already. Beach shut the bathroom door and examined his dishonestly cheerful face in the mirror. And it wasn't lying. If Tai asked if Beach had heard from his father, he would definitely tell him. Yes. That was perfect. He'd leave it up to fate. If Tai asked, Beach would give him the truth.

Tai didn't make it into the shower. When Beach climbed into the king-sized bed, Tai was under the sheet, dark-colored boxers visible through the thin cotton, despite his bare chest. "Sorry. I'm feeling beat."

Beach nodded and sat on the edge of the bed, flattened under a pile of uncertainty.

Maybe Gavin had said something to Tai about the D/s. Or the police knew Dad was back in the country. Beach could tell Tai. Surrender the decision into Tai's control—and what was left of family honor with it. Or Beach could do this one thing. One simple thing to help his dad and be free of that burden forever.

Beach switched off the lamp and looked over his shoulder at Tai. "The trust in D/s, it goes both ways, right? You'd tell me if—"

Tai grabbed Beach from behind and pulled him against a hard, warm chest. "I'm not angry with you, David. Or bored. Or planning to stop being your Dom. I'm just tired."

Beach let out a long breath. It shook at the end. He hadn't realized how really awful the possibilities were until Tai said them. Losing this, losing Tai—Sir—wasn't something he could stand to think about.

Tai untangled the sheet between them and dragged it on top of them both. His palm settled hot and rough on Beach's hip.

"Do you want me to jerk you off?"

The rumble against back and neck reassured Beach more than the offer. "I'm good."

Tai gave Beach's shoulder a quick kiss. "Good. Now go to sleep, boy."

BEACH WOKE to a sharp smack on his ass and then a shower-damp kiss under his ear. "Didn't know when your meeting was. Set the alarm for eight," Tai murmured before he dropped another kiss.

Beach contemplated turning toward the soft mouth, the fresh tang of aftershave and tickling brush of damp whiskers. Tai didn't always have to be at work an hour early. They could—

Another stinging swat hit his ass. "Later, boy. Don't oversleep."

When the door closed behind Tai and Jez, Beach lunged out of bed, a sickening tilt in his guts as he remembered what had happened last night.

His father was here. Hiding in Beach's apartment. Waiting for him to clean out his bank accounts so Dad could safely disappear.

And the person Beach most wanted to talk to about that was the last person on earth he could tell.

It only took the first five minutes of the video conference to remind Beach why he put more effort than most people thought he possessed into avoiding them. After Tai's comment about practicing last night, Beach had entertained a fantasy of running the meeting not only pantsless, but with a steel plug in his ass, body tingling with sensation and secret ownership. That would have made all this boring crap so much easier to deal with. It wasn't hard to follow what was going on. Profit and loss statements, return on investment, market share, growth projections, all of it in nicely color-coded charts and spreadsheets. It was the endless ego-stroking, making sure everyone had a spotlight on a pet project. Then the repetition of what had already been decided.

But he still would have rather kept the meeting going instead of haring off to the bank. He might not have had a safety deposit box with cash in it, but he did have accounts at three different banks.

He had stories prepared for the cash withdrawals. A shame-faced admission of gambling debts, buying some art from an eccentric dealer, a vacation. But no one cared. And two hundred and ninety-three Benjamins took up surprisingly little room in his freshly purchased briefcase. Nothing like the movies.

He rocked the case between his ankles as he sat in a cool leather chair and waited for the receptionist to lead him away to complete the last transaction, the wire transfer of one point six million to Blue Elephant Antiquities in Malta. He supposed he could have asked Gavin for cash. Gavin would hand over any amount, no questions asked. But Beach was done dragging Gavin into things like this.

The best way to sell a lie, Beach knew, was to believe it. He pictured what he was pretending to buy, a beautiful marble bust, third century BC. But again, aside from asking for his signature on six different forms and then on the touch pad, no one wanted anything from him. He felt a hell of a lot lighter when he dropped off the briefcase and the transfer receipt to his father, and more relieved when neither of them tried to prolong the exchange.

He supposed he should have been disappointed that his father barely acknowledged the gift, the risk, God—the brush of that damp, soft beard on Beach's chin that morning—what he was risking.

"I'll be in touch when I find someplace else to land for a while."

Beach nodded, though at that moment he was perfectly fine with the idea of this being his last father-to-son chat, despite how much of his life he'd felt he'd been missing that very thing.

The hug was a halfhearted effort, more of a handshake with some shoulder contact. Over his father's shoulder, David noticed what stuck out from under the pizza box on the counter. A nautical chart, and based on the number in the corner, one covering Cape Hatteras to the Bahamas. His eyes went to the hook—the empty hook—where the keys to the *Nancy* should be hanging. He should have been furious, demanded the return of the keys.

Instead the betrayal left him empty. Hollow.

All that fucking time defending honor, family honor, seeking the magic key to his father's return, wasted. A lifetime of believing in a man who'd steal from his son without a backward glance.

"You're the only one who didn't let me down, David. Thank you." His father's backslap landed high up, near Beach's neck, and it made his skin crawl. "And I'll be out of here as soon as I can. Going to try—"

"You were right before, Dad. It's better if I don't know."

His father could have the fucking boat. Beach didn't need to hear another lie. His father drew back. "I trust you."

Nausea roiled through Beach's stomach, a mix of acidic shame and bitter guilt. He'd given it freely to his father in this fantasy of a relationship for a wild chance to get it back. Real trust was what he'd earned from Tai. Given Tai. Beach was a bigger asshole than even Jamie could imagine.

Tugging his shirt down over his cuffs, he backed away. "I'd better get going."

"She's really got you hopping, huh?" His father shook his head. "Never figured you'd give up your balls so easily."

Beach was still half a coward, since he said it from the safety of the door with no intention of staying. "It's a he. And he can do anything he wants to my balls."

TAI COULDN'T believe he'd let Gavin make him overthink everything. The answers were right in front of him. The crate David had set up for Jez in the hotel room. The way David stood up for him in front of his friends. The way the cuffs never left his wrists. Those weren't the actions of a man planning his exit strategy. If David needed variety, Tai could give that to him. He'd fuck him in so many different ways David would never be bored.

After giving Jez a good, long walk after work, Tai showed up at the hotel with plans coming together nicely in his head. He used the keycard David had provided and found his boy on the couch, tapping at his computer.

"How did your meeting go?" Tai asked.

David shut his laptop and slid it onto the coffee table. "Good."

"Good to hear. Now get over here and kneel for me."

David moved as if his leg was bothering him, taking his time to square it off before using his hands to get fully into position.

But his "Yes, Sir" held the same husky bliss that drove Tai out of his mind with the need to push him further, faster.

"Take off your shirt."

David yanked the golf-style shirt up and over his head.

"Mmm." Tai leaned to stroke a hand across his pecs, tugging and pinching at a nipple until David flinched. But when Tai's hand slid to the other side, David swayed into the contact.

His boy. Always ready to surrender to new sensations. No hesitation. David dove right in.

"Hold out your hands."

Tai retrieved the heavier cuffs with the D-rings from his overnight bag, but as he buckled on the first one, David shuddered and said, "Red."

Tai unbuckled the cuff and stepped back, studying David's face. He wasn't frightened, his breathing in the early stages of arousal.

Putting the cuff away gave Tai a moment to catch his own breath. What had he done? Too much sensation on the nipple?

"Don't go. Please," David said.

The sharpness of that plea hit like a helmet to Tai's sternum. He turned back to find David still kneeling. "I won't. Unless you want me to."

"I don't want you to. I just can't…." David's gesture waved over his own kneeling position. Tai offered a hand, and David took it, standing up.

"Your leg bothering you?"

With a tight shake of his head, David said, "Sat too long without moving. It's only stiff." David used Tai's helping hand and pulled them closer, head resting against Tai's neck.

Okay. So it wasn't that David was suddenly sick of the sight of him.

"Want to sit?" Tai was careful to keep it as a suggestion instead of a demand.

"Yeah. I think so."

Tai liked being the one in charge, but that kind of halfhearted agreement was anything but reassuring. He suddenly felt like he was the target on a firing range. No time to take cover. Just to hope it wouldn't be a fatal shot.

"I need to tell you something. And it couldn't be when we were—I didn't want that part of us to get in the way." David sat on the couch, fingers wrapped around one of his braided cuffs, twisting it around and around.

This was what Gavin had warned Tai about. The passion burned out. David moved on. "Okay." Tai stared back down the barrel and waited.

"This is really hard." David's fidgeting had unsnapped his cuff, or maybe it was deliberate. Either way, it didn't take a PhD in psychology to read into that. Tai stopped himself from snatching it back from David's lap.

"Would you sit down too?"

His sub had safeworded out of a scene. So Tai should be offering whatever aftercare he needed. But his boyfriend was about to break up with him, and Tai wanted to take it on his feet. He put one hand on the back of the couch. "Just say it."

David ran his hands up the sides of his face and into his hair before locking them behind his head. It was a gesture Tai had never seen on David before, but one Tai made when he was trying to keep his temper. What did David have to be pissed about? He was the one doing the ending.

The words came in a rush. "My dad came back."

"What?" The grip on the couch came in handy. Tai's body hadn't been braced for that.

"My dad, last night, when I stopped off to get my suit. He was there, at my apartment." Now that David had uncorked, the words kept spilling. "He wasn't in my apartment. I let him in. He had to leave Venezuela for some reason, and my uncle won't send him money, so he got on a cargo freighter."

Tai's hands were interlaced on top of his head before he realized he'd done it. He squeezed as if that could keep the bomb of anger from going off. "This happened last night, and you're just telling me now?"

"I wanted to say something. I thought about it."

"And why the fuck didn't you?"

David jumped, though Tai thought his volume had been pretty tightly contained. "I didn't want to put you in a difficult position. I mean, because of your job."

"Because of my job? How about because of the fucking law?" Christ, Gavin had been right. David couldn't do anything without a big show. He'd never change. "And for fuck's sake, take some responsibility. It wasn't about me. You lied about it because you wanted to."

"I didn't lie. I just didn't tell you."

"Same goddamned song. I told you the one thing I needed was honesty. All the time."

David deflated, sinking into the couch. "You're right. I'm sorry. I didn't want to have to deal with it, and I hoped it would all go away—that he'd leave and I wouldn't have to tell you." He raised his head. "But I did. I couldn't have something like this going on and not tell you. So I'm learning."

Tai preferred the burn of anger to the hollow nausea of disappointment. "Twenty-four hours later, you do something close to the right thing. Yeah. That's learning."

"But I did. And I know I could have done it better." David slid off the couch and came toward Tai. "And I'm ready to accept the consequences."

David's hands were easing his shorts down over his legs before Tai realized what David meant.

"You think that can fix this? I spank you and everything is fine? You're aiding and abetting a criminal." God, David could go to jail. None of this pretrial probation to prove he'd learned his lesson. He could be in prison for years.

David hitched his shorts back up, face flushed dark. "But in some countries they do that. I've seen it on the news."

"They beat them. They draw blood and leave permanent scars. It's not like a game you play to see how much you can get away with."

"But you told me"—David's voice shook—"you told me that first time I came to you it wasn't a game. That it was who you are. And this is who I am now. I'm different."

"Really? Because I'm seeing the same guy who thought he could use an anonymous round of consensual sex to manipulate his probation officer into doing whatever the fuck he wanted. Consequence-free."

David stared at the floor. "I'm not him anymore. God, I'm so ashamed of that."

"You tell me that, but I don't see it."

"He's my father, Tai. I had to help him. What if it was your mother?"

Tai snatched at a sharp breath. He wanted to grab that excuse. But it wouldn't fly. Not with everything else David had done. And it didn't fix the betrayal.

"He'll leave," David continued. "Now that he has what he wanted—"

"What did he want?"

"Money."

"Jesus." Tai turned away and barely kept from putting his fist through the wall. He felt David behind him. "Don't touch me right now, David."

"I'm not afraid of you."

"You fucking should be. I'm afraid of myself."

"Why?"

"Because there isn't anything I wouldn't do to keep you out of jail." He grabbed Jez's leash and snapped it against his thigh. "Jez. Here. Now."

She slunk up to him with a whimper. He hated stressing her, but his control was slipping faster and faster the harder he clung.

"Tai, wait. I want to fix this."

He clipped the leash to Jez's collar and hooked his bag over his shoulder. "I don't think you can."

Chapter Twenty-Four

BEACH SAT on the couch in silence. It echoed around him, thick and heavy like thunder too far off to hear. But he could hear Tai's last words just fine. As soon as Beach realized the truth behind them, he got up, went to the mirror, and punched the stupid son of a bitch responsible for this mess in his stupid, smiling mouth. The first punch didn't do much damage, so he did it again.

Finally the pain sank in, and he stared down at his bleeding hand. After twenty minutes and most of the towels, Beach knew his hefty security deposit was going to not only have to cover replacing the mirror but the carpet too.

As he tied off the last towel as best he could in preparation for the drive to the ER, the one thing he could be thankful for was Tai wasn't here to see his latest act of idiocy.

Sixteen stitches and two and half hours later, Beach was back in his empty hotel room. He thought of checking on his dad, but all he really wanted was to forget the last two days had happened. Unfortunately the endless throbbing in his hand wouldn't let him forget anything.

Maybe there wouldn't have been an issue with the Toradol the ER doctor had prescribed, but the lidocaine hadn't worn off yet, and Beach turned it down. He'd say he was being responsible and not wanting to risk his probation, but his real refusal had much more to do with the someone who wasn't even there to hear it.

I'm taking responsibility for it, see? I'm not avoiding the consequence of being stupid enough to punch a mirror.

But his imaginary conversation was one-sided. He glanced at his phone but left it on his bedside table. Dialing that number would provide proof a real-life conversation would be just as one-sided. This way he could hang on to hope.

He wasn't really asleep when the solid pounding hit his door in the early morning. Tai.

Beach came off the bed in a surge of hope. But Beach had given Tai a room key. "Police. Open up."

Apparently Tai's desire to keep Beach out of jail hadn't lasted long.

Beach had been through it before, though as he knelt with his hands on his head, he couldn't help but find the humor in being in the same spot he'd been in a few hours ago under much more enjoyable circumstances.

"Is this blood?" One of the officers peered at the spots on the carpet.

"Yes, Officer. It's mine."

"Was there a fight?" The cuffs were clamped on immediately, and a very thorough pat down followed.

"No. I punched out the mirror."

One of the cops dragged him to his feet. "What for?"

"I didn't like the way I was looking at me."

At the station, instead of booking him, a procedure Beach had been through a few times in his life, they put him in an interrogation room and took off the handcuffs. It occurred to him no one had said he was being arrested. What the cops had said, after a brisk round of exchanging identities, was, "We need you to come down to the station with us."

Here in the room with the one table and a few chairs, there wasn't a clock Beach could see, only the usual one-way glass on the wall facing him. His hand hurt. His head hurt. And his insides were so empty they made everything hurt.

God, how he'd fucked everything up. He should have called Tai the second he saw his dad yesterday. Hell, Beach should have called the cops on his own.

When the door opened, his chest gave a lurch of hope. Tai. Somehow he'd found out and was here to tell Beach they could still fix it. But it wasn't Tai. It was two men, both in suits and ties. Not cheap cop suits either.

"David Beauchamp?" Without waiting for a response, the first guy introduced himself. "I'm Special Agent Wallace, and this is Special Agent Duprey. We appreciate you coming in to talk to us."

Beach nodded. "The officers were very polite."

"What happened to your hand?" Wallace asked.

"I punched a mirror. Am I under arrest?"

"Should you be?" Wallace selected the seat opposite, taking up space, leading the conversation while his partner hunched at the end like a vulture waiting to pick over what was left.

Beach shrugged.

"Your father is Stephen Thaddeus Beauchamp, also known as Tab Beauchamp." That was from Duprey.

Beach nodded.

"Are you aware of his criminal record?" Duprey's voice was reedy.

"He left the country when I was ten. I don't know much."

Wallace and Duprey exchanged a glance, and Duprey handed a folder to Wallace. "Your name is on the lease for Apartment 514 at the Tides, 947 Fell Street." Wallace had the floor again.

Nothing had been phrased as a question, but Beach kept nodding.

"But when the officers met you tonight, you were staying at the Exemplar Inner Harbor."

After Beach's nod, Wallace said, "Seems strange to take a hotel room when you have a fully functional furnished apartment you're already paying for."

Beach gave that a shrug.

"Why don't you explain that one to us?" Wallace spread his hands out on the table, one covering the folder.

Beach gave the same answer he'd given to his parole officer. It was all window dressing anyway. Either they had him, had his father, and were nailing things down for the court case, or they were fishing. The one thing he could do was keep Tai out of it.

"I had a difference of opinion with my landlord. I didn't want any trouble because of my pretrial probation, so I called my PO and changed addresses."

"What was the nature of the difference of opinion?" Wallace smiled like it was a shared joke.

"Dog breeds."

"Do you have a dog, Mr. Beauchamp?" Duprey put in.

"No."

Wallace lifted the folder, tapped it, and put it down. "The manager at the Tides said you had a frequent guest with a dangerous dog. He described the guest as mean-looking. Like a bodyguard. Big and swarthy, he said."

"Swarthy?" Beach looked at Wallace's brown hand covering the folder.

"Do you need a bodyguard, Mr. Beauchamp?" Duprey asked.

"No."

"Do you know where your father was living after he left the US?" Back to Wallace.

It wasn't a good-cop-bad-cop game. It was more like a tennis match, a constant volley of shots. Beach lobbed the ball back. "I was told he was in Venezuela."

Wallace opened the folder. "Recognize anything?" He turned it around so Beach could see a picture.

But upside down or not, it was a dark splotch on a carpet. He didn't think the special agents were indulging in Rorschach tests. Then he remembered what had happened with the mirror and said, "Blood."

"On your apartment floor. One of two types. Too soon for DNA, but we're pretty sure at least one of them was your dad."

Beach swallowed. "Two types? What happened?"

"What? You're not surprised to hear your father was in your apartment?" Duprey's voice sliced through Beach's ears.

He'd almost forgotten the other man was there.

"Is this your father?" Wallace produced another picture. A blowup of a security shot, his father glancing over his shoulder as he tapped in the code at the door. Then a side view, his father running down the hall. God, was that blood on his arm, his shoulder? A gun in his hand?

What—? Beach stared at the pictures, trying to make his mouth work.

"Mr. Beauchamp?"

"Yes. I think so." But the wild man darting through the door to the parking garage bore no resemblance to the man with a hunt-jumping trophy that had been the image Beach had carried throughout his life.

"And this. Your bodyguard maybe?"

Beach clenched his freshly sewn-up hand and forced sharp, hot agony up his arm, clinging to it because the picture could not be, would not be Tai. Tai had not gone over to confront Dad. Tai had common sense. He followed the law. And Tai's blood was definitely not the second type they'd found.

"Look at the picture, Mr. Beauchamp." Duprey. He wasn't a vulture. He was a weasel.

The man was sitting in the hall, blood pouring from his leg. He had medium brown skin, long black hair, and a beard, but it wasn't Tai. Not even close.

Beach looked back at Wallace. "I've never seen him before."

Wallace nodded and closed the folder. "David, you're in a lot of trouble. You were doing a good job on the pretrial release, but now you're fucked. You let a wanted international criminal stay in your apartment. That's aiding and abetting. That's serious time. Federal—prison time."

He wasn't telling Beach anything new. The question was how much of it did he have coming? "This other man—was he a policeman?"

Wallace made a sound that might have been a laugh if he wasn't an FBI agent. "He wasn't there to arrest your father. He planned to kill him."

"What did—? International criminal?"

"Your dad did the same thing in Venezuela he did here. Only to the wrong guy's little girl." Duprey's voice was even more nasal.

"Little—" Beach seemed to be trying to think through a half a bottle of bourbon. No, she'd been older, after Dad's money, ran afoul of a statutory restriction. Not—

"This one was only eleven."

Beach's stomach heaved, and he clenched his jaw to keep from spitting bile onto the table. Tai's daughter—God, any sweet little kid—He slapped his hand over his mouth, welcoming the pain as a distraction.

"Look. We talked to your uncle. He says you didn't know." Wallace's voice was cajoling. "So you didn't know. And your dad shows up, and hey, you haven't seen him since you were a kid yourself, he gives you a story, you want to help. But he's not a nice guy, David. He shot someone last night. But you're a good guy, right? You're not going to keep trying to protect a guy like that. You help us out, we'll help you out. Tell us where he went, and we'll see what we can do about the charge against you."

Beach heard him, he just couldn't get the words to line up and make sense consistently.

Everything was a lie. His uncle lied. His whole life was a lie.

Duprey got up and went to the door. Wallace joined him for an instant, then turned back.

"You think about that for a minute, David. What are you going to do about helping out a man who rapes little girls?"

Thinking was the last thing Beach wanted to do. "I don't need a minute. I know where he went."

TAI'S PHONE started ringing before his alarm went off. He jammed it to his ear. "Fuck. You."

For a second, he thought it was David. Then DiBlasi's thick Delaware Valley accent registered. "You motherfucking, shit-sucking asshole." DiBlasi was reaching new heights in creativity, even for someone who swore as much as he did.

Tai managed a grunt that could have been interpreted as a "What?" before DiBlasi went on.

"This was why you dumped that Beauchamp prick on me. You knew this shitstorm was coming."

Tai shot upright, heart thumping. "What happened?"

"What happened?" DiBlasi's voice was practically a screech. "What happened is the fucking Feds have been up my ass with a microscope. Fucking Interpol had a nice, long look too. Everybody wants to know every fucking step that son of a bitch has been taking for the last two weeks. I spent a goddamned hour answering over and over about the goddamned address change. You ever deal with the fucking Feds?

They ain't got no personal lives, so you don't get one either."

"Where's Beauchamp?"

"The fuck do you care? They picked him up hours ago. His dad is wanted in some kind of international shit. Probably running heroin on the fucking boat. Jesus Christ, I do not need this shit."

"Is his lawyer with him?"

"A big fucking fuck do I know or care about who's holding his hand. I called to tell you you are on my shit list, Fonoti. Next time I see you, you better duck, you big bastard, because my fist is headed for your ugly face." DiBlasi hung up.

Tai jumped off the bed, pulling on jeans and a shirt. *Shit.* Why couldn't he remember David's lawyer from the file? Why hadn't he skipped all the crap about trust, about letting David tell him what he needed, and copied all the contacts from his phone?

Tai didn't even know Gavin's number. But that Tai knew how to get. As he waited for someone at the Dundalk Precinct to pick up, he prayed David had enough sense to keep his mouth shut and ask for a lawyer. He'd been arrested before. Except this was David. Who honestly believed that with charm and a smile, he could be excused from anything.

Christ, if you're ever going to find some common sense, David, now would be a good time to do it.

As THE agents turned back to Beach, the door was shoved open the rest of the way and Algernon Butler, Esquire shoved himself in too. His baby brother Gilbert had gone to school with Beach, and Al was a pretty damned good lawyer. He'd gotten Beach loose when the DA labeled him a high flight risk. But as nightmarish as the last twelve hours had been, Beach was sure he hadn't called Al—or anyone else, for that matter.

"Why is my client being questioned without counsel, and what happened to his hand?"

"He never asked for counsel." Duprey scooped up the pictures and papers and put them back in the folder.

"Was it offered?"

"He is not under arrest at the present."

"Then he'll be leaving," Al said.

Normally Beach would be off and running. But a sickening and unfamiliar inertia held him in the chair. None of it mattered. All that mattered was keeping his father from—Beach swallowed back bile—from touching another child. "Al, I want to tell them—"

Al held up his hand. "Not a word, Beach. What happened to my client's hand?"

Beach glanced down. Something had happened underneath the layers of gauze, because there were fresh spots of blood.

"He told us he punched a mirror," Wallace said.

"Al, I don't really care. I just want to—"

"Mr. Beauchamp," Al began in a voice that drowned out the rest of the room, "is clearly acting with diminished capacity, as the attempt at self-harm indicates. I doubt anything he has revealed will be considered admissible."

Duprey's narrow gaze turned on Beach. "So you're just going to let your dad keep getting away with it?"

"No." Beach pushed away from the table and leaned in close to Al. "They said they'd drop the charges if I told them where my father went."

"I need a moment to confer with my client. And we're going to need to talk to the prosecutor about any deals," Al told the agents.

It was another hour at least before Al would let Beach tell Special Agent Wallace that Dad had taken the *Nancy* and was headed in the direction of the Bahamas. The *Nancy* had all the latest in GPS tracking in case of theft. There was no chance he'd be able to disappear. Even after he'd made his statement, under Al's assurances that they'd force a trial if they tried to hit him with anything but probation on the harboring charge, Beach stayed deep in boneless lethargy.

Not the good feeling when he gave up control to Tai. That still had an energy to it, an awareness and focus despite the floating sensation.

This was utter apathy. He let Al call the shots, moving and speaking like a puppet. The prosecutor declined to file charges at present, trusting his current release status would keep him available for further questions.

Even Al's rant at him about knowing better than to answer questions without a lawyer and why the hell hadn't he called when his father first showed up didn't spark much of a defensive protest. It wasn't anything Beach couldn't tell himself—hadn't already told himself. Though the personal consequences were proving far more difficult to live with than the potential criminal ones.

AT LAST he was released to find Gavin waiting, looking completely out of place among the dingy seventies-style cement-and-glass lobby.

"If it isn't my fairy godmother."

Gavin rolled his eyes. "I prefer deus ex machina."

"Thanks for calling Al, my god machine, but how did you know I was there?"

A crash bar slammed against a door off to the side, and Beach looked up just in time to see Tai disappear through it.

"Tai. Wait. Please." Beach took off in that direction, but Gavin dragged him to a stop before he reached the door marked Official Personnel Only.

"I'll tell them I left my—"

"Jesus Christ, Beach, we just got you out of there. I am not letting you go back."

"You act like it's the ninth circle of Hell. It's only—"

"He doesn't want to see you."

Beach stopped trying to pick Gavin's hands off his arms. "He—" It hurt too much to repeat, words sharp as glass slicing curves through his lungs. But he forced himself to ask, "He told you that?"

Gavin maintained his grip as he nodded.

"Then what the hell was he doing here?"

"I think he wanted to make sure you were okay. He's the one who called me, told me the cops had picked you up, said you needed your lawyer called right away before you ended up locked in prison for the rest of your life."

Then how could he not want to see me? Why bother if he's done with me?

"God, Beach, what did you do? Who did you fight with?" Gavin looked at his hand.

"No one worth mentioning."

Chapter Twenty-Five

Tai's 2:00 p.m. voicemail from David went, "I don't even know where to start to apologize. It got out of control so fast. I hope nothing happened to cause problems with your job."

His job? That was what David was worried about?

DiBlasi had taken the rest of the day off, so Tai didn't have to watch out for retribution.

So far, he was Teflon. Nothing in David's explosion of family crap had stuck to Tai.

At four thirty the voicemail said, "I would like to offer an apology in person. If you don't want to come here, I could meet you somewhere after work. Just tell me what to do here."

How lucky was the bastard that the *here* wasn't lockup. That he was free to roam around until his next selfish choice dragged in friends and innocent bystanders.

The voicemail at eight was almost the last one his phone would ever be able to take. A pause so long Tai thought David was going to let it go like that, silent, and then, "Sir. Please. I can't—" David's swallow was audible and then he disconnected.

Fiery need and icy rage battled along the nerves under Tai's skin. His David. That betrayal. The plastic housing on the phone cracked, and Tai dropped it like it burned him, shoving it away from him on the couch.

Jez picked her head up off his thigh, ears raised. "How? How can I make it work if he can't even see what he did?"

She huffed a deep sigh and settled her head back down. He stroked her ears. "It's just you and me, Jez. Donte, Sammie. I'm not settling for almost again."

Six hours later Tai was still awake. The window unit AC couldn't do much when it was swamp-humid and still eighty degrees long after midnight. Jez was parked underneath it. Sprawled out on his bed, sweating from every pore, Tai thought about joining her.

He got as far as considering a shower first when his phone rang. After hours of silence, he'd wondered if David had given up, but his name—and that grin—popped up on the screen.

"What?"

"Uh, ah, oh. It's you." Live, David's voice was harder to resist. The surprise, undeniable relief. Tai wanted to watch those feelings in David's beautiful eyes.

"You called my phone."

"Right. I did."

"Just wanted to recite some vowel sounds at two in the morning?"

"No."

"Well?" Tai prompted after a minute of silence.

"I'm sorry. I made a mistake."

"Well, that we can agree on."

"Do you—? You called Gavin—I thought—You do care about me?"

"I can't believe you're asking that."

"I miss you. And I need Sir. I feel like I don't know how I work anymore without knowing that's there."

And whose fault was that? Tai sat up. "Selfish much?"

"What?"

"You can't start a sentence without *I*, can you?"

"I guess not." There was a trace of David's humor there, but warped into something so broken Tai had to clench his hands into fists to keep from reaching for him, reassuring him. Then David came back at him. "But you're the one who told me to stop hiding. To tell you what I was feeling."

"You're right. I'm not saying I was perfect here. I thought I was a good Dom for you."

"You *are*."

"If I was, maybe we wouldn't be here."

"Where are we? I'm sorry. I don't know how to prove to you that I know—God, I helped that disgusting—I feel like shit and I can't—Please."

Tai felt the pull, like David was there at Tai's feet. The tug to take away what his boy was suffering. Make it right. And when the next time came for David to choose between easy and right—what then?

Pressure squeezed tight at the base of Tai's skull, everything hot and heavy, making it impossible to breathe. "I'm sorry too. But right now, I need some time. Some space."

"You know—you know I didn't choose him—I wouldn't choose anyone over you." But in a way he had.

"Give me some time, David. Good night."

BEACH OPENED the hotel suite door to Gavin's knock.

"Since when do you turn down an invitation to go anywhere?" Gavin strode in and took up a seat on the couch with the air of a man who was not leaving until he was good and ready.

"Since it sounds like a snoozefest." Beach had been expecting Gavin to pop up since turning down both the invitation to meet the newest little Montgomery and the earnest plea to come condo shopping, but he didn't have to like it. It was harder to wallow without bourbon, but he was giving it his best shot.

"Hamish Tolliver Montgomery and mother are doing quite well, thank you for asking."

"Hamish? Good luck at school, kid."

"It's impossible not to want to call him Hammie, as he looks like a freshly boiled haunch, down to the curse of red hair."

"Thought you liked redheads."

"And I therefore know that my half brother already has a chip on his shoulder. I am removing myself to a new address posthaste."

"Why don't you move in with Jamie?" Beach slunk into the opposite corner of the couch. "Don't you practically live there already?"

"I wasn't invited."

Beach's eyes widened. He wasn't overly fond of Gavin's choice of boyfriend, but seeing them make eyes at each other left no doubt things went deeper than skin. And somebody ought to be happy.

Gavin shrugged. "It's just about an address. We're comfortable with things the way they are."

Right. What did Beach know about successful relationships? The only two he'd ever put effort into had blown up in his face. Speaking of, "They caught him."

"Who?" Gavin asked, as if there were another criminal apprehension Beach might be mentioning.

"My father. Al says if we don't contest the forfeiture of the money and the *Nancy*, they'll drop any aiding-and-abetting charges, so I'm back to just my original criminal trespass sentencing on Tuesday." Beach picked at the edges of tape holding down the gauze on his hand. Al said it would be Beach's own doctor taking out the stitches next week, but hedging his bets, Al also added that the worst-case scenario was thirty days in jail. Beach found himself surprisingly uninterested in the outcome.

"The *Nancy*? Oh, Beach, I'm so sorry."

It wasn't as if he could fit the cuff over the big wad of gauze. But he couldn't bring himself to put on the other one. He'd lost the right to wear it.

He dragged up a smile for Gavin. "Yeah. She was a good lady. But I can get another boat."

"True." Gavin stretched out a leg and kicked Beach's knee. "You know what else you could easily get. A shower. You look like shit and smell worse."

Beach held up his bandaged hand. "I ended up tearing two stitches. I'm under dire orders to keep it dry."

"Nice excuse." Gavin stomped over to the kitchenette and grabbed a plastic bag that held the leftovers from his trip to the hospital. Tossing aside the blood-stained shirt, he pulled out the discharge directions. "And you were supposed to change this bandage yesterday. Here." He came back over with the bag. "I suppose it's too much to hope for that one of the principal owners of Midland-South Health has any bandages or tape in his hotel room."

"You suppose right."

"It's all right, my brother's a doctor. I can swing it." Gavin shoved the plastic bag over Beach's hand and began tying the ends over his wrist.

It hit like a wave. Like the worst kind of sub drop. It shoved him sideways and rolled him under, and he couldn't breathe. His eyes burned with tears.

Jerking free, he tore off to the bathroom and spun on the shower to full blast as sobs choked his chest. Gone. He'd never ever have that back. Never know what it felt like to put himself in Tai's—in Sir's hands and feel the weight and freedom of that control. Never ride that high of endorphins, ache with what Sir wanted him to feel.

And what had he given that up for?

A pedophile of a father. How could he not have known? Because he didn't want to. It was easier, less complicated not dealing with truth, which was inconvenient and boring and inflexible. He'd hated anything that locked him in with those limits. Black and white, either/or.

Until Tai.

He made the rules worthwhile. Made them mean something besides an obstacle to slide around.

"Beach. C'mon." Gavin hammered at the door. "Beach. You're freaking me out."

He was freaking himself out. How could he never have that again? There wasn't anything like it. Not X. Not liquor. Not coke. Yeah, there were other Doms out there. A world full of them, men and women, from what he'd learned online. But none of them were Tai.

Beach yanked off his shirt and shoved his head under the spray to get rid of the worst of his tears and snot, though he was pretty sure he'd been crying loud enough for Gavin to hear him.

"I'm fine." He grabbed for a towel with his unbandaged hand and opened the door a crack. "Showering."

"Do you need help?"

"I thought you didn't want me getting into any more trouble with the police. I should think you washing my dick would piss off one in particular." Beach unfastened his shorts and kicked them away.

"Fine. But I'm staying right here."

"I'm not going to kill myself, Gavin. I'm only taking a shower."

"You didn't see your face."

Beach didn't have to. He'd felt it. Could still feel it. He squeezed his eyes and managed a scraping off of funk with one hand.

A few minutes later he yanked open the door, holding the towel at his hip with his plastic-wrapped hand. "See? Everything intact."

Gavin had perfected a polite demur that at the same time was as clear as an emphatic *Says you*.

"You get dressed, and we'll go pick up some supplies to change your bandage."

"You go play doctor with Sergeant Boyfriend." Beach stripped off the plastic and handed it to Gavin, letting the towel fall to the floor. "I'm fine." He went into the bedroom and dressed, but he knew Gavin was still out there.

Which became obvious when Gavin said, "So when's the last time you left the hotel?"

"Let me think, since none of your fucking business."

Gavin pushed open the door. "So you're in love with him, huh?"

The flash of anger evaporated. Beach sat on the bed and stared at his bare feet. "I was in love with you once, remember?"

Gavin shrugged then came over and sat beside him. "Guess I've always been just that good."

Beach shoved him—"Ow"—with his bandaged hand.

"And you've always been that stupid." Gavin caught Beach's wrist, then looked at the knuckles before freeing it. "So when that didn't work out, what did you do?"

"Became your best friend and told myself it didn't matter that much."

"Did you try that this time?"

"No." Beach cracked his ankles. "I already have a best friend."

"So what are you going to do?"

"I know the D/s freaks you out, but it's more than that. And at the same time—everything, every thought in me is that I want to be with him. That I need to belong to him."

"You did seem pretty happy."

"You thought I was high."

"Like I said." Gavin turned his head to study Beach. "You really like him telling you what to do, like with dessert when we went out?"

"I really do." Beach flopped back on the bed. His leg had begun hurting since he'd stopped doing the exercises. "You know, it's kind of crazy. Even if by some miracle he forgave me, my life would never be easy again. And I want that. It doesn't make sense, but I want it."

"Shit." Gavin's voice was oddly urgent. "I guess your fairy godmother needs to dust off her wand."

TAI GRABBED the phone and kept typing up the probation report. It was hard to keep his mind off David, but doing two things at once helped.

"It's Gavin Montgomery. I'm so sorry to trouble you at work, but I wasn't sure we had established that more personal contact was appropriate."

Tai translated that as Gavin wasn't sure Tai would take the call if he knew it was from David's friend.

"Yeah?"

"I know it's short notice, but this Saturday we're doing a volunteer cleanup at the residence. You were kind enough to make a generous donation, and I sensed you were really interested, so I thought you might want to come down and help out."

Right. And in no way was this some kind of ploy where he'd end up either listening to another one of Gavin's for-your-own-good speeches or trapped working side by side with David.

He had to admit Gavin was good at manipulation, though. He already felt bad about turning him down.

"I do think the shelter is worth working toward, but it is kind of last-minute. And besides, Gavin, I thought you wanted me to let David go."

"I'm sorry about my intrusion. I misread the situation. But I didn't even tell Beach about the cleanup. Even if his hand wasn't all messed up, it's not his sort of thing."

"What happened to his hand?" Tattoo *sucker* on Tai's forehead, but he couldn't help himself.

"He won't really talk about it. All I know is it happened the night he was arrested. Twelve? No, sixteen stitches."

David had a smart mouth, but the cops would be used to worse. Tai hadn't heard anything about resisting arrest.

His phone lit up. "I've got another call."

"Will we see you on Saturday?"

"If I'm there, I'm sure you will."

Tai spent the rest of the day digging around, but there was no arrest record because David hadn't been arrested. Just held for questioning. But the lawyer was as sharp as money could buy, and if David had been hurt by the cops, there would have been press all over it. Unless that was how the lawyer got David out without charges?

No matter what Gavin said, Tai was pretty sure David would be down at the shelter on Saturday. He could ask him then. He'd see David. And then?

Then Tai would know.

TAI SAW the dumpster first, hard to avoid when it seemed to take up half the street. But though he saw Gavin's matte-black car next to a shining '60s Ford truck, David's Spider wasn't around.

Tai buried his disappointment as he climbed out of the car. The letdown told him what he should have already known. They weren't done. After he put in some help, he was going to go see David and make this work.

"Looking for something, Fonoti?" Jamie passed him and hurled an overstuffed trash bag into the dumpster.

"Just the man in charge."

"Hmph." Jamie's cheeks were red under his freckles. "Gavin's throwing stuff down the chute." He jerked his thumb at the spot where a funnel made of plastic spilled from the upper story into the dumpster.

There was a rumble, and the plastic buckets shook. A cloud of dust billowed up. "Did he get a permit for this?"

Jamie shrugged. "I've learned it's better sometimes not to ask."

On the first floor, a guy with salt-and-pepper hair was working a crowbar on the boards over the windows. As Tai climbed the stairs, he heard laughter and the sound of tiles clanking together. In the hall a tall, thin blond with a medical mask on and a kid with dark curly hair were emptying trash cans into the chute.

The kid was doing most of the giggling.

The blond punched him in the arm. "For fuck's sake, Marco, enough with the what-should-we-stuff-in-the-hole crap." He lowered his mask and narrowed his eyes at Tai. "Can I help you?"

"Gavin?" Tai said.

"Back there." The blond waved behind him.

In a bathroom a guy too small to be Gavin stood in the tub, knocking out the tiles. "Hey, Gavin. Did you ever think of designating the bathrooms by orientation?" He spun around. One hand on his heart, he tugged down his mask. "Yowza. You are not Gavin."

"What? Another rat's nest?" Gavin came to the door. "Tai. I'm glad you came. This is—"

The guy in the tub stripped off his glove and offered a hand. "Eli. And I am deeply regretting a commitment to monogamy at the moment."

At Gavin's chuckle, Eli turned to him. "What, like you're the only size queen in the room?" Still hanging on to Tai's hand, Eli delivered a slow once-over. "Hon, you are proof that God loves queers and wants us to have lots and lots of dick."

"Thank you, I think. Nice to meet you, Eli."

Eli's hand went back over his heart. "That voice."

"Gavin, how can I help?"

Gavin led Tai through the doorway. "I really appreciate you coming. Especially after my behavior the other night."

"Forget about it." Tai would rather not spend too much time thinking about Gavin's opinion of David.

"I wish I could. I was wrong. I can see how much he's changed for the better. And I'm going to be horribly inappropriate again, but I feel like I owe him. If you don't want to be there for him in that capacity any longer, do you think you could steer him toward someone else to offer it?"

Tai's head hurt trying to wrap around Gavin's words. The guy wanted Tai to send David to another Dom? Or was that coming from David?

"You got something you want me to do, or you just want to pimp your friend?"

"You could start in there." Gavin gestured toward a room like he was doing Tai a huge favor by letting him clean up a pile of broken furniture.

"Fine."

However "horribly inappropriate" David's friends were, Tai had made this commitment to help out and for a good cause. He knew what happened when kids didn't have a place where they felt safe. He'd seen too much of it.

So he'd do this thing and then go find David and figure out what the fuck Gavin had been talking about with his "steer him toward someone" bullshit.

Hauling furniture—and smashing some of it into more portable bits—then flinging it into the dumpster was a productive way to burn off some anger. Tai figured he'd made four trips to one of Jamie's with whatever he was hauling in trash bags. During one slog out to the dumpster, he saw two more guys come in. One ended up helping yank down the boards over the windows while the other spent as much time making suggestions as he did tossing stuff in one of the wheeled bins.

All that was left from Tai's pile was an armchair with an exploded seat cushion courtesy of the rats Gavin had mentioned. As Tai lifted it, the kid, Marco, called from the hall, "¡Oi, papi! Throw that one from the window. I want to watch."

Tai looked through the dirty glass. It was a clear shot to the dumpster, and that would be one hell of a satisfying toss.

As Marco shoved open the window, another car rolled to a stop in the alley. "Thank God, more people."

Eli came up behind them. "I hope it's the lesbians Gavin said were coming. We could use some butch help."

Marco giggled and shoved Eli.

"Nope," the blond called from the hall. "Hair's too long. It's Zeb." He took off down the stairs, almost instantly appearing in the alley below.

A man with hair down to his shoulders only had a foot out of the car when the blond grabbed him for a solid kiss.

"You going to throw it now, papi?"

The passenger door opened, and David stepped out, balancing a bakery box and a tray of coffees.

Tai sucked in a hot breath of air, more aware—more alive—in his body than he'd ever been. The expansion deep under his ribs was big enough to take in all the dust motes flying out into the sunshine, all the thuds and bangs and rumbles of the city. And more. To take in all of the man now turning to look up, to know David held a big piece of Tai in return. And that was all right.

He gave the chair enough momentum and arc to land squarely in the middle of the dumpster.

David's eyes grew wide, the chair crashed and shattered, and the big tray of coffees wobbled. His bandaged hand shot forward, and then the whole tower spilled and splashed against the side of the car.

"Whoops?" Marco patted Tai's arm.

Chapter Twenty-Six

BY THE time Tai made it outside, David was mopping at himself with a shirt. Judging by the tank top on the guy who'd been driving, Tai figured out where it had come from.

"Why did it have to be the coffee?" the tall blond muttered. "How could you put it in Beach's hands? How much more proof of klutz do you need besides a bandaged hand and a cane?"

The driver laughed it off. "In his defense, there was an incoming chair."

One of the other recent arrivals stared at the scattered cups as if they were the fallen bodies of his friends. "Did anything survive?"

The driver reached back into the car. "Cooler full of water."

"Great," the blond said. "Just don't let Beach carry it."

Tai stepped forward. "I'm the one who threw the chair."

"Yeah, you are." The blond eyed him. "Fuck you very much."

"Anytime." Tai nodded. He moved closer to David. "Did you get burned?"

David held the shirt off himself. "No."

"Is your hand okay?"

David examined the brown-streaked gauze. "Probably should change the bandage."

"Good idea." Tai grabbed the shirt and tossed it back to its owner. "Thanks." He put his hand on David's arm way above the bandage, a zing from the touch like a freshly completed electrical circuit. "Get in my car."

David glanced up, and the hope in his eyes made Tai want to say the hell with anything else and kiss him.

"Yes, Sir."

With the AC blasting and the windows down enough to let out the heat, Tai gripped the wheel, though he left the car in park. "What happened to your hand?"

"I punched a mirror, sliced up my hand." David's voice was uninflected.

Tai exhaled. "Why did your buddy Gavin ask me to hook you up with another Dom?"

"He did what?" David's voice cracked. "Jesus. I'll fucking kill him."

"Not your idea, then."

"No. God, no."

"Good." Tai slid his hands over the wheel. "Because you're mine."

"Am I?" David's voice held a grin.

"Yes, you damned well are. Don't be a brat."

"No, Sir."

Tai turned to look at him.

The smile faded. "I'm sorry. I fucked up."

"You did."

"And today—I didn't plan it. Gavin said he needed help and sent Zeb to pick me up."

"He's a manipulative bastard."

"You have no idea. Everyone thinks I'm the wild one. He just doesn't get caught."

"Yeah. I'm thinking that asking me about another Dom for you was also part of his setup." Tai didn't realize how hard he was gripping the wheel until it squeaked.

"If I thought of it, I might have tried it. But I want—I don't want you to be here only because of that."

"I'm not." Tai let his hands slip from the wheel. "I'm crazy about you."

"Ah—is that why you threw the chair at me?"

"I didn't throw the chair at you." Tai snapped his head around to glare and got a face full of David's grin. "C'mere, brat."

David leaned in. Tai rested his hand on his cheek and then slid it down to his throat.

Chin arched, David pressed forward.

"No." Tai gave him a soft kiss. "Don't push."

David relaxed, and Tai slowly increased the pressure until the motion of first David's larynx, then his breath, and finally his pulse were in Tai's hand. They stayed like that, David settling in deeper, eyes blinking, dark even in the bright sun. With that dreamy look, no wonder his friend had thought he was stoned.

Tai had never seen a sub slip under so fast, no stimulation to rev the endorphins, nothing to trigger it but a light touch and this connection humming between them. And it was all his.

"I'm going to do better for you, David." Tai let his thumb sink in against David's pulse, a hint of pressure.

David made a small sound, a sigh and a groan barely escaping his throat, straining as he tried to get more sensation.

"Stop that." Number one, Tai was going to make the boundaries clearer, stop letting David jump ahead. Tai released him. "Who is in charge?"

"You, Sir. But I missed—" David stopped himself. "I'm sorry. So sorry about everything."

Tai slid his palm under David's arm and eased the bandaged hand into closer view. "Tell me about this."

"I was frustrated. That night when you left. I knew I'd fucked up. I was just—I looked in the mirror, and the anger flew out of me."

"Did you break anything?"

"Only the mirror. In addition to whatever bad luck I accumulated, they had to dig a few shards out from under my skin."

David wasn't the only one who'd fucked up.

"If we're going to do this, you need to understand this. You do not punish yourself. Ever. You can ask. But I'm the only one who decides. And your punishment might be no punishment at all."

David's eyes rounded with anxiety, but there was no rebellion in them.

"I forgive you for not telling me about your father. I understand it was an impossible situation. But if something big is going on in your life, I want to know about it. Not just because I'm your Dom, but because I love you."

David blinked rapidly, throat working, then lowered his head.

"David?" Tai reached for David's chin.

"Yes, Sir." His eyes were wet, and he bit his lip. "I meant it when I said I wasn't choosing him over you. Not even when I didn't know—" There was a catch in his breath, and he tried to look away. "—what he was. But God, I should have known. I should have asked. Found out."

"No. That's not on you. That started when you were only a child. David, he never...?" Tai let the question trail away.

David shook his head violently. "Never. I remember fishing and riding and learning to shoot a rifle. Guess I was lucky to be a boy."

"Okay." Tai released him. "You aren't wearing the cuffs."

David glanced at his unbandaged wrist. "I wasn't sure if I still had a right to."

"You did and you do. Are you ready to put them back on?"

"Yes, Sir."

BACK IN David's hotel bedroom, Tai put his boy on his knees, wrists bound together, Tai's cock headed for his throat, like the first time. David waited, all sweet obedience and hunger, while Tai rubbed his dick over David's lips and cheeks.

"Open."

It started okay, and then David jerked, a tooth catching Tai on the edge of his glans, and he yanked his hips back.

"God, I'm sorry. So sorry. I've been practicing. I know I can do this." David's words ran together.

Tai wanted to make things clearer this time, not let David push so hard, but he didn't want him groveling. "It's okay."

David swallowed and settled back into position.

"Easy." Tai caressed David's cheek and traced fingers through his hair. "Open."

Just the head in, David's mouth soft-hot-wet around him, Tai rocked, rubbing against the silky pressure of palate, the motion of David's tongue lapping underneath.

"That's it. Suck now."

He did, a solid pulse of pleasure flooding out from the heat and the tug on the head. Tai let his head drop back and cradled David's skull. "Good. Now." He slid forward until he felt the back of David's tongue flutter against him. "Relax. Swallow."

David gagged immediately, choking, eyes watering.

Tai pulled off.

"Sorry. I can do this. You know I can do better than this." Tai knelt and removed the clip connecting David's wrists. "Wait. I can do it." David's plea held more than frustration.

"It's okay. Things don't always have to be perfect." Tai pulled David up onto the bed, tucking him close, pinning his forehead under Tai's chin.

David didn't resist, but there was a waiting stillness in his body. Not fear. But not the patient anticipation of sub space either.

"Worried about your sentencing on Tuesday?" Tai suggested.

"I'm trying not to think about it. Not much I can do now."

That was a reasonable answer, but something about it coming from David was off. "Maybe I should be in jail anyway. I know I have it coming. If not for dragging Gavin out there, then for everything else."

Tai squeezed him. "You're a good man, David. Just impulsive sometimes."

"Like in harboring a pedophile."

"I told you that wasn't your fault."

"And hiding it from you."

"I forgave you for that." Then it hit Tai like a bat to the back of the head. *Christ.* He'd forgiven David, but David hadn't forgiven himself.

"I'll tell the judge everything. I deserve to be in jail."

"No, you do not." Tai shifted him so he could see David's face. His eyes were flat—when he would even meet Tai's gaze. Tai grabbed his chin. "You don't punish yourself, remember."

David jerked his head free. There was some spark. Then he sighed. "Yes, Sir."

Tai let his body remember the shock of David's admission, the anger. In a quick motion, Tai rolled them off the bed and put David on his feet. "Kneel, boy."

David sank down immediately.

"You broke the law. And then you betrayed me by not telling me."

David hung his head.

"That is something very serious."

"I know, Sir." But there was something new in his voice. Hope. David lifted his head.

"It's not something that can be made up for with a simple punishment."

"I know."

Before David could slump again, Tai put his hands on his boy's shoulders. It had to be something harsh. But quick. Tai couldn't stand to hurt his boy like this over something he'd already thought was behind them. "Do you deserve to be punished for it, boy?"

"That's up to you, Sir."

"Yes. It is."

David looked up at him expectantly. Tai had thought he understood the dynamics of D/s. The trust. Power exchange. Control. But as his boy waited, Tai realized he'd missed the biggest part, though he'd claimed to be aware of it all along. David wasn't only trusting him with his body, with sensation, with control over what he felt, but with who he was, with his soul.

For the first time, Tai trusted back. Believed that this man, his David, understood what they needed.

"Your punishment starts right now. You will go in and take a shower and then go to bed. I will leave you directions for what you do tomorrow. After you tell me you understand, no more talking."

"I understand, Sir."

IT HAD been a long time since Tai had swung a cane, and then only in play with heavy-sensation subs. He had the pressure right, but his aim, that needed to be perfect. No wrapping or shifting. He lined up the swing and snapped it against the cushion, checking the indentation against the mark he'd set.

"I'm sure we could have lined up quite a few volunteers to be your practice dummy." Nic peered at the indentation. "You're dead-on, but it's not flesh. That tends to bounce a bit more."

"Are you offering your ass?" Tai asked.

"Absolutely not."

"Then step back." Tai patted more chalk dust on the cane and lined up the next swing.

"You're that sure he'll pick the cane?"

"Yes." He knew his boy. For all the claims of being easily bored, once David got an idea in his head, he followed through. If he'd researched criminal corporal punishment, he'd landed on caning.

The stroke made an even line under the last three. No overlap. Tai exhaled and wiped his forehead on his shoulder.

"Six is traditional."

"Thanks for the bulletin."

"Going to bar the gate?"

For the first time, Tai saw David's flesh there instead of the pillow. Five raised welts. A sixth one slicing across them. Blood drained from Tai's head, and he bent over, hands on his knees.

Nic put a cool hand on Tai's neck. "A few million schoolboys can attest to the fact that it's not fatal. Even on bare skin, that cane won't leave a mark longer than a week."

Tai exhaled steadily. Christ, he hadn't been this shaky since he'd been doing two-a-days under the August sun with the rest of the Terps. "What if I'm wrong? What if it's too much? I can't lose him."

Nic ruffled Tai's hair then moved away. "From what you've told me, you'll lose him if you don't do this. Do you trust him?"

"Yes." Tai didn't have to think about it at all.

"Then do it. Trust him. He'll show you what's too much."

Chapter Twenty-Seven

BEACH'S STOMACH rode a pendulum between anticipation and jittery fear. The swing tightened, grew shorter with every minute that brought him closer to his seven o'clock appointment with his Dom. The delicious dread, the shivering promise that had been a part of his life since Tai had first mentioned the word *punishment*, ratcheted right up with that tension. Even knowing this would be uncomfortable—*Man up, Beach, it's going to hurt*—couldn't stop the dizzying buzz that came from submitting to Sir.

He'd followed every one of Tai's instructions, gotten up to the alarm he'd set, done the physical therapy exercises. The mundane took on a shine when the actions were for Tai. Even the discomfort of leaving off underwear under his baggy shorts.

Being sent to a strange address was curiously reassuring. Beach needed this to be intense. Different. That he'd been sent here was proof Tai understood how badly Beach needed to fix the shame and guilt he'd never be able to outrun the usual way. He didn't even want to try. He deserved whatever Tai had planned.

The GPS took him to a big-for-the-city three-story brick house with black trim. Beach wished he'd seen it when it had last been on the market. He'd have grabbed it—assuming it wasn't haunted. He stood on the stoop and pressed the intercom button.

The door buzzed an instant later, and he remembered the direction to take off his shoes. The place was nicer inside. Solid Mission furniture in the foyer, all restored hardwood floors, oak if he wasn't mistaken. And he knew focusing on all those details was a way of trying to distract himself from what was waiting up those stairs.

Which turned out to be Tai, and Beach was so happy to see him he almost forgot to hand over the note he'd been instructed to write, explaining why he deserved to be punished. Tai took the note with a nod and Beach knelt, sinking back onto his heels, hands on his thighs. That hadn't been in the instructions, but it felt like the right thing to do. Overhead the paper whispered in Tai's hands, and then Beach's heart was beating too loud to hear anything but the ocean-wave rush of blood in his ears.

"Up."

As Beach stood, another man stepped into the hall. He was slight and dark, with a sharp nose and ink-black hair, thick and cut close to his head. Something about him suggested a thin blade, compact and lethal, with a power radiating from him that made Beach want to kneel again.

"David, this is Nic. It's his house."

Nic offered his hand. "Nice to meet you, David." There was a trace of a Greek accent in his consonants.

"Your home is lovely. Thank you for having me." The polite response was formulaic, but he was sincere. Though it held a touch of the absurd, considering they all knew why Beach was here. He didn't need to be told Nic was also a Dom.

"Nic can stay and help, or he can leave us alone. Your choice, David."

"It's up to you, Sir."

"I want you to decide." Even the choice was a command.

"How would he help?"

Nic's brows were dark and curled like commas toward the bridge of his nose, a powerful addition to a sardonic smile. "Not being involved directly, I can make sure you're both safe and comfortable."

"I trust Tai."

"Of course, but I mean hydrated or comfortable with the room temperature."

Once they started, Beach really hoped they wouldn't have to stop until it was over. In fact, he wanted to fast-forward all the way to where this was over and the guilt was gone. "You can stay."

Those quirked brows made it hard to tell if Nic was surprised or smug. "After you." He waved Beach toward the open door.

Eli had mentioned dungeons briefly, but if that was what this was, it wasn't anything like Beach had imagined. The long, open room might have been an expansive home gym—though a second look showed that the equipment here and there was all about restraint, holding someone still for spanking, beating, fucking.

"Do you need the bathroom?" Nic asked.

"No." The room was bright, with warm track lights. If he wasn't there to be strapped down and spanked, the room would be comfortable, inviting.

Tai walked over to a large wardrobe and opened it. Inside were paddles and straps and whips and lengths of bamboo. Beach held his breath.

"Come here and pick out two implements."

When Tai had opened the cabinet, Beach dreaded the possibility of any of those smacking into him. Having to pick made it worse. He skipped past one paddle the size and shape of the bath brush. The strap looked deadly. Beach unhooked a clear plastic paddle that was heavier than it should have been. But he was getting the hang of this. A bigger surface area spread out the pain.

He'd avoided looking directly at the bamboo cane, but it had been at the front of his mind since Tai opened the case. Essentially it was a thick switch, right? Beach already knew how bad that was and that he could get through it. He gripped it and lifted it down, handing them both to Tai.

"Take off your shorts and put them on that stool."

If Beach didn't have so many good associations with Sir's stern voice, he'd have been terrified. Still, his stomach had cement-shoed butterflies bouncing in it. He was reaching for his shirt when Tai said, "Leave that on."

"Yes, Sir."

Tai led Beach to the equipment that looked like a low vaulting horse. There were no pommels to grip, and Tai had Beach stretch out across the length of the padded top, the naugahyde cool under his skin, even through his shirt. Gripping his hips, Tai adjusted

Beach until his weight was mostly on the horse, legs spread outside the metal supports.

Usually Tai's hand on Beach's dick was a guaranteed case of wood. But as Tai tugged to make sure Beach's junk was hanging free between his open legs, he might as well have been saying *Turn your head and cough* for all the juice Beach got pumping.

Tai stepped around to Beach's face and put each of his wrists in cuffs that kept him tight against the faux-leather padding. "I know you're a good boy, but I need to make sure you don't move. I don't want to hit anything but your ass."

Another strap went over the small of Beach's back, and his ankles were cuffed to the metal legs. Since his dick and balls were dangling, exposed, Beach didn't want Tai to miss his target either.

Tai came back around and put his hands on Beach's face, tipping his neck up. "I already forgave you, David. But I'm giving you this because we both need you to forgive yourself. We don't stop until you're done. So I want you to tell me what's going on in your head."

"Yes, Sir. I'm nervous."

Tai's thumb rested for an instant on the spot where Beach's skull had been depressed on that trip off the bridge. One stroke across the scar and then his hands were gone. "This is serious punishment. You don't get a warm-up. It's going to hurt, and you're going to be very sore when we're done." Tai released Beach's head.

Beach settled against the padding with a sigh. That was what he wanted. Well, he didn't want it. He couldn't stand feeling like this, thinking he'd betrayed Tai for that abomination.

Beach had been so stupid to miss his father, to try to help him, make him proud. If Beach could find the part of him that had done that, he'd cut it out himself.

Tai moved behind Beach, and the cane swished in the air. Beach jumped, but the rattan only rested against him, cool and smooth as silk. Tai tapped with the cane, quick and light, then harder. Then a jarring bounce. *Shit.* It hurt. The swishing noise became a whistle, and the solid rod slammed into Beach's ass, sharp, burning.

He blew out a surprised yelp. Then, in that narrow spot where the cane had hit him, pain exploded, a fiery line with acid etching it deeper and deeper with every pulse from his heart. The sensation didn't fade; it got worse, blazing like a knife cut. "Jesus." What the fuck had he been thinking? That was nothing like the switch. He tried to lift up, but there was no room to move.

Tai patted him with the cane, under the first spot, and before Beach could form a no-way-in-hell protest, the cane zipped and sliced into him again, doubling, tripling the pain from the first stroke.

"Stop. I can't. Sir. Please. I'm sorry. I can't take this. Not the cane anymore. Anything else. I know it was wrong." His ass burned. Just the cane resting against him made his body try to leap away, but the straps held him there.

Tai's hand stroked Beach's back under his shirt, and the deep, sexy voice rumbled in his ear. "You can take it, boy. You will take it. You know what to say if you want it to stop."

Red. It hung there between them, binding them together. Beach had the choice to stop it if he really wanted to. And what made that word, this whole balance between them so powerful, was Beach knew it would stop. Nothing he'd ever done before to chase away being disappointed or disgusted with himself could be stopped so easily. He'd flung himself into those sensations without brakes.

"Yes, Sir."

The cane rubbed, and Beach's body wanted to know why he was so fucking insane that he didn't make this stop when the third stroke buried itself into his skin.

Something came out of his throat. Half sob, half scream.

"Talk to me, David." Tai stroked, then squeezed those cuts etched deep into Beach's nerves.

David couldn't find any words. Just sounds. No thoughts. His body trying to find a way to take this pain. His ass was burning, cold, hot.

If he apologized more, would it stop? What had Tai meant "until you're done"?

"I don't want any of this." But that was a lie. Because he wanted the other side. The part where he'd earned Tai's praise. Where Beach knew he was good. Why the fuck did this have to be so goddamned hard? If he had the timer, if he knew how many swings from the cane, and then God, the paddle—

Beach tried to get up. He jerked at the cuffs, kicked his trapped feet. Tai put a hand at the top of Beach's ass.

Yes. That was why. That was the promise. Like an orgasm, it was hanging just out of reach. Tai's hand lifted, and the cane came down sharply, making Beach groan out another desperate "I'm sorry."

Tai put a hot hand on Beach's ass, squeezing out more pain. Though it was different, closer. "That's it, boy. Give it to me. Tell me."

The cane slid back and forth in the groove where Beach's ass met his thighs. No. Not there. No. "No." It slipped out, and then he couldn't stop the words. "I'm sorry. I'm sorry I hurt you. I'm sorry I do these stupid things. Why do I always do this? I hurt people I love. All those times I tried to help. Thought I wasn't good enough. And he was never fucking worth it."

The stroke slammed into that crease, a flood of pain, washing through him until it made him shake, and before the shock of impact had faded, another whipped across every single fiery line, lighting them up like brands. The flush spreading out from his ass, down his thighs and back up, buzzing, tingling, until it reached his head and rippled along his scalp. He sagged into the cushion. The straps weren't holding him in place for the cane now; they were keeping him from floating up to the ceiling.

It hurt. God, it hurt, but it didn't matter. Nothing mattered. Nothing was here but Sir and David.

Sir pushed the hair away from David's face. "So good, boy."

"Thank you, Sir." David knew how his drunk voice sounded. And that was definitely it. Sir kissed his cheek. "Is it gone, baby?"

David remembered that horrible feeling, the way he couldn't stop thinking about whether any of the times he'd done his father a favor, sent him money, if he had helped him rape a little girl. David had written it all down and given it to Sir. And Sir had taken it away and smashed it with the cane. Now there was a memory of it and that was all. He blinked.

"Yes, Sir."

"Good." Sir kissed David's cheek, his forehead, his neck, then released his hands.

"But the paddle. I betrayed your trust. Lied to you."

Sir's hand slapped down over bruised skin, pain shooting out along the lines, a match on lighter fluid. "Who decides if you're punished?"

"You, Sir."

"Good. And if I decide you need it, you'll feel it. I forgive you, David." He kissed him, slow, hot, hard.

"I love you, Sir."

NIC LEFT two bottles of water close by and put away the implements before fading into the woodwork to let Tai soothe and pet his boy back down alone. Nic had also offered to let them stay, and Tai knew how generous an act that was for Nic, but David had some real-world consequences, like a curfew. He was going to have to ride home on his freshly striped ass.

It was a shame he couldn't ride home without his shorts. Tai was fascinated by the lines he'd put on David's skin. He couldn't stop touching them. The tight smoothness of the raised double edges, the dip where the tip had sunk in deep. He carried David to the couch in the corner and settled him on his lap.

"How do you feel?"

David gave him a smile. "Better. I can think about it without feeling sick. Thank you, Sir."

"Thank you for trusting me with it."

"You're welcome." David shifted. "Um. This doesn't fade to the good kind of glow like the other spankings do."

"No. It doesn't."

David gave a rueful laugh. "I guess that makes it a good reminder to think things through."

THEY WENT back to the hotel in Tai's car. He wanted to be sure David was safe from a drop, and damn it, Tai wasn't letting his boy out of his sight until he had to. He fed David from a stash of honey-roasted nuts in the kitchenette and made sure he drank lots of water. And then Tai couldn't wait anymore, and he tugged David into the bedroom and started sucking him off, fingers sunk into the welts, David's cock deep in Tai's throat as he gulped and sucked, sliding up enough to flutter his tongue under the ridge before sinking back down. He read the signs in David's body, the involuntary jerk of his hips, the tightness in his ass and thighs, the pace of his breathing and moans, the sharper cry of "Jesus" a final warning.

Tai pulled off, wrapping his fingers tight around the base of David's shaft. "No." David's fists ground down against his thighs, but he got control.

"Good." Tai ran his hands along David's chest and flanks.

David opened his squeezed-tight eyes. "Damn. I really want to learn how to do that." His gesture took in his cock and Tai's mouth.

Tai's lips quirked. "I wouldn't mind that myself. We'll work on it. I enjoy your practice efforts."

"I'm getting pretty badass with bananas."

Tai laughed. "Roll over, boy."

"Yes, Sir." David flopped eagerly.

Tai kissed and traced his tongue along the cane strokes showing dark through the light fuzz on David's cheeks. Dark bloodred, purple in spots. Tai's marks. A perfect barred gate, but what made them better was who wore them. How much David had fought and suffered before he could surrender. It was as sweet as if he had his name tattooed there. Tai wrapped himself around David, holding him everywhere, chest expanding as if he could fit David whole inside him. *Mine. To keep.*

"If you had any other plans for the future, you need to change them," Tai said as he rolled them onto their sides.

"Plans like what?" David rested his head on Tai's shoulder.

"Anything."

"Change them to what?" David turned back, brow wrinkled.

"To me."

David smiled. "Yeah. That works for me."

Tai fucked his boy, slow and steady until he came, rubbing and pressing on the bruises to teach him how to slide between the pain and pleasure, letting him know with body and words that Tai would always give him both, feed the hunger he'd found in his boy.

He clamped down with his muscles to hold back his own orgasm as David's ass pulsed on Tai's dick and the thick shots coated their fingers where they were wrapped around David's cock.

He jerked free and pushed David facedown, stripped off the condom, and worked himself against the ridges on David's ass, stroking back and forth until he painted him with spunk.

An hour later, David flopped and sighed for the fifth time, and Tai pinned him under a thigh and arm. "Settle down."

"They still burn."

A spark of doubt had Tai studying David's face.

"I don't think I want to do that again."

As hot as the marks were, Tai had thought he'd wear a hole in Nic's floor from pacing by the time David got there. "Me either."

"But if I need it, would you?"

Tai tightened his arm around David's waist. "Always."

BEACH FELT so relaxed, he managed to completely forget about the sentencing until his alarm went off Tuesday morning.

Tai followed him into the bathroom.

"Thanks for coming with me today. I don't want you to get into trouble."

"Well, if we can keep it under the lid around my boss and coworkers, that might help. I can take DiBlasi in a fair fight, but if he knew why I traded you off to him, he might get inventively dangerous."

"What is his report going to say?"

"That's another reason he's pissed." Tai tugged the plastic bag over Beach's hand and taped it down. "The boss said in the interest of public and interdepartmental relations, he had to stick to only matters pertaining to your pretrial release."

"Oh." Holding his hand outside the door, Beach ducked under the spray. "You know, it's not too late for me to move to someplace else. I don't think they'd hound me to the ends of the earth over a misdemeanor charge."

Tai grabbed David's arm and pulled him dripping out onto the mat. "What—"

Tai bent Beach forward over the sink, an arm around his waist pinning him against hard marble and an equally hard hip, while a harder-than-either hand slammed into his ass. Between wet skin and the cane marks, it hurt like hell. Beach yelped, shock keeping him speechless for the first five swats.

"I was joking."

"Do I seem amused, boy?"

"No, Sir." Beach relaxed in Tai's hold.

Tai rubbed the skin his palm had been scalding. "Still nervous?"

Beach didn't even want to lie. "Yes, Sir."

"Concentrate on this, then." Tai stung his ass with a slap. "Count backward from fifteen."

"Fift—"

"Okay. Make it twenty."

Beach let out a long breath. Tai squeezed his ass. "Yes, Sir."

By fifteen, Beach was having trouble not moving his feet. He didn't know why his body thought shifting his weight from side to side could make his ass hurt less, but he kept trying it.

Jesus, Tai's hand was so big it hit every one of the bruises at the same time.

"Thirteen," he managed through gritted teeth. If he'd kept his mouth shut, he'd be halfway done.

"Twelve." His right hand came up off the counter.

"Do you need me to hold that for you?"

"No, Sir." He put it back down and rocked forward under the next spank.

At eight, he made up his mind to never get smart-mouthed in the shower again. He'd survived through the caning, and his eyes were watering from Tai's hand on wet skin.

But then Beach's body moved toward the sensation, back arching to push his ass out to meet Tai's palm. Beach knew his mind wouldn't be far behind.

"Five." His head went quiet, nothing to do but count and process the sensation of the thud and sting on his ass.

"Four." Pain slammed in, swelled, and broke away like a wave, washing clear anything that didn't matter.

The last three left him swaying, and Tai held him there for a minute after the last spank had landed.

When Sir let him up, David went to his knees. "Thank you, Sir."

Sir stroked a hand through David's hair. "I love you, boy."

FOR ALL that the criminal trespass charge had ended up changing Beach's life completely, the resolution happened in front of a bored-looking judge in less than ten minutes. After Beach pled guilty to a misdemeanor charge, the judge said, "Close supervision seems to serve Mr. Beauchamp well. Three months suspended jail sentence, five hundred hours of community service, and a year's probation, with continued monitoring of sobriety."

With a quick tap of the gavel, they were done. Al shook his hand and winked. "If you think that was bad, wait until you see my bill, Beach."

Gavin had come, despite Beach telling him not to bother. "Five hundred hours would come in really handy sanding and painting and cleaning. I think I'll contact the probation office."

Beach thought of the miles of walls in the three-story building of Gavin's shelter. "I hate you."

"I'd treat you to a bottle of Krug Grande Cuvée, but…." Gavin shrugged.

"You are really spending way too much time with Sergeant Boyfriend."

Gavin arched his brows. "And here comes your Sheriff de Sade now." Gavin hugged Beach and walked away.

Tai maintained a respectable distance, but Beach felt him like they were touching, skin humming, everything sparking to life.

"David." His voice was softer than Beach had ever heard it. Beach faced him.

"A whole year in one place. Feeling antsy?"

His skin did tingle, and his ass was throbbing, but both those sensations only let him know how much could happen when he was standing still.

"No." Beach smiled as the happiness bubbled up from his landlocked feet to his head. "I'm pretty much ant-free."

"Pretty damned free considering your ass isn't in jail," Tai said.

"Yes. I had one hell of a probation officer. Got me time off for good behavior."

"Boy, your ass is in no shape to cash the check your mouth is writing."

"Those overdraft fees can be steep." Beach nodded.

"I need to buy you a muzzle."

"Hm. What about a collar?"

"Don't push, brat."

Author's Note

THANK YOU for reading this story. There will be more stories with the characters from the Bad in Baltimore books. I can't seem to say goodbye. I hope you enjoy visiting them as much as I do. After *Bad Habit*, Marco needs to grow up a little before he'll be ready for anything permanent. Nic isn't ready to settle down, but he's very interesting. Gavin's brother-in-law, Lee, has started poking at me. I'd love to hear your opinions on which couple should be first to get married.

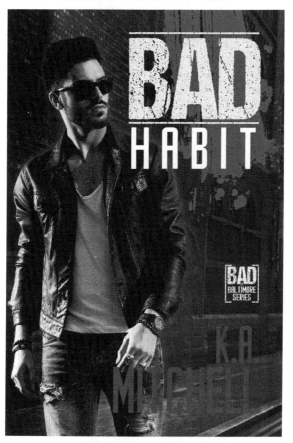

Bad in Baltimore: Book Six

Life is always looking for ways to screw you over. Scott McDermott survived the foster care system and knows better than to let anyone close, but Liam Walsh is his one vulnerability.

Twice Scott let down his guard, and twice Liam vanished from Scott's life. So when Scott comes face-to-face with Liam for the first time in five years, he punches Liam in the nose. Only after Scott's friend—and Baltimore County police officer—Jamie reads him the riot act does Scott discover that in the intervening years Liam has been to war and lost his leg.

Liam hasn't had the easiest life either. He took care of his drug-addicted mom when she was unable to take care of herself. He's fallen in love with Scott twice, but when Liam saw Scott going down the same path as his mother, Liam left. The lesson that he can't save everyone has been a painful one for Liam to learn. Maybe what he and Scott had can't ever be fixed.

Scott and Liam have never fallen out of love—which becomes obvious when they start working together—but what will make this time any different from all the others? Will the third time really be a charm?

Available now at
www.dreamspinnerpress.com

Chapter One

Twelve years ago

THE NEW kid Liam was a fucking punk. Everyone knew not to touch Scott's stuff.

Scott ran his tongue on the inside of his fat lip. He'd won anyway. Hit the motherfucker in his eye, mouth, and gut before Derrick pulled them apart. Scott shot a look over at the chair three spots away where Liam sat. Fuckface smiled back at him.

Scott rolled his eyes and went back to staring at the door to the conference room. Some social worker was supposed to show up and counsel them on resolving their issues. Scott had been through the drill before. He thought things were pretty simple. Don't touch me or my stuff and there won't be any fucking issues to resolve.

But Scott had done a few stints in the hole, which was what everyone at St. Bennie's called the lockdown rooms over the gym. A mattress and a bucket to piss in and food when someone got around to bringing it. He'd play the game with the social worker. Anything beat what had happened to him when he first got here, being held down for a shot of Vitamin H in his ass to turn him into a zombie for forty-eight hours.

"Hey," the Liam-ratfucker said.

Scott stared at the wood grain of the door. Part of it looked like a freaky skeleton with a big alien head.

"Let's just settle this now," Liam-can't-buy-a-clue went on.

Scott dragged his feet in from his sprawl to get ready. If he had to go to the hole, so be it. Rep was all he had. "You wanna go again, bitch?"

But Liam didn't make any moves toward him. "No. I mean, I'm sorry I touched your box of whatever."

There wasn't much in the old shoebox. Two fading pictures, a Batman valentine his older sister had given him, and a Rugrats washcloth—though where he'd gotten that, he couldn't remember.

"You put it in the fucking trash."

"I said sorry, okay? I didn't know it was important."

That was a problem. As soon as people knew something mattered to you, they could hurt you with it. Scott shrugged. "Just don't touch any of my shit, and it won't be a problem."

"Okay."

Scott stared at Liam. He wasn't acting scared of another beatdown, didn't sound sarcastic. He sounded nice, and not even fake-nice like a new social worker. Liam had been at St. Bennie's for a month and people liked him. Reason enough for Scott to hate him. Not that he needed a reason.

The social worker finally showed up. Shit. It was that bitch Kristin who hated Scott. Their hall staff Derrick was with her.

She started in on him before she even opened the conference room door. "I've told you before, Scott, violent behavior is not going to help you get out of here. A foster family is not—"

"It was my fault, Miss Kristin." Liam-can't-keep-his-mouth-shut cut in. The number one rule of survival here was *Don't volunteer information.*

That stopped her midbitch, though. "Liam? Derrick, let me see the incident report."

"Put it in your mailbox an hour ago." Derrick leaned against the wall behind Scott.

"Well, can you at least tell me what it said?" Bitch Kristin sighed like Derrick should have been able to whip the paper out of his ass.

"Eight twenty, Scott came into the common room, hauled Liam off the couch by his left arm, and punched him in the mouth. Liam swung back, striking Scott in the face. I initiated a restraint on Scott. Gerry restrained Liam."

Derrick was big, solid muscle. If he took you down, you didn't get back up. Gerry was big too, all of it in his gut. Scott wondered if that was the first time Liam had been restrained and how he liked 300 pounds pressing into his back.

"So it was unprovoked." Bitch Kristin was happy about that.

"I did provoke him." Liam must have wanted to spend a couple of days in the hole. "I threw his belongings in the trash."

Belongings? Who the fuck said that kind of shit?

Kristin deflated. "Why would you do that, Liam?"

"Someone dared me to."

"Who?"

Liam was smart enough to shut his mouth then. Henry, Scott bet, or Curtis. They'd both been laughing next to Liam on the couch.

Liam turned toward Scott. "I'm sorry, Scott. I promise not to touch your stuff again." Liam stuck his hand out.

Scott felt the adults' eyes burning into him but concentrated on Liam's. They were a weird light brown, one swollen from were Scott had punched him, but the other looked friendly.

What the fuck. Guy like Liam would probably be out of here in a couple of months. Scott flexed his sore knuckles and slapped at Liam's hand in a brief shake.

They'd missed the main lunch, but Derrick took them down to the cafeteria so they could make sandwiches before going to class.

"Jesus, that Kristin has it in for you." Liam reached in front of Scott to grab a giant scoop of institutional peanut butter from the can. "Whadja do?" He licked the knife and stuck it back in, barely missing Scott's belly.

He curved his spine out to avoid touch, but it still made the hair on his arms stand up.

"Got born, I guess. Plus I'm unplaceable."

Liam dropped a dab of jelly on his mountain of peanut butter and folded the bread over, then repeated the process on the other half.

Scott had never seen anyone make a sandwich like that, but it looked like a good way to get some extra food.

"My mom will probably get clean in a couple of months, and she'll petition to get me back." Liam folded his second slice. "At least this place is better than the one I got sent to in Florida."

They hadn't said more than ten words to each other since Liam had been shoved into Scott's room a month ago.

"What's so better?" Scott said, slapping margarine on a slice of bread.

"Smaller roaches." Liam laughed.

But Scott remembered there was more of an issue to resolve. They grabbed juice cups and the least soft apples from the bin and sat at a table, eating slowly to kill more time.

"Who dared you?"

Liam wiped his face on the back of his hand and shook his head. He moved his eyes toward where Derrick was leaning on the counter, peeling an orange. "Later."

"Yeah, whatever." Scott could find out himself.

"No. Really. Promise." Liam tried a big smile, then winced.

Fuck it. Scott wasn't apologizing for hitting him. Ratfucker had it coming.

In the room that night after showers, they had about fifteen minutes before bed check. Scott checked to see that nothing was disturbed in front of his new hiding place for the shoebox, then hung up his towel before hauling up his boxers to get in Liam's face. "Who the fuck dared you to mess with my shit?"

"No one."

"I swear to God—"

"No one. I did it on my own."

Scott was so surprised he sat down on the bottom bunk. Should have known better than to believe Liam was anything but another asshole trying to fuck with Scott.

"I wanted you to talk to me."

"You'll be talking to my fist again in a minute." Scott jumped back up.

"You never talk to me, but I've seen you shoot me looks. When you think I don't notice."

Scott froze. Liam couldn't mean it like that. No one could know that. Not ever. Scott had that safely locked away. Safer than the shoebox, safe as it could be, deep inside. Even he only let himself think about it late at night, staring at the ceiling and hating it even when it made him so fucking hard he ached. Liam had been the first one he thought of with a face. Before it had just been pieces. The curve of some guy's ass. The cut of a hip. Width of a shoulder. Mouths. Dicks.

"In your dreams, queerbait." Safest thing was to throw it back on him.

Liam rolled his eyes. "Yeah. I am."

Scott's mouth went dry. This little fa—he could just say it?

Liam put a hand on Scott's chest.

Hot. Shivery. Terrifying.

Scott froze under those sensations, which was how Liam managed to shove him back onto the bunk, so hard Scott bounced against the bolted furniture and thin mattress.

It was why he couldn't say a word when Liam knelt in front of him.

Barry, the night staffer, yelled for everyone to get in their rooms.

Liam winked his unswollen eye. "Fifteen before bed check. Wanna fight some more or want me to blow you?"

Ten months later Scott stared hard at the filthy ceiling through dry eyes as Liam wiped some snot on his shoulder.

"I'll write you. And remember the email address I told you to get so I can find you when you get out." He pressed quick short kisses along Scott's collarbone.

"Yeah. I got it."

"I love you." Liam's tears made their kiss salty. But that wasn't the reason Scott couldn't make himself kiss back. Or say what Liam wanted to hear.

"Uh-huh."

"Scott."

"What?"

"Can't you, like, even agree that this sucks?"

Scott's lips cracked as he opened them. "It sucks."

But he'd known this would happen. Hadn't hoped for one fucking second that things would stay like this. Happy was for people too stupid to know better. And Scott sure as shit knew better.

But it would have been nice to get more than ten months of this. Of Liam. It wasn't only the blowjobs and quiet frantic grinding that Scott kind of liked even better. It wasn't just a body to hold, the idea of having contact that wasn't meant to hurt but make him feel better.

Together they were more. No one dared start shit with them, because it meant taking both of them on. Scott might be good at landing a punch, but Liam was sneaky and mean. He could twist staff around his finger, and no shit ever stuck to him. The assholes could call them fairies and cocksuckers, but when Liam laughed at them, Scott didn't care as much either.

He swallowed. "I'll miss you."

Liam lifted his head from Scott's chest. "Holy fuck. Did it actually hurt you to say that?"

"Yes. Like someone punched my nuts. Kiss 'em and make 'em better."

Liam shoved at his shoulder. "Say it first."

Scott sighed. "When we get out of here…," he forced out in a monotone.

Liam took the next line. "We'll get a place."

"And you'll go to college."

"And you'll be a fireman."

"You'll go to med school."

"And become a doctor and buy you your own Batmobile."

Scott had to laugh. Liam always jacked up the game till it was stupid.

"And while I'm driving in my Batmobile, you can give me roadhead, Robin. Better get your practice in now or I'll never let you in the Batcave."

Chapter Two

Now

MAYBE THE second weekend in August was a great time to stand out on an open field with hundreds of shining steel heat reflectors. Maybe in Antarctica. At the car show at the state fairgrounds in Timonium, Maryland, way too fucking far from any place to catch a decent breeze, it was hot as fuck.

Which was exactly what Scott said to Jamie as they both studied the '65 Ford Galaxie Jamie had his eye on.

"And how hot is fuck, ya think?" Jamie said.

Scott leaned over the engine as he inspected the connections on the plugs. "Don't know about you, but for me, depends on how tight his ass is." He kept his voice low enough so only Jamie could hear.

They'd waited until the owner had gone to lunch, not wanting to show too much interest, but some things didn't mix with the car show crowd. Openly gay guys talking about ass fucking was high up on that list.

Jamie snorted a laugh and lifted his head out from under the hood. "Ain't that the truth." He wiped his face on the sleeve of T-shirt. "At least this is a dry heat."

"Yeah, only about ninety percent humidity today." Scott squinted around the popped hood at the glare on the windshield where the For Sale sign was. "So what's he want for it?"

"Seventeen fifty."

Scott whistled. Christ, what he could do with a spare grand, let alone almost two. Not have to sell his Mustang for rent money for starters.

Jamie pointed out the features. "The interior's okay, so's the frame, and it's one hell of a shiny paint job." They had both admired the two-toned red-and-white classic style. Nothing like classic Fords.

Scott straightened from his lean into the engine. "Engine's clean enough to eat off of. You been under her?"

Jamie nodded. "Exhaust needs an overhaul. I'm not giving him more than twelve if I decide to take it. Wanted a second opinion."

Scott dropped his overshirt on the dusty pebbled ground and wiggled under the frame. Damn. The seller obviously thought no one would bother getting a look from underneath. Good thing Scott had sent him a text. With the light from his phone, he scanned the transmission housing. "Fucking bastard."

"What?" Jamie squatted.

Scott wiggled out, and Jamie gave him a hand up.

"Sorry, man. You were right on the exhaust. Probably seizes up like a virgin. But there's an oil leak between the engine block and the transmission. Slow enough that you wouldn't know from starting it up, but I'm betting the main seal is going."

"Son of a bitch." Jamie sat and ducked under. Scott handed him the phone for light.

"Right at the transmission bell housing."

As Jamie muttered under the car, Scott bent back over the engine to check the manifolds.

"What do you want the Galaxie for?" Scott said to the beam of light flashing up through the engine. "Thought the truck was fine now."

Jamie had been working—mostly adding features—on a '68 F-100 for almost as long as Scott had known him. Back in May Scott had spent most of his free time helping Jamie take out the door motors and fixing it up after it rolled into the bay. Jamie hadn't wanted to talk about how, but since there was another guy involved, Scott bet on relationship drama.

"The Galaxie's not for me." Jamie's voice drifted back up. "What a fucking bitch."

"You see it?"

"Yeah." Jamie wriggled back out and sat there. "What did you want with Galvez this morning? You looking to sell your Shelby?"

It choked him to admit it. "Maybe."

"Ha. Warned you Mustangs were pussy magnets. Unless that's what's making your dick hard these days."

Scott made a disgusted sound in the back of his throat. "No."

Jamie patted the red-and-white walled tires. "Damn shame." He looked up at Scott. "You know, if I find another one and you put in some work with me, you can drive it sometimes. I mean, check that sweet interior. You can actually fuck a guy in it. Unlike your bitch Mustang." He pushed to his feet. "Even with room for your pathetic hair, punk." Jamie jabbed at Scott's shoulder.

"Fuck you." Scott didn't take the bait and touch the short tips of the inch-high mohawk he had glued up this morning.

Jamie had been ragging on him for almost ten years now, since he'd busted Scott for possession of stolen property when he was seventeen. Despite being a cop, Jamie wasn't a complete asshole.

Jamie sat back down like he'd been shoved. "Shit. The whole fucking circus. Sorry about this, Scott. Maybe they didn't see me." He rocked his shoulders back and forth as he tried to disappear under the car.

"Huh?" Scott looked over his shoulder. From Jamie's sudden panic, he expected bill collectors, process servers, zombie hordes. There wasn't anything out of place in the crowd of sunburned and sweaty people flooding the field at the East and Beast Car Show.

As Scott watched, a big guy built like the Rock with hair and a beard caught Scott's gaze and stared back, then nodded. Scott glanced to either side to see who the guy was nodding at. He sure as hell didn't know anyone who looked like he was starring in an action film franchise. Then he realized the guy was nodding at someone with him

"Are they coming this way?" Jamie called from under the car.

The big guy was weaving through the people in their direction, along with whoever he'd nodded at. Maybe Jamie's overcompensation for being short had led him to pick a fight with this the big man.

Scott studied the group. "If you mean a pro wrestler, two pretty preppy types, a Mr. Studly Salt-and-Pepper, and some goth kid with a camera, yeah, they are."

"Fuck," Jamie spat.

The goth kid in black jeans, black T-shirt, and a metal-spiked leather cuff got to the Galaxie first. He tossed his black hair off his face and kicked Jamie's ankle with a black-sneakered toe. "Why'd you ditch us, asshole?"

"Because I hoped you'd fucking take a hint." Jamie hauled himself out, movements slow and sullen. "Uh, not you, though," he said to one of the preppy guys in an apologetic tone Scott had never heard from Jamie.

However fun it might be to watch Jamie get harassed by this circus, it was too much drama for Scott. People were starting to stare.

He bent down and grabbed his phone out of Jamie's hand. "Gotta run. I'll keep an eye out for that induction hood you wanted. Catch you around."

The goth kid took in Scott with an assessing stare. "Nice sleeve." The kid nodded at the ink on Scott's left arm.

It was a part of him. And he was used to people commenting on it. But every time they did, he flashed back to getting that first small tattoo. Everything else he'd added had been to distract him from that symbol.

"Thanks." Scott nodded back.

That exchange went on exactly a half-second too long, so instead of being ten steps away, Scott was standing right next to the pale sweaty prep when he wobbled. Scott reached to steady the him, but he was dropping too fast. Mr. WWE got involved, lunging across the space. His bulk drove Scott a step back, and he fell backward over someone's cooler. Scott, the prep, and WWE hit the ice-and-water-soaked ground, taking out a nearby shade canopy on the way.

People crowded around the show, offering help.

"I got him." WWE growled. "Damn it, David. I told you to drink the water, not carry it around. He's okay." The force of his assertion—along with his size—moved some of the onlookers back.

Scott studied Preppy David who'd started the mess. He wasn't passed out, but he was pasty and shaking.

"He's not used to lifting anything but a drink outside air-conditioning," Jamie said from behind Scott.

Scott extracted himself from the mess on the ground, jeans muddied on his ass and legs.

"I'm fine," Preppy David said. "It's just fucking hot." He gestured at the destruction around him. "We should pick up this stuff for the owners."

Preppy David tried to move, but there was a reason Scott had named the other guy WWE. His grip on David meant he wasn't going anywhere.

"You are getting out of the heat and getting some fluids into you." WWE had what Scott knew all too well as a cop voice.

Hell, two of 'em. Obviously a good time to retreat.

A John Deere Gator pulled off onto the grassy edge where they stood, and people with first aid bags jumped out. Definitely time to go.

He took a step toward escape and ended up face-to-face with one of the first aid workers.

No.

With Liam.

His hair was cropped tight to his head, jaw clean of familiar scruff, but it was Liam. Six years since

Scott had last seen that face, since he'd woken up to a five-word note instead of the man who'd been sharing his bed. His life.

Rage flashed bright and hot.

Scott punched Liam right in his clean-shaven face. His knuckles made a satisfyingly solid connection to the side of Liam's nose as Scott followed through, driving from his shoulder.

Liam sprawled backward. The shock of anger fizzed out, leaving Scott with a flat hum in his head. He reached for Liam, maybe to shake an answer out of him, maybe to apologize and help him up. Scott would never know what he'd planned because his arms were barred behind his back and someone was shoving him, forcing him away from the chaos on the ground.

"I'm a cop. I got him." Jamie snarled the words, along with some revolting moisture, into Scott's ear. Jamie had to be talking to someone else, though, because Scott already knew that.

A guy in a ball cap and flag T-shirt beater slammed his fists into Scott in a boxer's quick uppercut and gut jab. His body tried to curl in to protect itself, but Jamie still had his arms. Blood flooded Scott's mouth from a split lip, breath trapped in a spasming diaphragm. That hurt, was going to hurt a lot more in a few minutes, but in that instant there was too much adrenaline in his system to deal with it.

Jamie spun Scott away from the free-swinger. "Police, asshole. Back off. I got this. You want an assault charge too?"

Without waiting for a response, Jamie marched Scott down the grassy center aisle between cars. A snapped-out "Baltimore County Police" cleared the way through startled faces. Scott stumbled along, his brain absurdly focused on how Jamie, a good five inches shorter, could completely control Scott with that grip on his arms.

At a point where a lone maple interrupted the line of cars, Jamie shoved Scott forward, releasing him to battle tree roots and momentum for balance. He caught himself, palms slapping into the rough bark.

He pushed away to get the tree at his back, not sure where the next attack might come from.

"What the fuck is wrong with you, asshole?" Jamie's face was as red as his hair. Scott was surprised fire wasn't shooting from Jamie's nostrils along with his heavy breath.

The question was reasonable. Jamie had no way of knowing this was the third time Liam had dropped in on Scott's life, like the whole thing was some kind of fucking game. *Hey, look, me again. Surprise.*

Okay, Scott's random punching-out of a stranger deserved an explanation. Though he couldn't help thinking Jamie should have grabbed the guy who'd punched Scott instead. He brought his thumb to his lip, ran his tongue over his teeth to see if they were all there. As always, he caught on the one Liam had chipped. Though that had been an accident. Still, he remembered Liam laughing in triumph, then the horror on his face. *Shit, I'm so sorry, Scott.*

So where to start with the explanation? Back in at St. Bennie's, a couple of years later in that dark garage, or when he'd woken up to that fucking note after the best and worst two years of Scott's life? None of that Jamie needed to know.

Scott settled on "It's complicated."

"Complicated?" In two steps Jamie had Scott pinned up against the bark of the tree. "You punched a paraplegic, probably a vet, in the face for no god-damned reason. Now you give me 'complicated.'" Jamie shoved him harder and stepped away. "If I hadn't hauled you out of there, they'd be mopping up your remains for a week."

Scott latched on to a single word in the spew from Jamie's lips. Paraplegic. But that was crazy. Liam wasn't in a wheelchair. He'd jumped out of the cart. "He wasn't a paraplegic."

"Quadrpl—" Jamie waved both arms. "What the fuck ever. Guy has a metal leg."

Scott didn't know how it happened, but he was on his ass staring up at Jamie. None of this was real. Some fucked-up version of one of his night terrors.

No. He could move. Focus. He'd gotten a text from Jamie asking him to come check out that '65 Galaxie, so Scott met him and then—

How did that end with him sitting in the grass thinking about Liam missing a leg?

What did you do, you dumb impulsive fuck? Shit. What did I do?

Scott scrambled off the ground. He had to find Liam. Find out what happened.

Jamie shoved him back down. "No way. I'm telling you, people back there wanted to gut you. I thought about it myself. Poor guy goes to war and gets his leg blown off and you take a punch at him for…." Jamie squinted at him. "You gonna finish that sentence for me sometime?"

Scott shook his head. "Gonna arrest me?"

Jamie shrugged. Scott reached for the cigs in his pocket before he realized the denim shirt was back on the ground next to the Galaxie where they'd crawled under the car.

He glanced up at Jamie. "Got a cigarette?"

Jamie's hand moved reflexively to his chest, then stopped. "I quit."

"Fuck this." Scott shoved his hands through his hair, fucking up his 'hawk.

Jamie leaned over him. "You make a habit of punching handicapped people?"

"No." Scott bit off the rest of his response. *No, asshole.* He had a feeling he wasn't talking to Jamie who shot the shit when they worked on cars together, but Officer Donnigan and his damned badge.

"So why's he special?"

Scott shook his head.

"Don't give me more of that 'it's complicated' crap, McDermott."

Scott ripped up some grass, less painful than ripping out his hair. "He had both legs last time I saw him. Honest to God, Jamie, I didn't see that—" he swallowed. "I didn't even notice. Fuck, how could I not notice?" His guts clenched and spasmed, bile coming up sharp to burn the back of his throat, his sinuses.

Liam. Torn apart somewhere on the other side of the world. Blood pouring onto pale dusty ground. How could Scott not have known about it somehow, not have felt it?

Jamie sighed and shoved his hands in the front of pockets of his jeans. Did he carry a spare set of cuffs? He knew Jamie's job these days was more about cleaning up after drunk assholes in the harbor than chasing down teenagers who had only been trying to earn some cash, but he wondered if he was going to get to hear Jamie tell him "You're under arrest." Again.

"So, I'm guessing you've seen more of this guy than just his two good legs?" Jamie arched his brows.

"Yeah."

Every hard inch. But it wasn't just that. The sight of him laughing, singing, *coming*. Knew every taste and touch and smell and sound.

Scott had thought he'd known the rest of Liam too. Who he was. What he thought. What he wanted. Until he disappeared like he'd never existed. Like *they* had never existed.

"Jesus fucking Christ." Jamie blew air noisily through his lips. "The fuck I need another round of some gay soap opera. What happened to just getting your dick sucked?"

Scott straightened away from the tree. "This from the guy whose truck I just helped clean up because it went off a pier after a fight with his—"

"Finish that and I swear to God I'll arrest you right now." Jamie took a deeper breath, steadier. "Okay. Here's what we're going to do. I'm going to go back and check on the fallout, find out if he's pressing charges."

Liam wouldn't press charges. If it hadn't been a sucker punch, he'd have come back swinging before Scott could shake out his hand. But Scott had just remembered he didn't really know Liam. And he definitely didn't know the Liam who'd been to war, had come back missing—Scott pushed himself up from the ground. He had to see him.

"Oh no. You are not coming with me. You are going right home where you will eat, sleep, shower, and shit with your phone next to you so if I call you, you better pick up."

"Fine."

"That does not mean go home after you go looking for the ex you just punched in the face, you got it?"

"I got it."

"Anything on your record I should know about?"

He shook his head. "Shouldn't be."

"Why the fuck do I keep ending up in the middle of all this shit?"

Maybe because you're an asshole wasn't going to help Scott out much. And it was only half true. Jamie could act like a total asshole, but he actually did give a crap. Had when Scott had been seventeen, did now.

Scott shrugged. "You know what they say. Look for the common denominator."

"And for those of us who failed algebra?"

"Maybe you just attract it."

"Lucky me. You stay the fuck out of this, McDermott. Stay far, far away. Go home, you got me?"

"Absolutely," Scott lied.

Chapter Three

AIR-CONDITIONING WRAPPED a chill around Liam and Kishori as they steered the gurney into the fairgrounds' first aid building.

Their patient, still pasty and shaking, let out a dramatic sigh. "Oh, excellent. Five minutes in here and I'll be good as new." David call-me-Beach Beauchamp hadn't wanted to get on the gurney, but a look from one of his friends had cut his argument off mid-sentence. Good thing, because Beauchamp wouldn't have made it ten steps before collapsing again.

"Walsh," their supervisor snapped at Liam from behind the dispatch desk.

"With a patient." Liam wrapped the arm cuff around Beauchamp's upper arm while Kishori pulled out an IV kit.

Gillespie came out to stand behind Kishori's shoulder, towering over her. "Prakash here can handle him."

Liam stared at Gillespie in shock. The guy was a micromanager, but mostly about paperwork.

"She might not even bleed on him."

At Gillespie's words, Liam became aware of the copper filling his mouth, the drip of blood from his nose. Everything he'd forced out of mind to concentrate on his job slammed back into his consciousness.

Scott.

Just as angry as he'd been the first time Liam had seen him.

And twice as fucking hot.

Liam stopped himself from bringing his hand to his face. "I'm fine."

"I'm sure you are, but you're not working on a patient until you clean up." There was no arguing with the glare behind Gillespie's glasses.

Kishori gave him an I-got-this look with her brows. "I'm sure Mr. Beauchamp won't complain."

"Not about being left in your lovely hands, ma'am." Beauchamp's voice was thin, but the drawl was clear.

"Walsh." Gillespie jerked his thumb toward the bathroom.

Liam barely had time to take off his gloves and turn on the tap before Gillespie shouldered through the door.

"What the hell happened out there? Victim clip you?"

"No."

Liam soaped up his hands and then let himself examine the damage in the mirror. It was pretty gory. His nose was still bleeding. Fat drops, bright with fresh oxygen, rolled over his mouth and chin to join the spreading stain on his light blue uniform shirt. It throbbed and stung, pain forcing itself into notice now that the hyperfocus on his patient was gone. He soaked some paper towels and wiped off the blood.

"Walkies lit up with chatter about a fight breaking out. That you?" Gillespie passed Liam some gauze.

"Don't know. I was focused on the victim." Liam felt his nose, no popping or shifting, just pain that radiated into his eye sockets. The right nostril had stopped bleeding already. He rolled the gauze and stuffed it up the left. "Anyone else come in with injuries?"

"No. Apparently there was a cop on the scene." Gillespie folded his arms. "So get your statement ready."

Liam wiped his face off again, then washed his hands and spoke to the mirror. "When the victim fainted, he took out one of those pop-up canopies. Maybe I got whacked with a pole. There were a lot of people crowding around."

Gillespie still blocked the door. "I know you've got stuff to prove"—he glanced down at Liam's prosthesis—"but that doesn't mean you gotta put up with crazy bastards taking a swing because they got issues."

Issues. Interesting way to put it. He and Scott were a long way past issues. Or proving themselves. Had Scott seen Liam's prosthetic? It shouldn't be possible but sometimes Liam forgot about it himself, until he tried to take a step. "I'm sure it was some kind of accident."

As they walked back down the hall, Gillespie's walkie spat out a call about someone's foot getting run over in front of the Miller Building. "Copy. On our way."

Liam reached for fresh gloves. "I can ride—"

"You can stay here and not run into any more poles, clear? I'll call Saunders and have her meet me." Gillespie went out the back.

As the door closed behind him, a rush like the opening gates at the track hit the front door.

"Beach?"

Before Liam had time to answer, the crowd pushed into the treatment bay.

Was Scott friends with the victim? Was he there now?

Liam charged in behind, but none of them had dark brown hair, darker eyes, and a ready snarl on full lips. He caught a glimpse of their patient, who now reclined on the bed like a Roman emperor, the similarity reinforced by the way his friends hovered like attendants.

Kishori's voice was clipped but polite. "If you insist on declining intravenous fluids, you need to sign this refusal form."

One of the new arrivals, the man built like a pro linebacker, intercepted the clipboard before Kishori could hand it to the patient.

Liam took as deep a breath as he could through one nostril and started on crowd control. He slipped in between two of the five men—did they travel in a group in case of random volleyball games?—and turned to face them. Being blood-spattered had usually given him some authority as an Army medic. Maybe it would have an effect on these guys. "I know you're concerned about your friend, but you need to give us a little room to work." He bit back a grimace at the nasal whine in his voice.

A short redhead in a tight blue T-shirt rolled his eyes and started helping. "The man's right. Let's hit the waiting room. Want to show me where that is?"

The redhead pinned Liam with a stare. There were only three welded-to-the-wall plastic chairs near the desk, but there was a lobby in the administration offices that shared the building.

Liam led them to the staff-only door. "Through here. I'll come tell you when he's finished." A look over his shoulder showed that the big guy was still hovering around the patient.

When Liam went back to urge him out, he found the redhead still at his elbow. "Officer Donnigan. Baltimore County Police." He flipped open a badge and then put it away in his back pocket. "I want to talk to you about your bloody nose."

"It'll have to wait until after I see to my patient."

The policeman gave a nod. "I'll wait."

Kishori was swabbing Beauchamp's arm for the IV, the big guy looming behind her. Her braid had slipped out of its bun and hung over her shoulder. "Make a fist for me, please." She looked up as they came back. "Officer Donnigan, would you please ask Mr. Fonoti to step aside for a moment."

The policeman choked off a sound that sounded like a laugh. "Sure thing. Mr. Fonoti?" He smirked as the big man stepped out and followed him toward the desk.

Beauchamp gritted his teeth as the needle slid in. "I really don't mind him staying, ma'am. After all, he got me to take your advice on sticking that needle in me."

Kishori leaned over. "Mr. Beauchamp—"

"Call me Beach, please."

"—do you feel safe at home?" she finished.

He blinked, blue eyes wide behind long lashes. "Safe?"

"Yes. Does anyone hurt you or make you feel that they will?"

"Uh… not—" Beauchamp stammered, looking down. "No. Ah, to tell you the truth, I'm safer than I've ever been." His cheeks had a hint of a flush.

Liam had already picked out at least three of the guys as gay. Now some other stuff fell into place. He glanced down at a leather cuff on Beauchamp's wrist, its mate clutched in his fingers. Kishori must have had him take it off for the IV. Liam didn't get all that leather and bondage stuff, but there was no reason to make Beauchamp sweat about it. Beauchamp saw the direction of Liam's gaze and made an appeal with blinked eyes.

Liam nodded. "I'll tell the officer your friend can come back in, then."

Beauchamp sighed with relief. "Thank you."

Liam found himself alone with the cop when Beauchamp's boyfriend rushed past them to get back to his bedside.

"You going to tell me about your bloody nose now?"

Liam shrugged. "There was a crowd. It happens. No big deal."

The cop grunted in disbelief. "Maybe. But a lot of witnesses might say someone aimed right at you."

Liam met the guy's gaze and gave him the nothing-to-hide half smile that had worked on social workers and judges and lieutenants. Though it probably was less effective with the bloodstains. "I didn't see anything like that."

"Anything like what?"

"Whatever hit me."

The cop scrubbed at his face. "You two are peas in a pod."

Liam's skin prickled with awareness. Donnigan meant Scott. Did he know Scott?

The kickstart to Liam's circulatory system made his nose throb with pain. "Us two?"

"Something you want to add?"

"No, Officer."

"So you don't know what hit you. You interested in finding out?"

"No."

"'I don't know what hit me' is your official statement?"

Liam hadn't done multiple rounds with the social welfare system and not learned a few things. "Do I need a lawyer?"

"Fuck no. Psychiatrist, maybe." The cop turned and slammed through the door to the administration side of the building.

LIAM BRACED a hand against the dash as Kishori parked the Gator back in its slot behind their building. They'd delivered a rehydrated David Beauchamp and stern boyfriend to Gate 4. Over the stink of exhaust from the Gator, Liam's one working nostril delivered a dose of cigarette smoke. The hair on his arms stood up. There was no reason it had to be Scott—probably half the people at the car show smoked. But Liam knew he was here.

He went inside with Kishori but grabbed his afternoon energy drink from the fridge and waved it at her. "Taking five outside if you need me."

Liam tapped the top of the can and pulled the tab as he stepped out. Cigarette smoke hung in the hot air. Scott sat on top of the broken picnic table out back, Doc Martens on the seat, muddy jeans ripped at the knees, puffing away like he waited for Liam there every day.

Oily doubt twisted Liam's stomach, self-consciousness robbing him of the coordination he'd spent five thousand hours of physical therapy to regain. He should have worn jeans. Except it was the third ninety-plus day in a row, and he'd never given a shit if people saw his prosthesis before.

None of those people had been Scott.

Liam forced himself to take a long drink from his can of Brooks Blast before making his stiff, halting way across the baked-dry grass and powdery dirt.

As Liam reached the picnic table, Scott leaned back and took a long inhale, then blew the smoke off to his left.

He pointed the cigarette at the can in Liam's hand. "Don't you know those things will kill you?"

Laughter and tears fought for space in Liam's throat. Jesus. Scott. Liam had missed him. Missed *them* in a thousand different ways.

He couldn't say that out loud, though. Not when he'd been the one to leave. Though he'd left *for* Scott. Because of what Liam had forced Scott to be. Liam tried to push something through his dry mouth, a word, a sound even, anything to let Scott know why.

I'm sorry. I was scared. I was stupid. Damn, you look good.

The only sound he could make was "Scott."

Scott made a disgusted sound in his throat and put the cigarette back to his lips. This time the exhaled stream came right at Liam's face.

"So." Scott rested his arms on his knees. "You've been keeping busy, huh? Still gonna save the world?"

"Scott." Liam wanted to tell him everything. How losing his leg had been his own fucking fault. That he fucking knew better now. Some things you couldn't fix. But God, how he wanted to fix this now.

"You said that, yeah." Scott tapped his cigarette out lightly, brushed away the end, and tucked it in the pack. "I just came to say sorry for punching you."

"Sorry? You admit you know the word?"

Scott's lips thinned. "Yeah, well, I didn't know about"—he pointed at Liam's prosthesis—"all that."

He'd missed this too. The rush and challenge of sparring with Scott.

"So you're only sorry about hitting me because I'm down a leg? Fuck you."

Scott's mouth twisted, offering a glimpse of his gap-toothed smile.

Liam pulled the gauze out of his nose. He wasn't having this conversation honking like a goose. "Besides, not like it was the first time." He put the gauze and the can on one of the cracked wood planks.

Scott nodded, then pushed off the table and stood in front of Liam.

"Wasn't fair. You didn't see it coming." Shaking out his arms, Scott lifted his chin. "You get a free shot."

Liam stared at him.

"One-time offer, here." Scott made a *c'mon* motion with his hand. "Try not to break any teeth this time."

"I'm not going to hit you."

"Why not? I owe you one."

Jesus, Liam owed him so much fucking more. He'd been afraid of doing even a tentative online search for Scott after rehab, terrified of what could have happened. But he was here. Alive. Safe.

"I don't want to hit you."

"No?" Scott dipped his chin and arched a scarred, pierced brow in the infuriating superior expression Liam knew better than his own reflection.

Liam moved, though he'd swear it wasn't a conscious decision any more than the contraction of his heart that kept his blood moving. He grabbed Scott's shirt and kissed him.

Motor oil, menthol smoke, and cinnamon gum. Scott. The instant their mouths touched, the familiar jolt pulled Liam closer, reminded him how he'd never been able to get close enough.

Scott shoved a hand between them and pushed Liam away. He staggered, then caught his balance with a hand on the table. They stood glaring at each other, Scott breathing hard in the heavy air. Scott took another step back. "What the fuck was that?"

"Me taking my free shot. Didn't see it coming?"

"Crazy ratfucker." Shaking his head, Scott sank onto the bench.

Liam sat next to him and scooped up the can to take another drink, remembering when he'd asked Scott about his favorite insult.

"It's like saying the guy has a small dick, right? Because how small would your dick need to be to fuck a rat?"

Now Scott pulled out his lighter and flipped it through his fingers, despite the swelling on his knuckles. "The fuck happened to you?"

Liam had seen him do that same trick with a knife, knew the fluid fingers had dozens of white nicks from the learning curve. He watched the shining barrel flash in the sun. There were so many ways to answer him. Starting with why he'd run. Why he'd needed to run to something that would keep him from coming right back.

He deliberately stretched out his right leg, the ankle joint pointing his fake foot toward the sky. Watching it always gave him the sensation of floating, disconnected from his body. His leg, but not a part of him. After two years he was used to it, except for all the times when he wasn't.

"I joined the circus." He turned to see Scott's expression. "Lion taming isn't as easy as they make it look."

Scott snorted a laugh; then the lighter made the pass across his fingers again. "Yeah. Guess it's none of my business."

"Army. Afghanistan. Twenty-eight months ago. I don't like to talk about it." But not for the reasons most people thought. Explaining that what had happened was his own fucking fault didn't make him—or them—feel any better. Didn't make him less maimed. Or Ross any less dead.

Scott flicked the lighter on. "Shit."

"Yeah."

"But you're—I mean, they'll pay for school now that you—" Scott exhaled in a rush. "Doctors only need a good set of hands."

"There are programs, if I decide I want to go back."

"Decide?"

Liam finished off his Blast, trying and failing to ignore the stare that burned into the side of his head. Maybe being a doctor was all he'd ever talked about back then. But he'd earned a little time to think about it. Right?

He stuffed the wad of gauze in the empty can and crumpled it against the bench. "How many cars do you have now, Batman?"

"Just one. Might be selling it, though."

"Time for an upgrade?"

"There is no upgrading a '68 Mustang GT Fastback."

Liam gasped. "Why the hell would you sell a car you claimed was a blow job you can drive?"

Scott swung a foot, kicking the bench. Vibrations ran up into Liam's socket.

"Beats selling blow jobs."

"Huh?" Liam lifted his foot off the bench.

Scott pocketed his lighter. "To make rent."

Shit must really be bad if Scott was planning to sell his dream car.

"I don't have a lot, but I banked most of my service pay."

Scott leaped off the table. "Don't. Jesus, Liam. Just don't."

"You put me through two years of school. Kind of the least I can do."

Scott shook his head. "You don't owe me shit." A laugh that was mostly disgust made his lips curl. "Except maybe a why."

Fear. Guilt. It started a fresh tumble of what Liam always thought of as guilt worms wriggling in his stomach. The nights he'd felt Scott's heart jittering under a palm pressed to his chest, even in exhausted sleep. Finding a prescription bottle full of dexies with a stranger's name on it. Scott trying to kill himself or ending up an addict like Mom because he was working two full-time jobs to pay the bills and keep Liam in school.

"I had to."

"Yeah. Read the note." Scott relit his cigarette. "Forget I asked."

Admitting Liam had made a terrible mistake then—about all his mistakes—wasn't going to fix anything now. Wasn't going to slow the writhing bundle of worms making him nauseous.

"Is that why you came looking for me, to ask that?" Liam picked up the crushed can.

"Point to you, genius. Guess college wasn't a complete waste."

"I'm sorry."

"Don't be. At least it gave me a chance to say this to your face: bye, Liam. Have a nice life." Scott walked away

K.A. MITCHELL discovered the magic of writing at an early age when she learned that a carefully crayoned note of apology sent to the kitchen in a toy truck would earn her a reprieve from banishment to her room. Her career as a spin-control artist was cut short when her family moved to a two-story house and her trucks would not roll safely down the stairs. Around the same time, she decided that Ken and G.I. Joe made a much cuter couple than Ken and Barbie and was perplexed when invitations to play Barbie dropped off. She never stopped making stuff up, though, and was thrilled to find out that people would pay her to do it. Although the men in her stories usually carry more emotional baggage than even LAX can lose in a year, she guarantees they always find their sexy way to a happy ending.

K.A. loves to hear from her readers. You can email her at ka@kamitchell.com. She is often found talking about her imaginary friends on Twitter @ka_mitchell.

Email: ka@kamitchell.com
Twitter: @ka_mitchell
Website: www.kamitchell.com
Blog: authorkamitchell.wordpress.com
Tumblr: kamitchellplotbunnyfarm.tumblr.com

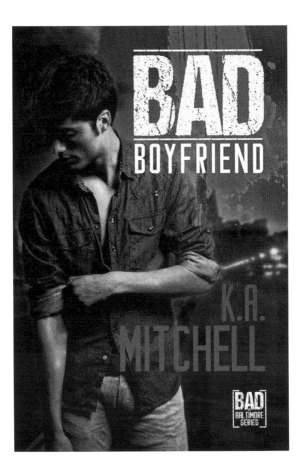

Bad in Baltimore: Book Two

Causing trouble has never been more fun.

Eli Wright doesn't follow anyone's rules. When he was seventeen, his parents threw him out of the house for being gay. He's been making his own way for the past five years and he's not about to change himself for anyone's expectations. For now, romance can wait. There are plenty of hot guys to keep him entertained until he finds someone special.

Quinn Maloney kept the peace and his closeted boyfriend's secrets for ten years. One morning he got a hell of a wake-up along with his coffee. Not only did the boyfriend cheat on him, but he's marrying the girl he knocked up. Inviting Quinn to the baby's baptism is the last straw. Quinn's had enough of gritting his teeth to play nice. His former boyfriend is in for a rude awakening, because Quinn's not going to sit quietly on the sidelines. In fact, he has the perfect scheme, and he just needs to convince the much younger, eyeliner-wearing guy who winks at him in a bar to help him out.

Eli's deception is a little too good, and soon he has everyone believing they're madly in love. In fact, he's almost got Quinn believing it himself....

www.dreamspinnerpress.com

BAD
ATTITUDE

BAD
BALTIMORE
SERIES

K.A.
MITCHELL

Bad in Baltimore: Book Three

Saving lives never used to be this complicated.

Gavin Montgomery does what's expected of him by his wealthy and powerful family—look good in a tuxedo and don't make waves. When a friend takes a leap off a bridge, Gavin tries to save him, only to fall in with him. At least at the bottom of the river he won't feel like such a disappointment to his family. But he's pulled from the water by a man with an iron grip, a sexy mouth, and a chip on his shoulder the size of the national deficit.

Jamie Donnigan likes his life the way it is—though he could have done without losing his father and giving up smoking. But at least he's managed to avoid his own ball and chain as he's watched all his friends pair off. When Montgomery fame turns a simple rescue into a media circus, Jamie decides if he's being punished for his good deed, he might as well treat himself to a hot and sweaty good time. It's not like the elegant and charming Gavin is going to lure Jamie away from his bachelor lifestyle. Nobody's that charming. Not even a Montgomery....

www.dreamspinnerpress.com

BAD
INFLUENCE

K.A. MITCHELL

BAD
BALTIMORE
SERIES

Bad in Baltimore: Book Four

Can a future be built from pieces of a broken past?

Jordan Barnett is dead, killed as much by the rejection of his first love at his moment of greatest need as by his ultraconservative parents' effort to deprogram the gay away.

In his place is Silver, a streetwise survivor who's spent the last three years becoming untouchable… except to those willing to pay for the privilege. He's determined not to let betrayal find him again, and that means never forging bonds that can be broken.

No matter how hard he tried, Zebadiah Harris couldn't outrun his guilt over abandoning his young lover—not even by leaving the country. Now, almost the moment he sets foot back in Baltimore, he discovers Silver on a street corner in a bad part of town. His effort to make amends lands them both in jail, where Silver plans a seductive form of vengeance. But using a heart as a stepping-stone is no way to move past the one man he can't forgive, let alone forget….

www.dreamspinnerpress.com

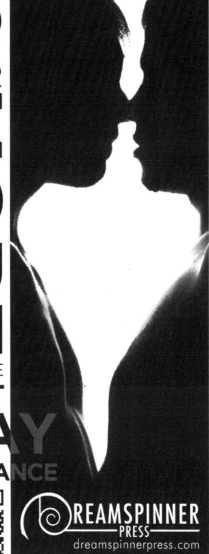